DARE ME

MEGAN ABBOTT

DARE ME

PICADOR

First published 2012 by Picador
an imprint of Pan Macmillan, a division of Macmillan Publishers Limited
Pan Macmillan, 20 New Wharf Road, London N1 9RR
Basingstoke and Oxford
Associated companies throughout the world
www.panmacmillan.com

ISBN 978-1-4472-2115-9

9 8 7 6 5 4 3 2 1

A CIP catalogue record for this book is available from
the British Library.

Printed and bound by CPI Group (UK) Ltd, Croydon, CR0 4YY

Visit **www.picador.com** to read more about all our books
and to buy them. You will also find features, author interviews and
news of any author events, and you can sign up for e-newsletters
so that you're always first to hear about our new releases.

The curse of hell upon the sleek upstart
That got the Captain finally on his back
And took the red red vitals of his heart
And made the kites to whet their beaks clack clack.

— John Crowe Ransom

DARE ME

Prologue

"Something happened, Addy. I think you better come."

The air is heavy, misted, fine. It's coming on two a.m. and I'm high up on the ridge, thumb jammed against the silver button: #27-G.

"Hurry, please."

The intercom zzzzzz-s and the door thunks, and I'm inside.

As I walk through the lobby, it's still buzzing, the glass walls vibrating.

Like the tornado drill in elementary school, Beth and me wedged tight, jeaned legs pressed against each other. The sounds of our own breathing. Before we all stopped believing a tornado, or anything, could touch us, ever.

"I can't look. When you get here, please don't make me look."

In the elevator, all the way up, my legs swaying beneath me, 1-2-3-4, the numbers glow, incandescent.

The apartment is dark, one floor lamp coning halogen up in the far corner.

"Take off your shoes," she says, her voice small, her wishbone arms swinging side to side.

We're standing in the vestibule, which seeps into a dining area, its lacquer table like a puddle of ink.

Just past it, I see the living room, braced by a leather sectional, its black clamps tightening, as if across my chest.

Her hair damp, her face white. Her head seems to go this way and that way, looking away from me, not wanting to give me her eyes.

I don't think I want her eyes.

"Something happened, Addy. It's a bad thing."

"What's over there?" I finally ask, gaze fixed on the sofa, the sense that it's living, its black leather lifting like a beetle's sheath.

"What is it?" I say, my voice lifting. "Is there something behind there?"

She won't look, which is how I know.

First, my eyes falling to the floor, I see a glint of hair twining in the weave of the rug.

Then, stepping forward, I see more.

"Addy," she whispers. "*Addy* . . . is it like I thought?"

1.

Four Months Ago

After a game, it takes a half-hour under the shower head to get all the hairspray out. To peel off all the sequins. To dig out that last bobby pin nestled deep in your hair.

Sometimes you stand under the hot gush for so long, looking at your body, counting every bruise. Touching every tender place. Watching the swirl at your feet, the glitter spinning. Like a mermaid shedding her scales.

You're really just trying to get your heart to slow down.

You think, *This is my body, and I can make it do things. I can make it spin, flip, fly.*

After, you stand in front of the steaming mirror, the fuchsia streaks gone, the lashes unsparkled. And it's just you there, and you look like no one you've ever seen before.

You don't look like anybody at all.

At first, cheer was something to fill my days, all our days.

Ages fourteen to eighteen, a girl needs something to kill all that time, that endless itchy waiting, every hour, every day for something—anything—to begin.

"There's something dangerous about the boredom of teenage girls."

Coach said that once, one fall afternoon long ago, sharp leaves whorling at our feet.

But she said it not like someone's mom or a teacher or the principal or worst of all like a guidance counselor. She said it like she *knew*, and understood.

All those misty images of girls frolicking in locker rooms, pom-poms sprawling over bare bud breasts. All those endless fantasies and dirty boy-dreams, they're all true, in a way.

Mostly, it's hard, it's sweaty, it's the roughness of bruised and dented girl bodies, feet sore from floor pounding, elbows skinned red.

But it is also a beautiful, beautiful thing, all of us in that close, wet space, safer than in all the world.

The more I did it—the more it owned me. It made things matter. It put a spine into my spineless life and that spine spread, into backbone, ribs, collarbone, neck held high.

It was something. Don't say it wasn't.

And Coach gave it all to us. We never had it before her. So can you blame me for wanting to keep it? To fight for it, to the end?

She was the one who showed me all the dark wonders of life, the real life, the life I'd only seen flickering from the corner of my eye. Did I ever feel anything at all until she showed me what feeling meant? Pushing at the corners of her cramped world with curled fists, she showed me what it meant to live.

—

There I am, Addy Hanlon, sixteen years old, hair like a long taffy pull and skin tight as a rubber band. I am on the gym floor, my girl Beth beside me, our cherried smiles and spray-tanned legs, ponytails bobbing in sync.

Look at how my eyes shutter open and close, like everything is just too much to take in.

I was never one of those mask-faced teenagers, gum lodged in mouth corner, eyes rolling and long sighs. I was never that girl at all. But I knew those girls. And, when she came, I watched all their masks peel away.

We're all the same under our skin, aren't we? We're all wanting things we don't understand. Things we can't even name. The yearning so deep, like pinions on our hearts.

So look at me here, in the locker room before the game.

I'm brushing the corner dust, the carpet fluff from my blister-white tennis shoes. Home-bleached with rubber gloves, pinched nose, smelling dizzyingly of Clorox, and I love them. They make me feel powerful. They were the shoes I bought the day I made squad.

2.

Football Season

Her first day. We all look her over with great care, our heads tilted. Some of us, maybe me, even fold our arms across our chest.

The New Coach.

There are so many things to take in, to consider and set on scales, tilted always toward scorn. Her height, barely five-four, pigeon-toed like a dancer, body drum-tight, a golden collarbone popping, forehead high.

The sharp edges of her sleek bob, if you look close enough, you can see the scissor slashes (did she have it cut this morning, before school? she must've been so eager), the way she holds her chin so high, treats it like a pointer, turning this way and that, watching us. And most of all her striking prettiness, clear and singing, like a bell. It hits us hard. But we will not be shaken by it.

All of us, slouching, lolling, pockets and hands chirping and zapping—*how old u think? looka the whistle, WTF*—the texts flying back and forth from each hiccupping phone. Not giving her anything but eyes glazed, or heads slinging down, attending to important phone matters.

6

How hard it must be for her.

But standing there, back straight like a drill officer, she's wielding the roughest gaze of all.

Eyes scanning the staggered line, she's judging us. She's judging each and every one. I feel her eyes shred me—my bow legs, or the flyaway hairs sticking to my neck, or the bad fit of my bra, me twisting and itching and never as still as I want to be. As she is.

"Fish could've swallowed her whole," Beth mutters. "You could've fit two of her in Fish."

Fish was our nickname for Coach Templeton, the last coach. The one plunked deep in late middle age, with the thick, solid body of a semi-active porpoise, round and smooth, and the same gold post earrings and soft-collared polo shirt and sneakers thick-soled and graceless. Hands always snugged around that worn, spiral notebook of drills penciled in fine script, serving her well since the days cheerleaders just dandled pom-poms and kicked high, high, higher. Sis-boom something.

Her hapless mouth slack around her whistle, Fish spent most of her hours at her desk, playing spider solitaire. We'd spot, through the shuttered office window, the flutter cards overturning. I almost felt sorry for her.

Long surrendered, Fish was. To the mounting swagger of every new class of girls, each bolder, more coil-mouth insolent than the last.

We girls, we owned her. Especially Beth. Beth Cassidy, our captain.

I, her forever-lieutenant, since age nine, pee-wee cheer. Her right hand, her *fidus Achates*. That's what she calls me, what I am. Everyone bows to Beth and, in so doing, to me.

And Beth does as she pleases.

There really wasn't any need for a coach at all.

But now this. This.

Fish was suddenly reeled away to gladed Florida to care for her teenage granddaughter's unexpected newborn, and here she was.

The new one.

The whistle dangles between her fingers, like a charm, an amulet, and she is going to have to be reckoned with.

There is no looking at her without knowing that.

"Hello," she says, voice soft but firm. No need to raise it. Instead, everyone leans forward. "I'm Coach French."

And you ma bitches, the screen on my phone flashes, phone hidden in my palm. Beth.

"And I can see we have a lot to do," she says, eyes radaring in on me, my phone like a siren, a bull's eye.

I can feel it still buzzing in my hand, but I don't look at it.

There's a plastic equipment crate at her feet. She lifts one dainty foot under the crate's upper lip and flips it over, sending floor-hockey pucks humming across the shiny floor.

"In here," she says, kicking the crate toward us.

We all look at it.

"I don't think we'll all fit," Beth says.

Coach, face blank as the backboard above her, looks at Beth.

The moment is long, and Beth's fingers squeak on her phone's pearl flip.

Coach does not blink.

The phones, they drop, all of them. RiRi's, Emily's, Brinnie Cox's, the rest. Beth's last of all. Candy-colored, one by one into the crate. Click, clack, clatter, a chirping jangle of bells, birdcalls, disco pulses, silencing at last upon itself.

After, there's a look on Beth's face. Already, I see how it will go for her.

"Colette French," she smirks. "Sounds like a porn star, a classy one who won't do anal."

"I heard about her," Emily says, still giddy-breathless from the last set of motion drills. All our legs are shaking. "She took the squad at Fall Wood all the way to state semis."

"Semis. Semi. Fucking. Epic," Beth drones. "Be the dream."

Emily's shoulders sink.

None of us really cheer for glory, prizes, tourneys. None of us, maybe, know why we do it at all, except it is like a guard face against the routine and groaning afflictions of the school-day. You wear that jacket, like so much armor, Game Days, the flipping skirts. Who could touch you? Nobody could.

My question is this:

The New Coach. Did she look at us that first week and see past the glossed hair and shiny legs, our glittered brow bones and girl bravado? See past all that to everything beneath, all our miseries, the way we all hated ourselves but much more everyone else? Could she see past all of that to something else, something quivering and real, something poised to be transformed, turned out, made? See that she could make us, stick her hands in our glitter-gritted insides and build us into magnificent teen gladiators?

3.

Week One

It isn't immediate. No head-knocking conversion.

But, with each day that week, the New Coach continues to hold our interest—a feat.

We let her drill us, we run tumbles. We show her all our routines and we keep our claps tight and our roundoffs smooth.

Then we show her our most heralded routine, the one we ended last basketball season with, lots of chorus-line flips and toe touches and a big finish where we all pop Beth up into a straddle sit, her arms V split above her head.

Coach seems almost to be watching, her foot perched on top of the crunking boombox.

Then she asks us what else we got.

"But everyone loved that number," peeps Brinnie Cox. "They had us do it again at graduation."

We all want Brinnie to shut up.

Coach, she's just tighter, fleeter than we'd expected and, that first week, we take notice. Planted in front of us, her body held so lightly but so surely.

We can't fluster her, and we are surprised.

We can fluster everyone, not just Fish but the endless sad parade of straw-man subs, dusty-shouldered geometry teachers and crêpey-skinned guidance counselors.

Let's face it, we're the only animation in the whole drop-ceiling, glass-bricked tomb of a school. We're the only thing moving, breathing, popping.

And we know it. You can feel that knowingness on us.

Look at them, that's what we can hear them—everyone—say when, Game Day, we stride the hallways, pack-like, our ponytails rocking, our skirts like diamonds.

Who do they think they are?

But we know just who we are.

Just like Coach knows who she is. It's in the click and tap of both her aloofness and nerve. So unconcerned with our nonsense. *Bored* with it. A boredom we know.

Right off, she won something there, even if—or because—she didn't ask for it, care about it. Not because she's bored but because we're not *interesting enough for her*.

Not yet, at least.

The second day, she takes a piece of Emily's flab in her fingers. Pixie-eyed, apple-breasted Emily lifts her arms languorously above her head in an epic yawn. Oh, we knew this routine, this routine which so provokes Mrs. Dieterle and makes Mr. Callahan turn red and cross his legs.

Coach's hand appears out of nowhere and reaches for the spot laid bare by Emily's tank top lifted high. She plucks the baby fat there and twists it, hard. So hard Emily's mouth gives a little pop. The gasp, like a squeeze toy.

"Fix it," Coach says, eyes lifting from the skin between her fingers to Emily's stricken eyes.

Fix it. Just like that.

Fix it? Fix it? Emily, sobbing in the locker room after, and Beth rolling her eyes, her head, her neck in annoyed circles.

"She can't say things like that, can she?" Emily wails.

Emily whose balloony breasts and hip-cascades are such the joy of all the boys, their ga-ga throats stretched to follow her gait, to stretch around corridor corners just to see that cheer skirt dance.

All those posters and PSAs and health-class presentations on body image and the way you can burst blood vessels in your face and rupture your esophagus if you can't stop ramming those Hostess snowballs down your throat every night, knowing they'll have to come back up again, you sad weak girl.

Because of all this, and Coach surely *can't* tell a girl, a sensitive, body-conscious teenage girl, to get rid of the tender little tuck around her waist, can she?

She can.

Coach can say anything.

And there's Emily, keening over the toilet bowl after practice, begging me to kick her in the gut so she can expel the rest, all that cookie dough and Cool Ranch, the smell making me roil. Emily, a girl made entirely of donut sticks, cheese powder and Haribo.

I kick, I do.

She would do the same for me.

—

Wednesday, Brinnie Cox says she might quit.

"I can't do it," she pules to Beth and me. "Did you hear my head hit the mat on the dismount? I think Mindy did it on purpose. It's easy for a Base. Her body's like a big chunk of rubber. We're not trained for stunts."

"That's why we're *training* for stunts," I say. I know Brinnie would rather be pom-shaking, grinding and ass-slapping during half-time, or all the time.

Brinnie's the one Beth and I have always ridden the hardest, out of irritation. "I don't like her big teeth or her chicken-bone legs," Beth would say. "Get her out of here."

Once, practicing double-hook jumps, Beth and I made loud comments across the gym about how Brinnie's slutty sister got caught making out with the assistant custodian until Brinnie ran off to the far showers to cry.

"All I know," Brinnie lisps now, through those big teeth, "is my head is killing me."

"If you ruptured a blood vessel," Beth replies, "you could be slowly bleeding inside your head."

"You probably already have brain damage," I add, eyeing her closely. "I'm sorry, but it's true."

"The blood may be squeezing your brain against the side of your skull," Beth says, "which eventually will kill you."

Brinnie's eyes wide and wet and brimming, and I know we have achieved our goal.

On the last day of that first week, Coach calls a special meeting.

14

There are anxious texts and twitterings. Talk of cuts to the squad and who might it be?

But, standing before us, her announcement is simple.

"There isn't going to be a squad captain anymore," she says.

Everyone looks at Beth.

I've known Beth since second grade, since we braided our bodies together in sleeping bags at girl camp, since we first blood-brothered ourselves to each other. I know Beth and can read her every raised eyebrow, every toe pivot. She holds certain things—calculus, hall passes, her mother, stop signs—with a steely contempt that drives her hard.

Once, she dunked her mother's toothbrush in the toilet, and she calls her father "the Mole," though none of us can remember why, and there was that time she called our Phys Ed teacher a cunt, though no one could prove it.

But there are other things about her, that not everyone knows.

She rides horses, has a secret library of erotic literature, barely five feet tall and yet has the strongest legs I've ever seen.

I might also tell this: in eighth grade, no, summer after, at a beer party, Beth put her scornful little-girl mouth on Ben Trammel, you know where. I remember the sight. He was grinning, holding her head down, gripping her hair in his hand like he'd caught a trout with his bare hand, and everyone found out. I didn't tell. People still talk about it. I don't.

I never knew why she did it, or the other things she's done since. I never asked, that's not how we are.

We don't judge.

The main thing about Beth, though, is this: she has always been our captain, my captain, even back in pee-wee, in junior high, then JV, and now the Big Leagues.

Beth has always been captain, and me, her badass lieutenant, since the day she and I, after three weeks of flipping roundoffs together in her backyard, first made squad together.

She was born to it, and we never thought of cheer any other way.

Sometimes I think captain is the only reason Beth even comes to school, bothers with any of us, any thing at all.

"I just don't see any need for a captain. I don't see what it's gotten you," Coach says, glance passing over Beth. "But thank you for your service, Cassidy."

Hand me your badge, your gun.

Everyone pads their sneakers anxiously, and RiRi peers dramatically at Beth, arching her whole back to see her reaction.

But Beth gives no reaction.

Beth doesn't seem to care at all.

Doesn't even care enough to yawn.

"I was sure it'd be bad," whispers Emily to me, jump squats in the locker room later. "Like when she got mad at that math sub and keyed his car."

But, knowing Beth, I figure it will be some time before we see her true response.

"What'll cheer be like now?" wonders Emily, lunging

breathlessly, paring that body down to size. Fixing it. "What does it mean?"

What it means, we soon see, is no more hours wiled away talking about the lemonade diet and who had an abortion during summer break.

Coach has no interest in that, of course. She tells us we'd best get our act together.

End of that first week, new regime, our legs are loose and soft, our bodies flopping. Our moves less than tight. She says we look sloppy and juvenile, like Disney tweensters on a parade float. She is right.

And so it's bleacher sprints for us.

Oh, to know such pain. Hammering up and down those bleacher steps to the pulse of her endless whistle. Twenty-one high steps and forty-three smaller steps. Again, again, again.

We can feel it in our shins the next day.

Our spines.

We can feel it everywhere.

Stairwell to hell, we call it, which Beth says is just bad poetry.

By Saturday practice, though, we're already—some of us—starting to look forward to that pain, which feels like something real.

And we know we will get a lot better fast, and no injuries either because we're running a tight routine.

4.

Week Two

The bleacher sprints are punishing, and I feel my whole body shuddering—*pound-pound-pound*—my teeth rattling, it is almost ecstatic—*pound-pound-pound, pound-pound-pound*—I feel almost like I might die from the booming pain of it—*pound*—I feel like my body might blow to pieces, and we go, go, go. I never want it to stop.

So different from before, all those days we spent our time nail-painting and temp-tattooing, waiting always for Cap'n Beth, who would show ten minutes before game time after smoking a joint with Benjy Grinnell or gargling with peppermint schnapps behind her locker door and still dazzle us all by rocketing atop Mindy and Cori's shoulders, stretching herself into an Arabesque.

Back then, we could hardly care, our moves so sloppy and weak. We'd just streak ourselves with glitter and straddle jump and shake our asses to Kanye. Everybody loved us. They knew we were sexy beyotches. It was enough.

Cheerutantes, that's what they called us, the teachers.

Cheerlebrities, that's what we called ourselves.

We spent our seasons prowling, a flocked flock, our ponytails the same length, our matching Nfinity ripstop trainers, everything synchronous, eyelids gold-flecked, and no one could touch us.

But there was a sloth in it, I see now. A wayward itch and sometimes even I would look at the other kids who filled the classrooms, the debaters and yearbook snappers and thick-legged girl-letes and the band girls swinging their battered violin cases and wonder what it felt like to care so much.

Everything is different now.

Beth is tugging at her straw, the squeaking grating on me.

I should be home, drawing parabolas, and instead, I'm in Beth's car, Beth needing to get out of the house, to stop hearing her mother's silky robe shushing down the hallway.

Beth and her mother, a pair of impalas, horns locked since Beth first started speaking, offered up her first cool retort.

"My daughter," Mrs. Cassidy once slurred to me, sluicing her neck with Crème de la Mer, "has been a delinquent since the day she was born."

So I get in Beth's car, thinking a drive might do some kind of soothing magic, like with a colicky baby.

"The test's tomorrow," I say, fingering my pre-calc book.

"She lives on Fairhurst," she says, ignoring me.

"Who?"

"French. The coach."

"How do you know?"

Beth doesn't even give me a shrug, has never, ever answered a question she didn't feel like answering.

"You wanna see it? It's pretty lame."

"I don't want to see it," I say, but I do. Of course I do.

"This isn't about the captain thing," I say, very quiet, like not quite sure I want to say it aloud.

"What captain thing?" Beth says, not even looking at me.

The house on Fairhurst is not small. A ranch house, split-level. It's a house, what can I say? But there is something to it, okay. Knowing Coach is in there, behind the big picture window, the light tawny and soft, it seems like more.

There's a tricycle in the driveway with streamers, pink and narrow, flittering in the night air.

"A little girl," Beth says, cool-like. "She has a little girl."

"Don't think of a pyramid as a stationary object," Coach tells us. "Don't think of it as a structure at all. It's a living thing."

With Coach Fish, when we would do pyramids, we used to think of it as stacking ourselves. Building it layer by layer.

Now we are learning that the pyramid isn't about girls climbing on top of each other and staying still. It's about breathing something to life. Together. Each of us a singular organ feeding the other organs, creating something larger.

We are learning that our bodies are our own and they are the squad's and that is all.

We are learning that we are the only people in the world when we are on the floor. We will wear our smiling masks, tight and meaningless, but inside, all we care for is Stunt. Stunt is all.

At the bottom, our hardcore base girls, Mindy and Cori, my feet on Mindy's shoulders, her body vibrating through mine, mine vibrating through Emily above me.

The Middle Bases in place, the Flyer rises not by climbing, not by being lifted, it's not a staircase, a series of tedious steps. No, we bounce and swing to bring everyone up, and the momentum makes you realize you are part of something. Something real.

"A pyramid is a body, it needs blood and beats and heat. ONE, TWO, THREE. What keeps it up, what keeps it alive is the bounding of your bodies, the rhythm you build together. With each count, you are becoming one, you are creating life. FOUR, FIVE, SIX."

And I feel Mindy beneath me, the sinew of her, we are moving as one person, we are bringing Beth up and she is part of us too, and her blood shooting through me, her heart pounding with mine. The same heart.

"The only moment the pyramid is still is when you make it still," Coach says. "All your bodies one body, and you DO NOT MOVE. You are marble. You are stone.

"And you won't move because you won't be able to, because you're not that hot chick bouncing down the hall-way, that ponytail-swinging girl, mouth filled with nothings. You're not dainty, you're not pretty, you're not a girl at all, not even a person. You're the most vital part of one thing, the perfect thing. Until, SEVEN, EIGHT, and . . .

"We blow it all apart."

After, our bodies spent, our limbs slick, we query her.

Sweatless and erect, she looks down our wasted loins, water bottles rolling over our chests and foreheads.

"Coach, where'd you go to high school?" one of us asks.

"Coach, what's your husband like?"

"Coach, is that your car in the faculty lot, or your husband's?"

We try every day, most of us. The information comes slow, wriggling out. She'd gone to school over in Stony Creek, her husband works in a mirrored office tower downtown and he bought her the car. Barely information at all. As little as she can share and still share something.

So focused, so intent, she'll only answer questions when we've done our sprints, our bridge bends, our hundreds of searing crunches, backs sliding, squeaking on the floor.

That prettiness, that bright-beaming prettiness she wears almost like a shameful thing, a flounce she keeps pulling tight, a tinkling charm she stills under her hand.

It's when she's walking away from us, it's when she's dismissed us that RiRi calls out, "Hey, Coach, hey, Co-o-ach. What's that on your ankle?"

The tattoo creeps above her running anklets, a violet blur.

She doesn't even turn her head, you wouldn't even know she heard.

"Coach, what *is* it?"

"A mistake," she says. That hard little voice of hers. *A mistake.*

Ah, steel-strung coach with a reckless past, a bawdy past.

"Bet we find her in an old episode of *Girls Gone Wild: The Prehistoric Years*." That's Beth, of course. On Emily's laptop. Beth typing Coach's name into youtube, bottom-trawling.

She doesn't find anything. Somehow I knew she wouldn't. Someone that steely-strung, there's nothing you could find.

After practice, dwindling Emily, back flat on the locker-room linoleum, curls her stomach upon herself over and over, fighting to get tighter, to whittle herself down to Coach specs. I stay with her, hold her feet down, keep her pudged ankles from swiveling.

And it turns out Coach hasn't left either. She's in her office, talking on the phone. We see her through the glass, opening and closing the blinds, hand coiled around the plastic wand. Staring out the window to the parking lot. Open, shut, open, shut.

When she hangs up, she opens the office door. The shush of the door swinging open, and it's beginning.

She opens the door and sees us, and the nod of her head, permitting entry.

The office smells like smoke, like the sofa in the teachers' lounge with that hard stain in the sunken center. Everybody has a story about that stain.

There's a picture on her desk of her little girl. Coach says her name is Caitlin and she's four years old with a bleary mouth and flushed skin and eyes that glaze so dumbly I wonder how does anyone have kids.

"She's so cute," spurts Emily. "Like a doll or something."

Like a doll, or something.

Coach looks at the photo, like she's never seen it before. She squints.

"They get mad at me, at daycare," she says, like she's thinking about it. "I'm always the last one to pick up. The last mom, at least."

She puts down the photo and looks at us.

"I remember those," she says, nodding at the flossy bracelets banding up and down our forearms.

She tells us she made them when she was a kid and she can't believe they're popular again. Friendship bracelets, she calls them. But we would never call them that.

"They're just bracelets," I say.

She looks at me, lighting a cigarette with a twiggy old match, like the man who sells us jugs of wine out of the back of his store on Shelter Road.

"We called this kind 'snake around the pole,' " she says, lifting the one on Emily's wrist with a crooking finger, her cigarette flaring.

"That's a Chinese Staircase," I say. I don't know why I keep correcting her.

"What's that one?" she says, poking at my wrist, the cigarette tip flush on my skin.

I stare at it, and at Coach's cool tanned finger.

"A Love-Me-Knot," Emily grins. "That's the easy one. I know who made you that."

I don't say anything.

Coach looks at me. "Guys don't make these."

"They sure don't," Emily says, and you can almost see her tongue flicking.

"I don't even know who gave it to me," I say.

But then I remember it was Casey Jaye, this girl I tumbled

with at cheer camp last summer, but Beth didn't like her and camp ended anyway. Funny how people you know at camp can seem so close and then the summer's over and you never see them again at all.

Coach has her eyes on me, and there's a shadow of a dimple in the corner of her mouth.

"Show me," she says, poking out her cigarette. "Show me how to love-knot."

I say I don't have any of the thread, but Emily does, at the bottom of her hobo bag.

We show her how to do it, then watch her twist the strands, to and fro. She picks it up so fast, her fingers flying. I wonder if there's anything she can't do.

"I remember," she says. "Watch this one."

She shows us how to make one called Cat's Tongue, which is like a Broken Ladder crossed with a simple braid, and another she calls the Big Bad that I can't follow at all.

When she finishes Big Bad, she twirls it on her finger and flings it at me. I see Emily's face flicker jealously.

"Is this all you guys do for fun?" she says.

And no, it's not.

"It was like she was really interested in our lives," Emily tells everyone after, her fingers whisking across my new bracelet.

"Pathetic," Beth says. "*I'm* not even interested in our lives." Her finger slips under the bracelet and tug-tug-tugs until it snaps from my wrist.

—

The next day, after school, the parking lot, I see Coach walking to her sprightly little silver crawler of a car.

I'm loitering, fingers hooked around my diet-soda bottle, waiting on Beth, who is my ride and occasionally sees fit to make me wait while she talks up Mr. Feck, who gives her reams of pink fluttery hall passes from his desk drawer.

I don't even realize Coach has seen me until she beckons, her head snapping toward her open door.

"Well c'mon then," she says. "Get in."

As if she knows I've been waiting for the invitation.

Driving, Coach is shaking one of those strange, muddy-looking juices she's always drinking, raw against your teeth. I don't think any of us have ever seen her eat.

"You girls have lots of bad habits," she says, eyeing my soda.

"It's diet," I say, but she just keeps shaking her head.

"We'll get you right. The days of funyuns for lunch and tanning beds—they're over, girl."

"Okay," I say, but I must not look convincing. First of all, I've never eaten a funyun in my life.

"You'll see," she says. Her neck and back so straight, her eyebrows tweezed to precise arches. The glint-gold tennis bracelet and shine-sleek hair. Teeth white enough to blare. They blare. She is so perfect.

"So, which one of those footballers is your guy?" Coach asks, staring out the window.

"What?" I say. "None of them."

"No boyfriend?" She seems a little more interested, sits up a little. "Why not?"

"There's not a lot to interest me at Sutton Grove High," I say, like Beth might say. I'm eyeing the cigarette pack on the console between us, imagining myself plucking one and putting it in my mouth. Would she stop me?

"Tell me," she says. "Who's the guy with all the curls?" She taps her forehead. "And the crook in his nose?"

"On the team?" I ask.

"No," she says, leaning forward toward the steering wheel a little. "I see him run track in those high tops with the silver skulls."

"Jordy Brennan?" I say.

There was a group: ten, twelve guys you might loiter with, might lap-shimmy, beer-breathed at parties, might letter-jacket him for a week, a month.

Jordy Brennan wasn't one of them. He was just there, barely. Scarcely a blip on the screen of my school.

"I never thought of him," I say.

"He's cute," she says. The way she breathes in, turning the wheel, you can feel her thinking all about Jordy Brennan, for just that second.

And then I think of him too.

My shirt scraping up my back, the nervy-hot hands of Jordy skittering there, and before I know it, my cheer skirt twisting 'round my waist, nudging up my belly, his hands there too, and mine coiled into little nerve-balls, and am I going to do it?

This is in my head, these thoughts, as I rustle under my

Sutton-green coverlet in bed that night. I've never had it happen like that before, a sharp ache down there, right there, and a put-put-put pulse, so breathless.

Jordy Brennan, who I never blinked at twice.

After, I'm about to call Beth for our nightly postmortem, but then I decide not to.

I think she will be mad at me for not waiting for her after school. Or for something else. She is mad at me often, especially since last summer at cheer camp, when things started to change with us. I grew tired of all my lieutenant duties, and her no-prisoners ways, and I started stunting with other girls at camp. It goes deep with Beth and me. Our history is long and lashed us tight.

So I call Emily instead and talk with her for an hour or more about basket tosses and her shin splints and the special rainforest wax Brinnie Cox bought in Bermuda to tear off all her girl hair.

Anything but boys and Coach. My head a hot, clicking thing. I want to quiet it. I want to hush, hush it and I hold my legs together, tense as pincer grips, and clutch my stomach upon itself. I listen endlessly to Emily's squeaking voice, the way it sputters and pipes and dances lightfoot and never, ever says anything at all.

5.

Week Three

We're getting better all the time.

We are all locking stunts, focusing. Emily nailed her standing back handspring, which we never thought she would, with those soft-rise breasts she once had. We are stronger and we are learning how to feel each other's bodies, to know when we will not fall.

Nights, in bed, I hear the thuds on the gym floor, feel that thud through my bones, through the center of me.

Already, I can feel my muscles thrusting under my skin. I even start eating because if I don't, my head goes soft. The first week, I pass out twice in calc, the second time hitting my head SMACK on the edge of a desk.

Can't have that, Coach says.

"You can't slap the treadmill before school and then expect to make it to lunch on your a.m. diet coke," Coach says, coming at me in the nurse's office. Charging in with such purpose, making even lumberjack-chested Nurse Vance, twice her size, jump back.

Her hands are riffling through my purse, thwacking the bag of sugar-free jolly ranchers at my chest.

I'm meant to throw them away, which I do, fast.

"Don't worry," Coach says. "No one gets fat on my watch."

So I start with the egg whites and almonds and the spinach, like wilting lily pads between my teeth. It's so boring, not like eating at all because you don't feel the sweet grit on your tongue all day and night, singing on the edge of your teeth.

But my body is tight-tight-tightening. Hard and smooth, like hers, my waist pared down to nothing, like hers.

The walk, her walk, feet planted out, like a ballerina. I wonder if Coach was a ballerina once, her hair pulled into a fierce dark bun, collarbones poking.

We all do the walk.

Not Beth, though, and not some of the girls, like Tacy Slaussen, who cotton more to Beth's dusky glower, the way she hitches her cheer skirt low, the way she slinks over to the freshmen squad, perched in the stands to watch us. The way she reaches up and yanks the pom off one of the girl's socks and sinks it purposefully into the bottom of her plastic cup.

This is what Beth does, while some of us make ourselves hard and beautiful.

Jordy Brennan, fleet around the track, a soft tangle of cord skimming from his ear buds.

I watch him four days in a row, under the bleachers, my wrist wrapped around one of the underhangs, fingers clenching and unclenching.

"You got a thing for deviated septums, Addy-Faddy?" Beth asks.

"I don't know," I say, scratching my palms.

"What's the story, anyway," she says. "He's dull as a plank of wood." She pings the bleacher post, which is actually aluminum.

"He looks like he's thinking things," I say, jumping a little on my toes, feeling like some dumb cheerleader. "Like maybe he actually thinks about things."

"Deep thoughts," Beth says, pulling her ponytail tight, "about puma treads."

I didn't tell her what Coach said, somehow didn't want her to know Coach had even given me a ride home.

Beth drifts forward from the bleacher skeleton and lingers on the edge of the track.

He's pounding toward us, the huff-huff rattling in me, churning between my hips.

"Jordy Brennan," Beth shouts, voice deep and clear. "Come here."

There's a rollicking in my chest as he slows to stop just past us, then does an about-face and slows to a cool-man stride as he makes his way over.

"Yeah," he says, up close his eyes green and blank as poker felt.

"Jordy Brennan," Beth says, throwing her cigarette on the ground. "It's your lucky day."

Fifteen minutes later, the three of us drifting along in his pocked Malibu, Beth directs Jordy to the convenience store on Royston Road, the place where the football players all buy their beer from the grim-faced man behind the counter, extra five-dollar charge just for the plastic bag.

We take the Forties, which I never like, all warm and sour by the time you get halfway in, and the three of us drive up to the Sutton Ridge where that girl jumped last spring.

Seventeen and brokenhearted, she jumped.

RiRi saw the whole thing, from Blake Barnett's car.

Right before, RiRi spotted a screech owl burst from behind the water tank.

Her eyes lifted up, so did Blake's, to the top of the rutted ridge. A place haunted by ruined Indians, or so we heard as kids spooking on Halloween. Apache maidens swan-diving over lost love for white men who abandoned them.

Together, RiRi and Blake watched.

Blake recognized the girl from St. Reggie's, and nearly shouted out to her, but didn't.

Arms stretched wide, her hands strangely spinning, and walking backward fast.

RiRi watched it, the whole thing.

She said it was terrible and kinda beautiful.

I bet it was, jumping from so high, so very high, into the dark plush of that grieving ravine.

All us girls might look down into that same gorge on nights steeped in the sorrows of womanhood. I never felt so much, but looking now, I thought I might yet.

Beth walks up extra high on the ridge, swinging her Forty with surprising grace, and Jordy ducks his big boyhead against me and kisses me smearily for a half-hour or more.

He tells me this is a special spot for him.

At nights sometimes he runs up here, playing his music and forgetting everything.

"Maybe," he says, "that's how cheerleading is for you."

Then he ripples his hands up and down me, gentle and with those great empty eyes of his shut tight, lashes long like a girl's. That funny way his nose bends slightly right, like a boxer.

"Isn't she pretty, Jordy," I hear Beth's rippling voice from somewhere, "when she looks into your eyes?"

I rest my lips on his cheekbone, near the crook of his nose, and he shudders.

The way his eyelashes flutter so, and his hard heavy boy hands, grave and turbulent, I can feel all kinds of wonder and surprises charging through him.

All of this moves me, strangely, and the day feels rare, the dusk falling purple and I must be drunk because I think I hear Beth's voice far away, saying crazy things, asking me if I feel different, and loved.

Jordy Brennan's name buzzes on my phone that night, a spare text with "u"s and "r"s and cautious wonderings. But the thing that was there, the feeling huddling in me at the gorge, is already gone.

His wanting, so easily won—well, it bores me. I know every flex and twist of it, because there are no flex and twists to it.

And instead I want to see Coach again, and tell her about it. I wonder what she'll say.

Beth calls after, and we have a long-winding talk, the forty-ouncers still heavy on us both.

She is asking if I remember how we used to hang on the monkey bars, hooking our legs around each other, and how strong we got and how no one could ever beat us, and we could never beat each other, but we'd agree to each release our hands at the count of three, and that she always cheated, and that I always let her, standing beneath, looking up at her and grinning my gap-toothed, pre-orthodontic grin.

Such reminiscence is unlike Beth, but she is drunk and I think she may still be drinking, her mother's V.S.O.P., and she sounds affected by our time at the gorge, and possibly by other things.

"I hate how everything changes, always," she says. "But you don't."

In the parking lot the next day, Coach tilts her head and gives me a whisper of a smile.

Wanting to present this to her, I felt a funny kind of pride. Like she'd asked me to do a stunt for her— "Give me that pop cradle, Addy. Straight up, straight up". —and there I am, legs arrow-piked, and the feeling when my feet land on that hard floor, the fearsome quake through my ankles, legs, hips.

So I tell her, my hand sweeping across my mouth, like I can barely say it. *Just messed around a little. Jordy Brennan. Jordy Brennan. Just like you said.*

"Which one is that," she says.

I feel something slither a little loose in me. Which one?

"You see him on the track," I insist. "You were talking about him. You talked to me about him and his high tops. The crick in his nose."

She looks at me, quiet like.

"So was he a good kisser," she asks, and I still don't know if she remembers him.

I don't say anything.

"Did he open his mouth right away," she asks.

At first, I think I misheard her.

"Or did you make him work for it?" she continues, grinning slyly.

"It wasn't like that," I say, and is she making fun of me?

"So," she asks, her voice softer, straighter, "what *was* it like?"

"I don't know," I say, not meeting her eyes, my face burning. Somehow it feels like I'm talking to a boy, a guy, an older one, or from another school. "I don't think I want it to go anywhere."

She looks at me and then nods, like I've said something wise.

"You're a smart girl, Addy," she says. She pauses, then adds, "You can make a lot of mistakes, Addy, just wondering about boys."

I nod back, thinking about the word she uses, about the word "boys." Because that's what Jordy Brennan is, a boy. A boy. Not even a guy.

Coach, after all, is married to a man. Coach, after all, has known the world of men. Who even knows how many or what kinds.

She jangles her car keys into her fingers, sliding into her car.

She looks at me through the window, a winking look, but it's between us. We've shared something.

And it brings her closer to me.

6.

Week Four

"Where is she?" RiRi whispers, her honey curls whipping side to side.

Beth is late for practice, and I wonder if she's going to show at all.

Something's been shifting in her and I think it's sort of like she's still captaining with nothing to captain, itching some phantom limb.

Twice last week she didn't call for our late-night recap, our laying forth of the maneuvers of the day, who humiliated herself, whose bra is tatty and whose fat ass is fatting up the whole squad. We've done these calls nightly since forever. But Tuesday I forgot to call and Thursday she didn't pick up. Still, I could feel her breathing somehow, could feel her watching her phone screen blinking ADDY, ADDY.

Coach rolls the media cart into the gym, fingers wrapped tight around the remote.

"Progress has been," she says, "not bad."

We watch ourselves. That bouncing yellow frill on the screen. Malibu-tanned and jerking ponytails, as ever. But we are no longer hip-shaking, pop and locking. We are bounding in perfect time, marching into a three-rowed V., jumping into our toe touches with matching precision. When we do our transition, I can't even believe it, not quite, the way we seem like one long centipede snapping and unsnapping.

We are in sync. We are tight. We are martial and precise.

"Where's Cassidy?" Coach asks, and all our heads turn from the screen.

If you're even ten seconds late—seconds she counts out with toe taps, like our third-grade gym teacher—you don't get to practice. Emily once skidded in at the five-count, blood pouring from her forehead, hurrying so fast her face had caught in her own slamming locker door.

"I think she—" I start, trying to generate an excuse.

As if on cue, I see Tacy's hoodie pocket, red blinking from the top seam. A bass kicks up, the chorus of that song about the club, the way the heat presses tight and you know you're getting some, at da club.

She forgot her phone was on, and now she's trapped.

And I know that ring is Beth's.

Every year there are ones like Tacy Slaussen, with big ole girl-crushes on Beth, the kind who will skip fourth period to go on Monster Energy runs for her, or do dares, like running through the Sutton Grove Mall, hitching jeans low and flashing thongs at security guards. Beth likes to make these girls run.

I glare quick at her, try to get her to steady herself, but her face is panic-stitched.

A flash, and Coach is right there, her hand in Tacy's pocket.

The phone skitters across the floor, spinning madly all the

way to the stretched accordion doors behind which the junior squad shouts buoyantly, *We do it like stomp-stomp-clap-clap, we do it like stomp-stomp-clap-clap.*

Tacy's jaw shakes.

Since we've never actually seen Coach have to lay it down, I don't know why we all feel it like a hammer on our chest. But we do.

Coach, though, doesn't say anything. Not for ten, twenty seconds.

She doesn't look angry exactly.

Instead, she looks bored.

It's a dismissal.

"You girls, with your phones and your sad little texts," she says, shaking her head. "Ten, twelve years ago, it was still folding notes, passing them in class. Just as fucking sad. No, this is sadder."

In an instant, it feels like all our hard work, still frozen on the TV screen, has been wiped away.

And I feel so stupid with my own stupid fucking phone, with the little skins I have for it—hot pink, butterflied, leopard skin—and how it never leaves my curled palm, a live thing that, it seems now, beats instead of my heart.

And we all know whose fault it is.

Tacy's head is shaking back and forth, worse, much worse than the time Beth kicked her out of the car on Black Ash Ridge for spilling peach brandy all over Beth's new leather boots, licorice-shiny and magnificent and ever since creased with ruin.

"I'm sorry, Coach," Tacy blurts. "I'm sorry."

Coach just looks at her, and the look makes me think of the needle valve on that Bunsen burner, turning tight. Shutting off.

Later, Coach, smoking in front of the propped-open window of her office, ponders poor Tacy, and her lank, whippet-straight hair and startled eyebrows.

"She's a sheep," sighs Coach.

I feel relieved I am not one of the fucking sad girls with her sad fucking phones.

"Squad needs sheep," she says. "So fine."

I nod, pressing my temple to the cold window pane, legs still shaking from practice.

"But I don't spend my time on sheep," she says. "There's no payoff."

I nod, slower now, my forehead squeaking on the window pane.

A flicker in Coach's eye, like she can spot the flare of insecurity on my brow.

"But you, Hanlon. You're figuring out what you want," she says, staring at her cigarette, like it's telling her something. "Which is what you should be doing."

I keep nodding, lifting myself straight, straightening myself for her.

Still staring at her cigarette, her face slowly loosens, turns soft with youngness and fear and wonder.

I've not seen this on her, and it's like the years shuttling backward and it's two girls behind the bathroom stall, hiding from the horrors of the world together, burning their throats, their lungs, for rude courage to face those same horrors with big smiles and white shoes.

Beth shows up at next-day practice, a note from See-Yu at the Living Heart Medical Spa assuring Coach that Beth had been suffering from severe menstrual cramps the previous day and needed an emergency acutonic session.

"Coach, no lie, they ding these big forks, like the kind you use to flip steaks on a grill," Beth says, and none of us can watch her, "and the sound just zings through you and straightens your ovaries all out."

Beth, she runs her hand over her hips, like she's showing us how quiet and subdued her ovaries now are. How she has vanquished them.

"It's hard being a girl," Beth adds, shaking her head with elaborate weariness.

Coach looks at her, hands curved lightly around her clipboard. Face blank.

She will not play.

Instead, she looks right through Beth.

"The timing is way off on the tuck jumps," she says, turning away from Beth.

That's it?

"And I know why," Coach says. "I can see sugar glazed all over you girls. You're all shiny with bad living."

Suddenly, I've forgotten all about Beth and I can only feel all the grease on me. As hard as I try, there are slips, and I feel like Coach is looking just at me, seeing the cinnamoned snack puffs I'd snuck that morning. My teeth ache with it. My stomach is soft and swollen with it. I feel weak and desecrated.

"We're going to hit it extra hard today," Coach says. "Hit you in places no tuning forks can. Line up."

That's when we know: we're paying for Beth's sins.

The jump drill comes, and then the high kicks and then floor crunches and then running the gym track until RiRi throws up in the corner, a sloshing mix of Slim Fast and sugar-free powdered donuts.

Beth, though, she sacks up. I'll give her that. At least she doesn't make it any worse for any of us. Sweat glittering on her, dappling her eyelashes, she kills it.

She will not sit down after, when we all collapse on the mats, our sweaty limbs criss-crossing. She will not sit down, will not let the steel slip from between her shoulders.

She has so much pride that, even if I'm weary of her, of her fighting ways, her gauntlet-tossing, I can't say there isn't something else that beams in me. An old ember licked to fresh fire again. Beth, the old Beth, before high school, before Ben Trammel, all the boys and self-sorrow, the divorce and the adderall and the suspensions.

That Beth at the bike racks, third grade, her braids dangling, her chin up, fists knotted around a pair of dull scissors, peeling into Brady Carr's tire. Brady Carr, who shoved me off the spinabout, tearing a long strip of skin from my ankle to knee.

Tugging the rubber from his tire, her fingernails ripped

red, she looked up at me, grinning wide, front-teeth gapped and wild heroic.

How could you ever forget that?

We all want to "take it to the next level"—that's what we keep calling it. For us, the next level means doing a real basket toss, with three or four girls hurling a Flyer ten, fifteen, twenty feet in the air, and that Flyer flipping and twisting her way back down into their arms. And not even Beth has ever done a stunt like this, not this high, not without a mat. We were never that kind of squad, not a tourney squad. Not a serious squad.

Once we master a basket toss, we can do real stunts, real pyramids because they are pyramids that end with true flying, with girls loaded up and slingshot into the air. The gasp-ahh-awesomness we've always dreamed of.

We have been youtubing basket tosses all day, watching sprightly girl after sprightly girl get thrown by her huskier squadmates into the air and then try to ride it as far as she can. Arms extended, back arched, she is reaching for something, and only stops when she has to.

Mostly, though, we watch girls fall.

"A girl over at St. Lou's died doing a basket toss that high last year," Emily says, her voice grave, like she's giving a press conference on TV. "She landed chest down in everyone's arms and her spleen popped like a balloon."

"Spleens don't pop," Beth says, though how she knows this is unclear.

"But I heard she had mono," someone says.

"What's that got to do with it?"

"It makes your spleen swell."

"No one here has mono."

"You don't always know."

"They banned it in my cousin's school," someone says.

"You can't ban mono," Beth says.

"You're not even allowed to do them on spring floors."

"Who could get their heels over their head like that?" spiral-curled RiRi wonders, lifting one of her legs off the floor.

"You do," Beth says. "Every Saturday night."

"So are you ready for it, Beth?" Emily grins.

"Ready for what?" Beth asks.

It's a relief to see her avert her eyes a little, which shows me how much she wants it. When Coach gives it to her, it'll make everything better. *Maybe*, I think, high on hunger, *they will even become friends.*

"Like it'd be anyone but you, Beth," Tacy says, rolling her eyes. "You're top girl."

Beth almost smiles.

Of course, we all want to do it. (Even me, five inches taller than Beth, a tragedy of birth.) It's the star shot, and we feel our bodies hardening, we feel our speed quickening, our blood pounding, thick and strong.

Tosses, two-and-a-half pyramids, table tops, thigh stands, split stands, wolf walls—Coach says they're what separates you from just another ass-shaking pep squad.

"So we're not an ass-shaking pep squad?" Beth mutters, her voice smoke-thick, her eyes shot through with blood and boredom. "If I wanted to be an ath-lete," she says, "I'd've joined the other dykes on field hockey."

Three-oh-seven and Coach strolls into the gym, her hair wound softly into a ponytail.

"Let's get started on that toss," she says. "We need four to make the cradle underneath—two Bases—and a Back and a Front Spot to get enough power. But who's going to be our Flyer?"

Our two killer Bases, Mindy and Paige, their legs like titanium pikes, saunter over, eyeing all of us. Wondering which one of our lives will depend on the strength of their flintlock collarbones, our feet lodged there, rising high.

I think, for a second, it might be me.

And why shouldn't it be me, twisting high, propelled skyward, all eyes lashed fast on me, my body bullet-hard and glorious?

But it has to be Beth. We all know it. Beth practically stepping forward, all five feet and ninety pounds of her, stomach tight as anyone fed solely on tar and battery acid.

She's our Flyer. Missed practices, insolence, but still she is our Flyer. Of course she is.

(Except the voice inside that says, Me, me, me. It should be me.

But, if not me, Beth.)

"Slaussen," Coach says, turning to Tacy, the ewe.

I feel myself stone-sinking.

"You ready to fly?" she says to Tacy.

There's a hush to everything, and a closeness in the air.

Not Beth.

And *Tacy*?

Tacy Slaussen, that little pink-eyed nothing, the one Beth used to call "Cottontail"?

But then I see it. Coach is putting Tacy—Tacy of the barking phone, Tacy, Beth's baby bitch—on the guillotine.

In my head, I hear the ear-popping snap, head clacking against the gym floor. Spleen splattered. So many ways to go wrong, to ruin yourself. Your legs like barrettes bent back, your body matchstick-snapped.

A pretty world of being pretty decimated in one splintering second.

That's what I secretly wanted, just moments ago?

I did. I still do. Those five inches, and no one will ever ask me.

None of us dare look at Beth, but we all watch Tacy, her flush face. You can see her heart beating all over her skin.

When I do sneak a look at Beth, I see she's not even looking up, coiling the drawstrings on her hoodie into a candy cane twist.

"Coughlin," Coach says to Mindy, whose boulder shoulders are ringed with bruises two seasons a year. "She'll be all yours. What do you think?"

Pausing, Mindy appraises Tacy.

"I could totally base her," she replies, looking at Coach as if with a thick wagging tail.

Coach nods. "Elevator her up and let's see what she's got. *One-two.*"

Mindy and Cori Brisky grab wrists, make a square.

"Three-four," Coach counts.

Tacy, her tendril limbs limply offering themselves, plants her foot in their wrist-weaved basket. One pancake palm on Tacy's back, the other just below her behind. Back Spotter Paige loads her in.

"Five-six," and Mindy and Cori lift Tacy from waist to shoulder, Tacy clambering frantically for their shoulders, Paige Sutcliff scrambling to back base her.

And up she goes.

"Seven-eight!"

And the girls, fingers flicking, legs rocking, toss her into the air.

Tacy's mouth open, struck.

Airborne.

Her whole body quivering like a plucked string.

Too scared to tuck, pike, toe touch, anything.

"Soften," shouts Coach.

Tacy sinking back down, all three girls scrambling, one of Tacy's legs jamming into Mindy's collarbone.

But they catch her. They don't let her hit the floor.

Tacy, walking it off, crying like a little bitch.

For an hour, Tacy falls and falls, over and over again.

Foot to face. Shin to shoulder. Face to mat.

Mindy and Cori angrier and angrier, the more knocks they take, elevatoring her up with greater and greater force.

Tacy starts sobbing a half-hour in, and never stops.

Off to her office for a phone call, Coach deputizes Beth to count in her absence.

Beth, looking at her, her mouth a straight line, says nothing. But when Coach's office door shuts, she starts counting.

One-two-three-four,

—*fucking ex*-tend, *Slaussen!*

Who can deny it is a masterful play? Take away the princess's crown and give it to the lady in waiting. The handmaiden. The servant.

Never, in all my lieutenant years, have I seen anyone go toe to toe with Beth. Never anyone who couldn't be felled with an errant Facebook rumor, a photoshopped image (*RiRi skanking it up over spring break*), the pilfered text message sent to the entire school. This was different.

Different because no one had ever taken her on and different because no one had ever wanted to do so on our behalf. Coach did it for us.

And her will was strong as Beth's maybe. Maybe even.

Watching Tacy, shin red-streaked, a long bone bruise readying to bloom on her forearm, we all know what's happened.

We all know why, that Saturday, Tacy will be landing, at terrible and just velocity, in our meager arms—arms weary from ten hours of Dieter's Tea and celery shreds—we all know why.

Because Coach sees Beth for what she is and knows she has to overthrow her.

And Tacy?

A pullet-pawn.

—

Two days till the game, we are practicing like Tacy's life depends on it, since it does.

I'm the Front Spotter because Coach says I have in focus what I lack in heft.

We start with a straight ride, no twists or toe touches or kick-arches. We've practiced all week, and never once missed, our hands wrapped around each other's locked wrists, steeling our arms so tight, bolting them in place, a safe little girl-cradle for Tacy's quaking feet.

Then, rubber-banding our arms to spring her shaking body up into the air, all our eyes on Tacy, making that promise to her, the birdy panic on her face as she flies, flies, flies.

But, had we slipped, any of us, had one of our arms weakened, her leg curled the wrong way, her body twisted an inch or less, she'd have hit a spring floor.

And when we try to get her higher, Tacy's landings are rougher. There are incidents: elbow to the eye, index finger bent back, Tacy's grasping hand clawing my face.

But I focus on Tacy, and I don't show my fear. That's what Coach tells me. "Don't let her see it on you, or it'll swallow her."

I won't let her see it.

Coach tells us you can fall from eleven feet and still land safely on a spring floor, our practice floor.

She says that knowing that, game time, Tacy will be flying high over not a spring floor but the merciless ground of the Mohawks' football field.

"Slaussen," Coach says, "you gotta want it. Don't do it if you don't want it."

And Tacy, her back straighter, her eyes clearer, her chin higher than I've ever seen on this meek and weak girl, replies, "I want it, Coach. I want it."

Tacy. Here was the head-smacking convert.

I can feel Beth's eyeroll without even looking.

"I knew that one was wasting our time," Beth says.

But I don't say anything. I am watching Tacy's avid eyes.

Friday night, when we set foot on the Mohawks' field, the frosted ground beneath us, how can we not picture Tacy's skull splitting daintily in two?

And two of the Mohawk squad bitches, the rangiest with legs like spires, circle us before and start gaming us with tales of bloodsport. A mix of fish tales, trash talk and camaraderie.

"JV year, the girl was fronting a new Flyer learning her twist," the blonde says, gum popping, "and when the Flyer spun around her legs came apart and knocked out both Bases. One popped a lip and the other had to get a face cut glued shut. Coach caught it on video and replays it at all our after-parties."

"I was practicing my back handspring," the scrubby red-head says, "and I kicked Heather and knocked her teeth right out of her face. It was insane. Teeth and blood were flying everywhere. I felt soooo bad."

There is a breathless momentum to it. I know how it goes. It's fun when you're doing it, like hearing a ghost story.

Forty-five minutes from now, it will not be fun for Tacy,

standing fifteen feet in the air, two spindly girls holding you up, ready to toss you.

Tacy is gray, into green.

Beth saunters over. She gives me a look, one I know from her captain days. I nod.

"That's enough," I interrupt everyone. "Don't know about you hardcore bitches, but we'd rather spend our pregame time getting pretty."

But the blonde Mohawk, eyes hard on Tacy, won't stop working her. "This one kid, she had a body just like yours. And she hit the tramp bar, hard. Her head was bleeding a *lot*, and she had to go to the ER. Turns out the skin on her head had split and you could see all this pink stuff underneath. She needed staples to pull it back together. We couldn't get her to come back to cheer no matter how hard we tried. Now she isn't doing anything at all."

"Slaussen," Beth shouts, looming over us now. "Coach wants you."

Rabbit-like, Tacy skitters away.

For a second, I think it's done. But it's not.

Beth surveys the Mohawk girls.

"Once," Beth starts and I know what she's going to do, and this is why she was captain, "I was standing on this girl's shoulders and I slipped and fell flat on my back."

Everyone gasps politely.

"The crack was so loud they heard it in the parking lot," I add.

"My first thought," Beth says, shaking her head, "was how am I going to tell my mom?"

Everyone nods appreciatively.

"I was lucky," she says, her cool gaze on those Mohawks, shivering a little now in their long timbers. "I was only paralyzed for six weeks. They bolted this metal ring into my skull with pins to hold my head and neck in place. It's called a halo, if you want to know."

We two, in such sync, like the old days, like before Coach, before last summer.

Reaching up, I touch Beth's hair lightly with my fingertips. "The doctors said if she'd been an inch to the right or left," I say, "she would have died."

"But I didn't," Beth says, "and nothing would ever stop me from cheering anyway.

"They gave me the coolest purple cast. And Coach tells me I'm the best Flyer she ever had."

Under the bank of stadium lights, Tacy's face poppy-pink with purpose and mania, we raise her up, her hands releasing our trembling shoulders, and she rockets herself, thrusting her legs in either direction, arms pressed against her ears and flying higher than I've ever seen.

So high that a wild shake ripples through all of us, our cradled arms vibrating with awe and wonder.

Vibrating so strongly that it runs through me, it does, and I feel my left arm slacken, ever so slightly, and a shudder bores through me and if it weren't for RiRi next to me, feeling my tremor, flashing me her terror, a starry span of panic before my eyes, I wouldn't have driven that steel back into my blood, my muscles, my everything.

Made it tight and iron-fast for Tacy, who seemed to be in the air for minutes, hours, a radiant creature with white-blonde hair spread wing-like, finally sinking safely, ecstatically into all our arms.

It's hours later, and we're in Emily's dad's car sneaking swigs of blackberry cordial, swiped from RiRi's garage, where her brother hides it.

We're waiting in the parking lot of the Electric Crayon, its neon sign radiating sex and chaos, making the cordial tickle our mouths and bellies almost unbearably.

We've never been on Haber Road before, except the time we went with RiRi's sister to Modern Women's Clinic to get ofloxacin and she told us after how she almost choked when they stuck that big swab down her throat, but it was still better than what Tim Martinson had stuck down her throat.

We all laughed even though it didn't really seem funny and none of us want to end up at Modern Women's Clinic ever, the matted-down wall-to-wall, and the buzzing fluorescent lights, and the girl behind the front desk who sang softly to herself, "*Boys trying to touch my junk-junk-junk. Gonna get me some crunk-crunk-crunk.*"

An hour drifts by before Tacy finally comes out of the Electric Crayon, tugging her jeans down so we can see the Sutton Grove eagle soaring there, the envy so strong almost makes me burst.

Coach, she wouldn't come with us no matter how much we begged. But she did slip Tacy forty bucks for it. Two smooth twenties, tucked in our new Flyer's trembling hands.

We never heard of any coach doing that, ever.

Nudging my fingers under the sticking bandage on her lower back, I touch that red-raw eagle, making Tacy wince with pained pleasure.

Me, me, me, it should be me.

7.

"I've heard some things about Ms. Colette French," Beth tells me. "I have contacts."

"Beth," I say. I know this tone, I know how things start.

"I don't have anything to report yet," she says, "but be ready."

Like bamboo slowly sliding under fingernails. She has started.

But Beth also grows easily bored. That's what I have to remember.

I am glad, then, when Beth seems to have found something—someone—else to do.

Monday morning, the recruiting table is struck in the first-floor hallway, by the language labs.

The posters blare red, the heavy ripple of the flag insignia. *Discover Your Path to Honor.*

Recruiters, out for fresh, disaffected-teen blood.

"Who needs cheer?" Beth says. "I'm enlisting."

They came last year too, and always sent the broadest-shouldered, bluest eyed Guardsmen, the ones with arms like twisted oak and booming voices that echoed down the corridor.

This year, though, they have Sergeant Will, who is entirely different. Who, with his square jaw and smooth, knife-parted hair, is handsome in a way unfamiliar to us. A grown-up man, a man in real life.

Sarge Will makes us dizzy, that mix of hard and soft, the riven-granite profile blurred by the most delicate of eye-lashes, the creasy warmth around his eyes. And he speaks quietly, gently, with a little burr to his voice. His eyes seem to catch far-off things flickering in the fluorescent lights. He seems to see things we can't, and to be thinking about them, with great care.

He is older, he may be as old as thirty-two, and he is a man in the way that none of the others, or no one else we know or ever knew, are men.

Before practice, or during lunch, a lot of the girls like to hang around and finger the brochures. *Spread Your Wings*, they say.

Fresh off her latest breakup with Catholic Patrick, lovely RiRi spends pass time lingering at the table, leaning across it, arms pressed tight against either side of her breasts, framing them V-like and drawing one foot up her other leg, like she says men like.

"Personally, I find they like it when I lift my cheer skirt over my head," Beth says, side by side with me on the floor in front of her locker. "You might try that next time."

"Maybe you need some new tricks," yawns RiRi, eyes hot on Sarge Will. "What worked with your junior high PE teach might not roll with the big brass here."

This is how it starts, Beth rising to her feet like them's

fighting words, and asking RiRi if she'd care to make it interesting.

I can tell from RiRi's face that she would not care to do so at all, but it's the prairie whistle of the Old West, high noon at ole Sutton Grove High. You can hear Beth's tin star rattling against her chest.

So much better to have Beth face off with party-girl RiRi than Coach.

It's not that Beth just rolls for anybody or even most people, but when she does, it's a star turn, it's page one. Like with Ben Trammel, or the time everyone saw her and Teddy LaSalle, ebony against her ivory, in the holly hedges at St. Mary's after the game. All those forked nettles studding his letterman jacket, all up and down the felted arms, and his neck bristled red.

Everyone talked about it, but I was the one who saw her after. The bright pain in her face, like she didn't know why she'd done it, the alarm in her eyes, pin struck.

We've been angling, I have. *Coach, what's your place look like? Coach, we want to meet little Caitlin too, we do.*

Coach, show us, show us, let us in.

None of us ever think she will. We've tried for five weeks. I dream of it, driving by her house like a boy might do.

The next Saturday at the home game, Tacy kicks out that basket toss like she's been doing it all her life, and she adds a toe touch, and we do a hanging pyramid, with Emily and Tacy, swinging like trap doors off RiRi's arms, which whips up the crowd to fierce delirium.

There is such an ease to it. In the parking lot after, we're all feeling so good, like we could annihilate an invading army, or go to Regionals or State.

Beth is hoisting between her fingers a very fine bottle of spiced rum from some boy on the Norsemen team. He wants to party with us, and promises big excitement at his uncle's apartment, up on the Far Ridge.

Just the kind of wild night we'd all maneuver endlessly for, trading promises and fashioning elaborate lies, a string of phone calls home to marshal a fleet of alibis no parent could pierce.

Beth is the dark mistress of such nights and seems always to know where the secret house party is, or the bar with the bouncer who knows her brother, or the college boy hangout by the freeway where no one ever cards anybody, and the floors are sticky with beer and the college boys are so glad for girls like us, who never ask them even one question ever.

But as we conspire around Beth's car, my hand stroking the borrowed bottle, mouth clove-streaked and face rum-suffused, Coach walks past us, car keys jangling loudly.

"Going home, Coach?" Emily asks, swiveling her Nutra-slimmed hips madly to the music thudding from the car stereo. "Why don't you come out with us instead?"

We all look wide-eyed at Emily's pirate-boldness, Tacy's head curled merrily on Emily's shoulder, like a parrot.

Coach smiles a little, her eyes, thoughtful now, drifting past us, into the dark thicket of trees banded around the parking lot.

"Why don't you all come to my house instead?" she says, just like that. "Why don't you come over?"

"The smell of desperation," Beth says, "is appalling."
Beth does not wish to go to Coach's house.
"It's not my job," she adds, as we all look at her blankly, "to make her feel like she matters."

Standing in the front hallway, we wait while she sends off the babysitter, an older woman named Barbara in a peach chenille sweater that hangs to her knees.

Coach lets us poke our heads in and see little Caitlin fast asleep. The room is blushing pink with one of those rotating lanterns that flickers pretty ballerinas all over the walls.

Caitlin, strawberry blonde, nestles under rosy gingham with a doilyed edge through which she hooks one pink thumb.

Her breath is light and fast and we can hear it even huddled in the doorway, Emily and me, we're the ones who want to see. We look at her, the soft ringleted hair and the peace on her flushed face and wonder what that peace is like and if we ever had it.

We sit out on the back deck—me and RiRi and Emily and the newly brave Tacy, the lil cottontail whom we once ignored but whom we now gird to our chests proudly, our newly branded recruit, our soaring rocket.

Our cold arms buried inside our varsity jackets, at first so formal, we sit legs crossed tight, backs straight, speaking in light hushy tones, asking questions about the house, about Caitlin, about Coach's husband Matt.

We sit in the chilling air, on long benches flanking two sides of the deck. And there's Coach, on a lounger, slowly sinking back, hands tucked in her jacket pockets, her hair spreading across the teak slats, her face slowly, slowly releasing itself from its school-day tethers, its rigor and purpose.

The night feels important even as it's happening.

Once, Beth and I had a night like this, the night before we started high school. Kiddie-like, we'd hooked her brother's Swiss Army into our palms and pressed them tight against each other, and later Beth said she could feel my heart beating in my hand, her hand. She swore she could. We knew that meant something. Something had passed between us and would endure. We don't talk about it anymore and it was a century ago, wars won and lost since then.

And Beth, you're not even *here* now.

On Coach's deck, we all talk in the echoey night, first shyly, awkwardly, of nothing things—the Mohawks' forward with the bow legs, the way Principal Folger spins on one heel like a lady when he turns in the hallway, the doughy chocolate-chip cookies in the cafeteria, the tang of the raw eggs and baking soda churning in your stomach, making you sick.

Slowly, slowly, though, we feel the dark night opening among us, between us, and RiRi talks about her dad, who moved out last month and cries on the phone whenever they talk, and Emily shows us the very first ballet step she ever learned, and Tacy says she never felt so perfect as when she was flying in the air.

Would a boy ever make her feel that way, she asks. Would a *man*?

We all look at Coach, who's smiling and nearly laughing even, slouching low on the lounger and flinging one leg over the other.

"Girly," she says, lively and light, like you rarely hear, "you have no idea the wonderful things men will make you feel."

Tacy smiles, we all do.

"And terrible things too," Coach adds, her voice tinier now. "But the terrible things are . . . are a kind of wonder too, I guess."

Tacy props her feet up on the foot of Coach's lounger. "How can something terrible ever be wonderful?" she asks, and I cringe a little, *I know how,* I want to say. *I know how, everything wonderful is terrible too.* I don't know how I know it, but I do.

"You don't know enough about wonderful yet," Coach says, her voice tinier still, her face growing more grave, more meaningful. "Or terrible."

We're so close in that moment it feels like a humming wire between us, and no one wants to say a word for fear of snapping it, silencing it.

It's very late when RiRi plucks the pint from her boiled-wool pocket. Smirnoff vodka, the slummer's choice.

RiRi's move is bold, but without Beth here, somebody has to be.

"How about we all do one shot," she says, rising, stretching her arms to either side, as if to insist on the importance of the moment, "to toast the squad, and most of all Coach, who's made us . . ."

She pauses, then looks around, all of us watching nervously, eagerly. Watching her and watching Coach, who hasn't moved from her luxuriant slouch, whose eyes lock with RiRi's, as if deciding.

"To Coach," RiRi stutters, then, her voice building, "who's made us women."

Who's made us women.

This from RiRi, who's never said anything significant, ever.

Suddenly, I'm on my feet, my toes even, raising my arm high too, as if I held a champagne flute, a whole frosty magnum in my grip.

Emily and Tacy follow fast and we're all standing now, looking down at Coach, her chin lifting regally to receive us.

RiRi takes a gentle tug from that pint, then rocks her head back and forth from the kick of it. The rough, smutty smack of it. We all do. I feel it heating in me, firing up my whole body.

Then, I tender the pint to Coach, my hand trembling a little, wondering what she'll do, if we've done something here, swept her up in something with us, something we all want.

Her arm lifts serenely, without pause, her hand slipping around the pint.

Tilting it, her fingers nuzzled tight, she drinks.

—

Hand to hand, our warming fingers, we pass the pint until it's empty. My eyes tearing, my body blazing and strong.

Emily and Tacy go home, and RiRi is drunken-texting a new boy, who seems just like the last one and may even be the last one's brother, so Coach and I drift into the house.

"Hanlon—*Addy*," she says, and we pluck fruit from the big wooden bowl on her kitchen island as we walk by. "And you can call me Colette. These are Smirnov rules."

She snags a tangle of grapes and we slide them into our mouths one after another as she gives me the big tour.

Coach's eyes are a little blurred, and it's just a nice buzz we have, and I drop a grape on the carpet, and it smears beneath my sock, and I apologize four times.

"Fuck it," Coach—Colette—says. "You think I care about this carpet?"

And soon enough we're both kneeling on the carpet, woven wool in the deepest forest green.

"It's the face weight," she says. "That's what counts. Matt says you have to have forty ounces per square. And at least five twists per inch. He read it on the internet."

"It's beautiful," I say, and I've never really looked at carpet before. But now I can't seem to get enough of the feel of it on my knees, between my fingertips, dug deep.

"Addy," she says, pulling me up to my feet, dragging me from room to room, "you should've seen the wedding. We had a picture pool filled with rose petals. A harpist. Pin spots on every table."

She tells me they couldn't afford any of it, but Matt worked harder, until they could.

Five, six days a week, he left for work at five, came home at ten. He wanted to give her things. He let her have whatever she wanted. She didn't know what to want, but she cut out pictures from magazines. Assembled them in a book. *My Wedding*, it was called.

"I was barely twenty-one," she says, "what did I know?"

I nod and nod and nod.

"He found the house," she says, looking around, eyes blinking, like it's all new to her. Like she hasn't ever seen any of it before.

And so, age twenty-two, she had this house. And had to fill it.

He said *whatever you want*. So she cut out more pictures from magazines. She made a big bulletin board and called it *My House*. He saw what she wanted and he made it happen— as much of it as he could.

"He's very hardworking," she says. "He looks at numbers all day. And at home, that laptop is always open, those long columns of numbers, flashing and blinking. They never stop blinking."

Her hand skates across the pleated shade of an amber lamp.

"He does it for me, Addy," she says. But the way she says it, it doesn't match what she's saying. The way she says, it's like it's some leaden thing.

My head isn't straight, though, the vodka still stirring in me.

But I'm not so drunk that I don't understand that the house is like any of our houses. Not as nice as Emily's, where everything is white and you can't sit on anything, but nicer than RiRi's, which has brown ceiling stains and wall-to-wall.

But the way Coach—Colette—walks through it, her voice hushed, her feet treading so softly, it starts to seem like the whole place is glowing, like the spinning lantern in little Caitlin's room, casting enchantment everywhere.

"Beautiful," I say again, my fingers slipping around a curtain pull. "Beautiful." That's the word that keeps sliding from my mouth.

"Beautiful, beautiful," she says, singsongy, as we walk past it all, as I lace my fingers through everything.

"And this is the last of it," she says, and my feet are nestling in the bedroom carpet, which is deep, rich. It's a quiet, caramely space, like a nice hotel room where everything feels soothing and featureless.

But then I think of how she chose it all, Coach—Colette—with fabric swatches, tile samples, paging endlessly through those thick magazines you see fanned on tables at the white-walled boutiques on Honeycutt Drive. From the wrought-iron chandelier, its arms looping up, nearly stroking the ceiling, to the sheer curtains dangling, twisting sinuously around the drooping spider plant. Everything touching everything else.

She made it up inside her head, and he made it real for her.

It starts to seem like so much more, swelling before my eyes. Like everything is throbbing lightly, and if you rested your forehead against it, you could feel its heart beating.

"This is my favorite room," I say.

She looks at me, then looks around, like she's already forgotten all of it. Like she hasn't noticed any of it in years, since she tacked it together on her bulletin board. *My House.*

Our eyes float to the creampuff of a bed, its linen whipped up high. The princess and the pea.

Wearily, she sinks down into it, and everything seems to puff up, tiny cream-colored pillows scattering to the corners, the carpet.

"All these pillows," she says. "Every morning I put them all back. He's already at the office by six and I'm here, putting all these little pillows, these hundreds of pillows back on the bed."

I feel my foot sink into one of them as I stumble toward her. I've never seen so many pillows, every shade of brown, from pale honey to something the color of chicory, like the French teacher drinks every day at lunch.

She takes my hand and sets it on the duvet, soft as spun air. Her touch, a coach's touch. Feel this. Now.

"Lie down," she says. "Get under it."

My bare legs cocooned under the filmy duvet, I want to kick them in circles. The bed is a tremendous cream-filled pillow, no, air-filled cream, and the tickling in my belly, unbearable.

"Pretend you're me," she says. I can barely see her over the frothy mound.

And it happens just like that.

A feeling of sinking, a falling deep inside.

And I'm her.

And this is my house, and Matt French is my husband, tallying columns all day, working late into the night for me, for me.

And here I am, my tight, perfect body, my pretty, perfect face, and nothing could ever be wrong with me, or my life, *not even the sorrow that is plainly right there in the center of it. Oh, Colette, it's right there in the center of you, and some kind of despair too. Colette—*

—that silk sucking into my mouth, the weight of it now, and I can't catch my breath, my breath, my breath.

Everything's changing in me.

I guess I'd been waiting forever, my palm raised. Waiting for someone to take my girl body and turn it out, steel me from the inside, make things matter for me, like never before.

Like love can.

8.

Noonish, at the Guard recruitment table, we're watching the bet unfold.

All week, Beth has kept Sarge Will in her sights, determined to take RiRi down. They both agreed: whoever can get him to do a below-the-waist touch.

Beth works those school corridors like a gunslinger, spurred boots click-clacking. They curl over her knees, tall and shiny, and you're not supposed to wear boots with your cheer skirt, you're not supposed to wear boots like that at all.

As for RiRi, her cheer skirt hoists heavenward, waistband tugged high enough to show what her mama gave her. The two of them, they're dangerous.

Sarge, though, is above all this. All the girls are hurling themselves at him, but he never blinks, not once. He smiles, but his smile doesn't really seem like a smile but the kind of thing you do with your mouth when you know everyone is watching.

Sometimes it's like each hip swivel is a burden he strains under. So he just smoothly shifts such attentions over to the corporal, the private, whoever the hard-jawed thug next to him is, the one we never look at, that brush of acne on his chin, that angry look on him, like the boys who get into fights after one beer, who shove their girlfriends at parties and knock their shoulder blades loose, who pop their collarbones like buttons. We never look at them. Or I don't.

The worst is Corporal Prine, the one with the barrelhouse shoulders and the broad head like an eraser stub. A few weeks ago, I spotted him standing in front of the door of my English class. He seemed to be staring right at me, his razor-burned cheeks studded red. I tried not to pay attention, but then he did something with his tongue and hand that could not be ignored.

But Sarge, he can do anything. Yet the more we try, the less interested he seems. Most days, he seems to be some other place entirely, some place in which girls like us have no place at all.

Even Beth at her tartiest can't provoke him.

I don't see it, but I hear about it—the flash of her skirt, the star-spangled panties—and I don't believe it. *I didn't flash any-thing*, she tells me later. Just curled her index finger, made him lean close, and asked him if she could feel his weapon.

But Sarge doesn't bat a downy eyelash.

Oh, the daily frustration on RiRi's candy-mouthed face, and worse still Beth's glower, which she wears like a black veil all day.

Between Coach and Sarge, she has much to be unhappy about.

But instead of wrath and plots, she is quiet, brooding.

There's a witchiness to it, and it worries me.

Two weeks later, maybe three, and the special magic of Coach's house is gone. We've been there a half-dozen times, and in daylight, our sneakers skittering through the house, sheets of hair whipping around the corners.

If we come after practice, Coach disappears for the first half-hour into Caitlin's room, unpacking her from daycare, swabbing her caked face with a bristly hand cloth.

While we slide out yoga mats in the living room, tall bottles of gurgling kombucha, fermented tea we chug until we feel we'll never need to eat again.

In her bedroom, Coach sets Caitlin high on the mountain of cushions and loads up the princessy DVDs, the cartoons of long-haired, switch-waisted girls with dinner-plate eyes and chirping voices. Five minutes in, music swollen and voices purling endlessly about dreaming and dreams and following them and making them come true.

They give me a somber feeling I can't account for, something old and half-forgotten, panting inside me, so deep I can't name it.

Then Coach joins us, shoes flipped off, body loosening, hair slipping from its rubber band.

We're on our mats, pelvises high in the bridge pose, supine.

We're waiting for her.

It's during those weeks that I see Coach's husband for the first time, through the half-open study door. He's reading a sheaf of paper while slowly pulling off his necktie. I can't even tell you what he looks like except there's nothing to notice at all.

The next time, and the time after, it's always like this presence. *Matt's here. Oh, that's just Matt, finally home. That's the pizza guy for Matt.* And sometimes just *"he." There he is, oh, we can't turn on the stereo, he's here. Oh, you know him, he's working. He never, ever stops.*

Even knowing all the things he gave her, there is not much enchantment to actually seeing Matt French. He is always on his cell phone and he always looks tired. Once or twice, we see him in the backyard, talking into his bluetooth, pacing around the yard. We see him sitting on a stool at the kitchen island, spreadsheets spread across the table, his laptop swiveling, screen glowing green on him.

He works very hard, and he's not interesting at all.

Or maybe he is, but Coach never seems interested. And when he's there, it feels strangely like Dad's home. A nice-enough Dad, and not a buzz-kill Dad except, it seems, for Coach, who seems to sink inside a little. Once, he tried to ask about how we planned our pyramids because he studied real pyramids in college engineering and wondered if it was similar. But no one knew what to say because we were all a little drunk and Coach said, her eyes shifting away, that we were just tired because we'd been working on sequences all night.

"Man fears time," he said, as he walked off into his study, smiling at us all and kind of saluting good night, "yet time fears the pyramids."

Once, I'm passing the door to his study and I see him there, and the computer screen flickering, reflected on the window behind him. And I see he's playing Scrabble online. And something about it makes me crashingly sad.

—

"Beth, just come, will you? Just once, come with us."

We have been trying for the last three weeks. But when Beth does concede, I don't like how easy it is.

"Let's see what all of you have going on over there," she says, eyes flashing. "I'd like to see for myself."

Three Saturdays in a row, we've lounged, grown-up like, at Casa French, the grill fired up, Coach flipping salmon on cedar planks. Nothing ever tasted so good, even though we all only pick at it, shred it to pink pilings on our plates, our mouths focused eagerly on the tickly white wine served in fine stemware that *tinggged* when your nails clicked it.

It's harder to enjoy it with Beth there, feeling her dismissive eyes on everything. But the wine helps.

We have a routine down, Emily and me lighting all the candles, the hurricane lanterns with the hand-painted ladybugs that Matt brought all the way from South Carolina, and the tall gas torch that Coach says is just like what they have on the beach in Bali, though she's never been there, none of us have. Beth, dull-eyed and afflicted, says it's the same ones she's seen in Maui, or even San Diego, or the Rainforest Café out on Route 9.

Eventually, though, the wine whirls even through Beth and it's so fun looking around the table at everyone's blooming, candlelit faces.

Mostly, it's all of us chicken-jabbering and Coach, her silent, half-smiling self. She listens and listens, and the stories, as before, get darker and more intimate. RiRi's endless stories of abuse at the hands of callous boys and Emily's hollow stomach and bottomless hunger. And we twirl them into nasty jokes, into epic silliness, *Oh, RiRi, maybe one day you'll find a boy who loves you for more than your double-jointed jaw. And Emily, six weeks running on Splenda and cabbage broth, as caved-in as your belly looks you'll never get that round face of yours any thinner at all unless you take a hammer and chisel.*

At some point I realize Beth's gone and someone says she went to use the bathroom.

When she returns, she has a pleased-with-herself look that lets me know she was prowling the house and who knew what damage was done.

I remind myself to ask her about it, but then the thought drifts away.

By the time Husband Matt comes home around eleven we are all pretty drunk, Coach maybe even a little bit, that bloom to her face and her tongue slipping around words, and when RiRi takes off her top and runs around the yard, shouting into the bushes for boys, Coach just laughs and says it's time we met some real men, and that's when we see him standing at the kitchen island, and we all think that's hysterical, except Matt French, who looks tired and flips open his laptop and asks us if we could be quiet, which we can't possibly be.

Beth, who keeps saying she isn't drunk at all, but she never admits to being drunk, starts talking to him and asking him questions about his job, and if he likes it, and what his commute is like. She squeezes her breasts together in her tank top and leans on the kitchen island, fingers grazing his computer mouse rhythmically.

He looks at her, his brow knitted high in a way that I do find sweet, and asks if her parents might wonder where she is.

Over Beth's shoulder, he's throwing these looks at Coach, who finally says she'll drive us all home and Emily and Beth can pick up their cars tomorrow.

When we're walking out, I look back at him, and his face looks troubled, like years ago, eighth grade, and my dad, who no longer bothers, watching me as I left the house with Beth, our bodies suddenly so ripe and comely and there was nothing they could do.

The next day, hungover on the L-shaped sofa in Beth's living room, I wake up to Beth's hair dangling over me. Leaning over the back of the cushion, she tells me she didn't have any fun at all. And she's talking big, which always feels ominous.

"Sitting there on the deck, like it's her throne," she says, cotton-mouthed and craggy. "I didn't like it there. I don't like the way she conducts herself." There's a hitch in her voice and I wonder if she's still drunk, or I am.

"So high on her seat," Beth says. "All of you mooning like schoolgirls."

But we *are* schoolgirls, I think to myself.

"You have always been soft to these things, Addy," she says. "Last summer you were."

And I don't want her to talk about last summer again, and all our bickerings at cheer camp when everyone thought we were busting up. Because this has nothing to do with that girly nonsense.

Suddenly, I remember something through the blur of

wine. "Beth, what did you do when you went inside the house last night for all that time?"

But she just looks at me, shaking her head.

"I tell you, Adelaide, I know her kind."

Climbing over the back of the sofa, Beth swings her bare legs, nestling into me, and I'm listening but not listening because I don't like that hitch in her voice.

"She better enjoy it while she can," she rumbles, burrowing her head into the pillow I've tucked under my arm, burrowing her head into me, like always. "Because in a few years she'll probably pop out another kid and her hips'll spread like rising dough and before she knows it, she'll be coaching field hockey instead."

Twisting her fingers in my hair, she tunnels into me and the pillow behind me, hiding herself.

"Who will want her then?" she asks.

Then answers.

"None of us."

9.

There is a golden period, a week, two, when Beth seems to have settled herself, when all our days are brimful with cheer, when everything seems, for a moment, like it will be golden-grooved forever.

Homecoming Week is starry and sublime.

For much of the school year, the rest of the student body views us as something like lacquered lollipops, tiara'd princesses, spirit whores, chiclet-toothed bronze bitches. Aloof goddesses unwilling to mingle with the masses.

But we never care because we know what we are.

And at Homecoming, we are given full rein.

At the pep rally, they see our swagger, our balls, our badassery. They get to see what we can do, how our bodies are not paperdolls and how our tans are armor.

How we defy everything, including the remorseless sugar-maple floor planks nailed a half-century ago, ten feet below, our bodies tilting, curving, arcing, whipping through the air, fearless.

Homecoming Week, even those who dislike us the most —the painted Goths, the skater rats, the third-sex drama freaks—gaze with embarrassed wonder as we spring into our hanging pyramid on the open quad at lunch, our bodies like great iron spokes on a massive wonder wheel.

And at the game, as we catapult Tacy to the heavens—the

woozy screech from the stands as they seem to believe that we have flung her to her death—it inspires shock and awe.

I'm the one, strutted high on Mindy and Cori Brisky's shoulders, who kicks off the pep rally, waving a long pole looped with streamers, Tacy running alongside with Custodial Services's pilfered leaf blower, blowing against the streamers, which unfurl like so many roman candles.

The bonfire is the highest we've ever had, our torches whirling, all the circles of light, a foam-toothed Rattlers' mascot going up in flames, swinging high above the cindery tips and all of us screaming to voicelessness, our faces hot and exploding.

Dropping our torches, we run across the dark field, Coach's voice calling out *Toe touch, lock arms, spread eagle . . .*

And there she is, ringside, watching us, eyes darting and everything about her glowing.

I remember, age twelve, watching this. From up high in the bleachers, watching the high-school squad in front of the wild inferno, flames vaulting, their silhouettes doing mad jumps, leaps, death defiance. One girl picking up her fallen baton rolling across sparking grass and knowing now, knowing having held that baton, that it is searing but she smiles and dances and leaps higher than anyone else.

And twelve-year-old Beth beside me, saying:

"Look at that, look at that," her voice when it was still filled with wonder.

But, after Homecoming, returning from our glory paths, something has shifted.

In Coach's eyes there is something burning moodily. We all note it and wonder what goes on with Coach. We try to chalk it up to post-Homecoming comedown, but we do nothing with it.

But two days that week, Coach cancels practice. We think it must be an adult thing in which we have no interest. Mortgage payments, a broken dishwasher, a flood in the basement.

Still, everyone wonders: what could go wrong in Coach's lovely life, with her nice home and her smooth hair and all those adoring girls wreathed at her feet in the gym stands?

But, of course, I know better. I know things, even though I'm not sure what, exactly.

The way she never meets Matt French's eyes. Watching him help her unload the dishwasher one evening, late, and she would not turn her head.

And the thing I saw, felt, under that creamy duvet of hers, that silk sucking into my mouth, the feeling of something weighing on me, on her, and I couldn't catch my breath.

Friday, Coach doesn't cancel. She just doesn't show up for practice at all.

"Maybe it's feminine medical problems," RiRi says. "That happens to my Aunt Kaylie a lot. Sometimes she has to take off all her clothes. She sits on the sun porch in her bra, rubbing ice cubes all across herself."

"That's for old ladies," Beth groans. "Maybe she's just sick of your face. Can you blame her?"

Emily, dizzy from Coach's x-treme juice fast, sucking on ginger peel all day, has to lean against the padded gym wall.

"She was going to bring me the potassium broth recipe," she whispers, her face feverish.

She starts to tell everyone about the broth, counting off the ingredients on her gum-sticky fingers: *raw garlic, beet tops, turnip tops, parsley, red pepper seeds, it alkalizes and then you—*

I nod and nod while Emily chirps and peeps, her little twigged legs trembling against the wall.

"Someone give her a fucking Kit Kat," Beth growls.

I throw an energy bar at Emily because I can't stand it anymore either.

We all watch as she eats it slowly, picking at it with shaking fingers, and then, turning greenish white, throws it all back up again in the wrapper.

Beth leans back on the long bench, extending one Aruba-tanned leg and examining it.

"Personally, I am sick of every one of you," she continues, eyes on perpetual roll. "Sick of everything and everybody."

Beth touches these things inside us sometimes. Inside me. It is one of her gifts, deeply misunderstood by others. It sounds like she's being mean, but she's not. Sick, sick, sick. It's something you feel constantly, the thing you fight off all the time. The knot of hot boredom lodged behind your eyes, so thick and grievous you want to bang your head into the wall, knock it loose.

I wonder if that's the thing Coach feels, at home, standing next to Matt French, loading the dishwasher, scrubbing her daughter's face.

"Hanlon," Beth says, jumping to her feet. "Let's trawl."

I look at her. "But if Coach shows . . . "

But I can tell where that will get me, Beth with her clenched jaw, about to unsnap. It reminds me of something I learned once in biology: a crocodile's teeth are constantly replaced. Their whole life, they never stop growing new teeth.

I get up, I follow.

There's something—always, even as late as junior year, us weary veterans now—about walking the echoing school corridors after school. The whole cavernous place, a place we know so well that all our dreams happen here, feels different.

It's more than the new stillness, more than the heavy bleach swabbed over every skidded, gum-streaked inch.

By day, we walk as if in a force field, surrounded only by one another—our great colored swirl of cheerness. It is not aloofness, superiority. It's a protection. Who in this ravaged battlefield doesn't want to gather close her comrades?

But after three o'clock, the schoolday's gush of misery rushing into the streets, TV rooms, fluorescent-lit fast-food counters all over town. And the school-after-school becomes a foreign place, exotic.

There are kids here, and teachers in strange lurking pockets, you never knew when or where, a huddle of physics grinds on the third-floor landing timing the velocity of falling superballs, the barking Forensics Clubbers snarking about capital punishment in the language lab, shaggy stoners slouching, their eyes bliss-glazed, outside the shop room—now called industrial design lab—the flash of nervous Mrs. Fowler flitting out of the ceramics studio, a foot-tall coiled candleholder thick with shellac in her shaking hands.

We stalk the halls, looking, hunting, scavenging.

I want to find something for Beth. No captain glory, no stable to call her own, not even a glance from Sarge Will to distract her, she needs *something*. Something to knock the gloomy ire from her: an abandoned joint, a senior boy and freshman girl doing furtive nastiness in some far-flung corner, his arm jammed up her shirt, up over her babyfat girl belly, her eyes wide with panic and excitement, already, in her head, practicing the telling of the moment even as the moment slips from her.

By the time we reach the fourth floor, there's a desperation to it. Beth flashes her eyes at me, and it's really a taunt. *Get me something, get me anything.*

But it's always complicated with Beth and me, where her desire ends and mine begins. Because when we first hear the sound, I realize it's me who wants it more. Wants something to happen.

And then it does.

A yard or two from the door to the teachers' lounge, we hear something.

The rough rhythmic sound of a chair skidding, lurchingly, across the floor behind the teachers' lounge door. It seems, suddenly, to be just for me.

Scrape, scrape, scrape.

Listening, Beth's eyes nearly pop with pleasure.

We're standing outside the door.

I'm shaking my head back and forth and whispering soundlessly *don't, don't, don't* as Beth, bouncing on her toes, leaning against the teachers' lounge door, dancing her fingers along it and mouthing things to me, *I'm opening it, I am, yes, yes, I sure am, Addy.*

I put my hand on the door too, which vibrates with all that clamor inside, that squeaking and thudding. My ear against the humming door, I can hear the breathless pant. It sounds so pained, I think. It sounds like the worst hurt in the world ever.

Like after RiRi lost it to Dean Grady at that party on Windmere and bled for hours in the bathroom and we kept pulling toilet paper from the roll in long, sloping drifts, like she was gonna die. Like she was gonna—

Just like that, Beth pushes her hip against the teachers' lounge door, and it swings open, and we see it all.

Every bit of it.

There, seated on one of the old swivel chairs, is Sarge Will, National Guardsman Will, and Coach spanning his lap, her legs bare and looped around him like a pale ribbon, feet dangling high, and his dress blue blazer wrapped asunder around her snowy nakedness, his hands pressed against her breasts, his face red and helpless. Her thighs are shuddering whitely and his hand curls around the back of her head, buried in her dark hair, sweat-stuck and triumphant.

Her face, though, that's what you can't take your eyes off of.

The dreamy look on her pinkening cheeks, all elation and

mischief and wonder, like I never saw in her, like she's never been with us, so strict and exacting and distant, like a cool machine.

It's the most beautiful thing I've ever seen.

I feel myself jostle backward into Beth the instant Coach's eyes meet mine, alarm and dread there. I feel myself hurling both Beth and me out the door, Beth's laughter clanging through the corridor, my hand dragging the door shut, closing my eyes to it. Wondering if I even saw what I saw.

But looking at Beth's gleeful, mocking face I know I have. I've seen it.

Later, I think about it. It wasn't like in the movies, soft-lit bodies writhing creamily under satin sheets.

It lasted only a second, so how could it pierce me with such thorny beauty—but it does.

Coach's face that long, hectic second before she saw me.

Like someone climbing her way out of the darkest tunnel, her mouth wide and gasping for air.

And his eyes shut so tight, face locking itself into place, as if to let go would destroy everything, would bury her again, and he only wants to save her, to breathe that hot life into her.

And she, gasping for air.

Within twenty minutes everything's changed.

By the time Coach finds us in the locker room, Beth and me jackrabbity with titillation, everything that had opened, gloriously, is shut again.

She is once more that iron ingot, hard and feverless, walking with purpose but without hurry, with no wilt or lilt in her step, no hair out of place from that shiny crest of hers.

In her office, she pulls the blinds down on the door then shakes out a handful of cigarettes on the desk.

This has never happened before, this offering.

Beth and I each take one, and I know what it means for me, to me.

And I know what it means to Beth, high on her new power perch, nuzzling her new wisdom close to her freckled chest.

But this, the extent of this, I can't think about yet.

Coach lights mine and when she does I look in her eyes and that's when I see she hasn't put on all the calm she wants. Those flat gray eyes are jumping.

Beth, slouching in Coach's seat, kicks her legs up and props her feet against the front of the desk. Scuffing its laminated edge.

She is very pleased.

As Coach walks past me to the window, I catch the scent, just barely. Sharp and fleshy and stinging my nose and *making me think of Drew Calhoun's bedsheets that time, the smell on them, even though we didn't, but he did.*

"I need you to understand what Will—what the Sergeant and I have is a real thing." She lets her gaze flit over us quickly. "A true thing."

Out of the corner of my eye, I see Beth piano-keying her fingers along her chin.

"I never thought it would happen," Coach says, and I think she means cheating on her husband. But then she says, "I never thought I'd feel like this."

I look at her, her arms curling around herself, her hands pulling at the wand of the window blinds, lacing around it and tugging like a little girl with her whole hand wrapped around her father's index finger.

Feel like what, I want to ask, but don't.

"Do you guys understand?" she asks, tilting her head, a strand of that perfect hair slipping across her face, grazing her mouth.

I do not look at Beth.

"I waited my whole life for it," Coach says, and I feel a buzzing in my chest. "I never thought it would happen. And then it did."

She looks at us.

"Wait until it happens to you," she says, breathing hard and her body twisting with it. With these magic words.

"Wait until it's you."

Don't tell anyone.

That night, fingers plucking the buttons on my duvet cover, thumbs on my phone, Beth's texts blipping under my fingers, *Agreed. This is just us. We keep quiet 4 now.*

I shut off my phone.

Wriggling there, thinking it all through, I start to see, for the first time, how it might be for Coach, young and pretty and strong. Why should she be stuck all day rousting chickens like us, or at least like some of us, on the shellacked floors of the Sutton Grove High School gym, our hapless ponytails flying, smarting off, being lazy, spitting gum on the floor, whining about periods and boys? She spends all her days like this and then home to her kid, pucker-mouthed and red-faced, a day of sugar and agitation in preschool, and her husband at work until the nightly news sometimes.

I start to think of it differently, as a home filled not with ease and liberty but with irritation and woe. Who wouldn't need the ministrations of the likes of Sergeant Will, and what he might give her? I wonder what he gives her and why what we give her isn't enough.

10.

"I *knew*," Beth says, before practice the next day, lifting her leg into a heel stretch. "I knew there was something wrong with her. What a fake, what a liar."

"Beth," I say. But the warning flare in her eyes says I better tread lightly.

"Beth," I say, "can you show me how you get your foot behind your head like that? Can you help?"

We are in Coach's backyard after practice, just the two of us. She has invited me. Just me.

We haven't spoken about Sarge Will, not yet.

Coach is trying to help me with my standing back tuck, which is weak at best. It's really just a tight back flip from a standing position and is one of those stunts all real cheerleaders can do in their sleep. RiRi says college cheerleaders do them at parties—"Tuck check!"—to test each other's drunkenness.

One of her hands on my waist, Coach uses the other to pull my knees up, flipping me hard as soon as I'm off the ground, her arms like a propeller.

She is in that focus mode where she doesn't even look me in the eye but treats my body like a new machine with parts not yet broken in. Which is what it is.

"If you can't back tuck," she says, "you can't land most

tumbling stunts." What she doesn't say: since I don't fly or do bottom Base, I need to be able to tumble.

I need to nail it.

"The pull is just as important as the set," she is saying, her breath fogging in near dusk. I can feel it on my face as she knocks her hip against mine. "You can have the best set in the world but if you don't pull your legs around after it, you're still going to land short."

Over and over, I start strong, arms up brace-tight, only to land on my hands, my knees, the tips of my feet.

It's a head thing. I feel certain I will fall. And then I do, my foot twisting beneath me.

"You think too much," Beth used to tell me.

She's right. Because if you think about it, you realize you can't possibly jump into the air and rotate yourself 360 degrees. No one can do that.

Beth, of course, does a flawless standing back tuck, and it's something to see.

It is incredibly high and perfect.

But Beth grabs from behind the thighs, not the shins like Coach likes.

"I don't want that sloppy stuff from you," Coach says. "Don't waste my time with that."

Again and again, my shins grass-streaked and the sky heavy with dusk.

"Chest up," she shouts, every time I land, to keep me from falling forward.

Finally, I'm getting cleaner and she stops flipping me. And I start falling. She lets me fall every time.

"It's a blind landing, Hanlon," she says. "You're trying to find the ground. You gotta know it's not there."

I try to pretend I'm her. Try to feel tight like she does, so tight nothing can touch her. I think of squeezing my whole body into a tight ball.

"Ride that jump longer," her voice out there somewhere, vibrating in my ear, her hands there but not.

And then releasing.

"Open your body," she keeps saying, and it's shuddering through my whole head. "Open it."

And I feel myself doing just that, an explosion from the center of me to my toes, my fingertips.

It is just after dark, the timered deck lamps flickering to life, when I start landing it.

The feeling is majestic, and I know I can do anything.

I feel like I could rotate myself forever and land every time, arms upraised, chest high, body both shattered then restored. Immaculate.

The night outside her front picture window is blue-shivery, but we are curled on her sofa, our legs folded under ourselves, our bodies loose and victorious.

"Addy, I know how it probably looks," Coach is saying to me, leaning close, cigarettes and tall plastic cups of matcha green tea as my back tuck reward. "But you have to understand how things are. With Will and me."

She runs her finger around and around the rim of her cup. Her eyes are ringed darkly and it's like I always hoped it would be. I'm the one she's telling. She chooses me.

"And Matt, Addy . . . " She sighs and arches her back, looking vaguely to the ceiling. "Maybe you think when you're as old as I am, you couldn't want things anymore. When I was your age, twenty-seven might as well be a hundred."

"You don't seem old at all," I say.

We sit for a while, and she talks. She tells me how it started.

Seeing her in the parking lot after the college fair, he told her she looked sad and wondered if she would like to sit with him in his car, parked on Ness Street, and listen to music. "Sometimes it makes me feel better," he said, and maybe it would make her feel better too.

She hadn't known she looked sad.

So they sat and they listened to some black singer she'd never heard of, a woman with a croony, needy voice, *don't go to strangers, darling, come to me.*

And the music did something, and suddenly they were talking about big things, personal things.

She told him the way she felt after Caitlin was born, like the secret of life had been told to her at last and the secret was this: in the end all the things you think matter are just disappointment and noise.

And then he told her about his wife.

"Do you remember the story on the news," she whispers to me, leaning close. "A couple years ago. That meth head from upriver drove through the front window at Keen's pharmacy? And the customer inside who died?"

I didn't remember exactly, these stories like static on faraway currents, but something about a photo they ran on the news and in the papers that alarmed everyone. A plate-glass window sheeted red. A figure slumped behind it.

"That was Will's wife," Coach says, so solemn. "She was five months pregnant."

Sitting together that night, under the pin oak on Ness Street, he told her all about it. About the things it had done to him, the way he saw the world. His year in Afghanistan nothing like the dark hole her loss drilled in him.

They talked for an hour, two, and by the time his hand dropped, almost as if by mistake, into her lap, it was like it was meant to be there.

The feeling took her by such surprise, a buckling in her stomach, and he saw it, and then everything started and, eyes shuttering back, she thought, *This is happening, right now. And it had to happen. How did I not know this.*

You have something that I need, he told her. But he had it backward.

The backseat, the seatbelt buckles cutting into her, her foot sliding on the window pane.

After, her own hands tingling and helpless, he buttoned her shirt back up, slid her barrette back in her hair. The tenderness, like when Matt French buttoned Caitlin's pinafore, when he tied her little shoes.

When I get home, Beth is waiting in the middle of my front lawn, which she hasn't done since she was nine, and it has the same quality of ominousness it did then. *Why did you go to Jill Randall's birthday party when we said we hated her?*

Or last summer, legs dangling from my upper bunk at

cheer camp, asking when I decided I wasn't bunking with her after all.

"Where were you?" she asks. "We have items to discuss."

"At Coach's," I say, unable to stop the giddy hiccup in my voice. My body still feels stretchy and my heart proud and strong.

"She is so transparent," she says, eyeing me head to toe. "Now she wants to be your best friend, huh? Sharing secrets on her outlet mall sofa? She thinks she can work us like two-dollar whores. I hope you are not a whore, Addy. Are you a whore?"

I don't say anything.

"Are you a whore," she says, walking toward me, "and is Coach your sweet-lipped Mack Daddy whispering promises in your ear?"

"I was practicing," I say. "She's the coach."

Beth folds her arms and stares me down.

I don't say anything.

"Haven't you learned anything, Addy," she says. I'm not sure what she means, but I know I have to settle her.

We are both quiet, my hands getting cold and Beth in her puffy jacket unzipped.

I see the quality in her eyes I know from back when, from some girl-recesses of time spent hiding in playground tunnels together, nursing schoolyard wounds.

Nobody might understand about Beth because her seeming power overwhelms. But I can see behind things.

And so I find myself reaching my pinkie out to twine hers, and she shakes it off and gripes some more, about Coach's treachery and false friend ways, but I do see her rest the smallest bit inside, her shoulders unhunching from a toadlike curl.

We end up back at her house, down in the basement. No one ever goes down there except Beth's brother when he used to robotrip with his friends.

We lie on the sectional and the moonlight tumbles through the high window and I start it this time, our favorite thing. Or what used to be our favorite thing, but we haven't done it in so long.

Taking the Vitamin E oil from my backpack, I do a soft massage on Beth's right knee, where she tore ligaments landing on the marble floor of the school hallway, which is the kind of thing Beth sometimes does.

I do these light-as-feather tap taps with my fingertips, which she likes.

After, hands pearled with her sweet almond salve, she does her hard magic on me.

We started this at age ten at PeeDee Tumbling Camp and it was our thing and it was the way, always, to soothe us. Sometimes it was like a visitation, a trance.

She once said, breathless after, that it was a coolness that stilled her like nothing ever did.

We stopped when we hit fourteen or so I guess, which is when everything changes or you realize it has. I wonder why we stopped? But time gets away from us, doesn't it? That's a thing I know.

In the basement now, there is a powerful nostalgia. This is a Beth I haven't seen for a while, the Beth of subterranean nights, our self-whipped adolescent fears and JV yearnings: *I will never what if we never will we ever.*

I'd forgotten we were like that, before we were everything.

Her hands move quietly to my calves, of which I am newly proud, the muscle there, tight as a closed bud.

Her thumb slides up the diamond-shaped middle of the calf, and notches there, working slowly, achingly, pressing down to the hardest place then sliding her thumb up, the two muscle heads forking. It's like her thumb is a hot wand, that's how I always used to think of it.

I can feel Beth unloose it the way the last back tuck unloosed it. It feels warm and wet under my skin, and everything is lovely.

"You were burning this tonight," she says, so dark I can see nothing but the whites of her eyes, the silver eyeliner.

"I was," I murmur. "Back tucks."

And there's this sense that somehow she knows.

"How did it feel?" she whispers. "To nail it."

"Like this," I say, curling under the hard pressure from her hand. "But better."

11.

"It's to thank you," I say. "It's like a thank-you."

We're in Coach's driveway.

"For the back tuck," I say.

She holds it up to the car light, examining it.

"It's my hamsa bracelet," I say. "You said you liked it."

When she saw me wearing it, she'd said, "What, you some kind of wicca, Hanlon?"

I'd shown her its hand-shaped charm—mirror-plated, with two symmetrical thumbs, an ancient amulet for magical protection from the evil eye.

"Sounds like something I could use," she'd said. And maybe she was kidding, but I wanted her to have it.

And now she's holding it, its crimson cord laced across three middle fingers, like she doesn't know what to say.

Reaching out, I spin the hand-charm with my index finger so she can see the big eye planted in the middle of its mirrored palm.

She holds up her wrist so I can put it on.

"It wraps around twice," I say, showing her.

"Twice the protection," she says, smiling. "That's what I need."

"You're Addy, right? Colette's favorite," he says, when I get in the backseat. Upfront, Coach is putting lipstick on in the mirror, a deep garnet shade I've never seen on her before. It makes her mouth look wet, open. It's distracting and I try not to look.

Addy, she'd said, looking at the hamsa bracelet tight on her wrist, *I have an idea.*

That's how it comes to be that it's late at night now and I'm in Sarge Will's SUV, so big inside it's like being in the center of a velvet-lined box, everything dark and buffered, soft sides and hard corners and the sense of nothing out there touching you.

I look at him, thinking how strange it all is. Sarge Will, but not in his uniform, and his shirt still finely pressed but some stubble on his jaw, and his eyes, most of all his eyes, not coolly watchful, as in school, as in when he scours the teeming, sweaty messes of students for recruits, pinpointing all the lost souls that fill our halls, all the ones who live close to the freeway and the ones I never notice at all.

No, his eyes aren't like that at all now. There's a looseness, and an openness and some other things I can't name. All the remoteness gone and he's this man, and he smells a little like laundry detergent and cigarettes, and he has a nick on one knuckle of his left hand and when he turns the steering wheel I see faint sweat scalloping under his arm.

Will is drinking from a pint he's holding nestled between his legs as he drives. When he hands it to me, the bottle is so warm.

Come with us tonight, she'd said. *I want you to understand how it is.*

And now I do.

We drive to Sutton Ridge, the fall air shivery and the smell of burning leaves drifting from somewhere.

"I thought there was no place left," Will says, "where people still burned leaves."

Because they do burn leaves here, the older folks do, and I remember now that I love it and always have. The way fall feels at night because of it, because of the crackling sound and walking around the sidewalks, like when you're a kid, and kicking those soft piles, and seeing smoke from back-yards and Mr. Kilstrap standing over the metal drum with the holes in the top, the sparking embers at his feet.

Where'd that world go, that world when you're a kid, and now I can't remember noticing anything, not the smell of the leaves or the sharp curl of a dried maple on your ankles, walking? I live in cars now, and my own bedroom, the win-dows sealed shut, my mouth to my phone, hand slick around its neon jelly case, face closed to the world, heart closed to everything.

It seems Will knows this older world and it binds us together and I realize we are meant to be close because, like she does, he opens deep pockets in the center of me I never knew were there.

"Let's go to Lanvers Peak," says Coach, voice light and high, a girl's voice. She's looking back at me now, that mouth of hers red and glorious. The excitement, and Will grab-bing her thigh so hard that I can feel it, I can feel his hand shaking my own thigh to gritty life.

Lanvers Peak is not a place for cars, but it is a place for Will's Jeep, because nothing will stop him.

Driving up, Will is talking about the gorges and how they were gouged by glaciers hundreds of times over two thousand years like God's own carving hand on the dark earth, or so his grandfather used to say.

We're higher than I've ever been and we're drinking bourbon, which is the most grownup thing I've ever had and I pretend I like it until I do.

Up high, where the sky looks violet against the peak, Coach and I kick off our shoes, no matter how cold it is, the silvered grass crunching under our feet.

"Show me," Will is saying, and he is laughing. "Show me."

He doesn't believe we can do the Shoulder Sit, just we two and dizzy on bourbon.

"You say it's so dangerous, but compare it to offensive tackle, which left me with these," he says, lifting his pretty lip to show me his front teeth, snowy white. "Caps, like my gramps. That's what real sports do to you."

Baiting us, he makes me want to turn my body into the lightest, most miraculous thing, makes me want to show him what I can do so that I will feel perfect and loved.

So we show him, without a spotter and in spitting distance from the depthless purple gorge so beautiful I want to cry into it.

I feel my phone buzzing and I don't even look at it, dropping it to the ground.

Coach and me, we're laughing now, Coach's mouth red and her hair tumbling against me as we scramble to the most solid patch of an unsolid turf.

Lunging forward, she calls to me and I set my bare foot high atop her bended thigh, lifting myself, swinging my other leg over her shoulder, as she rises to her feet. Wrapping my thighs around her, twining my feet behind her, and we are one.

We are one.

I never did a stunt with Coach before.

At first, we are a sorry case, weaving and laughing, and Will drill-sergeants us until we get focus, my thighs locking tight around her and Coach grinding her feet into the frosty grass.

Then I unlock my feet and thrust my legs forward, Coach reaching under and between my thighs to grab my clammy hands in hers. Dipping down, she gives me a pop, pulling me over her head, my legs swinging from behind her, then together again, my feet landing hard on the ground.

The sear up my leg is nothing at all. Nothing.

We are stupendous and Will is cheering and yelling and hip-hollering and it echoes through the ravine in majestic ways.

Up above her shoulders, fixed tight upon her, it is something. My eyes drift down to the icy bottom of the gorge and we are higher than we ever thought we'd be.

My house is farther, and Coach gets dropped off first, which is a mind-bending prospect.

He pulls over a half-block from her house and watching them kiss, watching the way he opens her mouth with his, her sneaky looks back at me, the pleasure on her, I feel myself go loose and wondrous inside. I want to be a part of their kiss, and maybe even they want it too.

It's only a five-minute drive to my house, but it feels like it lasts forever, all the misted lightness of Lanvers Peak gone.

"Tonight was the first time I ever saw you without that other girl," Will says. "The one with the freckles."

This seems the craziest way to describe Beth ever, but it makes everything go tight in my head and I remember, coming off the peak, flipping open my phone and seeing *missed call, missed call, missed call*. A text: *you'd best pay attn to me*.

He looks at me and smiles.

Suddenly, I want to hold the whole night close to my chest and I decide it is mine alone.

"Seeing her with you, I understand now," he says. "She needs this."

For a second I think he means himself. And, thinking of her that night, so carefree, all the antic restlessness blown out of her, I think he is surely right.

But then he gestures toward my Sutton Eagles duffel bag, and I see he means being coach.

"She needs you girls," he adds.

I nod, gravely as I can.

"I know what that's like," he says. "The way you can be saved without ever knowing you were in trouble."

These are the words he says, but they sound like something I'm overhearing, a conversation I'd never be a part of.

"I guess it's funny, me talking to you like this," he says.

I guess it is. Sometimes Coach doesn't seem that much

older than me, but Will, with his tragic dead wife and tours of duty, sure does.

"I know we don't really know each other," he adds. "But we know each other in a strange way."

I nod again, though really we don't know each other at all. It makes me think Will is one of those people who just tells everybody everything right away, and usually I don't like those people, those girls at summer camp sharing tales of cutting and kissing their babysitters. But this feels different. Maybe because he's right. Because we share a secret. And because I saw them together that day in the teachers' lounge, which felt like seeing everything.

"She has it hard," he says. "Her husband, he's not the guy you might think he is. She has it very hard."

Maybe it's the bourbon, or the bourbon wearing off, but this doesn't sound exactly right either, not really.

"He gave her that house," I say.

"It's a cold house," he says, looking out the window. "He gave her a cold house."

"It's her house," I say. "I mean, even if it's cold, it's hers."

He doesn't say anything, and I feel him drifting from me.

"And Caitlin," I say, but this sounds even less convincing. "There's Caitlin."

"Right," he says, shaking his head. "Caitlin."

We both sit for a moment, and I feel suddenly like we both might know something we can't name. About how, in some obscure way, Caitlin was another thing that wasn't a gift so much as the thing that stands in place of the gift. *My wedding, my house, my daughter, my cold, cold heart.*

12.

"Freaking rock star," RiRi marvels, finger spotting me.

I am doing perfect back tucks, one after another.

I know suddenly I was born to do them. I am a propeller.

"*This* is what a coach can do," RiRi grins. "Beth would never have let you get this good."

As soon as she says it, she seems almost to take it back, laughing, like it's a joke. Maybe it is.

"Knees to nose, Hanlon," Coach barks, a sneaky smile dancing there as she walks back into her office.

"*Pffht-pffht*," comes the sound from the bleachers, where Beth has slunk. "Watch that neck, Addy Faddy, or it's the ventilator for you. *Pfft-pffht*."

"Très J," whistles Emily. But I know Beth isn't jealous of my tuck. She can back handspring back tuck me into the ground, her body like a twirling streamer.

In the locker room after, Emily kicks her leg up, grabbing her toes as she stands on the center bench. Peashoot thin now, fifteen pounds lighter since the month before, she's set to fly with Tacy at the Stallions' game. All the hydroxycut and activ8! and boom blasters and South African hoodia-with-green-coffee-extract and most of all her private exertions have made her airless and audacious.

Eyeing her, Tacy is sullen, uneager to share Flyer glory.

Lying on the far end of the bench, Beth stares abstractedly up at the drop ceiling.

"Cox-sucka," she calls out to Brinnie Cox, who is curling her hair into long sausages and singing to the locker mirror. "How's your head?"

"What do you mean?" Brinnie lisps, her arm frozen. "My head is fine."

"That's a relief," Beth says. "I wondered if maybe you were still feeling the blood pushing against your brain. From that header you took a few weeks back. "

"No," she says, quietly.

"Beth," I say, a faint try at warning.

"As long as you're not a purger, you should be okay out there tonight. It's the regurgitators who drop like dead weight."

At the other end of the long bench, our girl Emily releases her leg and looks at the reclining Beth, who is staring straight up at the fluorescent lights.

"Chumming all the time," Beth says, "they bust all those blood vessels in their eyes. Then one day, out on the mat, they hit their head and . . . *ping*."

Beth snaps her fingers beside her temple.

"Once," she continues, "I heard a 'mia girl fell during a dismount and an eye popped out."

Propping herself up on her elbows, she looks down the long bench straight at Emily.

"But let's not talk of ugly matters," she says. "Our girl Em's going to rock it out tonight. Going out a youngster and coming back a star."

—

"She'd really miss the Stallions' game?"

Ten minutes before kickoff, Beth is nowhere to be found.

She's never no-showed a game. Everyone wonders if something happened, like that time she followed her dad and his paralegal to that Hyatt downtown and keyed the words MAN WHORE into the hood of his car.

Without her, we have to reconfigure the whole double-hitch pyramid. We count on Beth to be the middle Flyer, holding on to Tacy and Emily's inside legs as they swing out their other legs and stretch them sky high. She's the only one light enough to be that high and strong enough to support both girls. It's like juggling jigsaw pieces that don't fit and I can see Coach's face tighten.

"Should we skip the stunt?" I ask Coach.

"No," Coach says, eyes on the field, breeze kicking up her. "Cox can stand for her."

I look at flimsy Brinnie with her chicken-bone legs.

RiRi looks at me, squintingly. But I shrug.

"Coach knows what to do," I say.

Brinnie's right arm starts shaking during the double hitch.

I can see it from the back spot and I'm shouting at her, but the panic hurdles across her eyes and there is no stopping it.

On the half-twist Deadman fall, that pin-thin arm of hers gives entirely and Emily, now just an eyelash of a girl, her head dizzy with visions of blood burst, slips and crashes, knee-first, into the foam floor.

Oh, to see her fall is to see how everything can fall.

Her body popping like bubble wrap.

In the back of my brain, I know that the clap we all hear from Emily's knee, like a New Year's champagne cork, is about that back tuck of mine.

Is about Coach and me.

I had epic cramps, Beth texts me that night.

You had it last week, I say. We all had our periods at the same time, the witchiness of girls.

Infection, she texts. *Cranjuice all nite, and mom's Narvox.*

Come clean, I text. She has never missed a game, ever. Not even when her mother slipped on the living-room carpet and dented her forehead on the coffee table, forty-seven stitches and three years' worth of vicodin.

Clean as a whistle, Merry Sunshine, she texts back. *Cleaner than yr coach.*

U know what I mean, I text. *Em might have a torn lig.*

There is a long moment and I can almost feel something black open inside Beth's head.

I got a torn life. Fuck all of you.

"Two-game suspension," RiRi tells us. "No Beth for two games. Em's down. And with Miz Jimmy-Arm Brinnie Cox spotting us it means our heads'll be popping all over the mat."

"It sucks," Tacy Slaussen says, trying not to grin. She has her eye on the prize. With Emily and Beth out, she's the only bitty girl left to fly.

"Beth blames it all on Coach," RiRi says.

"Coach?" I say, my eyebrow twitching.

"She said Em fell because she's been living on puffed air and hydroxy for six weeks to hit weight for Coach."

I look at her. "Is that what you think?" I say, surprised at the hardness in my voice, the old lieutenant steel. It doesn't go away.

RiRi's eyes go wide. "No," she says. "No."

I find Beth lying on the bleachers out back, sunglasses on.

"I look at all of you, how you are with her. Your paper-heart parade," she says.

"You never like anyone," I say. "Or anything."

"She never should've back-based Brinnie Cox, she's too short and too stupid," she says. "And you know how I feel about her teeth."

"You should've showed up," I say, trying to peer behind the black lenses, to see how deep this goes.

"Coach can't top-girl anyone else," Beth says. "She'll beg for me back."

"I don't think so," I say. "She's a rule-keeper."

"Is that so." Beth wriggles up and stares at me, eyes like silver-rimmed globes, an insect, or alien. "That hasn't been my experience of her."

I look at her.

"She may have the clipboard and the whistle," Beth says, "but I have something too."

"We're not saying anything," I say, my voice going faster. "We said we wouldn't."

"Are we a 'we' again?" she says, sinking back down onto the bench. "And I didn't promise anything."

"If you were going to say something, you would've," I say.

"You know that's not how to play," Beth says. "That's not how to win."

"You don't understand," I say. "The two of them. It's not like you think."

"Yeah," she says, looking at me, nail-hard. "You know better? You've seen into her knotted soul?"

"There's things you don't know," I say. "About him, about them."

"Things I don't know, huh?" she says, something less than a taunt, more urgent. "Illuminate. Like what? Like what, Addy?"

But I don't tell. I don't want to give her anything. I see something now. She's building a war chest.

The next night, Coach has everyone over for a party for Emily, whose fall has put her on the DL for six weeks, maybe more.

No one can even imagine six weeks. It's a lifetime.

It's too cold to be outside, but after the wine swells in all of us, we're even taking off our jackets, lounging lovely across the deck, watching the sky grow dark. Emily gets prime seat, high-kicking her boot brace for all to see, her eyes stoned on percocet. The happiest girl in the world, for tonight.

I decide to banish Beth's hex from my head, *She fell because she's been living on puffed air and hydroxy . . .*

Coach maps out our Saturday stunts on napkins spread across the glass-top patio table. We huddle around eagerly, following Coach's sharpie as it plots our fates.

"We have three weeks until the final game against the Celts," Coach says. "That's our goal. We shine there, we have a qualifying tape to submit, we go to Regionals next year."

We are all beaming.

No one asks about Beth until Tacy, our little stone-drunk Benedict Arnold, bleats, "And who needs Cassidy? We don't need the haters. We're going to Regionals with or without the haters."

We're all a little nervous, but Coach smiles lightly, looping her bracelet around her wrist. I smile to see it's my hamsa bracelet on her wrist, the evil-eye flashing in the porch light.

"Cassidy'll be back," she says. "Or not. But she won't be our Flyer again."

She looks down at her squiggled hieroglyphics.

"She's not the straw that stirs the drink," she says.

Eyeing the Flyer spot on the diagram, I watch her pen skim right and left, a big black X right in the center.

It's not until very late that we're jarred by Matt French's car door slamming from the driveway and, the same instant, Coach's deck chair shakes to life.

Dad's home, that's what it's like, and everything jumps. We all scurry to the kitchen, start stacking plates and shaking wineglasses empty over our mouths, and I'm helping RiRi hide the empties behind the evergreen shrubs. The bottles clanging loudly. Matt French must know. He must hear everything.

We're swooping around the kitchen island, loading the dishwasher and chomping on our organic ginger gum, and

Coach is talking to him in the other room, asking him, her speech so slow and careful, about his day.

Through the swinging café doors, he looks very tired and he's talking but I can't quite make out the words.

He reaches out to touch her arm just at the moment she turns to hand him the mail.

I think how exhausted he must be, how maybe if he were my husband, even though he's not handsome at all, maybe I'd want to sit him down and rub his shoulders, and maybe get one of those lemony men's lotions, and rub his shoulders and his hands. And maybe that'd be nice, even if he's not good-looking and his forehead is way too high and he has little wiry hairs in his ears and I never think about him like that, really.

But he's tired after his long day and he comes home and there we are, bansheeing all over his house, all cranked high and slipping-free braids and ponytails, and Coach talks to him and it's like how she talks to the other teachers at school, holding their mottled coffee mugs and making the smallest talk ever.

Shoulders tucking in wearily, I see him flinching at all the clamorous girl energy radiating from the kitchen.

"Colette," I think he says, "I was calling all day. I called all day."

I'm not sure, but I think I hear him say something about Caitlin, about the daycare center phoning him, asking where she was.

Coach's hand is over her mouth, and she is staring at her feet.

Suddenly, there's a loud crash from the back deck, like glasses falling.

"Coach!" someone hollers from outside. "We're sorry. We're really sorry."

13.

"Everybody give the chicken a warm welcome," Coach says, giving a gentle shove to the latest recruit, a JV cheerleader getting her shot at the show. A hammer-headed girl with a body like a tuning fork. No one will mind her landing headfirst on the spring floor. She'll just ting.

"She's on me," Mindy surmises, curling her neck side to side. "I turn her out."

Mindy knows she can lift the shavetail rafters-high, a girl like that, not more than ninety pounds soaking wet, and she even looks wet, a dew on her that's probably flop sweat.

"Not before she pays her dues," RiRi says, arms folded. "We all fly her first."

New girls get tossed hard first time out. Initiate-style. And we like to rock them side to side.

"Mat kill," mutters Tacy, newly hard, suddenly a senior statesman of the squad.

No one asks about Beth. She's barely been in school these past three days, and Coach seems very calm in her victory.

It's after midnight when my phone hisses, rattling my bedside tabletop.

Can u pick me up? Cnr Hutch & 15.

Beth. The first call in five days. The longest stretch since she went to horse camp in the mountains after seventh grade, returning with a ringlet of hickeys from a counselor and fresh revelations about the world.

Creeping through the house, I hitch the car keys from the kitchen-door hook. Anyone could hear the car shaking to life in the garage, but if they do, they ignore it. My father nuzzled close to my stepmother, she muzzled by her nightly dose of sleep aids.

Beth is standing on the corner, and her face when the headlights hit it is a surprise. It's Beth bare-faced, which is scarier than her hooded eyes, her teengirl snarl.

Her face splayed open, like it almost never is, and mascara-spattered eyes blinking relentlessly, staring straight into the center of me.

With the headlights in her face, she can't really see me, but it feels like she can. She knows I'm there.

It's a thing to see, her face so bare. I almost want to turn away. I don't want to feel for her.

By the time she's in the car, her face is shuttered tight once more. She doesn't give me much of anything, not even a hello, and sets about punching text messages.

"Where were you?" I ask.

"Guard duty," she mutters, thumbs flying on her little keyboard.

"What?" I say.

Thump-thump-thump that thumb of hers, thumping.

"What?" I say again. "What did you say?"

"Sarge Stud . . ." she says, and I hold my breath, ". . . ain't the only stars and stripes in town."

She sets her phone down and glances at me, sly smile playing there.

"Which one?" I ask. All those raw-boned soldiers who stood at that table with Will, raw-boned and callow, steel-wool scrubbed.

"Bullet head," Beth says. "Prine. Corporal Gregory Prine. Gregorius, let's call him. You know the one."

I picture him, tongue waggling at me, fingers forked there, that acne-studded brow and sense of frat menace.

"Well," I say, feeling sick. "Bad Girls' Club for you, eh?"

"Hells-yeah," she says, a rattle laugh.

But I look at her hands, which are shaking. She clasps her phone to try to stop them. When I see it, something in me turns.

"Beth." I feel all the blood rushing from my face. I can't quite name it, but it's a sense of abandon. "Why?"

"Why not?" she replies, and her voice husky, her hair falling across her face. "Why not, Addy? Why not?"

I think she might cry. I think, in her way, she is.

14.

Little Caitlin, her doughy face with that cherry-stem mouth, baby soft hair sticking to her bulbed forehead.

Sitting on Coach's sofa, I watch her amble around her strewn toys, the pink plastic and the yellow fluff of girlhood, everything glitter-silted. She steps with such care through the detritus of purple-maned ponies, gauzy-winged tutus and all the big-eyed dolls—dolls nearly as empty-eyed as Caitlin, who reminds me of one of those stiff-limbed walking ones the richest girls always had, and we'd knock them over with the backs of our hands, or walk them into swimming pools or down basement stairs. Like stacking them up in pyramids just to watch them fall.

"I know, I know. Please, will you, will you . . . listen to me, baby. Listen close."

In the dark dining room, Coach is on the phone, fingers hooked around the bottom of the low-hanging chandelier, turning it, twisting it in circles until I hear a sickly creak.

For hours, she's been hand-wringing, jabbing her thumb into the center of her palm, molding it there, her teeth nearly grinding, her eyes drifting constantly to her cell phone. Ten times in ten minutes, a phantom vibration. Picking it up, nearly shaking it. Begging it to come to life. We can't finish a conversation, sure can't practice dive rolls in the yard. Any of the things she promised me.

Finally, her surrender, slipping into the other room and her voice high and rushed, *Will? Will? But you . . . but Will . . .*

Now, Caitlin's Play-Doh feet stomp over mine, her gummy hands on my knees as she pushes by me, and I want out. It's all so sticky and unfun and I feel the air clasp in my throat. For the first time since Coach let me into her home, I wish I'd gone instead with RiRi to her new boyfriend's place where they were drinking ginger-and-Jack in the back-yard and smashing croquet balls up and down the long slope of the lawn.

But then Coach, phone raised high in hand like a trophy, tears into the living room, her face suddenly shooting with nervy energy.

She is transformed.

"Addy, can you do me a favor?" she says, fingering her hamsa bracelet, its amulet flaring at me. "Just this once?"

She kneels down before me, her arms resting on my knees. It's like a proposal.

Her face so soft and eager, I feel like she must feel when she looks at me.

"Yes," I say, smiling. "Sure, yes. Yes." *Always.*

"It won't be long," Coach says. "Just a little while."

She tells me Will's having a hard time. Today, she says, is the third anniversary of his wife's death.

My legs tingling, it's like Lanvers Peak again and I have a sense of my grand importance. Jump, jump, jump—how high, Coach? Just tell me how high?

—

When he arrives, Will doesn't quite look like himself, his face sheet-creased and he smells like beer and sweat, a dampness on him that seems to go to the bone. A six-pack is wedged under his arm. He sort of burrows against Coach for a minute and I pretend to look out the window.

Coach hustling Caitlin off to the backyard, we sit on the sofa together, the cold beer bottles pressing against my legs.

There is a long, silent minute, my eyes following the milky rise and fall of his adam's apple, so hypnotized, and thinking somehow of Coach's fingers there.

"Addy," he finally says, and I'm relieved someone is saying something, "I'm sorry I interrupted you two. You were probably doing things. I'm sorry."

"It's okay," I say.

When I was seven, my dad's best friend died from a heart attack on the golf course and my dad locked himself in the garage for an hour and my stepmom wouldn't let me knock on the door. Later, I think, I crawled on his lap and I remember how he let me sit there for an hour, and never once asked me to move so he could change the TV channel.

I don't guess I should sit on Will's lap but wish I could do something.

"Can I tell you something, Addy?" he says, and he's not looking at me but at the furred white lamb on the coffee table, its head bent. "This awful thing happened to me on the way here."

"What?" I say, rising up in my seat.

"I was coming out of the Beer Depot on Royston Road and there's this bus stop out front. This old woman was coming off the bus, carrying her shopping bags. She had this hat with a big red flower, like a poppy, the ones you wear on Veterans' Day. That's what you're supposed to wear on Veterans' Day.

"When she saw me, she stopped in her tracks, right on the bottom steps. She just stopped. It was like she knew me.

"And this thing happened. I just couldn't move. I was just standing there, beer in my hand, and we just locked eyes. And something happened."

His stare is glassy, and he has one finger tracing the tops of the beer bottles sitting between his legs.

"What happened?" I ask. "Did she know you from somewhere?"

"Yes. Except she didn't. I never saw her before in my life. But, Addy, she knew me. She kept staring at me from under that poppy hat. And these black eyes, like lumps of coal. She would not let me go." He shakes his head back and forth. "She would not let me go."

I'm listening, but I don't know what I'm hearing. I wonder how many beers Will has had, or if this is what mourning can look like, diffuse and mysterious.

"Addy, I think . . ." He has his eyes fixed again on the toy lamb, its head tilted, like a broken neck. "She *knew* things about me. It all became clear. She *knew*. The things I did as a kid, the slip 'n' slide accident with my cousin and the sparkler bombs in the church parking lot and the time my dad showed up drunk at my job at the Hamburger Train and I shoved him and he fell on the wet floor and hit his head. And the first time in the Guard and the time there, and how now, after those bad drinking years, I only remember the Medcap missions, those little Allahaddin girls who slipped me love poems. I never remember any of the rest of it at all."

He pauses, his beer bottle tilting in his hand.

"She knew things I never told anyone," he says. "Like about my wife. Six years we were together, I never bought her a Valentine's Day card. I was a jerk, and I was a fuckup. I still am."

The empty bottle slips from his fingers, rolls across the sofa cushion.

"She knew all those things. And then I did."

I don't know what to say. I want to understand, to touch a bit of this shiny despair.

"What did you do?" I finally ask.

He laughs, the hard sound of it making me jump. "I ran," he says. "Like a kid. Like seeing the boogeyman. A witch."

We are both quiet for a moment. I am thinking of the old woman. I can see the poppy-blooming hat, and her face, her eyes inked black and all-knowing. I wonder if anything like that will ever happen to me.

Will leans down and picks up his beer bottle, setting it on the coffee table, its damp bottom ringing the wood.

"Remember that night we all drove up the peak?" he says, suddenly.

"Yes," I say.

"I wish it could always be like that," he says, twisting off a new beer cap.

I look at him.

Then he says, "Look at you," reaching out and flicking my blonde braid. "You're so easy to talk to, Addy."

I try to smile.

"Let me ask you," he says, pressing the beer bottle against his damp forehead. "Do people see you, so very pretty and your hair like a doll, and do they know about those things you hold inside of you?"

How did he know I held such things? *And what things?*

"Can I trust you, Addy?" he asks.

I say he can. Does anyone ever answer that question with a no?

And I wait for him to say more. But he just looks at me, his eyes blood-webbed and so sorrowful.

None of it makes much sense and I think Will must be very drunk or something. Something.

For a second it all overwhelms me, and all I want is to listen to music, or do a bleacher sprint, or feel the feather-weight of Tacy's elfin foot in my flat palm, her counting on me to hold her up, and it being so easy.

"I'm sorry I ruined your afternoon," he says.

I'm in the backyard, leaning on the enormous Dutch-door playhouse Caitlin occupies, jumbo chalk jammed in her chubby hands. Still half-breathless from my talk with Sarge Will, I smoke three of Coach's American Spirits and think about what's going on inside.

Nearly an hour goes by, and Caitlin falls asleep in the playhouse, her mouth sucked over the corner of the foam table inside.

Her hair scalloped into a ponytail, Coach runs barefoot across the lawn. I think she's going to hug me, but she's not a hugger, and kind of arm-hooks me, Coach-like, wringing my shoulder.

"Thank you, Addy," she says, breathlessly. "Thanks, okay?"

And she smiles, with all her teeth, her face taffy pink.

It's like I've just done the greatest thing I could ever do for her, like a single-based split catch, like a pike open-basket at the State Championship, like a balm over her heart.

For a moment, my fingers touch her hard back, which shudders like a bird.

Touching it is like touching them, their beauty.

15.

Party tonite, flashes Beth's text.

Rebs, I type back. *Away game.*

After, she says. *Comfort Inn Haber.*

Nu uh.

Uh huh.

That prickle behind my ear. The Comfort Inn. Older brothers and sisters are always talking about how it used to be called the Maid Marian, with a second-floor walkway that slung so low it looked like the hookers—real-live hookers like in the movies, only with worse skin—would slide right off into the courtyard. You'd only drive by when you had to go downtown, like a class trip to the museum and the teachers so embarrassed that you'd be passing the Maid Marian, with all those maids all in a row.

When it became the Comfort Inn, they tore out the walkway and you couldn't see the hookers anymore, but the whole place still quivered with a sense of dirty deeds.

And Beth, and her dirty deeds. I want to say no, but I want to say yes. I want to say yes to keep my eyes on Beth and want to say yes because it's a party at the Comfort Inn on Haber Road.

So I say yes.

—

"Whose party?" RiRi asks, reaching under her shirt, plucking first her right breast higher, then her left, so they crest out the top. "Your dealer's?"

"My dealer could buy Haber Road tip to tail," Beth says. Beth doesn't have a dealer, but there is a guy over on Hillcrest who graduated Sutton Grove ten years ago and he sells her adderall, which she sometimes shares and which feels like oxygen blasting through my brain, blowing everything away and leaving only immense joy that shakes tic-tac-like in my chest and then sinks away so fast it takes everything from me and my sad life.

"So whose party?" I ask.

She grins.

I didn't believe her at first, but there it is. There's five or six of them, all from the Guard.

All Will's men.

They're wearing regular clothes, but their haircuts and close shaves give them away, and the way they stand, feet planted apart, chests puffed out. One of them even has his at-ease hands behind his back, which makes it hard to hold his beer.

I recognize the PFC with the red brush cut who walks Sarge Will to his car every day and the other one, with the ham hock hands and the bow legs.

There's a little bar set up on the long plywood dresser and they're huddled around it, and no one's on the drooping beds with the nubby spreads, and the lights are pitched low and soft and there's almost a peacefulness about it.

It's just a place to have a party, that's all. A little party, two adjoining rooms, the clock-radio jangling softly and one PFC reaching above his hand, absentmindedly twirling the overhanging lamp, sending soft glades of light across the room like a mirror ball, like Caitlin's magic lantern.

Then, bullet-headed Corporal Prine steps out of the bathroom, his thumb dug in the neck of his beer bottle.

RiRi, looking at me, shaking her head, mouthing, *Hell-no*.

The other ones are all decked in ironed polo shirts and pressed everything, but Prine is wearing a T-shirt emblazoned with skulls and bones and a big knife wedged in one of the skulls. The words "Love Kills" are scrolled across it.

Nodding that big thick eraser tip head of his, Prine beckons us toward him.

Shrugging off her letter jacket, Beth, resplendent in a gold halter top, walks toward him, smiling slantily in that Beth way that feels like new trouble.

But RiRi is hipshaking and she curls her hand in mine, and RiRi's ease with boys is such solace and soon we are dancing, pop-pop-popping our hips and RiRi doing the robot arm.

There's rum and diet cokes mixed special for us and all the alcopops we can drink, and the PFCs are gentlemanly and suggest we play a game called beer blow. I never do figure out what the point is except it involves a lot of us bending over the table and blowing playing cards off an empty bottle, and then drinking, and then drinking again.

I don't care about anything, not the stain on the bedspread or the ceiling, or the way the bathroom sink drags from the wall when you hold on to it, when you try to stay upright, not the crusted carpet under my feet, my shoes flung off as I climb up on the bed with RiRi, when we dance together, our hips knocking, and the Guardsmen all watch and cheer. I don't care about anything at all.

I don't care because it's like this: the rum, and the hard lemonade, and the shot of tequila zoom and zigzag through me, and the spell cast so deeply.

The whole high school world of gum-stuck, locker-slamming, shoe-skidding tedium slips away and it's all just warm and gushing perfection.

"Tell Coach to come," RiRi is burbling. "Tell her we're with the Guard." She's fumbling with my phone, trying to send a text.

Because it's all okay because these are Will's men and nothing bad could ever happen, one of them is pressing our heads together, wanting us to kiss.

"Always ready," he says. "Always there."

"We could never be girlfriends like this before," RiRi says, hugging me close. "Until this year. You were always Beth's girl. She never wanted to share you. Girl has such a hard-on for you. I was even scared of you. I was always scared of both of you."

She's looking at me, eyes wide, like she's surprised herself.

This hot, sloshing feeling low in me, I've known it before, at house parties, at bonfires on the ridge with clanking kegs and plastic cups, and every boy becomes the prettiest I ever saw. But this is better somehow—the Comfort Inn on Haber

Road!—better still these men, grown men, Guardsmen—Will's men. Bearing somehow the sheen of Will.

Who am I not to curl myself under their hard, angled arms? Like Coach with Will. That could be me.

It's late when we can't find Beth.

At first I'm sure she's with Prine, but then PFC Tibbs, the sweet, gingered one with the whistle in his voice, like a gentle burr in the ear, shows me Prine passed out on the bed in the adjoining room, and there's no Beth.

Prine's jeans are around his ankles and his boxer shorts half yanked off, leaving a view of fleshy abandon. Even though he's alone, it feels sinister. Maybe it's the smell, which is ripe and unwholesome.

The PFC takes me for a walk down every hallway, and into every stairwell, talking about his sister and how he worries about her at State, hears tales of fraternity lap dances and early morning walks of shame.

We look for Beth for an hour or more, and I hold onto some kind of calm only because, walking under the long bands of humming fluorescents, I'm concentrating very hard and won't miss any deodorized nook of the motel.

But each burning hallway is like the previous one, all of them yellow-bright and empty.

I'm nearly night-air-sobered by the time we find her asleep in my car, face slack and childlike, except she has no shoes and, far as I can tell, her skirt riding up, no underwear.

When she jolts awake she says dark and woolly things about Prine.

How he took her to the adjoining room and tore her underpants off and pulled his pants down and all kinds of things are slipping from her drunken mouth.

He put his hands there, pushed down on my shoulders, my jaw, it hurts.

You're always supposed to believe these things. That's what they tell you in Health Class, the woman from Planned Parenthood, the nose-pierced college student from Girls, Inc. Females never lie about these important things. You must never doubt them. You must always believe them.

But Beth isn't like the girls they're talking about. Beth isn't like a girl at all. The squall in her, you can't ever peer through all that, can you?

You can't puzzle through someone like Beth who always knows more about you than you know about yourself. She always beats you to the punch.

"I better call someone," says the PFC, standing back from us, far from my ministrations, further still from Beth's sprawl, a seatbelt twisted around her bare ankle, her feet gravel-pocked.

I try to untangle her, and Beth's left leg drops to one side and we both see the flaring red mark on the inside, the shape of a thumb print. And a matching one on her other thigh.

"I better call the Sarge," he says, his voice strangled.

Suddenly, Beth jerks, her elbow jagging out at me, her eyes suddenly sharp and focused on the poor private.

"Call Sarge," she says. "Go ahead and call him. It's on him.

I've called him five times. I've called him for hours. It's on him."

Why would Beth call Will?

I look back at the PFC. I'm shaking my head. I'm giving him a look like *oh-crazy-drunk-girl.*

Beth is a liar. This is a lie, the only thing between Beth and Will is her failed campaign. This is just Beth blowing buckshot everywhere.

"I've got it," I say. "I've got her. You can go."

Standing back, the PFC lifts his hands up.

The relief on his face is astounding.

"You cannot bring her here, Addy," Coach is saying, my phone clamped to my ear. "Take her home. Take her to your house."

I'm looking at Beth, corkscrewed into the crook of my front seat, her eyes nearly closed but with a discomforting glistening there.

"I can't," I whisper, my varsity jacket sleeve snagging in the steering wheel, *sober up, sober up.* "She's saying things. About that Prine guy."

My eyes catch Beth's purse on the car floor, half unzipped.

That's how I see her bright lime panties inside.

Folded neatly, like a handkerchief.

You cannot judge how women will behave after an assault, the pamphlets always say. But.

"Prine?" Coach's voice turns spiky. "Corporal Prine? What are you talking about?"

I tell her about the party, the words tripping fast, my head spongy and confused. *Just let us come over, Coach, just let us.*

I don't tell her that I'm already driving to Fairhurst, to her house.

"Coach, she wanted us to call Sarge," I say, fast as a bullet. "She says she called him a bunch of times."

A pause, then her voice like a needle in my ear:

"Get the bitch over here now."

Like this, the car floating, the street lamps like spotlights coning in on us. And Coach's voice pounding, *Why would you go to that party, Addy? Is she saying Prine hurt her? He's no high school QB. They call him the Mauler. Fuck, Addy, I thought you were smarter than this.*

Climbing up Coach's front porch, I'm holding Beth up, her bare feet scraping on the cement.

She said not to knock, so I just send a text. Seconds later, Coach appears at the door, an oversize T-shirt with AURIT FINANCIAL SERVICES written on it, and a logo that looks like a winding road leading up to the sky.

The stony glare as she looks at Beth brings me straight to sober, sends my spine to full erectness. I even want to comb my hair.

"For god's sake, Hanlon," she says. *Hanlon* now. "I expected more from you."

I can't pretend it doesn't sting.

We are all hard whispers and shoving arms, hustling Beth to the den.

Just as Coach shakes the vellux blanket over Beth, hair streaked across her face, we hear Matt French coming down the stairs

It all feels very bad.

He looks tired, his face rubbed to redness, brow knotted.

"Colette," he says, his eyes taking it all in. "What's going on here?"

But Coach doesn't flinch.

"Now you see what I put up with all week," she says, almost like she's annoyed with him, which is a great technique. "And now Saturday night too. These girls are nothing but boxed wine and havoc."

They both turn and look at me. I don't know what to say, but I have never drunk boxed wine.

"Colette," he says, "can you come talk to me for a second?"

They walk into the next room for a minute and I can hear his voice rise a little, can make out a few words, *responsibilities* and *what if* and *young girls*.

"What do you want me to do? These girls' parents just don't care," she says, which feels funny to hear.

A few seconds go by and then they both reappear.

"Go back to bed," she says, trying for an aggrieved smile, one hand on his back. "You're exhausted."

Matt French looks over at Beth, buried on the sofa, and then away.

For a second, his gaze rests on me. His sleep-smeared face, the worry on it, and his bloodshot eyes on me.

"Good night, Addy," he says, and I honestly never knew he knew my name.

I watch him duck his head under the archway then ascend the carpeted steps.

Good night, Matt French.

Pulling me into the powder room, Coach sits me down on the bathtub ledge, the questions coming so fast and the pink lights flaming.

"I don't know what happened," I say, but Beth's words keep caroming back: *hand on the back of my head and shoved it down there and kept saying, "Do me, cheerleader. Do me."*

Coach makes me repeat everything five, ten times, or so it seems. I'm getting head spins. At some point I start to slink against the shower curtain, but she yanks me up again and makes me drink four cups of water back to back.

"What do *you* think happened?"

"I don't know," I say. "You saw her legs, the red marks?"

But then, my hand to my own leg, I think of the dusky violet bruise I have in the very same spot from Mindy's gouging thumb, lifting me to a thigh stand.

And there's the matter of those lime panties, folded tidily in Beth's purse.

But Coach isn't listening, isn't even looking at me.

She has Beth's phone in her hand. I never even saw her take it.

She's scrolling through call history. Outgoing calls and texts to "Sarge Will," six, seven, eight of them.

Suddenly, she flinches.

A text, *Come on by, Sarge Stud, we're all waiting.* There's a picture attached that looks to be Beth's zebra-print bra, breasts pressed tightly together.

Clattering the phone against the wall, she catapults it down the toilet.

As if it mattered.

Who knew, really, what digital obscenities swam around in that phone of Beth's, what electronic blight she'd hoarded in her deepest pockets.

My drunken head and all I can think is, *Oh, Coach, she's got you in her sights. Fair or not, she's got you. Please get smarter, fast.*

Later that night, I creep from the rolled-arm living-room sofa to the den. I see Beth, blanket twisted between her legs, her whole body twisting on itself like a snake.

"Beth," I whisper, tucking the throw blanket tighter around her, "is it true? Is it true Prine did things to you? Made you do things?"

Her eyes don't open, but I know she knows I'm there. I feel like I've tunneled my way into her dream, and that she'll answer me there.

"I made him make me," she murmurs. "And he did. Can you believe he did?"

Made him make me. Oh, Beth, what does that even mean? I picture her taunting him. Doing her witchy Beth things.

"Made him make you do what?" I try.

"I didn't care," she says. "It was worth it."

"Beth," I say. "Worth what?"

"She needs to see what she's doing to us," Beth says. "I will make her see."

This is the way Beth can talk. Her Big Talk, her campside spook story talk, her steel-toed captain talk. It's meant to put a shake on me, and it always works.

"She didn't even know we were at the party," I say.

"She thinks she can go about her sluttish ways and do whatever she wants. We're just girls and we were there, and anything could have happened to us."

"We wanted to go," I say, my voice hardening, "so we went."

"Because of her," she says, her hand lifting, coiling around her throat. Her hand, it's shaking. "We went because of her."

"Not me," I say, my voice a bark. "That's not why I went. What did it have to do with her?"

She looks at me through half-shut eyes, a glistening there beneath her lashes. Beth always knowing me. *Everything*, she is saying. *And you know it.*

"Those Guard boys, they see what they can get away with," she whispers. "They see what's okay, what's allowed."

Flashing on me, my own thoughts, hours before, hip rotating with RiRi on the slunken bed: . . . *it's okay because these are Will's men and nothing bad could ever happen.*

"Beth," I start, trying to turn the dial to the center. "Did he . . . did he—" I can't say the word.

"What does it matter," she says.

I breathe deeply. A breath so deep it nearly pierces me.

"Addy, he might as well have," she says, her eyes blinking open, and so very drunk and lost I want to cry. "That's what counts."

—

Near dawn, a shadow flits by me behind the living-room sofa. I feel the faintest weight dancing on the glossy maple floors. I don't rightly know the dream from the waking.

Rising, I creep through the living-room door to the hall-way, my stomach rising, the hangover scaling me with every move.

I see Coach in the den, leaning over the back of the sofa, whispering in Beth's ear.

Her face so hard.

Her fingers clasping the sofa edge too tight.

I think I hear. I know I hear.

You're lying. You're a liar. All you do is lie.

Then Beth, she's talking, but I can't hear any of it, or can't be sure I have. In my nightmared head, it's this:

He held my head, he bent my legs back, he did it to me, Coach. Monkey-see, monkey-do. Like us with you. Didn't I jump higher, fly higher, Coach? Didn't I?

16.

All Sunday long, still feeling drunk, my whole body wrung dry from it, I can't get Beth to return my texts. All I can do from my bedroom cave is wonder if she told her parents some version of her sordid story, or worse, the police.

And drifting in and out of hangover sleep, my dreams, so wretched, Prine's bullet head between Beth's tangled legs, doing tangly things with teeth, like a wild animal, the Mauler.

Or picturing Beth, teasing and goading him, slithering in her hiked skirt, saying who knew what, trying to get him to be rough with her, rough enough to mark her. I wonder how far he really got, or how far she would have let it go. Or why she did it to herself, to all of us.

Coach needs to see what she's doing to us. What does that mean, Beth?

It means nothing to me.

Sunday night, Coach calls.

"I don't know what happened," I say. "I can't get any more out of her."

"It doesn't matter anyway," Coach says, her voice flat, almost motorized. "All that matters is what she says happens. And who she says it to."

This sends a chill through me. How could it not matter?

But in some deeper way, I know what she means. There's a fog upon us and there seems no piercing through.

"They've been in there an hour," Emily announces, teetering on her crutches. On the DL but she won't ever miss a practice. "At first it was *really* loud."

We're standing recklessly close to Coach's office, she and Beth knotted in there, the blinds pulled shut, and I'm worried they can hear us.

No one knows about Beth and Prine. All they heard was she sidled off with someone, which Beth always does, anyway.

"Do you think Beth wants back on the squad?" Tacy whispers, and I can see her visions of glory slipping from her neon fingertips. "Do you think Coach'd let her back? What if Coach lets her be squad captain again?"

Little, battle-hardened Tacy, calculating three moves ahead. Time was, she was just Beth's gimp, then Beth's Benedict Arnold. Now she's Coach's gimp.

If Beth is captain again, Tacy will have to slink back into Spotter slots, or worse. No more awesomes or libertys or dirty birds or back-tuck basket tosses.

No more flying.

"Coach doesn't believe in captains," Emily reminds us. "Even if she changed her mind, why in the world would she let *Beth* be captain? Beth doesn't even show up anymore."

But they don't know what I know. Beth's new chit. Pay to play. I wonder, will that be Coach's strategy? It would be mine.

But it doesn't seem Coach's way. Meet swagger with swagger.

Swinging out of the office ten minutes later, Beth and Coach unaccountably snickering together, low, nasty laughs, we all watch, keenly.

I'm the only one who sees through them.

"She's a chicken," Coach says to me later. "She talks a good game, but she's just a baby chick."

About this, I know she could not be more wrong.

"You all think she's such a gamer," Coach says, shaking her head. "She's just marshmallow fluff. Like any of those JV tenderfoots. Just with bigger lungs and a better ass."

The two of them. Like liars dice at summer camp. But Beth always won because she was good at math and understood odds, and because, when looking under the cup, she'd turn over the dice with her thumb.

"But that Prine guy. And you said they call him the Mauler . . . "

Coach shrugs. "She told me she doesn't remember him ever hurting her. He passed out. And she guesses she didn't know what she was saying really, she was so drunk."

I look at Coach, and I wonder who's lying, or if they both are.

"So she's not going to do anything?"

"There's nothing to do," Coach says. "I asked her if she wanted me to take her to my doctor. She said absolutely not.

What she does remember is that Prine's a bantam rooster with nothing but squawk."

"So, bitch," Beth asks later that afternoon, chewing straws at the coffee place, "are you ever gonna give me my phone back?"

I picture Coach spiraling it down the toilet.

"Your phone?"

"Herr F told me you must've taken it Saturday night. Probably to stop me from drunk dialing. You're a scrub, you know that, Hanlon? You're auxiliary."

"I don't have your phone, Beth," I say.

"I guess she must be wrong," Beth grins, foam curled in the corner of her mouth. Her tongue uncoiling, swiping. "Funny she would think it was you."

"Beth," I say, "you said you'd texted Will that night. You said you'd called or texted him a bunch of times."

She doesn't say anything, but her mouth twitches just slightly. Then she pulls it taut and I wonder if I ever saw it at all.

"Did I say that?" she says, her bright tan shoulders slinking into a shrug. "I don't remember that at all."

17.

The next day, Beth is back on the squad.

And she is captain again. Honorifically.

She gets to skip Chem on Wednesday for captain–coach mentor time, and study hall means she can go to Coach's office by herself and smoke. I see her when I walk by and she waves at me, head tilted, smoke curling in malevolent plumes around her face.

Thank you, Coach, I think. *Thank you.*

"Is she really Cap?" Tacy whispers, everybody whispers, but Tacy shaking in her bright-white air cheers.

Because it appears she is.

And Beth, is that contentment I see there on your tan face?

Fuck me, I think, which even sounds like Beth, *is this all she wanted?*

It's not, of course.

"It's okay," says Coach. "I don't have time for her, Addy. And you don't either. Let's see that back handspring."

And I am trying, but my legs won't come together and my body feels strange and stiff.

"Push off," she barks, temple sweat dappled, and her hair limp and slipping from its elastic.

"Lock out"—and with each shout her voice stronger, and

my body tighter, harder—"stay tight, stay center, and, fuck it, Addy, smile. Smile. Smile."

The next morning, I spy Matt French pulling into the parking lot in his gray Toyota, with Coach in it.

When she gets out of the car she doesn't even look behind her. It looks like he's saying something to her, but maybe not.

But he's watching her, waiting, I guess, to make sure she gets inside the building.

More and more, when I see his face I think maybe he is kind of handsome in his own tired way.

That's the hardest part, she said once. *There's nothing bad I can say about him, nothing I can say at all.*

Which somehow seemed the cruelest thing to say, ever.

Which is maybe why I feel this, looking at him now. Matt French. I can't account for it, but his weariness amid all the bluster and strut of us sparkle-slitted girls—it speaks to me. Like seeing him the other night, the way he looked at me.

He's not the guy you might think he is, that's what Will told me.

But I'm not sure what he thinks I might think.

Matt French watches Coach as she walks down the center aisle of the parking lot, watches her walk through the glass doors. He watches for a long time, one arm stretched across the passenger seat, head slightly dipped.

Watching her in the way that reminds me of the way a dad might watch his daughter on the jungle gym.

She never looks back once.

—

"Her car's on blocks over at Schuyler's garage," Beth tells me later. "Davy saw it. There's a big punch in the front fender."

I don't know who Davy is, or how he knows what Coach's car looks like. Beth has always known people—friends of her older brothers, sons of her mother's exes, the brother of the woman from Peru who used to clean her house—that no one else knows or even sees. Her reserves of information, objects, empty houses, designer handbags, driver's licenses, and prescription pads seem limitless.

I ask Coach about it later, what happened to her car anyway.

She shows me a long cut skating up her arm.

"From the seam in the steering wheel," she says, cigarette hanging from her mouth, her voice throaty and tired, almost like Beth. "I hit a post in the lot over at the Buckingham Park playground."

I tell her I'm sorry.

"I was pulling in and had to swerve really fast. A little girl ran in front of the car," she says, her eyes losing focus. "She looked just like Caitlin."

"But you were both okay?" I ask, which seems like something you should ask.

"That's the funny part," she says, shaking her head. "Caitlin wasn't with me. I'd forgotten her. Left her at home, in her room, playing chutes and ladders. Or tipping over bleach, eating poison from the cabinet under the sink, starting fires in the backyard. Who knew?"

She laughs a little, shaking her head. Shaking her head a long time, flipping her Bic in her hand.

Then she stops.

"I must be the worst mother in the world," she says, eyes glassy and confused.

I look at her, all the blurry fear on her.

And I say, "Mos def."

Which always makes her laugh, and makes her laugh now, and it's unguarded, beautiful.

"She was trying to avoid hitting some kid at the playground," I say. "She hit a post."

"I don't believe it," Beth says.

"Why would she lie?"

"Plenty of reasons," she says. "I've been right before, other times. You believe people, just like cheer camp, with that St. Regina Flyer. That compulsive liar, Casey Jaye. And you licked it all up."

Beth, always sifting ancient history, scattering ashes at me. Always going back to last summer. It was our only fight and it wasn't a fight really. Just stupid girl stuff.

I never thought you'd be friends again after that, RiRi said after. But we were. No one understands. They never have.

"Beth, can't you leave all this alone?" I say now, surprised at the panic in my own voice. "You got what you wanted. You're captain again and you can do whatever you want. So stop."

"It's not my choice," she says. "Something gets started, you have to see it through."

"See what through? What, Beth? What, Captain-my-captain?"

She pauses, clicking her teeth, an old habit from the days we both slid retainers around in our hanging-jaw girl mouths.

"You don't understand it, do you? All that's happened. It's all her."

She leans back, spreading her long ponytail across her face, her mouth.

Then she says something and I think it's, "She has your heart."

"What?" I say, feeling something ping in my stomach, my hand fisting over it.

"She has her *part*," she says, brushing her ponytail from her face, "in all this."

But I can't believe I misheard her. Did I?

"It's not just me," she says again, teeth latching and un-latching. "She has her part."

I misheard.

18.

Monday: One Week to Final Game

Coach spends most of practice in her office, on the phone, her face hidden behind her hand.

When she comes out, the phone rings again, and she is gone.

In her place, Beth brandishes the scepter, or pretends to. We have a sloppy practice and Mindy wearies me, complaining about the red grooves and pocks studding her shoulder, the imprint of Tacy's kaepa toss shoe. Chicken-boned Brinnie Cox only wants to talk about her lemon detox tea.

My head bobbing helplessly, I look up into the stands and spot Emily, a white pipecleaner propped lonely there.

I keep forgetting about Emily. Ground-bound, it's like she dropped into the black hole of the rest of the school.

God, it must be terrible not to be on cheer. How would you know what to do?

Her head darting left and right, she is watching us from the cave of her letter jacket, her ponderous orthopedic moon boot nearly tipping her to one side.

Emily, who I've known for three years, borrowed tampons from, held her hair back over every toilet bowl in school.

"Skinny be-yotch," Beth calls out to her, as if reading my mind. "How we rate to your bony ass?"

Emily shudders to life. "Tight," she calls out, eagerly.

"Tight as JV pussy?" Beth shouts.

"Tighter!" Emily laughs, and I remember this Beth, Captain Beth when Beth was feeling most captainy, most interested in wielding her formidable powers, me at her side.

Thank you, Beth, for reminding me. Thank you.

Teddy saw Coach @ Statlers last week, Beth's text reads. *Drinking, talking on cell all nite, crying @ jukebox.*

So? I text back, nearing one a.m.

I want to turn off the phone. I want to be done with Beth for the night, done with her chatter about Coach, and her car, or even the things she used to talk about: Tacy's runty legs and the antidepressants she eyed in Mindy's bookbag, and the sex toy she found under her mother's pillow and how it looks like a pink boomerang made by Mattel, and maybe that's what happened to her Barbie surfboard, mysteriously lost a decade ago.

Like some polluted Little Red Riding Hood, Beth always creeping through everyone's lives.

So? I text again.

There's a long pause, and I can picture Beth pecking away her reply.

Sometimes, though, I think that how long she takes, these epic multipart texts, is all on purpose, making the dread mount each time: *What is Beth up to? What is she doing now?*

Zzzt, the phone screen flashes at me at last:

Said she ran outside + hit post in parking lot, peeled off.

So . . . ? I text back.

So why lie to us, to u? she texts. *Plus, crying abt what?*

I roll over in bed, let the phone slip to the carpet, its screen winking at me.

In the half dream that comes, the screen is a mouth, teeth gnashing.

19.

I'm deep into toes-curled sleep when I hear it.

The chirp from my cell, squawking from the floor.

I feel it hum under my grappling fingers.

Please not Beth.

Incoming call: Coach, the screen reads, and my favorite snap-shot, from the night after the Cougars' win, Coach sitting on the hood of my car, sated and exultant.

"Addy," the whisper comes. "Addy, I slipped on the floor. I saw him and I slipped on something and I didn't know what it was."

"Coach? What's going on?" Words sticky in my sleeping mouth.

"I kept looking at my sneaker and wondered what was on it. What the dark stain was."

I wonder if I'm dreaming.

"Coach," I say, rolling over, trying to blink myself awake, "where are you? What's going on?"

"Something happened, Addy. That's what I think. But my head . . ."

Her voice so strange, thin and wasted.

"Coach—Colette. *Colette, where are you?*"

146

A pause, a creaking sound from her throat. "You better come, Addy. You better come here."

I'm sure I'll be heard, but if I am, no one does anything about it, not even when the garage door shimmies open, when the car leaps to life. Sometimes I don't even try to be quiet. Sometimes I turn on all the lights, leave a trail blazing from my bedroom through the garage, until my dawn return, and no one has ever said a word.

But tonight, I don't.

I try not to look at my phone, which is spasming with texts that must have come in while I slept—all from vampiric Beth, who sometimes seems never to sleep at all and tonight seems especially wired with speculations and grim fancy.

I can't stop to read them now.

Nearly to Wick Park, I see The Towers, the large apartment complex, the only one in Sutton Grove, though it doesn't even feel like Sutton Grove but like the tenuous landing strip for some steel box dropped from high above.

I've been there once before, to pick up Coach and take her back to her car, which she'd left at school.

One of the new developments perched high on Redcap Ridge, it floats perilously over the edge, and still half empty because no one wants to live by the roaring interstate.

It's so great, Addy, Coach said, *like a deserted castle. You can scream and shout and no one could—*

I remember when I pulled up Will waved from the lobby's glass doors, his face and neck flushed, like hers. His hair wet and seal-slick. And Coach, still slipping on her left shoe as she ran to my car.

The sharp smell on her when she opened my car door, so thick it seemed to hover in the air around her.

Her face bright, her right leg still shaking.

I couldn't take my eyes off it.

But that was weeks ago, in the middle of the day, and nothing looks familiar at all now. It takes me three circuits of the complex to find the right building, and then find Will's name on the big lighted board out front.

All the while I'm thinking of Coach's voice on the phone.

"Is he there now," I'd asked, a sick feeling in my stomach. "Is Will with you?"

"Yes," she said. "He's here."

"Is he okay?"

"I can't look," she said. "Don't make me look."

She doesn't say anything on the intercom, just buzzes me in.

The buzz in my ear, it's like the tornado drill in elementary school, the hand-cranked siren that rang mercilessly, all of us hunched over on ourselves, facing the basement walls, heads tucked into our chests. Beth and me wedged tight, jeaned legs pressed against each other. The sounds of our own breathing. Before we all stopped believing a tornado, or anything, could touch us, ever.

In the elevator, the numbers glow and the funniest feeling starts up inside me. It's like before a game. Chest vaulting, bounding on my toes, everything ricocheting in my head (*lift arm higher, no fear, count it out, pull it tight and make it sing*), my body so tight and ready I feel like a spring coiled tight: *Let me free, let me free, I will show you my ferocity, my rapture.*

"Addy," Coach says, opening the door, startled, like she's almost forgotten she's called me, as if I've showed up at her own home, unaccountably, in the middle of the night.

The apartment is dark, one floor lamp coning halogen up in the far corner. A hooded fish tank effervesces on a table by the wall, the clouded water seeming almost to smoke, a fluorescent cauldron with no fish I can see.

She looks tiny, her iron-rod back slinking into itself. Bare footed, a nylon windbreaker zipped up so high it covers her neck and the tip of her chin. Her hair dankly tucked behind her ears.

"Coach," I start.

"Take off your shoes," she says, her mouth pinched. I think, somehow, it's because of the parquet floors, though they don't look that nice, and I slip off my flip-flops and rest them by the door.

We're standing in the vestibule, which gives way to a small dining area with a thick black-lacquered table. Just past it is the living room, strutted by the hard angles of a leather sectional.

Turning back to her, I see something's in her hands, her tennis shoes bundled there, soaking wet.

"I washed them in the sink," she says, answering my unasked question. Suddenly, she hoists them into my hands.

"Hold them, okay? Because I need to think. I need to get my head in order."

I nod, but, somehow, my eyes keep darting to the back of the large sectional sofa sprawling across the room like a spreading stain.

Maybe it's the gloomy dark, the phosphorescence from the glubbing aquarium.

But mostly it's the way Coach's eyes seem to vibrate when she looks at me, pupils like pins.

"What's over there," I say, angling my head toward the sofa. "Coach, what's over there?"

She looks at me for a second, running a hand through her hair, which looks so dark.

Then she lets her eyes drift over to the sofa, and I let mine too.

I'm holding the shoes tight, and inching toward the sofa.

I can hear her breathing behind me, in rasping gulps. Watching.

The parquet floors squeak and the sofa looms before me, crooking around the center of the room.

Walking slowly, the surging bleach from the sneakers nearly making me choke, I feel something skitter under my bare foot and spin across the floor. Something small, like a button or a spool of thread.

As I creep closer, ten-then-five feet away from the living-room area, the sofa back seems larger, taller than the football goalpost, than the Eagles emblem on the field, wings spread.

My right foot dangles over the circular rug in the center of the room. To step on it feels suddenly like to sink into black water.

Zzzt! My phone like Mexican jumping beans in my pocket. *Zzzt!*

I'm sure Coach heard the vibration, but if she did, she doesn't show it, so fixed is she on the sofa, what lies behind it.

Turning my body, I finger for, and press, the "off" button so hard I nearly knock the phone from my pocket.

Deep breath.

Deep breath.

Me, now only a few steps from the back of the snaking sofa, peeking around the sofa's sharp corner, around its scaly leather arm. I see flickers of something on the floor.

"I let myself in with the key he gave me," Coach is saying, answering more unasked questions. "I rang the door bell first, but he didn't answer. I walked in and there he was. Ohhh, there he was."

First, I see the glint of dark blond hair twining in the weave of the rug.

Then, stepping forward, I see more.

Coach's sneakers slip from my hands, shoe string tickling my leg as they drop to the carpet with a soft clunk.

There he is.

There he is.

There's Sarge. There's Will.

"Addy," Coach whispers, far behind me. "I don't think you want to . . . I don't think you need to . . . *Addy* . . . is it like I thought?"

—

His chest bare, wearing only a towel, his arms stretched out, he's like one of those laminated saint pictures the Catholic girls always brought from catechism. Saint Sebastian, his head always thrown back, body glorious and tortured.

"Addy," says Coach, almost a whimper. Like little Caitlin, just waking up and scared.

I just keep looking. At Will. On the floor.

In those saint pictures, their bodies are always torn, ruined, split, lacerated. But their faces so lovely, so tranquil.

But Will's face does not look righteous and magnificent.

My eyes fix on the thing that was Will's mouth, but is now a red flower, its tendrils sprawling to all corners and, like a poppy, an inky whorl at the center.

In those saint pictures, their eyes, lovingly lashed, are always looking up.

And, for all the ruin of Will's handsome face, his eyes, they are gazing up too.

But it seems to me not to the Kingdom of God but to the tottering ceiling fan.

Looking up so he doesn't have to see the ruin of his face.

Behind his head, the rug is dark and wet.

I can't stop looking at him, at the bright streak of his face.

It's like I'm seeing Will and I'm seeing something else too. The old woman getting off the bus, the one with the black eyes Will was sure could bore through to the center of him. That story never felt real to me, it felt like when someone tells you a dream and they can't make you feel what they feel. It didn't feel real to me except as something I wanted to understand but couldn't. But now suddenly I can. The woman's hat tilting up, eyes like shale. And we are all one.

"Stop crying," Coach is saying, begging. "Addy, stop crying."

"I didn't touch him," Coach says, and I cannot catch my breath, but she will not wait. "When I ran over, I slipped on those."

She points to three small white things dotted across the floor. The something I'd felt wobbling under my foot, that I'd sent spinning across the parquet. A button or spool of thread.

"What are . . . " But then suddenly I know.

Turning again to Will's poppy-struck face on the floor, the bottom half of it blown away, I know what they are.

I hear a moan come up from within me, my fingers clawing at my own teeth, as if to remind myself they're still there.

"Coach, *why am I here*," someone says in a voice I recognize, faintly, as my own. The words just tumble out, constricted and lost. "Why did you make me come?"

But she doesn't answer me. I don't even think she's heard me.

Zzzzzzt! My phone, my phone. Like a paddle over my heart.

Beth. I'm sure I've pressed that button long enough to turn it off until the end of time, but I must've pressed it so long I turned it on again.

The way it keeps ringing, it's like Beth is there in the room too. And I'm afraid to even touch the phone because it seems somehow Beth will know if I turn it off, like she can know everything. Like she's here right now, claws out.

"Do you see it," Coach says, still ten feet from me, she won't come any closer.

"I see *him*," I say, as calm as I can, my finger scratching at my phone, trying to hold the "off" button just long enough to shut it off. As soon as I do it shudders *Zzzzzt!* again. "Of course I see him."

"No," she says, her voice going quieter still but more insistent. "On the floor."

I don't want to look again, but I do. At his hands, palms faced up, his legs, which have a strange violet cast.

That's when I spot the gun peeking out from under his left leg.

I turn to face Coach, who's standing in front of the dining-room table, wending a dewy strand of hair behind her ear. She looks younger than me, I think.

"He did this to himself?" I whisper, not even wanting to say it out loud.

"Yes," she says. "I found him."

"Was there a note or something?"

"No," she says.

"You didn't call 9-1-1," I say. Maybe it's a question and maybe it isn't.

"No," she says. Before I can ask why, she adds, "I guess no one heard. He doesn't have any neighbors yet."

We both look at the walls to our left and to our right. The room feels impossibly small.

"I don't know when it happened," Coach says. "I don't know anything."

Thoughts come to me, of Will, and his self-puzzled depths. I feel a loss suddenly.

I can't hold on to it long enough to figure out why, but suddenly, shamefully, I feel sorry for myself.

In that moment, though, she's made a turn.

"So," she says, voice faster now, "where's your car?"

"I don't know," I say. I can feel a bolting energy from her, her body inching toward the door.

It's like she just showed me a triple-toe touch-back, three fast scissor kicks, landing, then springing back for the final back tuck. Her hands never touching the ground. Not once.

But something is niggling at me. Something holding me back.

"Wait, Coach," I say. "Where's your car?"

"At the mechanic. Remember?" She is curt, like I'm her slowest student.

"So how did you get here?" I ask, walking over to her.

"Oh," she says. "I took a cab. I snuck out of the house. Matt was asleep. He took two pills. I had to see Will. So I called a cab." A pause between each sentence like reading flash cards. "But I couldn't call a cab to take me back, could I?"

"No, Coach," I say. "I guess you couldn't."

"And I can't show up at home in a cab now," she says, her voice speeding up again.

Zzzzt!

My phone.

Zzzzt!

But this time she is right next to me, and she is back to

being Coach, her arm whipping out, her fingers clawing over my pocketed hand.

"What is that? Who's calling?"

"No one's calling," I say, her hot fingers clamping at me, like when she pushes your body to make that jump, support that weight, brace the weight of five girls, effortlessly.

In an instant, it's like I'm not in Will's apartment, but at practice, and in trouble.

"A text," I say. "I get texts all the time."

"In the middle of the night?" She jerks my wrist from my pocket and the phone rattles to the floor.

Mercifully, the battery flies out.

"Pick it up," she says. "Goddammit, Addy."

I start to bend down.

"Don't touch anything," she snaps, and I see one of my hands is almost resting on the shiny black lacquer of the table.

Rising, I look down at the tabletop and see my smudgy face reflected in it, black depthless eyes.

There's nothing there, not really.

"Addy, we have to go, we have to go," Coach says, her voice grinding into me. "Get me out of here."

Moments later, we dart across the bright-lit parking lot, my sapphire Acura like a beacon.

We're driving, the night vacant and starless, and the whole world is softly asleep, with furnaces purring and windows shut tight and the safety of people tucked inside with the warming knowledge of a tomorrow and a tomorrow after that of just such humming sameness.

The car windows down, the crystally cool on me, I imagine myself in that world, the one I know. I imagine myself curled in just such comforts, comforts so tight they could choke you. So tight they choke me always.

Oh, was there no happiness to be had the world over? There or here?

Here in this bleach-fogged car, she beside me, still holding her sneakers between her legs. Her fingers keep running around the tongue, her eyes thoughtfully, almost dreamily on the road.

I can't fathom what she's thinking.

Finally turning down her street, Coach asks me to pull over two doors from her house.

"Roll the windows up," she says. I do.

"Addy, it's going to be fine," she says. "Just forget about all this."

I nod, my chin shaking from the cold, from the wretched loneliness of that drive, fifteen, twenty minutes in the car. She never said a word, seemed lost in some kind of moody reverie.

"You just need to go home and pretend it never happened," she says. "Okay?"

When she gets out of the car, the waft of bleach from her shoes smacks me.

—

Unable to turn the ignition, I sit there.

Were I thinking straight, were I feeling the world made any sense at all, I might be driving to the police station, calling 911. Were I that kind of person.

Instead, I look at my cell. I need to text Beth back.

Fell asleep, be-yotch, I type. *Some of us sleep.*

Still sitting, I wait a minute for her reply. But my phone just lies there.

No Beth.

It should make me feel better—Beth has finally dervished herself into exhausted slumber, her reign of terror over, for now—but it does not.

Instead, I have a sickly feeling I know will sit with me all night, that will join the larger sickness, the sense of nightmare and menace that feels like it will be mine forever.

I roll down all the windows and breathe.

Then, I start the car and inch past Coach's house, just to see if there are any lights on.

Suddenly, I see something moving, fast, like an arrow, down her driveway and to my car.

Almost before I can take a breath, Coach's palms are slapping my windshield, my heart jammering to terrible life.

"I was just leaving, I was," I nearly yelp, shutting off the ignition as she leans into the passenger window. "No one saw—"

"You're my friend," she blurts, an ache in her voice. "The only friend I ever had."

Before I can say anything, she's whippeting back across her lawn, slipping soundlessly into the dark house.

I sit a long time, my hands resting in my lap, my face warm.

I don't want to start the car, move, do anything.

I never gave anything to anyone before. Not like this.

I never was anything to anyone before.

Not like this.

I never was, before.

Now I am.

Finally in my rumpled bed, my eyes jitterbug through all of Beth's texts.

2:03 a.m., 2:07 a.m., 2:10 a.m.

@ Statlers, Coach drinking ginger and jacks + on phone for hour kept saying 'why are you doing this to me why'

Bartend said she used to come when she was young and drink w. badasses from the speedway and once broke both wrists falling in that same pking lot

. . . kind of trash she is. She shld b glad Matt sunk so low to grab scruff of her neck cuz . . .

Then, by 2:18:

WHERE THE FUCK R U? You better txt back or I'm coming over. U KNOW I WILL. DON'T MESS WITH—

. . . and on until 2:27, the last one.

here I am, Pinetop Ct, looking at yr open garage door, but where's yr car? Hmmm . . .

She must be lying, I tell myself. But I know she's not. I know she was out there in front of my house at 2:27, hunched over the steering wheel of her mother's Miata. I know it.

I wonder how long she waited, and what she thought.

I wonder what I'll say and how I'll ever make her believe it.

In this knot of fear, I forget everything but Beth's canny slit eyes.

Those eyes on me, even now.

In the blackest of moments that night, when sleep finally sinks me, a dream of Beth and me, little kids, Beth raking the hard bars of that ancient merry-go-round they used to have in Buckingham Park, spinning us, spinning. And we lie flat on it, on its warty surface, our heads pressed close.

"It's what you wanted," she says. "You said faster."

20.

Tuesday: Six Days to Final Game

It's early, an hour before first period, but I had given up on sleeping, all those half-awake nightmares of my feet sunk in blood-wet carpet and aquariums pumping violet-red bubbles.

You saw a dead man last night, that's what I'm saying in my head. *You saw a suicide right before your eyes.*

You saw Will, dead.

So I'm slumped in front of my locker, curling the pages of my *The Odyssey of Man* textbook, fat green highlighter poked into my mouth.

Beth glides through the front doors of school.

I expect it to be immediate, her face a tanned snarl as she demands to know where I was last night, why I stopped texting her back.

But instead, hand out, she lifts me to my feet, her face bright and mysterious, and arm-in-arms me to the cafeteria.

We get a fat-slicked chocolate-chip muffin, which we heat up in the rotating toaster machine. Standing next to it, the heat radiating off its coils, I imagine myself suffering eternal damnation for sins not yet clear.

But then the muffin pops out, tumbling into my hands. Together, we eat it in long, sticky bites that we do not swallow.

No one else is there, so we can do it, and Beth fills tall cups with warm water to make it easier to spit it out after, into our napkins.

When we finish, I feel much better.

Until Beth starts telling me about her dream.

"It wasn't just any dream," she says, licking her fingers, under each slick fuchsia nail. "It was like before. Like with Sandy."

As long as I've known her, Beth has had these sinister dreams of dark portent, like the night before her Aunt Lou fell from her second-floor landing and broke her neck. In the dream, her aunt came to breakfast and announced she had a new talent. Then, taking one forearm to her neck, she showed them how she could turn her head 360 degrees.

Or, when we were ten and Beth came to school one day and said she dreamt she found Sandy Hayles from soccer camp behind the equipment shed, a sheet pulled tight across her face. That Saturday, our soccer coach told us Sandy had a blood disease and wasn't coming back to camp, ever.

"What was the dream," I ask, fighting off the nerves spiking up my neck, tickling my temples.

"We were doing toe touch jumps high on one of the over-looks, like that one time, remember?" she says. "But then we heard a noise, like something falling a long, long way. I walked over to the edge of the gorge to look down, but I couldn't see anything at all. I could feel it, though, because it was vibrating, like it was your throat when you scream."

And I'm thinking, yes, like when all of us scream at the game, with our throats vibrating and our feet pounding, and the bleachers shaking, everything. I can hear it all in my head now.

"Then I looked back up at you. It was so dark up there and you were so white, but your eyes were black, like one of those ash rocks in geology class."

Shoulders clustered, a preying black bird, she leans closer.

Suddenly it feels like I'm the one who's dreaming, who's still stuck in that grim nightmare of sinking carpets and bloody footprints and an aquarium pump glub-glubbing, opening and closing like the valves of a heart.

"But, Addy, the bottom part of your face was gone," she whispers, her fingers drifting to her chin, her lips. "And your mouth was just this white smear."

My breath catches.

"I started to slip," she continues, "you grabbed my wrist and were trying to pull me up, but it hurt and I looked down and something was cutting into me, something on your hand.

"And you lifted your other hand, and there was a mouth there, right in the center of your palm—and you were talking through it, and you were saying something very important."

I look down at my palm.

"What was I saying?" I ask, staring at the whiteness of my open hand.

"I don't know," Beth sighs, leaning back, shaking her head. "But then you did it."

"Did what?"

"You let go," she says, "just like before you learned how to spot."

Grab for the body, not the limb.

"You had my wrist, and then you didn't anymore. You let go. Like always."

My head hot, my stomach bucking, I press my napkin to my face. I can't remember the last time I ate anything and I almost wished I'd eaten that muffin. Almost.

"That's not a special dream," I say. "Nothing even happened."

"Everything happened," she says again, plucking lipgloss from her jeans pocket. "You know how it works. It will all be revealed."

I try to roll my eyes, and that's when my stomach turns hard, and I have to reach for the napkin. The gagging is embarrassing, but nothing really comes up other than chocolate residue, like a muddy slick dripping down my wrist.

"Lovergirl," Beth says. "We gotta get you your gunstones back. You're going feather soft. Now that I'm captain again, I'll get you tight. I'll get you good and tight."

"Yeah," I say, watching Beth swizzling that gloss wand like a magician. "How come I'm always the one doing bad things in your dreams?" I say.

She hands me the wand.

"Guilty conscience."

After World Civ, I see Beth again, she's waiting for me outside the door.

"Splitsville," she says. "I knew it. I knew something was gonna blow. Coach and Will, *c'est fini*."

"Huh?"

"He's not at the recruiting table today," she says. "It's just that stubby PFC."

So fast, I think. *So fast.*

"That doesn't mean anything," I say, turning. But she grabs me by the belt loop. Part of me is glad her morning spookiness is gone, and she's just regular badass Beth, but another part of me doesn't like all the jump and spark on her.

"I've done recon," she whispers, so close I can see the dent in her tongue where her stud used to be before she decided tongue rings were JV. "Bitty PFC says they don't know where the Sarge is. And he's not answering his phone."

I don't say anything, just spin-dial my locker combination.

"So get this: PFC says sometimes Sarge just AWOLs. And they don't bother him about it, don't report it. 'It's his way,' that's what the scrub tells me. They let it go because he's had some trouble in his life. Something about his wife and a plate-glass window," Beth says, not quite rolling her eyes.

"So why's that mean he broke up with Coach?" I ask, pretending to look for something in my locker.

"I'm telling you, Papa's got a brand new hag," she says, whistling a little. "Who d'ya think? I speculate Mrs. Fowler, Ceramics, always rolling those clay pots with her legs spread so the boys can see."

"I don't think so," I say.

"Well, if it was RiRi she'd've posted pictures of it on Facebook by now. I don't think he goes for young trim anyway. And we know it isn't *you*."

"Who cares, really," I try, my head blurred.

She pauses a beat, taking the measure of me, and smiles.

"Addy-Faddy, I wonder if that's what you were doing last night."

"What?" I whisper.

"Comforting our jilted Coach, of course," she says.

"No," I say, tapping my locker door shut.

"I have better things to do," I add, trying to match her crocodile smile, and maybe beat it.

I don't see Coach all day, until practice.

I text her four times, but she never replies.

Six hours of wondering about her, about how she's moving through her day. If she feels the swampy misery I feel leaching inside me.

Seeing the shiny brown leaf of Coach's hair from behind, her yoga-taut posture, I'm almost afraid to see her face. For our eyes to lock and for everything to come pitching forward until I can smell the smell, hear the gurgling aquarium.

What can it be like for her?

But when she turns around—shouldn't I have known?

Her eyes breezing past me, as if we hadn't shared anything at all, much less this.

Oh, the flinty grace, it's stunning. I think it must be pharmaceutical, and I look for the slight drag to her foot, the tug in her speech. But I can't be sure.

All I know is she's got her stunt roster, her purple gel pen with the click-click-click as she ticks us off, roundoffs, walkovers, handstands, handsprings, front limbers.

—

Tumbling drills, two hours' worth. Best distraction ever.

We do back tuck after back tuck, bounding from standing pike into flips, handsprings. Our bodies bucking, and when I spot RiRi and watch the row of girls I get a kind of calmness that hums in my chest. The promise of order.

My body, for instance, it can dip and leap and spring and I am as if untouched, no panic flapping behind my eyes can touch my body, which is immaculate and all mine.

It's when I'm spotting RiRi on the last turn that I spy Beth, lingering tardily by the locker-room door in practice shorts.

It unnerves me, but I brush it off, and instead my eyes drift to the flash of neon-pink daisies that sprinkle before me every time RiRi's skirt flips up.

How is it other girls' panties are always so much more interesting than your own, I think.

"Okay, let's see those Scorps," Coach says.

Everyone groans, quietly. RiRi says she's not nearly "stretchy" enough today, but she can't do a decent one any-way because you have to be small, small enough to fly. I am, or almost. I was. And I still can do it. The body remembers.

It was Beth who first taught me the Scorpion, her hands on my back leg, lifting it slowly behind me, easing it higher and higher until finally my left foot met my raised-up hand. Until my body became one long line.

She taught all of us, back when she was a real captain. She had us use dog leashes we'd tie to our ankles then try pulling it up. At the Centaur game, when I first got that foot just shy of my forehead and made myself go straight, I knew a pain so stunning I nearly saw stars.

After, Beth bought me a pink camo leash with my name on it in glitter.

Doing it now, I feel my body constrict, then loosen, warm, perfect.

Closing my eyes, I almost see the stars.

Opening them, I see Coach giving me a real smile, and Beth there, watching and nodding. And I forget about everything. I just do.

"It'll be okay, Addy," she says. "No one will ever know."

It's after, just after dusk, Coach driving, the two of us working things out.

"Jimmy—PFC Tibbs—told me. This afternoon, he drove out to the apartment and got the super to let him inside. He wanted me to hear it from him."

I don't say anything for a second, can feel her looking over at me. Then I say, "What did he say exactly?"

She faces the road again. "He told me something happened to Sarge. Then he couldn't talk anymore, for a long time. I kept waiting. It was like I almost forgot I already knew." She pauses a second. "Which was good, I guess. Because I think I really seemed surprised when he told me."

I find myself nodding because I don't know what else to do.

"He had this stuff he'd printed off the internet. *Wounded Warrior: Suicide in the Military.* He said it looks like Sarge suicided. That's how he put it. I never heard it put like that."

Suicided.

It reminds me how we'd all tried cutting. I never could break real skin. Beth scraped a big heart on her stomach and then wore her bikini top to the Panthers game. But then she decided it was a hobby for the supremely boring and it no longer seemed so gangsta to any of us after that.

Coach stops at a light and reaches for a cigarette.

"Life was always hard for him," she says, rolling the unlit cigarette up and down the steering wheel spokes.

She tilts her head a little, squinting like she's figuring out a puzzle. "I don't think he ever really got over losing his wife."

I guess maybe it's true.

"He came from a hard family," she says. "Came up hard, like I did."

I didn't know he came up hard, or that Coach did. I'm not even sure what that means. Suddenly I feel like I never knew the person who died, or the person right next to me.

"She helped him," she says, "and then she was gone."

She's not crying, doesn't even look sad precisely. But I feel like she is waiting for something from me.

"But he had you," I say. "Maybe you reminded him of her. How good she was. Maybe he found that in you."

But she shakes her head, and the look on her face is grim, knowing.

"That's not what he found in me," she says, softly.

I don't say anything. It feels like some kind of strange confession. But of what?

"I guess I knew it'd turn out this way," she says, and her voice speeds up a little, and she faces straight ahead, her foot churning on the brake pedal, inching us forward with tiny bursts.

"Not just like this, but near it," she says.

She nods, as if agreeing with herself, then nods again. It's as if she's saying, *That's it, that's it, isn't it? And there was nothing we could do.*

She looks at the road, we both do, and I think about it all. About how Coach is always so efficient, so precise, her moves sharp and tight, so it makes sense she could turn this all so quickly, doesn't it?

It makes sense she could, less than twenty-four hours after finding Will's body, come to understand that it was really as it was meant to be, there'd been no stopping it, and everyone was lucky they'd had some pleasures while they could.

When I get home, no one is there, they never are, so I pluck my secret bottle of Bacardi Silver Raz from the corner of my closet and take long gulps, then collapse on my bed.

But all I hear is Coach's voice, soft and nearly affectless: *Life was always hard for him, Addy. There was nothing we could do.*

Forcing myself to sit at my computer, eyes blurred, I make myself look.

I search for any news reports on Sarge but can't find any.

I even find the police scanner website, but I can't understand it, and I keep getting distracted *42 are we leaving the football game? didn't know you were there you told us to go here 841 Willard her back is broken that's what she said* and my eyes all loose and stinging.

—

It's nearly midnight when Beth calls. I pull the covers over me and press my lips to the phone.

"Hold on, little grit," she says. "Hold on and grip hard."

"I'm holding," I say, whorling myself into the wall, my head pressing into its solidness.

"Sarge Stud killed himself."

I feel my breath go tight. I don't say anything.

"I don't know the details yet, but I'm working on it. I dispatched my remaining minions. You used to be so much more help with that, Addy. Now I have to tend to everything. But the meat of the matter is he's dead. I heard he took his head off with a shotgun."

"I don't believe it," I say, which feels like the truest thing I've said in twenty-four hours.

"Well, Addy, truth is an ugly mother, especially for you. But it's the truth. The PFC told me. That boy thinks he's my Knight in Shining. On account of the other night."

It takes me a long minute even to remember the once-world-shattering quality of that night of Beth and Corporal Prine, barely ten days past. That feels like Holly Hobby time now.

"I told you something was going to happen," she says.

"No," I say, "you said you were going to *make* something happen."

"Well," she replies, "turns out I didn't have to."

"Why would Will do that?" I ask.

"Why wouldn't he?" she asks, her voice vivid, gossipy— like we have finally hit upon the thing itself, something she's been waiting for.

"Maybe, Addy Faddy, just maybe, he saw the pointless-ness of all matters of the heart and said I won't just sink in, I won't let her grab me by the ankles. Fuck me, I'll look her in the eye. I'll jump."

There is a pause, and I hear Beth's fast breaths, her tongue clicking in her mouth.

I have the sudden feeling that she might say something that will alarm and hurt me. Something I don't want to hear. About the way we are linked, my cheer shoe lodged in her steely palm. About last summer, when I said I was tired of being her lieutenant, tired of being her friend, and it seemed like the two of us were over forever, but we never could be.

"Beth," I say, my arms over my own head. "I can't talk to you anymore."

"Addy," she says, gravely, intimately. "You have to."

Something has passed between us, a secret knowledge about us, and what she needs from me. But I blink and I miss it.

21.

Wednesday: Five Days to Final Game

Meet me @ 7 at coffee place.

Coach's five a.m. text scissoring into my sleep.

I feel hungover, have felt hungover for two days straight, the early morning light laying dew and mystery on me as I walk the five blocks, wary of starting my car at 6:55 in the morning. Sometimes I see my dad then, lurking in the hallways, robe flapping, surprised to see me, like I'm his errant boarder.

Coach is slouched against the milk and sugar station, but when she sees me, her body seems to lift upward, her eyes jittering into focus.

She goes to the counter to get me a matcha green tea and when I reach for a pink packet, she smacks it from my hand, that familiar gesture of hers, and I almost smile but can't seem to.

We take our drinks to her car and sit there, windows rolled tight.

She tells me the police called last night and said they had some questions for her, just routine, but they thought she might wish to handle it discreetly and come to the station house.

At first, all her words just flap at me. I just listen and nod and slide my drinking straw behind my teeth, grate it along the roof of my mouth until it hurts.

"Luckily, Matt's out of town," she's saying. "Did I tell you that?"

I shake my head.

"He flew to Atlanta yesterday for work," she says, eyes lifting to the rearview mirror.

I hadn't even been thinking of Matt French. Or how she was going about her life with him amid all this, hiding such a monumental secret. But maybe it wasn't that different. Maybe it wasn't different at all.

"So I got Barbara to stay with Caitlin and I went and talked to them. And it wasn't like I thought at all. The detective told me that . . . he told me what we knew. And he said that they were conducting a routine investigation and they had found my phone number in his call log."

She pauses, her chest heaving a little. That's when I realize her voice is faster than yesterday, with a new wariness to it.

"He asked me if I thought Will was depressed. And if I knew whether he kept any firearms in his home. And about how we knew each other."

"Did you tell?" I ask, sinking my chin into the plastic lid of my drink. "What did you tell?"

"I was as honest as I could be," she says. "It's the police. And I have nothing to hide, not really."

I lift my head and look her in the eye. I wonder if I've heard her right.

"I mean, I *do*. Have some things I'd rather . . . " she says,

174

shaking her head, like she's just remembered. "I told him we were friends. And that Will probably did have firearms, which is all I really know."

"If he saw the call log," I say, trying to get her to look me in the eye, "wouldn't he know you're more than friends?"

"Will and I didn't really talk on the phone that much," she says, briskly. "Besides, all that has nothing to do with what happened."

I don't know what to say to this.

A voice spins from me, small and wild. "Will the police call me? Will they be calling all of us?"

It suddenly seems like it could happen, and I think: this is how your life can end.

"Listen, Addy," she says, turning to me. "I know this is all really a lot for you to take. I know it all seems scary. But the police are just doing their job, and once they confirm that this is . . . what it is . . . then they're not going to need to be bothered with me anymore. It's going to be just fine. Matt will come home, and it'll be like before. Before before. Believe me, they're not interested in my little life."

I nod.

It's not until a long time later, standing at my school locker that I think, *But I was asking about me. Will the police call me?*

But, Coach, what about me?

When we walk into school, Coach loops her arm in mine for a second, which she has never done and doesn't suit her.

Still, I feel her strain and want to clinch her tighter, but I don't. Now we share something. At last. Except it's this.

I fall asleep in Chem, my cheek on the tall tabletop of our lab station, a TV movie unreeling in my head: cheerleaders lined up at the station house in bright uniforms. On TV they always wear their uniforms all day long, and never stop smiling.

When I wake with a jolt to the sight of David Hemans flaring the Bunsen burner inches from my hair, I feel like I've just touched the tip of knowing, of realizing.

But then it goes away.

"You're the worst lab partner ever," he says, eyeing my Eagles letter jacket. "I hate all of you."

Second period, two minutes before the bell, and Beth slips into the seat next to me.

"Miss Cassidy," Mr. Feck says, hand on his hip like he does. "I don't believe I see you until fourth period. And not always then."

Full-on cheer-glamour mode, à la RiRi, Beth crinkles her nose with just a whiff of naughtiness and jiggles her index finger like a little inch worm, mouthing, *One second, Mr. Feck, please!!!*

Feck nearly bows his assent.

They are so weak. All of them.

Dragging my desk toward her, Beth whispers greedily in my ear.

"Did she tell you about it? Spill, soldier, spill."

"Did who tell me what?" A routine that's getting old, even to me.

"Fuck me, Hanlon," she says, hand gripping my wrist until both our tan hands turn white.

"Yes," I say, clipping my voice. "She can't believe it. It's terrible."

"Suicide is *no* solution," she says, and she says it lightly, cruelly.

Then she seems to catch herself, and something tangles messily in her face. For a second.

Seeing that, I feel my chin wobble, and heat rising to my eyes. Therein, somewhere, beats the heart of Beth.

"But Addy," she says, looking at me low-eyed, like *c'mon, give it up, girlie*, "did she have any *more* information? How did she find out? Who told her?"

"I don't know," I say.

"Miss Cassidy . . ." singsongs Mr. Feck, eager to reengage.

"Yes, m'lord," Beth says, and she curtsies. She really does.

Turning around at the door, her waist swiveling, she pokes two fingers out at me.

Later, be-yotch.

Later.

My finger poised over my phone, the text message screen blank and taunting.

UR nt gona tel abt Coach n Will . . . I start to type.

But then I don't.

And I start thinking of all the text messages Beth must have about everything.

One by one, text by text, email by email, I delete everything on my phone, my breath loud in my own ear. But I know it doesn't matter.

You can't erase it all, not even half of it. Half my life surrendered to gray screens the size of my thumbnail, each flare carelessly shot from my phone to another now rocketing back, landing in my lap like a cartoon bomb, its wick lit.

The thing is, when this happens, you just have to give Beth the thing she wants.

But what does Beth want?

And yet Coach goes on, and I marvel at it.

At practice, she hustles us while Beth sits on the top bleacher deck.

Perched up near the rafters, black wings tucked tight, she's staring at her phone, her face lit by it.

Counting off our beats, Coach is focused, intense. She rides us hard.

"I've got to move things fast," she shouts. "I have to pick up my daughter. Don't drag on me, dollies."

At first, the hurting is not the good kind, and I can't pound my way to it. And when Mindy fishhooks me during a tumbling pass, knocking me to the mat, I'm embarrassed to feel hot tears popping from me. For the first time ever on the mat.

"God, Hanlon," Mindy says, surprised. "You *are* Lieutenant Hanlon, aren't you?"

But there's no time to feel the shame and I make sure to hold nothing back when I jam my shoe into Mindy's hidebound shoulder next time around.

Soon enough, as we leap and tuck and jump, I start feeling better and my body starts doing wonderful things, tight and rock-hard, nailing it.

But then Beth starts talking loudly on her phone. I see Coach looking up at her, again and again, and everything starts galloping back, hoofs up.

"Cap'n," Coach calls out to her, and I feel myself tense. "Can you run some tumbling?"

Beth looks up, a strand of hair slipping from her mouth.

We all look up.

She does not remove the phone from her face.

I feel like if I were closer, I'd see her baring her teeth.

"I'd like to, ma'am," Beth shouts, in her whiniest teen girl voice, "but I only have one tampon left and I've had it in *all day*, so I think if I do mat work, it'll come loose."

We all look at Coach now, and no one says anything.

Coach, oh, Coach, why did you ask?

"Then we'll see your blood on the mat," Coach says, planting one dainty foot on the bottom bleacher.

Oh, Coach . . . these two, toe to toe, puffing their chests out, practically thumping them.

"I'd like to, Coach," she says. "Really, I would. But haven't we all seen enough blood lately? Shouldn't we really be thinking of our loss?"

Coach's face motionless, but I can see something in there, something caving in deep.

Look at her, Coach, I want to say. *Look at it. See how she is fearless now. See how long she has been waiting for her chance and now she has it.*

I have to make Coach see.

And I have to keep my eyes on Beth, ceaselessly.

We drive side by side down Curling Way, Beth play-gunning with the gas. We're driving out to Sutton Ridge, where the red-scalped PFC, Jimmy Tibbs, agreed to meet with Beth.

She's pumping him or someone's pumping someone, and suddenly they are like comrades, passing briefcases and taping Xs on telephone poles.

The spooky rustlings of the ridge are spookier than ever now that the air's gone cold and everything's glass-bright. Or maybe it's the strange pause I feel in Beth. Like a thing arrested between coming and going. Like the second before a crouch becomes a bound.

We're to meet the PFC in a clearing up by the eastern-most edge, and we walk in a hush, sneakers tramping, ankles twisting on strange clumps and roots and other things of nature. Why can't the world be as flat and smooth as a spring-loaded floor, as hard and certain as a gym's merciless wood?

We hear him before we see him because someone is whistling tinnily somewhere. It seems to put a little scare even in Beth, who doesn't suffer the red-tinted terrors behind my eyes.

But we get closer and the whistle sounds more like a young boy's. A whistle to ward off demons and night terrors.

He's whistling what I finally recognize as some quavering version of "Feliz Navidad."

Waving from the clearing, he heads toward us, jogging

soldier-like and extending his hand as we nudge down the crest of our twining pathway, shoes skidding.

Beth gives him her golden hand and a look of great charm, with the powerful illusion of delicate girlhood.

I see how this is with them.

Beth knows her mark.

"Listen, girls, I don't want to get anyone in trouble."

His freckle-rubbed face looking rubbed twice over, the PFC paces as he talks, scratching the back of his neck until it turns red.

"He was our Sarge," he says, "and he's still Sarge to me. And I got his back."

"Of course you do," I say. "None of us want any trouble."

"But the thing is, now our superiors are involved. The Army's doing their own investigation," he stutters. "And we have to cooperate fully."

He looks at us and it's then I realize he knows we know about Sarge and Coach, and I am guessing Beth told him.

"We understand," Beth says, all big-eyed sympathy. "It's your duty. What choice do you have?"

"We just want what's best for Sarge," he says, nobly. "And I want to protect your . . . sarge too."

Beth nods, slowly, her slowness a hint to him that maybe she has no "sarge" other than the truth.

"So they can't rule out anything yet?" she fishes. I marvel at her big-eyed frailing routine. It's like she can make her body smaller somehow just standing there. She can make her rough-skinned voice go soft and helpless.

"Well, the detective said that a lot of times the autopsy only tells you so much," he says, talking slowly, so we can understand. "You have to look at the behavior the weeks, days, hours leading up to the death. That's how you figure out what was going on in a guy's mind. To figure out if it's a suicide or homicide."

"Homicide?" I blurt, almost a laugh. Then it is a laugh.

He's not laughing, though.

There is a long second when both of them look at me.

"What are you two talking about?" I ask, trying to keep the laugh going.

"A young guy, prime of his life," the PFC says, swapping a grave look with faux-grave Beth, the two of them admonishing me. "There wasn't any note. They have to look at all possibilities."

"But his wife . . . he . . . " I start.

He bows his head, sighs, then looks at me intently. "The point is, they're trying to figure out what was going on with him, they're going to ask questions, and I've got to answer them."

I look at him, at Beth squirming delightedly beside him. These two. Who did they think they were, citizen soldier and good Samaritan?

"Just say it. You're going to tell them about how it was," I say. "With Coach."

"I have to."

I look at him, a bristling rising up in me.

"Sorry," I say, after a pause. "I was just thinking of the last time I saw you. Watching me knot this one's legs together in the parking lot of the Comfort Inn."

He looks at me, stricken.

"But back to your point. Yes, I guess you're going to tell him everything then. Like about all the booze you fed us, even fourteen-year-olds. You do know that JV is fourteen. And about Prine."

The PFC's face bursts redder than ever, a blaring siren.

Beth harrumphs like she's both annoyed and impressed. *My lieutenant, my lieutenant.*

"Girl looks out for her Coach, like she's a mama tit," Beth says to PFC, shrugging. "Point is, scrub, we all wanna protect our top dogs."

The PFC grates the back of his scarlet neck till it blazes, then nods, white at the mouth. White at the mouth like he's a little scared of both of us. Like he might need to start whistling again.

That word *homicide* snakes through my brain, its tail snapping back and forth.

Walking side by side back to the car, Beth twirls a finger through the bottom of my braid.

"*Foul play,*" I say, eyes rolling.

"He's no JV runt, Hanlon," she says. "You get more honey from that hive if you buzz softly in his ear. You with your fucking chainsaw. Bringing up the Comfort Inn."

"I studied at the feet of the master lumberjack," I say, sounding like no one if not Beth.

"But our goal, young buck, isn't to intimidate into silence," she says. "It's to find out what happened." She looks at me. "Isn't that right?"

Of course this is neither of our goals.

"And I'm sure Coach above all wants to know what happened to her man," she says, dipping her head closer to mine, so enjoying all this. "I'm sure she'll be grateful to know. I'm surprised you're not more eager to help her."

"I don't want him getting any of us in trouble," I say. "I'm looking out for the squad."

"Spoken like a born captain," she says, grinning. "I always knew you wanted to be captain."

"I never did," I say, turning from her to continue down the trail. It's so dark now, and I can hear her behind me.

"Of course not," she is saying, and I can hear a grin on her.

She's wrong, I never did. Not once. It was hard enough being lieutenant.

"Besides," she says, sidling next to me, "it *does* seem strange, now that I think of it. A man in the prime of his life. And bang, bang, puts a gun to his temple?"

"His mouth," I correct her.

As the words come out I feel myself go ice cold.

"His mouth?" Beth asks, lightning quick.

My whole life with Beth, under the hot lights. Standing beside her as she hotlights someone else.

"That's what I read, I think," I stumble. "Wasn't it his mouth?"

With her or against her, you better be on. Game on. Like

when you're out there, grandstands thrumming, sneakers squeaking on polished floor, and you gotta fake-smile till it hurts. Till you want to die from it.

Ramrod that back, hoist those tits, be ready, always. Because she always is.

"I don't know, Addy," she says, her eyes on me. "Was it Sarge's mouth?"

"No," I say. "I've got it all wrong. I'm blood-sugar bottomed out." I begin tugging my braid loose, bobby pins flying, scattering to the ground.

I can almost feel her disappointment at how poorly I've kept up with her, stayed in the game.

For hours after, I'm cursing myself for ever thinking I could run with Beth, for thinking I could keep up.

If you could have seen him, I want to say to Beth, you would know it was suicide. You would see. If you saw that dark smudge where his face was . . . you would feel his desperation and surrender.

Wouldn't you?

Is that what I felt?

I'm not so sure.

I think briefly, darkly, of that apartment, legions deep now in my head. A glugging, boggy cove in the center of the earth.

Still, to me, it had felt like stepping in the marsh swirl of a man underwater, a man drowning.

Hadn't it?

It had felt bad. That's what I knew. It had felt like the

worst place I'd ever been—and now that place, it was inside of me.

That night, at last, Coach calls.

"Addy, why don't you come over?" The warmth in her voice, and the desperation. "Stay at my place tonight. Matt's out of town, remember? It's so lonely."

I can't guess at the haunted feeling in her, given how it is with me. I'm glad to know she's feeling these things, because you'd never know it to look at her.

"I'll make us avocado shakes and we'll sing Caitlin to sleep and drag the velvet blankets out on the deck and wrap ourselves in them and look at the stars. Or something," she says, trying so hard.

I'd've dreamed of such courtship a month ago, and something about it does speak to me even amid all this, maybe even especially. It's a singular and troubling stake we share, but it binds us always, doesn't it? A stake that gives me new panics by the hour, yes, but now, for the first time, it warms me too.

So I go, but Caitlin's already asleep and Coach doesn't have any avocados, and it's raining slimily on the deck.

As I dangle on a kitchen island stool, without purpose, she makes a grocery list. She pays an electricity bill. She wrings out kitchen towels, twisting them across her hands and staring vaguely out the window over the sink.

It's almost like Coach doesn't want me there at all now that I'm here.

It's as if I remind her of bad things.

Once, I come back from the bathroom and see her look-ing at my phone, resting on the kitchen island.

"Can you just turn it off?" she says. "You didn't tell anyone you were here, right?"

I say no.

She pauses, fingertips still grazing the phone. Watching as I turn it all the way off, waiting for the screen to go blank.

"Oh, Addy," she finally says, "let's do something, any-thing."

And this is how we end up in the backyard close to midnight, doing backbends in the rain. Extended triangles. Dolphin plank poses.

There's a holiness to it, the wind chimes on the deck carrying us off to the deepest Himalayan climes, or wherever the world is peaceful and clear.

We sweat even in the cold, and I catch, amid a streak of light from some passing car out front, Coach's face looking untroubled and free.

The crying starts just after, when we're back in the house. Walking down the hallway, she bends over at the waist and sobs come hard and hurtful. I hold on to her shoulders, their tensile thew rocking in my hands.

She stops in the middle of the hall and I try to hold on and she cries for a very long time.

I sleep next to her that night, under that big dolloping duvet.

We face opposite directions and I think, this is where Matt French sleeps, and I think how big the bed is and how far away Coach is, the duvet snowbanking in the middle, and if she's still crying, I wouldn't know.

It makes me feel lonely for both of them.

Sometime in the night, I hear her talking, her voice strange and hard.

"How could you do this to me?" she snarls. "How?"

I look over at her, and her eyes almost look open, her fists wrenching the covers.

I don't know who she's talking to.

People say all kinds of things when they're dreaming. They never mean anything.

"I'm not doing anything," I whisper, as if she were talking to me.

22.

Turning my phone on, seven a.m., I see our squad Face-book page studded with new wallposts, from Brinnie, Mindy, RiRi:

Monday=FINAL GAME!

Go Eagles!

Slaussen, you better KICK ass! Our ticket to the tourney is on YOU!

I long to be a part of it. I long for it.

I find Coach in the kitchen, making toaster oven waffles for Caitlin, who chews on the bottom of her pigtail and watches the oven's orange glow, hypnotized.

"Did the phone wake you?" she asks, spoon in hand, slicing a banana over Caitlin's pearly lavender plate.

It's then that I realize it did.

"I have to go talk to them at the station again," she says, her eyes graying. "In a half-hour."

"They're talking to the Guardsmen," I say quietly, as if Caitlin might understand if I speak more loudly. "The red-head PFC. Tibbs."

The spoon, banana-slicked, slips from her grasp.

She pauses a beat, her hand still outstretched.

I go to reach for the spoon, but her hand shoots out to stop me.

"They have to talk to his men," she says. "I figured on that."

"But, Coach," I say, with as much knowingness as I can impart. "No one wants to get anyone in trouble. *No one* does."

She looks at me, searchingly, and I'm not sure why I'm being so mysterious—something about Beth, eyes on the back of her ponytail, something about Caitlin's blinking stare.

"There's plenty of trouble to go around," she says, holding my gaze.

"Right," I say. "I'm sure that's what everyone realizes."

"Is that what PFC Tibbs realizes?" she says.

"I think so," I say.

But Coach must see something on me, some dread gathering under my skin.

"So what might make the PFC share such details with you?" she asks, her sticky hands still lifted in front of her, her body frozen.

"He shares them with Beth," I say, after the quickest of pauses. It still feels queasy to tell her, but it would feel queasy not to.

It takes her a second for this new bit of knowledge to descend.

"It's Beth," I repeat.

"Got it," she says, those slippery hands still raised up, like a doctor ready for surgery. Ready to lay his hands upon your heart.

In the first-floor corridor, after second period, after her visit to the police station:

"It's fine," Coach says, brisking by me with a knowing face. Her French braid is very tight, temple vein pulsing. "No problems. It's all good."

After lunch, Beth finds me in the school library, where I never go and where no one should ever have thought to look. But she looks.

"Back in my day, libraries had books," she says, as we internet surf side by side at tall terminals, "and we walked five miles in the snow to school."

"So that's how you got such thick ankles," I say, clicking aimlessly through sundry nothingness. Celebrity crotch shots, Thinspiration: Secrets to Fasting Only Anas Know.

"The PFC went in this morning," she says. "He told me his sad, sad song over malteds."

"And?" I say, twirling my finger in ballerina circles over the touch pad.

"He said they'd called Coach in."

"Yeah, she told me. It went fine." I don't look at her. I don't like the feeling that's coming, that prickling in my forehead.

"Ah . . . " she says, and though I'm not looking, I know she's smiling, can hear the gum clicking to the corner of her grinning mouth.

It reminds me of the time Beth's mother swore to me over her morning coffee that Beth was born with sharp teeth.

Better to drink the blood of JVs, Beth had said.

"So," Beth says now, "what has Coach told you about the hamsa bracelet?"

"What hamsa bracelet?" I say, fingers to my prickling forehead.

"The one they found in Will's apartment."

I click on the ad for Wu Long Vanishing Tea.

"*Wait a minute*," she says, smacking her forehead. "Didn't you have one of those bracelets? The one you gave to Coach. Back in your puppy dog phase. To ward off the evil eyes of wronged husbands, I suppose."

I look at her. I hadn't even realized Beth knew about the bracelet.

"What about it?"

"Well, I guess she must have left it there, at some point," Beth says. "During some . . . encounter."

"Lots of people have those bracelets," I say.

She looks at me, and something pinches in my chest, a memory of something, a connection. But I can't hold on to it. She's watching me so closely, but I can't grab it.

"Do they think it's hers?" I stutter.

"*Is* it hers, Addy?" Beth asks, her left eyebrow lifting. "She must have told you they asked her about it. You two thick as thieves."

"We haven't really had a chance to talk," I say, holding tight to the edge of the terminal.

"Well, she's pretty busy," Beth says, with a slow nod. "Four days to the Big Game and all."

Turning away from the terminal, she flings one golden leg onto the nearest library tabletop.

"Look how tight I am," she says, surveying herself. "I'll grant Coach that. But you think Lil Tacy Cottontail's up for top girl? The balance is all. One of her calves is bigger than the other. Did you ever notice that?"

"No."

"I bet you have. Your balance is impeccable. Four inches shorter, you would've been a perfect top girl."

I pause a second.

"The PFC doesn't know she has one, does he?" I ask.

"Has what?" Beth asks, maddeningly, surveying my legs now with her cold-captain appraisal gaze.

"A hamsa bracelet," I say, fighting a panicky tilt in my voice.

"Not now, Adelaide," she says. "Not yet."

I grab my books and start to walk away.

"You're going to have to forget how pretty and interested she is in you, Addy," she calls after me.

Walking out, I hear her all the way.

"Tighten that gut, Addy. Lock those legs. Smile, smile, smile!"

Everyone is looking at me, but I only look straight ahead.

"Remember what old Coach Templeton used to say, Addy!"

I push open the shuddering glass exit doors.

"A good cheerleader," she is calling out, "is not measured by the height of her jumps but by the span of her spirit."

23.

Thursday: After School

"Four days, Bitches!!" shouts Mindy.

RiRi is doing waist bends, flashing her panties, this time lined with sparkles.

The JV is clicking through youtube on her laptop for the Celts' squad stunts.

Paige Shepherd is twanging—"Ima go for the gold, heart is in control, I'm a go, I'm a go, I'm a go getta"—lifting one long leg into a Bow 'n' Arrow.

Cori Brisky shushes her hair up into her trademark extra-long white-blonde pony whip, famous across three school districts.

Everything is as it ever was.

Still ground bound since her spectacular fall, gimpy Emily is passing around the temporary tattoos she ordered for the squad. She has one on the apple of either cheek and she's dotted her knee brace with them. Which all seems sad to me, like she's our mascot. No one respects a mascot.

We all feel sorry for her. She can't even hall-stalk with us, can't keep up with that club boot, and has already become a recruiting target of lacrosse players and the golf team, which could not be sadder, or of the predatory courtship of the field hockey furies, promising to get her knees skinned.

I remember, sort of, being friends with her. Holding her hair back while she gagged herself peashoot thin. Even calling her at night instead of Beth, confiding things. But now I don't know what we'd talk about.

At three-twenty, Coach, chin high, strolls through the doors to the gym.

Beth, standing in front of the mirror, doesn't even look up, too busy oil-slicking her lashes with a mascara brush, no cares furrowing her face.

"I have some news, guys," she says.

I reach out to hold on to my locker door.

"I heard from my source at State Quals. There's gonna be a scout at Monday's game. We rock them, we're rocking Regionals next year."

Everyone whoops and woohoos, jumping on the bleachers, grabbing each other around the necks like the ball-ers do.

Poor, boot-braced Emily bursts into tears.

"By next year, you'll be flying again," RiRi says, hand to her shoulder.

"But not on Monday," she whimpers. "That won't be mine."

"Let's focus," Coach says, clapping her hands sharply.

We snap front.

Looking at her I can't fathom it. I'd never guess anything else was going on at all. She is ready to ride us. She is sweat-less and bolt-straight.

"We need to think about the Celts," Mindy says.

The Celts squad has serious game, famous for cutesy expressions, head bobs and tongues stuck out and dropped jaws and wide eyes when their Flyers hit, when they spring back the ground gasp ah, ah, ah.

"They do two-girl awesomes," Brinnie Cox says with a sigh, which is how she says everything. "A girl my size can catch both the Flyers' feet in one palm."

"Their facials are hot," RiRi admits.

"I don't care about their wiggling tongues or bouncing ponytails," says Coach. "I don't care about the Celts at all. All I care about is that scout. That scout's gotta see our star power."

We all look uneasily at Tacy.

"Your Flyer isn't your key to the castle," Coach says. "It's about the squad. You gotta show you're the posse straight from hell. And there's only one way to do it. We're going to give that scout something that will guarantee our slot. We're going to show her a 2-2-1."

The 2-2-1.

It will be our shining achievement, if we nail it.

Three stories high of golden girls, two Bottom Bases holding up two Middle Bases in shoulder stands, the Flyer tossed through the center, Bottom Bases platforming her feet, the Middle Bases' arms lifted to hold her arms outstretched, crucifixion style. Spotters standing behind, waiting for the Flyer's death-defying Deadman fall.

It's illegal in competition, but not at a game.

And it's the kind of stunt you need to nail to make it to Regionals. To a tourney.

"Cap'n," Coach says, looking up at Beth, halfway up the bleachers again, her hovering black presence. "All yours today. Drill them hard."

She tosses Beth the whistle.

Beth, one eyebrow raised, catches it.

In an instant, a flare of energy seems to shoot up her body, that sullen slouch uncoiling for the first time in months, since . . . I can't even remember.

Coach has just handed her the Big Stick, and thank god she still seems to think it's worth taking.

"Gimme some handsprings, bitches," Beth says, making her slow, willowy way down the stands, arms dangling, snapping her fingers low.

"Don't fuck me with, RiRi," she says. "Loose limbs may fly for your Saturday night specials, but I need you tight as a cherry. Time-travel me back."

So Beth wrangles us for a while, and it does feel good. And Beth is so on, so animated.

She is enthroned and magnificent.

At some point, I see Coach slink into her office.

Later, while Beth's busy trash-talking Tacy for a weak back tuck, calling her a sad little pussy, I slip over and peer in, see Coach on the phone, her hand over her eyes.

I think: it's the cops. It's the cops. What now?

—

An hour in, we're ready to run the 2-2-1 pyramid.

Because I'm not too big and not too small, I'm a Middle Base, one of the two shoulder stands in the middle.

Beneath me stands eagle-shouldered Mindy Coughlin, my feet curled around her collarbone, her body bracing.

But I think it's worse for me, no floor beneath me, and 90 pounds of quaking panic above.

Once we're up, Tacy will get rocketed between RiRi and me, and we will grab her legs and lock her body in place.

Then she'll wow them all, flipping backward into a Deadman, falling into the waiting embrace of the cradle-armed Spotters fifteen feet below.

Everyone will gasp, grip their bleacher seats.

That Deadman, that's our moment of shock and awe.

Despite what Coach says, it really is all about the Flyer.

We can hold her steady as she comes, but if Tacy wobbles, twists, turns the wrong way: snap, crackle, pop.

Which is probably why she looks like a doomed tail-gunner waiting to be wedged into a quaking turret.

"You all need to sack up for Slaussen," Beth tells us. "Or she'll be mat-kill. Two years ago, at the Viking game, I saw a girl jiggle just an inch up there. Her girls didn't have her. Smack! Her neck hit the ground, skidded so hard that a piece of her blonde ponytail ripped from her scalp."

Tacy's face goes from green to white to gray. Beth, with that power to annihilate with a single breath. Two months ago, Tacy galloped hard at Beth's side, lackey under her mighty sway. Oh, the turns of fortune . . .

Eyes on Tacy's toned legs, which look like mini butter-fingers, Beth shakes her head.

I realize she's right. One calf is bigger than the other.

"You always were such a hoodrat," Beth says, shaking her head. "Always quick to hoist your legs in the air for my sloppy seconds. But I guess you were only hoisting the left one."

Beth kneels down on the mat in front of Tacy's dainty body.

Then, she wets her finger and runs it along Tacy's thigh and calf.

We all observe, like watching a gang recruit get jumped in.

"I thought so," Beth says, rising and wiggling her index finger, smudged with what looks to me like Mystic Island Radiance. "All the spray-tan in the world won't give you what you don't have. You either have muscle or you have twig. Or, in your case, Q-tip."

"I can do it, Beth," Tacy says, voice pitching. "Coach knows. I've earned my spot."

"Then let's see it, meat," she says, standing back. "Make a believer out of me."

Stepping back, she turns the speakers up and our game music, bawdy pop with baby-doll vocals cut through with a molasses-throated rap, *Get down, girl, go 'head get down.*

I swing up to Middle Base, above Mindy's ramming shoulder, her hand foisting, palm spreading over my bottom.

At that moment, Coach walks back into the gym.

"You got it, Slaussen," Coach nods, strolling past Beth to the back of the pyramid. Hearing her, such a relief. "You nailed it once, you'll nail it again."

Coach inexplicably becoming the good cop in this strange new world.

But RiRi, the other Middle Base, and I feel a joint twinge, our eyes on Tacy's legs, like little cinnamon sticks that might snap.

When we raise her up, air-puff light, she is shaking like a bobble-head doll, like Emily was. I can feel her try to make herself tight, can feel it radiating through me, but the cartoon terror eyes put a chill in me.

"Ride that bitch," Beth's voice booms at us. "Ride it."

Our arms shaking, we've got to lock it in place, but it's not locking. It's like trying to make a pair of gummy worms stand straight.

We bring her back down for a second.

"She can't do it," Beth pronounces. "Either no 2-2-1 or we need a new Flyer."

We are all quiet.

Suddenly, RiRi's voice rises from behind me. "What about Addy?"

I turn around and look at her, my heart speeding up. She smiles and winks.

"What if Addy were top girl?"

Coach looks over at me, eyebrows raised. I feel Beth's gaze on me too.

"Addy doesn't like to be on top," Beth says, poker-faced.

"Hey!" Tacy keens. "I've been flying all season."

Coach nods. "It's something to think about, long haul," she says. "But for now we need Addy right where she is, in the middle. She's our spine."

I don't like all the eyes on me. I wish RiRi had never said anything.

It doesn't matter anyway because, a second later, everyone is just looking at Tacy again.

"She can't, Coach," says Beth, as simply as she's ever said anything.

My hands fresh off Tacy's kindling hip bone, I feel certain Beth is right.

"Look at her," Beth scoffs. "She's not trained up."

These are fighting words and we all know it. It's spit in the eye to any coach.

"She just wants my spot, Coach," Tacy nearly whimpers. "I can do it. Elevator me up again."

"Slaussen?" Coach looks over at Tacy. "Are you ready?"

"Yes!"

Beth sighs loudly. "What happens," she practically sings, "when a pretty young coach takes a ragtag team of misfits and feebs under her wing? Why, they fly, fly, fly."

Coach looks at her.

"We just needed someone to believe in us," Beth finishes.

"Stop gaming her, Cassidy," Coach says, staring her down, duel-at-dawn, but her tone still flat, toneless, "or I'm gonna ground-bound you instead."

"Look at her leg," Beth says, "like a wishbone twanging."

"Cassidy," Coach says, like she's forgotten the caution she's supposed to use with Beth, or she's just stopped caring. "When you start showing me you can do more than flash your tits and treat your mouth like a sewer, then maybe we'll have something to talk about."

Don't, Coach, I think. *Don't.*

"You heard the coach," Beth says, turning to us with a smile. "Load her up and let her fall."

The music thumping again, Beth counting off, Mindy and Cori line up, Bottom Bases. Spotters Paige and a JV stand behind them and load up the second level, RiRi and me, our bodies springing up to shoulder stands, their palms cradling our calves.

Facing each other, we lift Tacy between us, throwing her above us into a stand, our arms lifted high, hands tight on her wrists. Her arms outstretched, Jesus-style, her left leg knee-bent in front of her, the girls beneath grasping her right foot to hold her in place.

For a second, she is solid.

Seven, eight Beth counting off until the Deadman and it is time. Time for us to drop her backward into a stiff-spined horizontal fall. Ready for Paige, the JV, all her Spotters, to catch her down below.

We let go.

Her eyes wild, Tacy drops, but her body seems to rubber-ize, limbs like spaghetti. As her hand clambers for me, I feel myself sliding down with her, Paige and Cori, on the ground, shouting, "Slaus, here, here, here. Hold it!"

But she plunges, our hands empty.

The sickly sound as Tacy, still half in Paige's sloping arms, hits the mat, face first.

RiRi and I still on high, I think my knees might give, but I hear Coach's voice, iron smooth, "Hanlon, slow down that dismount," as RiRi and I sink down.

I feel something clamping on me, and Beth is right there, her hand gripping my arm all the way down. Depositing me safely to the mat, feet first.

Coach is on the floor with Tacy, strewing from the Spotters' tangled arms, her feet still in their grip even as her head, neck tilted, her chin split wide open, swabs the mat.

"At least she can fall well," RiRi mutters.

Opening her mouth in a strangled sob, Tacy's teeth blare bright red.

"You come at the king," Beth says, "you best not miss."

RiRi and I take Tacy to Nurse Vance, who slaps on the butterfly bandages and tells me to take Tacy to the hospital for stitches, which sends Tacy into a new round of sobs.

"Your modeling career is over," I say.

Walking Tacy to her locker, she's purple-lipped and cotton-tufted, crying about the game and the scouts and how she's *got* to do the 2-2-1, she's the only one light enough, which isn't even true, and Coach damn well better let her cheer, no matter what she looks like.

Then, a new sob choking in her, she takes a deep breath.

"But it should be Beth anyway," she whispers, dramatically. "Beth's top girl."

For a second, I hear RiRi. *What about Addy? What if Addy were top girl?*

But it never has been me, has it? I never wanted it to. I was never a stunter, I was a spotter, a hoister. That's what I am.

And top girls were different than the rest of us.

I think of Beth last year, after the Norsemen game, all of

us drinking with the players up on the ridge, and Teddy Brun thrusting her above his head, hands gripping around her ankles, her feet tucked in his palms, one leg flung behind her, rendering her celebrated Bow 'n' Arrow, as she spun and lifted her right leg straight in the air, slipping it behind her glossy head, making one beautiful line of Bethness, all of us gasping.

It's all we could talk about, dream about, for days, weeks.

"It's always been Beth," she slurs, grazing the back of her wrist along her temple. "And the squad is what counts. Cheer, I never knew it mattered so much. Not until Coach picked me. She changed my life. Now it's all I can think about, Addy. I hear the counts in my sleep. Don't you? I don't ever want them to end."

I tell her to stop talking.

"Don't you see, Addy?" she says, words fumbling in her mouth, eyes shiny and crazed. "When we go out there Monday night, we need to show them what we can do. What we are. We need to make them know it. We need to give them more than awesomeness.

"We need to give them greatness."

It hurts to turn the steering wheel. I can still feel Tacy's grasping fingers, the fear my arm socket might pop. The sound of Beth, "Ride that bitch . . . ride her."

And Beth, the way her hand fastened on me, stopping my fall.

And after, Coach saying, as I walked the limping Tacy across the gym, "Next time, Hanlon, when you let her go, keep those arms to the side. Don't let her see your hands are there. If she does, she'll grab for them. Wouldn't you?"

Wouldn't you, I want to ask.

I think of injured Emily again, withering up in the stands. And I remember how, last week, she posted on my Facebook wall: "U never call me anymore. None of U." And I decided it was a joke, one of Emily's endless LOLs.

I couldn't be bothered.

At the games she sits, just barely separated from the bleacher crowd—in the borderland, the nowhere zone between our bronzed glory and the gray blur of everything, everyone else in this sad world.

At home later:

U put a hex on Slaus, I text Beth.

U shoulda given *her* the hamsa, she replies.

Like a hypnotist's cue, my head floods with the image of my bracelet in Will's apartment. A crimson ring on his carpet.

But I keep hearing Beth's words in my head: . . . *Coach must've told you they asked her about the bracelet. You two thick as thieves.*

Why hasn't Coach told me?

I think I should just call her and ask her about it. But I don't.

I want her to tell me.

It doesn't mean anything if I have to ask her.

A blipping text message comes hours later, but it's from Beth: *Guess who's flying Mon nite?*

Tacy's out, Beth's in. A peculiar mix of terror and relief floods through me—and then the taunting unknowingness of what kind of conversation transpired between Beth and Coach during those hours after practice to lead to this.

R U happy now? I text back.

But there's no reply.

It's the dark muddle of the night when I feel the phone hissing in my hand.

Come outside.

I flick my blinds with a finger and see a car out front, Coach behind the wheel.

The cold grass crunching under my feet, I skitter across the lawn.

We sit in the car, which is Matt French's and isn't as nice as Coach's car. It smells like cigarettes, though I've never seen Matt French smoke.

The cupholder is stained with three, four coffee rings like the center of an old tree.

Something's wreathing my ankle and I see it's the hand loops of a plastic bag, or the curled edges of an old receipt, or any number of stray Matt Frenchness left behind.

Something about how messy the car is makes me feel things, like that time I saw him, after midnight, drooped over a bowl of cereal, and understood it was his dinner, that gritty bowl of Coach's special holistic blend of organic gravel, soot and matches, and Matt French hunched over it by himself on the kitchen island, socked feet dangling, headphones on, tuning out all our hysteria and gum chewing.

And now. Poor Matt, in some airport or office tower in Georgia, some conference room somewhere where men like Matt French went to do whatever it is they did, which was not interesting to any of us, but maybe it would be if we knew. Though I doubted it.

Except sometimes I think of him, and the soulful clutter in his eyes, which is not like Will's eyes were because Will's eyes always seemed about Will. And Matt French's seem only about Coach.

"He's still gone?" I ask.

"Gone?" she asks, looking at me quizzically.

"Matt," I say.

She pauses. "Oh," she says, turning her face away for a second. "Yeah."

As if he were an afterthought.

Hands curling around the steering wheel, she says, "There's something new, Addy."

The bracelet, she's going to tell me at last.

"The police," she says. "I think they're hearing things. They asked me what the nature of our relationship was. That's how they put it."

"Oh," I say.

"I told them again that we were friends. They're probably just trying to understand his state of mind."

"Oh," I repeat.

"They had a lot of new questions about the last contact I'd had with him. I think they—and the Guard—they want to understand how he might have come to this," she says.

The words don't feel like hers, exactly. So formal, her mouth moving slowly around them like they don't fit.

"I'm sure it's fine, Addy," she says, her fingers clenching tighter. "But it seemed like I should tell you."

"I'm glad you told me," I say. But she hasn't told me anything at all. "Is that all?"

As if sensing my disappointment, she taps me on the shoulder.

"Addy, nothing can really happen if we keep tight," she says, resting her fingers there. I don't remember her ever touching me like that. "Keep strong. Focus. After all, it's just you and me who know everything."

"Right," I say. And I want to feel the dazy warmth of sharing things with her, but she's not sharing, not really, and so all I feel is Beth, the way she seems now, crouched, watchful, hovering.

"So we're good?" she asks.

Part of me wants to tell her everything, all the ways she needs to watch for Beth, knives out. But she's telling me only what she wants to. So I don't say anymore.

"I gave it to Beth," Coach says, reading my thoughts, like she can. Like they both can. "She's top girl. She's flying at the final game."

Coach, I want to say, what makes you think you can stop there? You have to give her everything until we figure out what she wants. Until she does.

"First I made her captain. Now I've made her top girl," she says, eyes on me, searching.

She didn't make *me top girl,* I can hear Beth saying. *I made me top girl. I made myself.*

She loops her fingers around the gear shift.

"I don't know what else to do," she says, a slightly stunned look on her face. "Jesus, she's just a seventeen-year-old kid. Why should I . . . "

There's a pause.

"She'll get bored with it all," she says, as if trying to convince herself. "They always do."

At home that night I spend an hour, forehead nearly pressed to my laptop screen, reading the news.

No Answers Yet: Guardsman cause of death still under investigation.

What would it mean if it were murder? What does it have to do with Coach, with me?

Coach, Coach, like my very own sergeant, who took me straight into the fog of war . . .

I wanted to be a part of your world, but I didn't know your world was this.

That night, I dream about that time with Beth, the first drunk I ever had, both of us climbing up Black Ash Ridge. She kept saying, *Are you sure you're ready, Addy. Are you?* And I promised I was, our heads schnapps-fuzzed and our bodies ecstatic. She said, *But you're not afraid, Addy, are you? Show me that lionheart.*

Later, I remember falling back, great big Xs for eyes and half-delirious, and Beth crawling over to me, her shirt off and blazing red bra. She says she will stop me from logrolling to my death. She promises she will save me, us.

Just don't look down, Addy, *just never look down.*

. . . and her voice, like it was coming from a deep gorge inside me, vibrating through my chest, my throat, my head, my heart:

When you gaze into the Abyss, Addy, she says, her eyes glowing above me like two blazing stars, laughing or even crying, *the Abyss gazes into you.*

24.

Friday: Three Days to Final Game

"Guess what I'm doing?" Beth asks, calling me crack o' dawn, while I'm standing at the mirror, trying to make my face over candy-clean. Streaming petal-pink across my cheeks, my eyelids, strutting it over my trembling lips.

I don't say anything. I don't like the way her voice sounds. Cat–canary-like.

"I'm reading the newspaper. I thought the old lady would faint. She said, 'Do you even know what that *is*, darling daughter?' Oh, the morning wit in the Cassidy household."

"Mmm."

" 'A National Guard source indicated increasing doubt that the Sergeant's death was suicide,' " she reads. " 'Results from a gunshot residue test on the victim's hands showed only trace amounts.' "

I don't say anything.

"Oh, and turns out you were right," she says, pausing as if taking a bite. I have a sudden image of raw meat shearing between her teeth. "It was a gunshot to the mouth, not the temple. You said you were confused, but it turns out you weren't confused at all, Addy."

—

The buzzing of the dying fluorescent lights above me prickles at me the whole time.

I'm in the first-floor girls' room, second stall, having just thrown up, my right cheekbone resting into the porcelain. I'd forgotten what that kind of throwing up could be like, the kind where you're not, Emily-style, nuzzling your finger down your fish-tailing throat, begging for release from the dreaded sluice of cupcakes or from the acidic sludge of too many Stoli Citronas—cheer beer, they call it, we call it. No, this is throwing up like coming off the tilt-a-whirl at age seven, like discovering that dead rat under the porch, like finding out someone you loved never loved you at all.

Now I'm sitting on the floor of the stall, damp newspaper still folded in my hands, the smeary sentences:

". . . while police would not comment on reports of conflicting evidence at the scene, a source close to the investigation questioned the position of the weapon near the body. Recoil will usually cause a handgun to land behind the body, the source noted, not next to his head where it was found."

I feel my stomach turn again.

Suddenly, Beth is there, standing above me, handing me a long sheaf of paper towels, still billowing, untorn, from the dispenser.

At first, I think I'm hallucinating.

"You wait your whole life for something to happen," she's saying, her face immaculate, princess-like, under the rimy fluorescents. "Then, suddenly, it's all the terrors of the earth all at once. Is that how it feels to you, Addy?"

She winds the trail of paper towel around me, leans down, dandling one edge into my sick-moist mouth.

"I'm just sick," I say. "It's nothing."

She smiles, tapping the newspaper in my blackened hands.

"I keep waiting for them to write about that hamsa bracelet," she says. "Put a picture of it to see if anyone recognizes it."

"They don't write about it because it's not important," I say. "They know it could've been left there anytime."

"It could've been. Except it wasn't," she says.

"How do you know?" I say, a fresh round of dread rising in me.

"Because of where they found it," she says. "Or didn't our fearless leader tell you?"

"Where they found it . . . " I say, fighting the panicky moan from my voice.

"Under Sarge's body," she says. "PFC told me. Riddle me that."

Her smile is so faint and yet so piercing, I feel I may go blind.

And the picture in my head, that nubbed carpet, Will's spent body, head black like a mussel's glistening shell.

Under his body.

"It doesn't matter," I say, shaking my head quickly, my words coming faster and faster. "Maybe it was lying there from before, kicked there."

"Hanlon," she says, bending down, a waft of coconut and

sweet vanilla, her girliest perfume worn only on days of biggest trouble and mayhem. "You should be careful here. After all, you may have given it to her, but it is *your* bracelet."

"Everyone knows I gave it to her," I blurt. Which is true, but I realize I've given Beth a new gift.

I'm ashamed of myself.

Smiling down at me, she extends her hand, but I don't take it.

"I know what she means to you, Addy," she says, hand dropping, "but this is bigger than your virgin crush. You best watch your back."

My head jerks back, smacking the wall tile.

"This is epic," she continues. "This is too big to girl out on me. Sack up."

She starts telling me about a show she saw on TruTV about a man whose wife killed herself, or so it seemed. It turned out he'd murdered her.

"You know how they knew? Her teeth. They were all fucked up, like the gun had been forced in there."

The blade through the center of me is sharp and exacting.

"What's that got to do with anything?" I whisper.

"PFC and his Captain ID'd the body. They said Sarge's top front teeth were shattered. Caps, by the way. In case you want to know."

I don't say anything, I'm picturing Will confiding in us at Lanvers Peak, showing us his counterfeit smile, like taking off a beautiful mask and revealing a more beautiful one underneath.

"So someone jammed a gun in Will's mouth," she says,

tapping her front teeth, I can hear the clack, "against those ivory tusks of his and went . . . POW."

Sliding back against the wall, I am too weary for her.

"That's not right, Beth," I say. "He jammed it there himself."

"How do you know?" she says, laughing with a kind of giddiness rare and unnerving on Beth. "Were you there?"

In class, in the hallways, trying to shake off Beth's grim hustle, the way she can whip me up into it with her, the way it can sweep through my body, like a fever.

What does she know, I think. She's just guessing. Wanting.

But the bracelet, the bracelet.

There are a million explanations, I tell myself. And Coach will tell me, she will.

This isn't like before, where the boom of Beth's voice in my head could drown everything else out.

Once it was, and I did what she said. Even last summer, when she told me about Casey Jaye and how Casey was lying about me behind my back. Finally I believed her. I surrendered to it.

But not this time. There's things I've seen she hasn't. Lanvers Peak, the three of us there, Coach, Will and me. The way the two of them nestled around me, knowing I'd take care of them. The smell of burning leaves, the way we shared it, that sense of a lost world of beauty and wonder.

The three of us, what we shared. It was a fleeting thing, but it has a radiant power. It is something just mine, and I won't have her take it from me.

And the boom of Beth's voice isn't enough to make me give it up.

Because Coach would never let anything happen to me.

You can, she told us, *fall eleven feet and still land safely on a spring floor.*

Except later that day, in English class, Beth's text popping up in my phone. The link to the second article, *Hunt for Answers at The Towers.*

It will not stop now.

It talks about police going door to door, interviewing every resident in the apartment building.

And about how lab technicians are going through everything found in the apartment, pulling up carpet samples.

My flip-flops, did they leave a print?

But I remember Coach, with what I now recognize as a stunning presence of mind, had us both remove our shoes. Staggering presence of mind, really.

But then the article says, in a throwaway line, really, the last in the piece:

"Detectives will be reviewing security camera footage of the lobby."

Security camera footage of the lobby.

Coach and I padding out, her sneakers in hand, at 2:30 a.m.

I feel a curtain fall over me.

A second text from Beth, just three words this time:

Truth will out!

—

In Coach's office, blinds pulled tight.

She's behind her desk, my phone lying on the blotter in front of her.

I have never cried in Coach's office and I don't intend to now.

"Beth sent this article to you?" she says, nodding to herself.

"Yes, yes," I say, waving my finger at the phone screen. "Security camera, Coach."

"What about it," she says. "If they'd seen me on that camera, you don't think they would have said so?"

What about *me*, I want to say. But don't.

"That's just newspaper stuff. They haven't even finished hooking up the security system yet. Half the time the door opens without the buzzer."

"Coach," I say, trying again. "They think it's murder."

"It's not murder," Coach says, with such firmness, flicking my phone with her fingers, swatting at it like a fly. "You can't let them scare you, Addy. The Guard's looking out for themselves. It's all about bad publicity."

I don't say anything.

"Addy," Coach says, "look at me."

I do.

"Don't you think I'd like to believe more than anything that Will didn't do that to himself? To me?"

I nod.

Something creaks open in her, a place she did not want to go.

"We saw him, Addy," she says, her fingertips to her mouth, her face sheeting white. "We saw what he did."

I want to hold tight to her hand and say soft things.

"Addy," she says, feverishly, her fingers fisting. "You have to understand. People will always try to scare you into things. Scare you away from things. Scare you into not wanting things you can't help wanting. You can't be afraid."

"Three days left!" shouts Mindy. "I hear scouts *always* seat high left in the bleachers. We gotta work toward that corner."

Our weird little universe where a word from Mindy, her face red and brutish, can suddenly make me care again about the Big Game. Our qualifying shot.

But Coach is nowhere to be found.

"Why does she keep going away?" Tacy asks, mouth-muffled with bandages. She's standing next to Cori, who's rotating her left wrist anxiously, taped tight where wavering Tacy's foot lodged.

And Emily. Gimpy Emily, still boot-braced, near-forgotten.

This array of casualties, and I wonder how I'm still standing.

We happy few, we band of bitches, Beth used to say. Don't you forget it.

As if on cue, Beth strolls in front of us, hip-slinging gangsta.

"Let's get started, kitties," Beth says. "The Celts wait for no sad-ass chicken-hearts."

This, I think, is good for her. I think, *Yes. Yes, Beth. Take it and let it feed you. Feed off this for a while, please.*

"The way to win is to sell it," Beth shouts, her voice rising high and thrumming in all our ears.

"Whip your heads," she says, and we do.

"Make your claps sharp," she says, and we do.

"Make your faces like you're wired for pleasure," she says, and we gleam ecstatic.

"Give 'em the best blow-job smiles you got," she says, and if she had a bullwhip, she'd be slapping it against our thighs. "Turn it on, on, on."

We ride rough and work hard for her. We have three days until the final game and we have to call up another JV whip-poorwill and we will work hard for Beth because we want to show our hot stuff, our epic impudence, our unholy awe-someness in front of the sneering Celt masses on Monday night.

But most of all, we work hard because it raises a din, a rabid, high-pitched din, that can nearly drown out the sound of the current and coming chaos. The sense that everything is changing in ways we can't guess and that nothing can stop it.

Or maybe that's not it at all. Maybe all we're trying to drown out is the terrifying quiet, the sense that all there is to hear is our own thin echoes. Our sense that Coach is drifting from our clasping hands, that maybe she is already gone. That there is no center anymore and maybe there never was.

All we have is Beth. But that is something, her thunder fill-ing up all the silence.

—

In the locker room, the din dissolving, girls scattered and then gone, I find myself alone, or nearly so.

With no Coach, everyone leaves a mess. This is how it was under Beth before. Flair strewn about, rolling empties of rockstar and sugar-free monster, pearly tampon wrappers and crushed goji berries. Even one cobwebby thong.

Bobby pins crunching under my feet, I walk through, surveying the damaged girl–ness.

My heart still hammering from the practice, I'm thinking of how hardcore Beth was out there today, like I haven't seen her since sophomore year, when it still beat in her so hard. When she hadn't gotten distracted by petty grievances and her own miseries of life, her own creeping boredom.

Maybe she has never been this good, cared so much.

This is what Coach has done for her, I think. *She helps us all.*

Then, lurking in the open doorway of Coach's office, she is there. The shadow she throws seems so large that her five feet swallow the office hall.

"Cap," I say, wanting to help sate her, "you bled us today."

Her back to me, I can't see her face.

I walk closer.

I'm hoping, praying for elation.

I mean, isn't she the Coach Itself now, for the moment at least?

"Beth," I say again. "Return of the King."

The sunfall flooding everything, her whole body lit darkly gold, I stop a few feet from her ambered back.

"Beth," I say, "you got everything."

Finally, slowly, a half turn of her head. A whisper of her profile, darkened by her shudder of black hair.

That's when I see that nothing's been had at all, nothing's been saved. She thought this would be it, and it wasn't.

"The sun's down and the moon's pretty," she says, her voice hushed. "It's time to ramble."

And I say yes. Of course I say yes.

25.

Sprawled on the hood of my car, we are high up on the south face of the ridge, right where it drops a thousand miles or more, into the deepest part of the earth.

We have been drinking cough-syrupy wine that clings to the tongue. Beth calls it hobo wine, and it feels like we are hobos now. Wanderers. Midnight ramblers.

For moments at a time, I forget everything and think that, hidden up here behind the sparkly granite of a thousand gorges and knobs, I am safe from all hazard.

But there is Beth beside me, breathing wildly and talking in ragged lopes that seem to streak around my head, across the sky above us.

At some point, I stop listening and instead focus on the loveliness of my own white hands, bending and canting them above me, against the black sky.

"Do you hear what I'm saying, Addy?" she asks.

"You were speaking of dark forces," I guess, because this is usually what Beth is speaking of.

"You know who I thought I saw yesterday," she says, "driving her whorey Kia over by St. Reggie's?"

"Who?"

222

"Casey Jaye. All last summer, cheer buddies in your camp bunk, giggling together in your matching sports bras, and that love knot she gave you."

"It wasn't anything—" I say, feeling an unaccountable blush. "It didn't mean anything."

"Opening her thighs to show you her tight quads. I knew her wormy heart. But I shot my wad too soon and you weren't ready to believe me. You didn't want to."

She will never let it go. She will never forget it.

But then she jerks up suddenly and I nearly slide from the car hood, hands grappling her jacket.

"Look out there," she says, pointing into the distance, the place where Sutton Grove would be if it weren't just nightness out there.

I peer off into the black, but I can't see anything, just a shimmer of some town somewhere that's mostly, if not fully, asleep.

A lush wino haze upon me, I guess I'd been hoping, with colossal foolishness, that Beth will determine she has won, that she is captain, that Coach is barely even a coach these days, ceding more and more power, and now she will let it go . . . she will let it go and Coach will be free.

It's all over, or nearly so.

The police will realize the truth, and it will all be over.

And Beth will be done.

Or nearly so.

I am drunk.

"With her sly smiles and her yoga orgies and her backyard

jamborees," Beth is saying, "all of you curled at her feet. Cleopatra in a hoodie. I never fell for any of it."

"You never fell for it once," I agree, trying to fight off the feeling of menace piercing the haze.

"But when I look out there," she says, sweeping her hand across the lightless horizon, "all I can think is that she's out there, *getting away with it*. Getting away with everything."

"Beth," I warn. My eyes on the velvety dark below. The expanse of nothingness that suddenly seems to be throbbing, nervous, alive.

What does lie down there?

In this state, the unruly despair of Will's life, the battered end of it, comes to me freshly.

I want sparkled cheeks, high laughter and good times, and I never asked for any of this. Except I did.

"Addy," she says, kicking her feet in the air, "I've got that fever in my blood. I'm ready for some trouble. Are you?"

I am not. Oh, I am not. But who would leave Beth alone when she's like this?

"Let's go look the devil in the eye, girlfriend," she says, tilting that wine bottle to my lips, to my open mouth, and I drink, drink, drink.

Beth now at the wheel, we are looping endlessly, in curling figure eights, and the street lamps overhead are popping over my eyes.

Then we're climbing back up again and there's a pause between songs and I hear a roar in my ear. Face to the window, I see the crashing interstate is newly below us.

We're nearly there before I realize where she's taken me.

"I don't want to be here," I whisper.

She stops the car in front of the lightboxed sign, THE TOWERS.

We sit, the light greening our faces.

"This is not a place I want to be," I say again, louder now.

"Can you feel the energy here?" she says, putting lipgloss on with her finger, like we are readying for our dates. "It's some black mojo."

"What are you talking about?"

"Our great captain's captain, the she-wolf. The li-o-ness. I can feel her here," she smiles spookily. "How it was for her that night."

I don't say anything.

"The night she done shot her lover dead," Beth says, curling her fingers into little guns.

Bang-bang, she whispers in my ear, *bang-bang!*

And there it is. She has said it.

"You have lost your mind," I say, the words heavy in my mouth. "You have lost it."

"*Hey, Coach,*" Beth sings, her grin wider and wider, "*where you goin' with that gun in your hand?*"

"Shut up," I say, my hand leaping out and shoving at her, a strange half-laugh coming from me.

But then I'm shoving harder and I'm not laughing, and Beth grabs my hands and locks them together, *when did she get so sober?*

"He killed himself," I say, so loud it hurts me to hear. "She didn't do anything. She'd never do anything like that."

My hands in hers, she leans toward me, very close, her wine-thick breath in my face, my hands knotted in hers so tight I feel a hot tear in my eye corner.

"She would never do anything like that," she repeats back to me, nodding.

"She loved him," I say, the words sounding small and ridiculous.

"Right," Beth says, smiling, pressing my hands against her own hard ribcage, like clutching in the backseat with a boy, "because no one's ever killed the person they love."

"You're drunk, you're drunk and awful," I say, and I'm trying to get my hands free, and we're rocking, our faces so close. "An awful bitch, the worst I ever knew."

She drops my hands at last, tilting her head and watching me.

Suddenly, the wine heaving in me, my hands palsied, I have to get out of the car.

Feet on the smooth, freshly poured asphalt of the lot, I breathe deep.

But this is what she wants because she gets out too.

We are standing high up on the ridge, my lips stinging with the last of the wine as I take it to my lips.

I look at her, face shot through not with moonlight but the wan blue of the bank of parking lot lights.

"Let's go," I say. "I don't need this—

"Do you smell something?" Beth asks, suddenly. "Like flowers or something. Honeysuckle."

"I don't smell anything," I say.

I smell all kinds of things, most of all chlorine. Bleach. Blood.

"Did you know the government is studying the possibility that people might give off these scents when they're lying?" Beth says, and I must be dreaming. "And each smell is very individual. Like a fingerprint."

I've dreamed my way into one of Beth's nightmares, the one where we're standing above the gorge, like an open throat.

"I wonder if yours is honeysuckle," she says.

"I'm not lying about anything," I say.

"Honeysuckle so sweet, I can taste it. You're good enough to eat, Addy-Faddy," she says, and I feel she's monstrous now.

"He killed himself," I say, my voice almost too low to hear. "It's the truth, if you want to know."

"You lie and lie, and I keep lapping it up," she says, clucking her tongue.

"He did. He shot himself in the mouth on his carpet," I say, and it's not even my voice, not even my words, but they come so fast and so sure. "It's the truth."

Beth is watching me, and there's no stopping me now.

"He shot himself," I say. I wish I could stop, but I can't stop until I convince her. "He fell on the carpet and his head was black. And he died there."

With those security floodlights glaring, her face like cold marble, she says nothing.

And I keep going.

"You don't know," I say, the wind whipping my hair into my face, my mouth. "Because you didn't see. *But I know.*"

"How do you know?" she darts back, and repeats her question from the girls' restroom. "Were you there?"

"*Of course I was,*" I say, almost a moan, my breath sliding from me.

"Of course you were," she says, fingers reaching out, lacing through my blowing hair.

"So that's how I know," I say, tightening my voice. "That's how I know more than you. I saw his body. I saw it lying there."

She is quiet for a moment.

"You saw him kill himself."

"No, after."

"Ah, so you saw him after he was already dead. After Coach shot him dead."

"No," I say, my voice loud. "We found him together. We got to his apartment and there he was."

"I see," she says, an unspeakably lewd leer arising, "so what exactly was going on that Coach would bring you to the Sarge's apartment, at all hours of the night. Were you some virgin prize—"

"No," I nearly shout, feeling stomach-sick. "She found him and she called me. I went and got her."

She smiles faintly. "Huh," she says.

My stomach turning, I lean against the car door, breathing in.

"You saw us that night," I say, heeling back onto the front seat. "You saw me come home after."

"I didn't need to see you," she says, toe-kicking at my

ankles. It's not really an answer, though. "I know all your beats, Addy."

"You know everything," I mutter. "Like God."

"I know you, Addy," she says. "Better than you ever could. You've never been able to look at anything about yourself. You count on me to do it for you."

I press my face into the car headrest.

"And what you've just told me," she continues, "I'm glad you finally fessed up, but it doesn't change anything."

Turning my head slowly toward her, my mouth drifting open . . .

"What?"

"All it proves, Addy, is that you lied to me. But I knew that already."

Later, in bed, the alcohol leeching from me, I cannot make my head stop.

Drunk and weak, I gave her everything.

I feel outmaneuvered, outflanked.

Because I was.

Don't you believe me now? I'd said, whining like a little JV, all the way home.

Don't you get it? she'd said, shaking her head. *He was done with her. And now she's done with him. And now she's sunk you down in it with her. And soon she'll be done with you too.*

She made you her accomplice.

She made you her bitch—but then again, weren't you already?

I think I will never sleep and then, finally, I do.

26.

Saturday Morning: Two Days to Final Game

I wake up with a start, and a picture flashes there.

Last Monday night, Coach opening Will's apartment door to me. The alarm in her eyes like she'd forgotten she'd called me. The shimmery dampness clinging to her thick hair.

The picture so vivid, it aches. My heart rocketing in my chest, I feel my t-shirt sticking to me, my hungover body blazing.

Grasping for the warm water bottle by my bed, I know something suddenly. Something I'd forgotten.

The dew on her.

Faint. Like someone who'd showered maybe a half-hour before.

And Will, lying on the floor in his towel.

I can't quite piece it together, but it reminds me of something.

It reminds of another time.

It reminds me of this:

Will, waving through the lobby doors, his hair wet and seal-slick.

Coach, slipping from behind him, walking toward me, her

hair hanging in damp lopes to her shoulders, darkening her T-shirt.

The first time I drove to The Towers, the time I came and picked her up. And I knew what they'd been doing before I arrived, because it was all over them.

Their clothes on but they seemed so naked, all their pleasure in each other streaked across their faces.

Fresh from their shower, their shared shower I'd imagined. I imagine now.

Monday night, Coach and Will, both shower damp, but Will is dead.

She didn't find his body, Beth said. *She was there when it happened. She was already there.*

The phone rings and rings and rings. I turn it off and stuff it under my mattress.

The thoughts that come are rough and relentless.

The days leading up to Will's death, the way Coach had been acting, missing practices, the car accident, and now I wonder if she'd lied about all of it. If she had felt Will drifting away and had been calling, had been begging him to come over, like that day at her house, when she finally lured him over. When she had me wait in the backyard with Caitlin.

And that night. The faintly damp hair. The bleachy tennis shoes. What had that been about, really?

And how did she get to Will's?

I took a cab, she'd said. *I snuck out of the house. Matt was asleep. He took two pills. I had to see Will.* That strangely robotic voice she had that night. *So I called a cab. But I couldn't call a cab to take me back, could I?*

Snuck out at two in the morning, and Matt French didn't hear her? It made so much more sense that she'd gone over earlier, made some excuse to Matt or gone because Matt wasn't home yet.

Could Will have been done with her, and she . . .

Suddenly, I think of last week, that sleeping snarl in the night as I lay beside Coach:

How could you do this to me? How?

Pow-pow, I can hear Beth say. *Pow-pow*.

A Post-it left for me on the kitchen island:

"A, Debbie says someone from police dept. called for you. Someone steal mascot again? Love, D."

Yes, Dad, I think, holding the edge of the counter. *That's exactly it.*

I'm running on Royston Road when the car pulls up.

I never run. Beth says runners are uncreative masturbators. I was never sure what that meant, but it made me never want to run.

But this morning, my stepmother's klonopin still sticky on my tongue, running seems right.

Like at practice, like at games, I can forget everything but the special talents of my special girl body, which does everything I ask it to, which is unravaged and pure, babyoil soft and fluttered only with the bruises of girl sport.

The feel of the concrete pulsing up my shins is near exquisite and when the release comes, it's like hitting a stunt but better because it's just me and no one can even see, but I'm doing it, doing it anyway and without peering out waiting for anyone to tell me I hit it, because I know I did. I know it.

So I keep running. Until all I feel is nothing.

And no one can touch me. My phone shut off, far from me, and no one even knows where I am, if I'm anywhere at all.

Except the detectives.

It's just like on TV. They pull up to the curb, and one of them is leaning on the door jamb.

"Adelaide Hanlon?"

I stop, ear buds slipping from my ears.

"Can we ask you a few questions?"

The man gives me a bottle of water. It gives me something to do with my hands, my mouth.

We sit in an office, and when the woman sees my sweated legs puckering a little on the seat, she offers me the desk chair, and she doesn't seem to care that I sweat on it.

"If you'd feel more comfortable with your parents present," the man says, "we can call them."

"No," I say, shaking my head. "That's okay."

They both look at me and nod, as if I am being very wise.

Then, they exchange a quick look. He leaves, and the woman stays.

In my head, I start doing my cheer counts. One-two, three-four. I count them until my heart finally slows down. Until I can empty my face, teen-girl bored.

"We're just trying to confirm a few details about last Monday night," she says.

She has a tight ponytail that reminds me of Coach's, and a dimple on one side of her mouth. She doesn't really smile, but she speaks softly.

Somehow I start to feel okay, like having to talk to the assistant principal about something you know about but had nothing to do with. If you just say as little as possible, they really can't do anything.

Or maybe it's just that it doesn't seem real, any of it.

And maybe I don't feel real, or even awake.

The questions start generally, more like a conversation. What do I like about school, how long have I been a cheerleader. Aren't some of the stunts dangerous.

When the questions turn, it's a gentle turn, or she renders it gently.

"So you and Coach French spend time together outside of school?"

The question seems strange. I think I've misheard it.

"She's my coach," I say.

"And last Monday night, did you see your coach?"

I don't know what to say. I have no idea what she told them.

"Last Monday?" I say. "I don't know."

"Try to remember, okay? Were you at her house last Monday?"

That second part, a gift. *At her house.* If Coach didn't tell them that, who would have?

"I guess I was," I say. "Sometimes I help her with her little girl."

"Like a babysitter while she goes out?"

"No, no," I say, calm as I can. Besides, who is she to call me a babysitter? "I don't babysit."

"So just pitching in?"

I look at her, at her bare lips and badly plucked eyebrows.

"I hang out there a lot," I say. "She helps me through stuff. I like being over there."

"So last Monday you were there with your coach and her husband?"

And her husband. "Yes," I say, because doesn't this have to be Coach's story and don't our stories have to be straight for both our sakes? "I was."

"And you knew the Sergeant?"

"I'd see him in school."

"Was your coach friends with him?"

"I don't know," I say. "She never said anything to me."

"You never saw them together?"

"No."

I have no idea what I've done or undone.

"And you like being at Coach's house. You like spending time there." She's watching me closely, but I can't get over the stitch of stray eyebrow hair to the side of her very groomed right brow.

How could she miss something like that? That detail, like spotting a slack move in another squad's routine.

It makes me feel strong.

Deputy Hanlon, stone-cold lieutenant, my old roles—I'd forgotten how good they felt.

"That's what I said, yes ma'am."

I lean back, stretch my legs long and adjust my ponytail.

"It was a comfortable place to be? They seemed to get along?"

"Yeah," I say.

"Seem like a happy marriage?"

I look at her with my head tilted, like a dog. Like I can't guess what she might mean. Who thought about the happiness of marriages?

"Yeah, sure," I say, and my voice clicks into something else, the way I talk when I have to talk to people who could never understand anything at all but who think they get me, think they get everything about girls like me.

"We like Coach," I say. "She's a nice lady."

And I say, "Sometimes she shows us yoga moves. It's really fun. She's awesome. The Big Game is Monday, you should come."

I lean close, like I'm telling her a secret.

"We kick ass Monday, we're going to Regionals next year."

"We may have some more questions," the detective says, as she walks me out.

"Okay," I say. "Cool." Which is a word I never use.

Walking past all the cops, all the detectives, I raise my runner's shirt a few inches, like I'm shaking it loose from my sweated skin.

I let them all see my stomach, its tautness.

I let everyone see I'm not afraid, and that I'm not anything but a silly cheerleader, a feather-bodied sixteen-year-old with no more sense than a marshmallow peep.

I let them see I'm not anything.

Least of all what I am.

27.

Saturday

At home, I drag my phone from under my mattress.

There are seven voicemails from Coach, and sixteen texts. They all say some variation on this: *Call me before anything. Call me NOW.*

But first, I decide to do some stretches, like Coach showed us.

Cat tilt. Puppy dog. Triangle pose.

She can wait.

I turn the shower on and stand under it a long time.

Then, I blowdry my hair, stretching each strand out languorously, my mind doing strange twists and turns.

Somewhere in the back of my head some old cheer motivational words sputter forth: *Time comes, you have to listen to yourself.*

That seems like something old Coach Templeton—Fish—would've said, or printed out from the internet, or typed in scroll font at the bottom of our squad sheets.

As if listening to yourself were just something you could do. As if there were something there to listen to. A self inside you at all.

My fingers touch my open computer screen, our squad

Facebook page, all the cheer photos from three years of death defiance and bright ribbons.

Cheerlebrities!!!

There's one shot of Beth and me in the foreground, our faces glitter crusted, our mouths open, tongues out, our fingers curled into the devil hand sign.

We look terrifying.

The picture was from last year. At first, I don't recognize myself. With all the paint, we are impossible to tell apart. Not just Beth and me, but all of us.

The front windows of Coach's house are still rimy from last night's frost, and Caitlin's paper snowflakes scatter across. A lamp glows inside.

It has the feel of a fairytale cottage, like one of those paintings at the mall.

Caitlin stands inside the front door, two fingers punched in her mouth. Usually so tidily groomed, her hair looking oddly knotted, like an uncared-for doll. Bread crumbs scatter up her cheek.

She doesn't say anything, but then she never does, and I twist past her, my legs brushing against the barbs of her ruffled jumper, which seems more suited for July.

She likes to look pretty, Coach always said, like that was the only thing she really knew about her.

"I didn't think they'd get to you so fast," Coach says. She's washing the windows in the den, wielding a long pole with a squeegee at the end, and a soft duster beneath it. "I was calling and calling. I thought for sure I'd get to you before they did."

There's a sheen of sweat on her face.

I don't say anything because I want that sweat there, at least for now. She's made me sweat enough.

"It just seemed easiest to tell them you were here that night," she says. "If you were at my house, then I couldn't possibly have been at Will's."

She looks at me, from under her extended arm, the pretty muscles spun tight.

"And you couldn't have been there either," she adds. "So we're both covered."

"What about Matt?" I say, dropping my voice.

"Oh, he's outside," she says, gesturing out the window.

In the far corner of the lawn, I spot him sitting on the brick edging of an empty flowerbed.

I can't figure out what he's doing, but he's very still.

I've never seen him like that, or outside at all. I wonder if he feels peaceful.

"No," I say, regaining my focus. "I mean he told the cops you were home asleep, right? Which is what he thought anyway?"

Why did you need me as your alibi, I want to say, *when you had him.*

"This is better, Addy," she says, the words just tripping from her tongue. "They never believe the spouse. And he was asleep, that's not much corroboration . . ."

She stops for a second, eyes fixed on something on the windowpane. A smudge I can't see.

"I used to use newspapers," she says. "Then Matt bought me this thing." She touches her fingers to the duster at the end of the pole. "It's lamb's wool."

I keep waiting for her to say sorry, *Sorry I didn't warn you, Sorry I didn't prepare you, Sorry I didn't protect you from all of this.* But she's never been a sorry kind of person, I guess.

"Coach," I say. "Don't you want to know what I said to the cops?"

She looks at me.

"But I know what you said," she says.

"How do you know?" I say, sitting on the sofa where she stands, barefoot. "I might have blown it without even realizing it."

"I know because you're smart. I know because I trust you," she says, and lifts the pole again, telescoping it higher. "I wouldn't have gotten you into this, otherwise."

"Gotten me into what?" I say, my voice scraping up my throat. "Coach, what am I in?"

She will not look at me. She's looking out the window.

"My mess," she says, her voice smaller. "Don't think I don't know that."

I follow her gaze.

Far back on the lawn, Matt French has turned and seems to be looking toward us. Toward me.

I can't make out his face, but it's as though I can.

"Coach," I say, "why was your hair damp?"

"What," she says, swooping the squeegee back up the window.

"When I got to Will's apartment that night," I say, my eyes

still on Matt French in the backyard, his rounded over shoulders. "Why was your hair wet?"

"My hair wet? What kind of . . . it wasn't wet."

"Yes it was," I say. "It was damp."

She sets the pole down.

"Oh," she says, looking at me at last, her voice hardening. "So it's you who doesn't trust me."

"No, I . . ."

"Did the police . . . did they . . . ?"

"No," I say. "I just remembered it. I'd forgotten it and I remembered it. I'm just trying . . . Coach, he was wearing a towel, and your hair . . ."

Something is happening, that vacant, efficient expression slipping away, revealing something raw, bruised. It's like I've done something powerfully cruel. "I took a bath before I went over there," she replies. "I always did."

"But, Coach . . ."

"Addy," she says, looking down at me, the pole piercing the cushion, like a staff, or sword, "you need to stop talking to Beth."

A burr rises up under my skin.

"Because she just wants her pretty doll back," Coach says quietly, lifting the pole again, pressing the squeegee against the window, making it squeak.

I feel something tighten in me and have a picture suddenly of Beth's fingers circling my wrist.

Then, at last, I say it. "You never told me about the bracelet."

"The bracelet?" she says, finally releasing the pole and descending from her perch.

"My hamsa bracelet."

"Your what?"

"To ward off the evil eye. The one I gave you."

She pauses a second. "Oh, that, right. What about it?"

"Why didn't you tell me the police found it?" I say, then wait a beat before adding, "Under Will's body."

She looks at me, squinting. "Addy, I don't know what you're talking about."

"You mean they didn't ask you about it? They found the bracelet under Will's body."

"They told you that?" her voice darts.

"No," I say, "Beth did."

I start to feel like my feet are going to slip out from under me, even though I'm sitting down.

We're standing in front of Coach's bureau, her smooth mahogany jewelry box before us.

She sets her hands on either side and lifts the top with a shushing sound.

We look at the tidily arranged bracelets woven into the soft ridges. Her tennis bracelet, a few neon sports bracelets, a delicate silver linked one.

"It's got to be in here," she says, fingertip stroking the velvet. "I haven't worn it in weeks."

But it's not.

I look at the box, and at her, at the way her face looks both tight and loose at the same time, veins wriggling at her temples, but her mouth slack, wounded.

"It's here," she says, sliding the box off her bureau, everything tumbling radiantly to the carpet.

"It's not," I say.

She looks at me, so helpless.

For a long time, maybe, we are both kneeling on the floor, fingers nuzzling into the carpet weave, shaking loose those filmy bracelets, tugging them from the caramel-colored loops.

That beautiful carpet with its dense pile. And at least five twists per inch.

"Addy, you've listened to Beth, now you need to listen to me. If they found that bracelet, a girl's bracelet like that, like one of yours—" she says, pointing to my arms, ringed with friendship flosses, neon jellies, a leather braid—"don't you think they'd have asked you too?"

There's nothing I can say. I watch her as she walks into the bathroom and shuts the door.

Neither of us wants to openly reckon with how deep Beth's trickery may go and neither of us wants to reckon with why I have believed her.

I hear the shower start and know I'm meant to leave.

Being part of a pyramid, you never see the pyramid at all.

Later, watching ourselves, it never feels real. Flickering youtube images of bumble bees swarming, assembling themselves into tall hives.

It's nothing like it is on the floor. There, you have to bolt your gaze to the bodies in your care, the ones right above you.

Your only focus should be your girl, the one you're responsible for, the one whose leg, hip, arm you're bracing. The one who is counting on you.

Left Spot, keep your focus on the left flank. Don't look right.

Right Spot, keep your focus on the right flank. Don't look left.

Eyes on the Flyer's eyes, shoulders, hips, vigilant for any sign of misalignment, instability, panic.

This is how you stop falls.

This is how you keep everything from collapsing.

You never get to see the stunt at all.

Eyes on your girl.

And it's only ever a partial vision, because that's the only way to keep everyone up in the air.

On my way out, I see Matt French still drifting around the backyard. It strikes me how few times I've seen him without his laptop in front of him, or his headset on. He looks lost.

I stop at the kitchen window, wondering what Coach has told him. What he believes.

Matt French reaches out to a branch spoking from a tall hawthorn bush, the one Caitlin is always cutting herself on, its hooks curling under her feet.

He looks no sadder than usual, which is sad enough.

Suddenly, he looks up and it's like he sees me, but I think I must be too far, too small behind the paned window.

But I think he sees me.

"You made it up," I say.

I'm at Beth's house, in her bathroom. She has her leg propped up on the toilet seat, where she's examining it with care.

"The Asian girl did the sugar wax on me, and she is comprehensive in her approach," she says, shaking a flame-colored bottle of Our Desire, her mother's perfume. "Except now I reek of Pop-Tart. Frosted. With sprinkles."

"You made it up," I repeat, smacking her leg off the toilet seat. "The cops never asked her about any bracelet. You made all that up."

"The hot fuzz called you in, eh?" she says, standing up straight, still shaking the perfume bottle, shaking it side to side like some dirty boy gesture. "They called me in too. I go right after practice today."

"They never found any bracelet at all, did they?"

"You'd best stay right, girl," she says, lifting her leg back up, sending a fine mist of bitter orange and ylang-ylang over it.

This, I don't like. She can't batter at me like I'm Tacy, like I'm some JV.

"What made you finally ask her?" she asks.

I knock her foot off the toilet seat again and sit down on its furred top.

"You made it up," I say. "If the detectives found a bracelet, they would've asked me about it."

"Addy, I can't make you believe me," she says, looking down at me. "And as for you and Coach . . . "

She lays her hand on my head, like a benediction.

"We are never deceived," she says, her voice deep and ringing. "We deceive ourselves."

We are lying on Beth's deep-blue bedroom carpet, as we've done a hundred, a thousand times, collapsing from our labors, the wages of war, one kind or another. Adrift on that speckless ultramarine, Beth would lay out all her martial machinations for me, her attaché, her envoy. Sometimes her mouthpiece. Whatever was required.

In some ways, Beth was almost never wrong in her judgments.

Paper-thin, Master-cleansed Emily wasn't strong enough to do the stunt.

Tacy didn't have the head game or the strong legs to be a Flyer.

With Beth, so full of lies, you have to push past the lie to see the deeper truth that drives it. Because Beth is almost always lying about something, but the lying is her way of rendering something else, something tucked away or confounded, manifest.

And you have to keep playing, and maybe the truth will reveal itself, maybe Beth will get tired and finally show her hand. Or maybe it'll stop being fun for her, and she'll just hurl that truth in your face, and make you cry.

I never liked you anyway.

You're just so goddamned fat it depresses me.

I saw your dad at the mall buying lingerie with a strange woman.

Casey Jaye said you can't throw a back handspring for shit, and she told RiRi there's something weird about you, but she wouldn't say what.

Oh, and I only pretended to care.

"It can't be easy," she says, surveying her lotioned legs, "knowing you were an accessory to a crime, even if it's *after the fact*. It's not really a position a red-blooded All-American teenage girl expects to be put in, especially given everything you've done for your Coach."

"Like the things I've done for you?" I say. "Did you think I was going to be your lieutenant forever?"

"What have you ever done for me," she replies, her eyes snake-slitted, " . . . that you didn't want to do?"

Flipping over on her stomach, she props her tanned chin on one palm and reaches out to me with her other.

"Oh, Addy. You can't even see it, you're so loveblind. I'm sorry about that. And sorry to have to do this to you. Really, I am."

"I'm not . . . loveblind," I stutter, the word throwing me. Which I guess it's meant to, but—

"But you're bringing a knife to a gunfight," she continues. "You can't see the facts, even laid out plain. Even when the *po-lice* department, Addy, calls you into the station to investigate her lover's murder. What will it take?"

I feel a sob creep into my chest, she's just so damned good and I can't breathe.

"You keep saying these things," I say, "but you've never

given me any real reason to believe why you think she would ever . . . "

Beth slants her head. "Why would she ever?" she repeats, singsongy. "Why *wouldn't* she?"

My head throbs, not knowing what to believe now, ever, except I believe them both—Beth and Coach, in different ways—when their words wormhole into my brain. They make everything seem real. Dark. Painful. True.

"It kills me, I tell you," Beth says, "the way you all fawn over her. The way you, Addy, the way *you* fawned over them both. She isn't what you think, and neither was he. They were not star-crossed. He was just a guy, like all of them. They fucked each other and he got tired of her before she got tired of him. She gets everything she wants, and she couldn't stand not getting him anymore."

The throbbing becoming something else, something worse and more insistent.

I lift myself up to sitting position, my head light and everything lifting lightly in me. The edge of hysteria sliding into her voice, it can come to no good.

"And none of us gets away with anything," she says, climbing up onto her knees in front of me. "None of us."

"You don't know anything," I say. "Neither of us knows."

She looks at me, and for a second I almost see all the misery and rage, centuries of it, tumbling across her face.

"She's not a killer," I say, trying to make my voice bore-thick.

She looks down at me, her eyes depthful and ruinous.

"Love is a kind of killing, Addy," she says. "Don't you know that?"

There are three hours before practice, the Big Saturday Practice before the Big Game.

I can't live in Beth's head a moment longer, so I spend a few hours at the mall, wandering, damp hands curling around my jug of kombucha, its fermented threads swirling around the bottom of the bottle.

Coach, my Coach. I think of that pearl-smooth face of hers and wonder if I can ever imagine it, try to picture her hard, ordered body doing the thing Beth says she's done.

It's impossible and I keep trying but the image that comes instead is of her, legs hooked hard around Will in the teachers' lounge, the elation, everything in her unpinned, untucked, unveiled. No one looking, no one watching, and everything hers.

He is mine, he is mine, and I will do anything to feel this always. Anything.

Feeling Will slipping from her, might she find herself doing something she'd never thought she'd do?

Maybe it's a feeling I know.

It's the feeling that sends me out to The Towers again, second time in as many days, some magnetic stroke tickling inside my antic self.

Pulling into the lot, I see no sign of police. There are even fewer cars than usual on this blustery day, the wind whistling under my windshield wipers and the sky thickly grim.

I sit for a long time, punching radio presets, then turning my car off, putting my earbuds in, drowning in the plaintive songs of adolescent heartache, then quickly becoming disgusted by them, and flinging my player to the floor of my car.

Then, the flinging seems to be part of the same counterfeit world of those tinny teenbox songs, and I hate myself too.

But that's when I realize that I've been on a stakeout, without even knowing it.

Because there, walking across the parking lot into Building A, is Corporal Gregory Prine.

I'd know that bullet head anywhere.

I watch him enter the building and then, without even thinking, I follow him, sneakers squeaking across the wet parking lot.

Stopped short by the locked lobby doors, I can't guess why he has a key and wonder if it's Will's key. I stand at the big buzzer board where I stood five days ago, and I try to be Beth-bold, my bright nails dancing over the silver buttons, pressing them all, waiting for any crackling voice, the ringing wail of entry.

"Sorry, I live in 14-B and forgot my keys. My mom's not home, can you buzz me in?"

Someone does, and before I know it, I'm in the elevator, a slick sweat on me now, and the fluorescent light buzzing, and then I'm in the empty hallway on Will's empty floor.

I'm not scared at all but seem to be fueled by the same kind of chemical rush as at a game, like when there's just been too much hydroxycut and nothing to eat but sugar-free Jell-O so you can get back the space between your upper thighs, it's a feeling most spectacular.

I have it now and it's so strong in me I can't stop myself from charging forward, my foot accidentally punting a piece of crime-scene tape, catching it on the tip of my puma.

And there I am, standing in front of number 27-G, a lone strip of tape still curled around its handle.

But before I can decide what I plan to do—ring the bell, burst in like some gangbanger—I stop myself, tripping backward against the stairwell door, inhaling deeply three times.

Prine, what if he . . .

That's when I notice that the door to the neighboring apartment is just slightly ajar, and a whoosh from the heating unit has nudged it farther open.

I walk slowly toward it, peeking in.

Inside, it's the mirror image of Will's apartment but spartan-bare.

The same parquet entry, the same sandy carpet.

The only difference seems to be the plastic lazy susan perched on the table in the entryway. Stuffed with brochures: *Luxury Living on Nature's Edge.*

Were I to step closer, to step inside, I'm sure I'd see the same leather sofa slashed across the center of the room.

But I don't step closer. Somehow, I feel if it were an inch closer, this sofa will became that sofa, and there on the carpet, I will see it. Him.

But mostly, the place just feels empty.

Except it's not.

A door thuds, then the sound of feet skimming across the carpet, and heading toward me is the bullet-head himself, a plastic grocery store bag clutched in that ham-hock hand.

It all happens so fast. Spotting me, he stops short in front of the open door.

Gorilla-puffed chest, sunglasses perched on his crewcutted head, he blinks spasmodically, red rushing up his thick neck and face.

It's as if he can't believe his eyes, and I nearly can't either.

"Oh," he says, "it's one of you."

Back in the near-empty parking lot, we sit together in my car.

"Listen," he says, the plastic grocery bag hooked daintily around his wrist, "I haven't said anything. So don't worry."

"What do you mean?" I say, marveling still at the idea of Prine in my car, us both here. Everything.

"I have some priors. I had a substance problem," he says, fingers prickling noisily at the bag. "So I'm not saying a goddamn thing to those cops. You can tell her not to worry. And you can tell her to leave me the hell out of this."

I don't know who "she" is, but I don't ask.

There is a palpable sense of revelation coming and I want to tread carefully. Finally someone not smart enough to lie to me, or even to know why he should.

Though, sitting there with him, his left foot ensnared by

the cheetah-print sports bra on my car floor, it strikes me he might be thinking the same thing.

"So you live here or something?" I ask, fingering my gear shaft.

"No," he says, watching my hand. He takes a breath. "Sarge let me crash in that apartment. He knew no one was living there. The realtors are always just leaving it open. He gave me the building key. For when things get tough at home."

He looks over at me, sheepish.

"My old man and me don't always see eye to eye," he explains. "Sarge understood . . . Sarge, he was such a good guy."

Suddenly, Prine's eyes fill. I try to hide my surprise. He turns away and looks out the window, flipping his sunglasses down.

"So why are you here now?" I ask.

"I had to see what I'd left behind," he says. Looking down, he opens his plastic bag, showing me a travel-size mouthwash, a single-blade razor, a dusty bar of soap.

He lowers his voice to a whisper, even though there's no sign of life anywhere. *Luxury Living on Nature's Edge.*

"Listen, the cops don't know I was here that night," he says.

I try not to let him see my flinch.

"Okay," I say.

"It doesn't matter anyway," he says. "I left before any gunshot. I don't know what the hell happened. But I did hear the two of them headboard banging for a good fifteen minutes before midnight and I couldn't get any sleep."

Coach, there, that night. When Will was still alive.

I take this fact, this staggering and harrowing fact, and put it in a far corner in my head. For now. I can't look at it. It is there for safekeeping.

"That's how it always was with them," he says. "I don't like hearing other people's private business. And, to be honest, the two of them, it made me sad."

He looks at me, fingers dandling through the bag loop.

"I mean, that was a messed-up situation, right?" He looks at me, raising his eyebrows. "You could see something bad was going to happen. Something was going to go down."

The way he's looking at me, I know he's waiting for some kind of confirmation, but I don't say anything.

"The point is," he goes on, "like I promised her, I'm not saying a goddamned word."

"Her?" I ask, measuring my voice. Hiding everything.

"Your friend," he says, a little impatiently now, "the brunette."

"Beth?"

"Beth," he says. "The one with the tits. I mean, you seem nice, but so did she at first. Girl like that, she could make trouble for me."

Craning his neck, he looks up at the apartment building, ominously.

"All of you, you're a whole lot of trouble," he says, softly. "I don't need that kind of trouble."

A whole lot of trouble, I think.

"Guess Sarge found out, didn't he?" He looks at me, grimly. "Queen of the hive. Don't mess with the queen."

I look at him and wonder which queen he means.

Driving away, I can't begin to unravel it all. Why would Beth want Prine to keep quiet about hearing Coach in Will's apartment that night? And why didn't she tell me, at least, if her aim is to convince me of Coach's guilt?

But the pulsing center is this: Coach was there with Will that night, Will alive. She and Will in bed.

The picture in my head now, Coach standing before me, bleached sneakers in hand.

Coach.

Tilting pyramid-top, reaching for me, clamoring for my arm, knowing what it will mean. Where it would take both of us.

"Two days, four hours," RiRi says, fingers tapping on her thighs anxiously. "Fifty-two hours till the game, hollaback girls. Where *is* she?"

We are all standing in the gym at five o'clock, waiting for Coach.

I haven't figured out what I will do when she does arrive, if I will let my face betray anything.

Lifting my highdrive monster energy, I slide two tylenol with codeine, leftovers from last year's thumb jam, under my tongue and wait.

But Coach doesn't show.

And Beth, well, she's not here either.

"I don't understand how Coach could do this to us," plaints Tacy, her battered lip now a frosted lavender. "Two days before the big game."

"It must be some kind of test," Paige Shepherd says, chin-nodding with unsure surety. "To show us we can do it on our own."

RiRi is doing a straddle stretch against the wall, which usually calms her down.

"No," she says. "Something's wrong. Really wrong. I've been hearing things. What if this is all about Sarge Stud?"

Oh, this causes quite a conflagration.

"My brother—listen to this!" Brinnie Cox gasps through those big chiclet teeth of hers. "My brother works at the sub shop next to the police station where the cops come in for lunch and he heard them mention Coach. And I don't know what they said, but . . . ."

There's scurrying and speculations spun like long sticky gum strands, but I am out of it.

Instead, I work it. I pound that mat. I'm doing my tucks, over and over, curling my body sharklike upon itself.

"You are so fucking tight," RiRi murmurs, strolling by.

I slap her thigh hard and grin.

"You're better than you ever were with Beth," she says.

"I'm working harder," I say.

"You were kicking it with Casey Jaye last summer," RiRi says. "You were so good."

"Why are you bringing that up now?" I say. "Why does everyone always want to talk about that?"

It's the thing no one can let go of. But I can. I'd like to never think of any of it again.

"I was glad when you two got together," she says. "That's all I'm saying."

I think suddenly of Casey, the ease of her light hands on me, flipping my hips up, laughing.

"You know," RiRi says, "Casey told me she thought you were the bravest, best cheerleader she ever knew and she's been cheering her whole life."

"She meant Beth," I say. "She must have meant Beth."

Addy, Casey whispered one night, hanging from the bunk above me. *She's never going to let it be you. Fuck your four inches. You're light as air. You could be top girl. You're a badass and beautiful. You should be captain.*

"And that fight between you and Beth, we all knew it was coming," RiRi says, shaking her head. "Four of us to pull you two off each other."

"It was an accident," I say, but no one ever believed me. "My hand got caught. She just didn't believe me."

One day, tumbling class by the lake, I was spotting her handspring. When my arm flung up, my fingers caught her earring, pulling it clean through.

I was trying to catch you, I'd told her. *You were bending.*

But she'd just stood there, holding the side of her head, a brick red trickle between tan fingers.

Everyone whispered that it was about Casey, but it wasn't. It was an accident. Beth and her big ghetto earrings. It just happened.

Sometimes now, when she's not looking, I stare at her ear lobe, and want to touch it, to understand something.

I never thought you'd be friends again after that, RiRi said later. But we were. No one understands. They never have.

"I stood with her when they stitched up her ear," RiRi says now. "I never saw her cry before. I never knew she had tear ducts. Hell, I never knew she had blood in her."

"It was just a fight," I say, remembering the two of us tangled up, someone screaming.

"I thought," RiRi says, " 'Addy's finally manning up to Beth.' None of us ever had the guts."

"A stupid fight, like girls do," I say.

"And, for what it's worth, Beth talked all kinds of trash about Casey," RiRi says, "but I never believed it."

But I had, and I stripped my bunk of sheets and walked down to the end of the cabin, to the bunk Beth had already vacated for me. And I never talked to Casey again.

"Addy, you could still do it," RiRi says now. "You could be captain, anything."

"Shut the fuck up," I say.

RiRi brushes back, like I've hit her.

"That was a long time ago," I add, setting my arms up for another tuck. "That was last summer."

A half-hour passes, everyone doing lazy tuck jumps and stretches, before we hear the sound.

Coach Templeton's ancient boombox sliding across the gym floor, blasting bratty girl rap: *take me low, where my girlies go, we hit it hardcore 'til there's glitter on the floor . . .*

All our heads turn, and there is Beth, white-socked and whistle swinging.

"Bitches," Beth hollahs, ringingly. "Front and center and show me your badass selves. I'm self-deputized."

"What do you mean," demands Tacy. "Where's Coach?" Our now-perpetual lament.

"Didn't you hear?" Beth says, turning the music up louder, the rattle in it sending a few girls to their feet, bouncily. "She got hauled in by the po-po."

"What are you talking about?" I say.

"She's at the station house. The cops picked her up in the squad car. Her ball-and-chain went with her."

I don't let her catch my eye.

"How do you know?" RiRi says, cocking an eyebrow.

"I went over there to see if Coach needed a ride. Barbara-the-Babysitter told me. She looked scared pantless. She said the cops came in with trash bags. Started hauling off stuff."

Everyone exchanges wide-eyed glances.

"But I'm not here for idle gossip," she says. "Show me you got something other than chicken-hearts behind those padded bras."

Everyone starts forming their lines, I can't believe how quickly.

Clapping tight and shaking their legs out and faces tomato-bursting.

Like they're eager for it.

Like anyone will do, if they're hard enough.

"And no more tantric chants and bullshit," Beth says. "I

want to see blood on the floor. And remember what old Coach Temp used to say . . . "

She steps back as everyone but me assembles for their back tucks.

"Cheer, cheer, have no fear!" they all chant. Some of them are even smiling.

Grinning, Beth gives the response: "When you're flying high, look to the sky, and scream Eagles, Eagles, Eagles!"

An hour later, we hit the 2-2-1, Beth our Flyer.

Tossed up between RiRi and me, already six feet up, our legs braced by Mindy and Cory beneath us. Tossed up, our ponytailed apex.

My arms lifted above, I have her right side, her right wrist, her arm like a batten, hard and motionless, and RiRi her left.

She, spine so straight, the line of her neck, her body still, tight, perfect.

I have her, we have her, and Beth is higher than I've ever seen anyone.

After everyone has scattered to the locker room, I spot a lone figure watching practice from high up in the stands.

No tan for her, no nothing, but thinner than ever, a bobby pin, and she seems to be saying something to me.

That mammoth brace on her knee and her mouth open, a big O, straining to rise.

It's Emily. And she's saying something.

"What?" I call up. "What do you want, Royce?"

Slowly, she gimps her way down the stands, each step meaning a wide swing of her leg.

It never occurs to me to climb up.

"Addy," she is saying, breathless. "I never saw it before."

"Saw what?"

"I never saw the stunts. From back there," she says. "I never saw us."

"What do you mean?" I say, a faint ripple in my chest.

"Did you ever really think about it? About what we're doing?" she says, holding tight to the railing.

She starts talking, breathless and high, about the way we are stacked, like toothpicks, like Pixy Stix, our bodies like feathers, light and tensile. Our minds focused, unnourished, possessed. The entire structure bounding to life by our elastic bodies vaulting into each other, sticking and then . . .

A pyramid isn't a stationary object. It's a living thing . . . The only moment it's still is when you make it still, all your bodies one body, until . . . we blow it all apart.

"I couldn't look," she says. "I had to cover my eyes. I never knew what we were doing before. I never knew because we were doing it. Now I see."

I am not listening at all, her voice getting more shrill, but I can't hear. A month on the DL, a month stateside, this is what happens.

I just look hard into her baby-blue eyes.

"Standing back," she says, mouth hanging in horror, "it's like you're trying to kill each other and yourselves."

I look at her, folding my arms.

"You were never one of us."

28.

Saturday Night

Nine o'clock, I drive by the police station and see Matt French's car. At eight, it's still there.

Prine heard Coach there that night. Which means Coach lied, which means Coach was there when whatever happened to Will . . .

These words still hang, sentence unfinished. I just can't finish the sentence.

I remind myself that, hard as she is, I have seen her grief blast apart her stony self. At least once I did, holding her by the waist in her bedroom hallway Wednesday night. Feeling the bed shake with it while we slept. How is that a killing soul?

But does anyone ever seem like a killer, I can hear Beth's voice squirming in my head.

To Beth, of course, everyone does.

I believe both of them and neither of them. All their stories poured in my ear, maybe it's time to start finding out on my own.

At ten o'clock, I drive by Statler's. I'm remembering Beth's texts.

Teddy saw Coach @ Statlers last week
Talking on cell all nite, crying @ jukebox.
Ran outside + hit post in parking lot, peeled off

The shaggy guy at the door won't let me in with my premium TIFFANY RUE, AGE 23 driver's license, but I don't need to go inside.

Instead, I walk from parking-lot post to post, hands on the peeling silver paint.

On the farthest one from the door of the bar, I spot the chewy dent, paint glittering the asphalt.

"What happened here," I call over to the door guy.

He squints at me.

"Life is hard," he says, adding, "and you're too young for the parking lot too, little miss."

"Who did it?" I ask, walking toward him. "Who hit the post?"

"A woman wronged," he says, shrugging.

"Was she late twenties, brown hair, ponytail?"

"I don't know," he says, pointing with one long delicate finger, at the Eagles patch on my arm. "But she had a coat just like yours."

I sit and tally the lies, but there are so many and they don't quite line up.

Why would Coach tell me she hit a post in Buckingham Park, instead of Statler's? One small lie, but there've been so many. Add them all together and they seem to teeter five miles above me.

It's eleven when I drive by Coach's house again.

At last, the car is there.

I find her on the deck, smoking clove cigarettes. One knee hunched up, her chin resting on it, she seems to hear me before I've even made a sound.

"Hanlon," she says. "How'd practice go?"

Have you lost your mind? I want to say. *Have you?*

"Awesome," I say, teeth grit. "We're tight in the fight. You should've seen us rock the 2-2-1."

"Make sure you don't lean down to pull your Flyer up," she says. "Bend your legs to reach her, otherwise you could pull the whole stunt down."

"I've never done that once," I say, wincing. "You weren't there."

"I'm sorry I missed it," she says, moving her ashtray from the deck chair beside her.

If it weren't for the faintest throb over one eyebrow this might be any other night at all.

"Well, you had a pretty good excuse." I sit down, our matching twin letter jackets zipped tight up over our chins.

"I'm guessing my captain ran the show?" she asks. "Or maybe you don't want to talk about that."

All the cold and loneliness of the night sinking into me, all I want is to hammer through that stony perfection. Hand heel to chisel, that's all I want.

"You were there," I say, "you were at Will's that night."

She doesn't say anything.

"You didn't hit a post in Buckingham Park lot," I say. "You

had a fight with him. You ran into a post at Statler's. Everything was falling apart with you two, or something. He was breaking up with you, he was done with you."

She remains statue-still.

"And you didn't find Will's body," I say, throwing my whole body into it, hammer, hammer, hammer. "You were with him. You were in his bed. You're a liar. You've lied about everything."

Jumping forward in my chair, I'm nearly shouting in her ear. "You're a liar. So what else are you?"

She doesn't move, doesn't even turn her head to face me.

A moment passes, my heart suspended.

"Yes," she says, finally. "I was at Will's earlier than I'd said. And I hit a post at Buckingham. And I hit another post at Statler's. I've hit posts, curbs, street lamps, all over town. I've forgotten to feed my daughter dinner. I've forgotten to brush my hair. I've lost eleven pounds and haven't slept, really *slept*, in weeks. I've lost my daughter in stores, and slapped her little face. I've been a bad influence and bad wife. I haven't known my mind in months.

"What's the difference, Addy. The thing that matters is this. Will's dead and everything's over."

She turns and looks at me, the porch light catching her for the first time. Her face swollen, soft.

"Is that what you wanted?" she asks. "Does that help you, Addy? Because making you feel better is what matters, right?"

I flinch at that. The rest is too painful to look at.

"You," I say, my voice rising, "*you* called me that night. You dragged me into this."

"I did, Addy," she says. "But don't you know I'd tell you more if I could?"

"Why can't you?"

"Addy, I called you that night because I knew you'd help me. You understood how it was with Will and me. You were a part of it."

I was. I was.

"So yes, I was at Will's that whole night, Addy," she says. "But I didn't do anything. I was with him, but I found him too. It's all true. Everything is."

I think about this a second, this riddle. But I can't decipher it, not with everything else happening, not with the hammer and chisel still trembling in my hand.

"So why can't you tell me?" I say, a pleading in my voice I can't stop. "I'm trying to help you. I am."

Suddenly, a band of light streams from the kitchen. I hear Caitlin's fretful weeps.

Coach turns her head, glancing through the patio doors.

"You better go home," she says, rising, her cigarette dangling from her fingertips.

"Not yet," I stutter. "Why can't you tell me? I need to know more than this. I need . . ."

Caitlin's weeps squall up into a sob, something about bad dreams. What about my bad dreams, I want to say.

"But, Coach," I say, my mind scattering madly. "Beth says she's going to the cops tomorrow."

She stops at the patio door, one hand on the handle. "To say what?"

"To say all this. The parts she's figured out. The parts she's guessing at."

She takes one last drag on her cigarette, staring out into the black murk of the back lawn.

"She thinks you did it," I say. "She thinks you killed Will."

The first time such words come from my mouth, and they sound more monstrous than anything ever.

"Well, I didn't," she says, dropping her cigarette to the deck, letting one foot tap it out, with infinite grace.

In bed, late, I'm whispering into my phone, to Beth.

"You didn't go today? To the cops?"

"You're a freaking broken record, Addy Hanlon," she says.

"If you're so sure you know everything," I say, squinting my eyes tight, trying to figure my way into her, "why haven't you gone already?"

"I'm still collecting the final pieces," she says. I swear I can hear her tongue churning in her mouth like a vampire. "I'm working on my deployments and flanking maneuvers."

I picture her, on the other end of the phone, plucking her marked lobe, the crescented scar, but then I realize it's me, fingers gnarled around my own ear.

"Beth, I have to ask you something," I say, gliding my tone elsewhere.

"I'm waiting," she says.

"Beth," I say. Without even planning on it, my voice slips into something from our past, the Addy who needs things from Beth—her skinny stretch jeans, the ephedra tea you have to mail order, the questions for the calc exam, someone to tell her what to do to make it all bearable.

The voice, it's not an act, it isn't, it never was, and it's like a message to her, to both of us, to remember things, because she needs to remember too, I need to make her step back and see.

"Beth, I could get in trouble here," I say. "I helped her. Can you give me one more day? Just one more day to see what I can find out. To see if you're right."

"You mean one more day for her to save her own skin."

"One more day, Beth," I say. "Wait until Tuesday. Monday's the game. Tomorrow you're top girl."

There's a pause.

"One more day, Beth," I say, softly. "For me."

There's another pause and its quiet feels dangerous.

"Sure," she says. "You take your day."

29.

Sunday: One Day to Final Game

She's given me one day and I have no plan for it, no idea.

All the voices from recent days, all the threats and calamity, and I can't think my way through any of it, least of all those words from Coach: *I was there, but I didn't do anything. I was with him, but I found him too.*

It's all true.

Everything is.

Crawling under the covers Sunday morning, three a.m., I take more codeine-dosed tylenol, and the dreams that come are muddled and grotesque.

Finally twisting myself into a trembling sleep, I dream of Will.

He comes to me, his arm outstretched, palm closed. When he opens it, it's filled with shark teeth, the kind they show you in science class.

"Those are Beth's," I say, and he smiles, his mouth black as a hole.

"No," he says, "they're yours."

—

When I wake up, there's a newfound energy in me that boosts me from bed that feels like the day before a Big Game. That feels powerful. It's the day of readying.

Standing in front of the mirror, toothbrush frothing, I feel certain things will happen and this time maybe I will be ready for them.

I try to find a way to reach PFC Tibbs. I think he might share more with me, reveal something, as Prine did. But I can't find a number for him, and there's no answer at the regional Guard office, so I have no way to reach him without Beth.

I drive to the police station, park in the back. Wait for an hour, door-watching.

I think about going inside, but I'm afraid the detectives will see me.

I was there, but I didn't do anything. I was with him, but I found him too. It's all true.

Beth or Coach, who do I believe when one never tells the truth and one gives me nothing but riddles?

Something about it reminds me of pre-calc. Permutations and combinations. *Consider any situation in which there are exactly two possibilities: Succeed or Fail. Yes or No. In or Out. Boy or Girl.*

Left or right. You're the Left Base, you know your only job is to strut that left side of the pyramid, hold that weight and keep your girl up.

But am I on the right side, or the left?

—

Watching the back door of the police station, I ponder a third way. I imagine going inside, telling them everything, letting them sort it all out.

But it's not the solider heart in me.

I'm just about to start my car when my phone rings.

I don't recognize the number, but I answer.

"Addy?" a man says.

"Yes?"

"This is Mr. French," he says. "Matt French."

I turn off my car.

"Hey, Mr. French, how are you?" I say, on babysitter auto-pilot, like during those long three-minute rides home with the fathers wanting to know all about cheerleading and what it does to our bodies.

Except it's not someone's dad, it's Matt French and he's calling me and I've been a party to his family's ruin.

"I'm sorry to bother you," he says.

"How did you," I say. "So you got my number from Coach? You . . ."

"This isn't weird, okay?" he says quickly. "It's not."

"No, I know," I say, but how is this not weird?

Matt French. I picture him standing in his yard, this for-lorn figure. I picture him always like he's looking at us through glass—windshields, sliding patio doors. I don't know if I could even picture his face if I tried, but the sight of that sad slump in his shoulders is with me now.

"Can I ask you a question, Addy?" his voice muffled, like his mouth is pressed close to the phone.

"Yes."

"I'm trying to figure something. If I tell you a phone number off my call log, do you think you could tell me if you recognize it?"

"Yes," I say before I can even think.

"Okay," he says, and he reads off a phone number. I type it in and a name comes up.

Tacy.

I say her name out loud.

"Tacy," he repeats. "Tacy who? Is she your friend?"

"Tacy Slaussen. She's on the squad," I say. "She's our Flyer. Was our Flyer."

There's a pause, a heavy one. I get the feeling something monumental is occurring. At first I think he's processing what I'm saying, but then I realize he's the one waiting for me to process something.

He wants me to remember something, mark something, know something.

It's like he's the one giving something to me.

I just don't know what.

"I was glad it wasn't your phone number," he says. "I was glad it wasn't you."

"What wasn't me?" I ask. "Mr. French, I—"

"Goodbye, Addy," he says, soft and toneless. And there's a click.

The phone call knifes its way through my head.

Matt French has found out something, or everything. It's all blown apart and he's going through her emails, her phone calls, everything. He's amassing all the pieces, pieces that will damn us all, will damn us both.

Adulteress, *Murderer*, and *Accessory to*.

But that doesn't fit with the call. With what he asked and what he didn't. And there's the way he sounded, too. Unsteady but reserved, troubled but strangely calm.

I tap Tacy's number. I almost never call her, maybe I never have, but we all have each other's numbers in our phone. And Coach has them all in hers. Squad rules.

Which is how Matt French might have Tacy's number.

Except I don't think he was looking at Coach's phone when he read off the number. If he were looking at Coach's phone, it would say, "Tacy" or "Slaussen." It would say something.

My call log, that's what he said. His phone.

His phone.

But why would Tacy call Mr. French? And if she did, why wouldn't he know who she was?

So I call Tacy's number, but it goes straight to voicemail.

Hey, beyotch, I'm out somewhere, lookin sick n sexified. Leave a message. If this is Brinnie, I never called you a bore. I called you a whore.

I'm glad it wasn't your phone number, he'd said. *I'm glad it wasn't you.*

Matt French, what is it you want me to know?

———

I drive to Tacy's house, but she's not there. Her jug-jawed sister is, the one who I always hear in the speech lab droning on about Intelligent Design when the Forensic League meets after school.

"Oh," she says, "you're one of those."

Slouched against the door frame, she's eating wrinkly raisins from a small baggie, which is just the kind of thing those kinds of girls are always doing.

"She's not here," she says. "She borrowed my car to go to the school. To practice her hip rolling and pelvis thrusts."

Looking at the cloudy Ziploc in her hand, at the sad gray sweater and peace sign nose ring, I say, "We don't need to practice those."

I see the ice-blue hatchback in the parking lot, and pull in next to it.

The gym backdoor is propped open with a rubber-banded wedge of dry erasers, like we do when we want a place to drink Malibu before a party. And now some of us use it to practice weekends, off hours, or we have since Coach drove our bodies to perfection, elevated our squad into sublimity.

I hear her first, her wheezy grunts and the soft push of pumas on airy mats.

Cheek still puffed from Thursday's fall, she's running tumbles. Throwing roundoff back handsprings, one after another. She should have a spotter because her technique, as ever, is pussy-weak.

"Stop throwing head," I shout. "Arms against your ears."

She stutters to a stop, nearly crashing into the padded wall at the far end.

"Fire, form, control, perfection," I count off, like Coach always did.

"Who cares," moans Tacy, breathlessly. "I'm ground bound anyway. With Beth back, my life is practically over."

She slides down the wall and collapses onto the floor, pulling cotton wisps from her glossed mouth. God love Tacy, full makeup on a Sunday morning, by herself, in the school gym.

"It's only one game," I say, even as I know it's the Big Game, the Biggest Ever, and who cared about cheering spring baseball?

"Besides," I add, "how long do you really think Beth can possibly last as captain?"

"I don't know," Tacy says, now picking cotton from under her grape-lacquered fingernails. "I think she might be captain forever."

"Why would you think that?"

"Because of what's happening," she says. "Coach French was the only one who could ever stop her. And now Coach is gone."

"She's not gone, she just—"

"She's not coming back. Face it, Addy, it's all over for Coach." She looks at me, that swollen face of hers, lapine-jowled. "Which sucks because Coach was the only one who ever saw it in me. My *potential*, my *promise*."

"Slaus, the only reason Coach put you up there is because you're ninety-eight pounds soaking wet and you're Beth's pigeon," I say, wanting to ring her little-girl neck. "If you care so goddamned much about Coach, why do you keep helping Beth?"

She looks startled but too dumb to be startled enough.

"I'm not helping Beth. Not anymore."

"But you were."

She takes a deep breath.

"Well, you don't know what's happened. Coach maybe did something really bad, Addy," she says, shaking her head. "It's Beth's fault, sort of. But that's no excuse. My dad says we're an excuse society now."

"Tacy," I say, my voice grinding, "tell me what you mean. Tell me what you know."

I press my foot against her bendy-straw leg, press it hard.

She looks at me, rabbit scared, and I know I need to slather some honey but keep that foot pressed too. That's what she loves. Both those things at once.

"Tacy, I'm the only one who can help you now," I say. "I'm the only one who can help."

Her tears come and I fight off the urge to slap those swollen jowls of hers. I fight it off because she's about to give me gold, and she doesn't even know it. She thinks her gossip, her petty grievances are significant, but they are tiny pin-holes. The things around them, though, the fabric of Beth's lies and fictions, they are the gold.

"Coach was sleeping with the Sarge," she says, eyes saucering up at me. "And she loved him. And then Coach found out. About Beth. About Sarge and Beth."

—

I'm leaning against the padded gym wall and Tacy's still on the floor, legs tucked tight, looking up at me, and talking, talking, talking.

She isn't what you think, and neither was he. That's what Beth said. *He was just a guy, like all of them.*

But Will, Will and Beth? I just can't make my head believe it.

"This was right when he first started coming to the school," she says. I'm relieved for that. Before Coach, before all that. Lost, wandering, wondering Will. "And they had that bet, her and RiRi. She wanted to beat RiRi. She said RiRi was all tits and eyeliner and she would eat her heart whole.

"So one day after school she was waiting by his truck for him. You know how he'd park in the back, behind the school lot, on Ness Street?"

I used to walk Coach there. Coach, whose face would flush at the sight of his SUV shadowed under the oak tree, its leathery leaves hovering, the shadows of them across her face as she turned to look at me, to say, *Here he is, Addy, here is my man.*

"My job was to wait by the tree with my phone," Tacy is saying, "so I could take a picture to prove she'd done it."

I don't know what's coming, but I feel a churning in my gut.

"So she's out there, waiting for him in her miniskirt," Tacy says, her fingers carelessly grazing my ankle as I stand above her. "Well, Beth, she's a hot bitch, and Sarge was a guy, right?"

He's a guy, right.

"But he couldn't go through with it," she sighs, resting her fingers on my ankle bone. "Just kid stuff. And I only got one half-decent shot, but you couldn't see much of anything."

I don't say anything.

"But here was the thing," Tacy says, shaking one of her fingers. "Beth never did show it to RiRi. Maybe she knew it wouldn't be good enough to win the bet. Finally I asked her about it and she had me text it to her. She said she was saving it. She just kept it on her phone. She loved to flash it at me."

This seems like Beth and I wonder why she never flashed it at me. But I guess I know. Once we found out about Coach and Will, she couldn't be sure where I'd stand. She couldn't be sure I'd play for her side. She was right.

"Then all of a sudden she tells me something happened to her phone," Tacy says, "and she lost the picture and she needed me to send it again."

The memory comes to me: Coach torpedoing Beth's Twizzler-red phone down the toilet.

"So I say: tell me what you need it for first," Tacy says, looking up at me, her smile coming and going as she tries to read me, read how I'm taking this, and if I want to play with her, to relish all this just a little.

"So she *had* to tell me," she, rocking in her seat, so eager to tell me, to recall the moment. "And that's when she said she was going to use it so Coach would stop giving her such a hard time."

I rest my back against the wall, not looking down at Tacy, sliding away from her, her hot breath on my legs.

"So that's when she told me about Coach and Will," she says. "She had to."

I look down at her, that lapin face squinting with conspiratorial pleasure, and I say nothing.

"So, after three years of hustling for that queen bitch, now I had something *Beth* wanted," Tacy says, her voice sharpening to something almost impressive. "Beth had lost the goods. She didn't even email the picture to herself or save it on her computer. She thinks she's so goddamned smart. How smart is that? But it was *me*. I saved the picture. And now she needed something from me."

That's a feeling I know so well it's like she's stuck her fingernail to my own beating heart. But it doesn't warm me to her.

You and me, Tacy? We share nothing.

"By then, I was Flyer, I was top girl," Tacy says. "But Beth warned me I'd better do what she said, or she'd make it bad for me."

Tacy's voice goes grave, the panic spiraling back through her eyes.

"She said I'd better not make her unhappy because I oughta know that she's never unhappy alone."

No, she's not, is she.

"So I gave in," Tacy says, sighing. "But I felt sorry for Coach. And then when the Sarge died, I felt rotten. I thought maybe Beth used that picture in some evil way. And that Sarge killed himself on account of it. Is that what happened, Addy?"

"I don't know what happened," I say, finally.

She stares up at me, glassy-eyed.

"Tacy," I say, "you better show me that picture."

"I deleted it," she says, too quickly.

"You did not," I say.

Sighing again, she reaches into the pocket of her yoga pants and pulls out her tiny phone, a searing purple.

The image on the screen looks like it was shot through a fuzzed screen door.

You can see Will's uniform, the green suit coat, the gold buttons shimmering, the braid on the lifted sleeve, and part of his face, the rest concealed by the back of a female head, a swamp of dark hair and bare shoulder blades.

For a second, I think it's Coach. It looks so much like Coach.

But then I recognize Beth's green hoodie, the one slipping down, his palm spread across her back.

The look on Will's face, how could I really name it, everything so pixilated into blurred nothingnesss.

His face, though, seems to me the saddest I've ever seen.

Both stricken and despairing.

Like the pictures you see of people standing in front of their burning houses, like one I saw once of a dad holding his night-gowned little girl in his arms, trying to put on her shoe, watching his house burn to the ground.

And I know, just like that, if Tacy had been standing on the other side of the truck, if her camera lens captured Beth's eyes instead, it would show the same thing.

The picture, I can't stop looking at it. Because it seems to me suddenly filled with truth. Because it seems to me so beautiful.

"I never wanted to get anyone into trouble," Tacy says. "But Beth, she scares me. I mean, she's always been scary. But since all this, it's been different. It's like she's gone up three levels of scary."

I stop looking at the photo and look at Tacy instead.

Things begin to shimmer into view.

"So you just gave Beth the photo, and that was it?"

"That's what I said," Tacy says, flipping over, lying back on the mat beneath her, "isn't it?"

Resting on elbows, she stretches her skinny little toothpick legs, observing them, admiring herself.

Looking down at her, all I can think of is the time she's cost me, these collusions, her weakness. The fact that this little tinkerbell got to be top girl.

Something in that puffball face of hers and I can't stop myself, my foot pressing against her face. Pushing into her blighted chin, still vein-mottled from her fall. I push it hard, harder than I meant to, its softness giving way.

"Addy," Tacy moans, scratching at me with her fingers. "Addy, what are you—"

"You sent that picture to Mr. French, didn't you?" I say, my voice husky and surprising.

Hands flinging up, she tries to shove my leg away, but she can't.

"Yes, yes," she whimpers, tears coming in long syrupy strands.

I drop my foot back to the floor. And she tells me the rest.

How Beth got Matt French's number from Coach's phone and made Tacy send it, claiming she didn't have a new phone yet.

And that Beth wrote the text herself: *Look at the kind of woman you're married to. Look at the trash she opens her legs for.*

Beth was always good with words. And knowing the times when simplest was best.

"But the picture didn't mean anything," Tacy insists. "A dumb prank. I guess Beth probably thought Mr. French would make her quit, or Coach would get fired. But wouldn't it have made more sense to send it to Principal Sheehan?"

I shake my head at this stupid girl.

Heels of hands to her mascara'ed eyes, she whispers, "Do you think that blurry little picture could have had something to do with all this? With Sarge and everything?"

I'm thinking of Matt French reading the text and looking at that picture. I'm guessing what he really thought:

Not, *There's some man with one of my wife's cheerleaders.*

No, instead: There's some man with *my* wife.

"And now Beth won't back off," she says, her hand back on my ankle, holding on to it, but eyes fixed straight ahead, at the locker-room doors. "She keeps saying I better not tell anyone what we did. At practice the other day, when I fell, it was like she was showing me what she could do to me."

Tacy's eyes fixed on the locker-room doors, strangely vibrating from the school furnace's blast, she doesn't even see me click a button on her phone and text the picture to myself.

"She showed me all right," Tacy says. "But I still told you, didn't I? I told Addy Hanlon. I guess I'm not such a cottontail. I guess I'm not the little pussy she says I am."

Her head dipping, as if by the weight of her ponytail slinging forward, she lets her body go lax.

"I was always afraid of you," she says, touching her cheek lightly, the tread of my shoe dancing faintly there. "Even more than Beth. I'd heard what you'd done to her. That scar on her ear."

This time, I don't correct it. What I'd done to Beth. What *I* had done to Beth, the scariest bad ass we ever knew.

I fold my arms and look down at Tacy. She looks so small.

"I just wanted to be Flyer," she says. "I'm going to be again."

"Sure you are," I say, handing her phone back to her.

She looks up at me as she takes it, and something passes over her face.

Dropping her phone into her pocket, she flings her hand upward, as if I should help her to her feet.

"Sure I am," she repeats, brightening. "I mean, you're gonna bust Beth now, right?"

A smile wiggling there, she adds, "Then I'll be Flyer again."

I was there, but I didn't do anything. That's what Coach had said.

I was with him, but I found him too. It's all true.

Matt French's phone blips, he looks at the screen, he sees that picture, reads those words:

Look at the kind of woman you're married to. Look at the trash she opens her legs for.

A mistake that also happens to be true.

So Matt French, he sees the military uniform and goes hunting. Finds out who the recruiter is. Or, he just checks his wife's phone, her emails, something. Anything.

He finds out where this recruiter lives, and he drives out there, to that empty steel tower on the edge of nothing, and he finds his wife and her lover.

And . . . and . . .

And he wants me to know.

And then there's Coach, the alibi she built for me.

"So last Monday you were there with your coach and her husband?" the detective had asked.

"Yes," I said.

Coach protecting Matt French, Matt French protecting Coach. The things between them, their webbed history and hidden hearts, and so instead of turning on each other, they are raising the ramparts high. The two of them locked in something blood-deep. Who knows what lies between them now? Wrists crossed, head to head, they are closing so tight, but they need me.

They do.

And Beth. There is Beth.

30.

Monday: Twelve Hours to Final Game

Work hard and believe in yourself, that's what they always tell you. But that's not really it at all. It's the things you can't say aloud, the knowledge of what you're doing, climbing high, jumping, hurling yourself into the air, hooking arms, legs around each other to create something that will collapse with the bobble of one knee, a twist of a wrist.

Standing back, Emily said, saying the thing you're never supposed to say, *it's like you're trying to kill each other and yourselves.*

The knowing that what you are all doing, together, is the most delicate thing, fragile as spun sugar, and driven by magic and abandon, your body doing things your head knows it can't, your bodies locking together to defy gravity, logic, death itself.

If they told you these things, you would never join cheer. Or maybe you would.

In the morning, it takes a long time under the shower head to get my blood moving. To pinprick my skin to life. To get my head game.

I stand under the bracing gush for so long, looking at my

body, counting every bruise. Touching every tender place. Watching the swirl at my feet.

I'm really just trying to jack up my heart.

I think, *This is my body, and I can make it do things. I can make it move, flip, fly.*

After the squall of a blow dryer, I gather my hair, sliding in bobby pin after bobby pin, pulling it all into place.

I stand in front of the mirror, my face bare, flushed, taut.

Slowly, my hands lifting, the sticky nozzle, dusty brushes, oily wands waving in front of my face, fuchsia streaking up my cheeks, my lashes stiffened to brilliant black, my hair stiff, gleaming, pin-tucked.

The perfumed mist, thick in my throat, settling.

I look in the mirror.

And it's finally me there, and I look like no one I've ever seen before.

"GAME DAY—KILL CELTS!!" shrieks the banner across the school entrance, a tissue-paper eagle, wings stiff and high, rising behind it.

I let my heart rise to it.

The morning passes, I don't see Beth at all, and Coach has called in sick. That's all anyone can talk about.

She's abandoned us twice, three times over. We are losing count.

She doesn't care about us at all.

She hates us.

"What did we do wrong?" the JV girl sobs, pressing her face against her locker door. "What did we do?"

School skitters by without touching me, and Tacy, face bleach-white, will not meet my gaze.

I am thinking of things, of the abyss and its greasy stare and how I won't blink. I can't.

At 3:15, we are in the gym, jumping high.

"Scout's a-coming!" RiRi hollers. "Wait till she sees what we got!"

Everyone screams.

And it feels like God touching me. What would I do without this, because here I am, propelling to heaven itself, soles resting on Mindy's knotty shoulders—or on the floor, knees sponging, lifting Brinnie Cox, nimble feet in my palm, surging her straight to God.

That feeling, it is God's greatest gift.

Just like that adderall. Found that morning in the corner of my hoodie from a long-ago act of Beth's generosity, it gallops through me, and I know I can do anything.

When you have nothing inside you, you feel everything more, and feel you can control all of it.

With Jesus in my heart, and with that seismic blast, who could stop my ascent? Any of ours?

In the locker room, forty minutes to game time, we are Vegas showgirl-spangled. The air thick with biofreeze and tiger balm and hairspray and the sugared coconut of tawny body sprays, it is like being in a soft cocoon of sugar and love.

There's RiRi, slinging her curling iron like a gunfighter, shaping the spring-shot ponytail, its helix curls.

There's Paige Shepherd, temp tattoo blazing across her tan face, kicking her leg high and twisting, tumbling into Mindy's arms, her wrists black duct taped like Roman gladiator cuffs.

See Cori Brisky, rubbing flexall on her numbing wrists, her smile showing all her teeth, and how sharp they are, and I know that there's a jungle princess in there who's ready for hot blood.

See even shell-shocked Emily, our fallen comrade, fingers glazed with icy hot, running it across Mindy's armor shoulder blades, whispering in her ear.

And there I am. If you could see me—tall, tight, lightsome and powerful, flipping my back tucks on the slippery tile, afraid of nothing, no one. Just try to stop me.

That's what people never understand: they see us hard little pretty things, brightly lacquered and sequin-studded, and they laugh, they mock, they arouse themselves. They miss everything.

You see, these glitters and sparkle dusts and magicks? It's warpaint, it's hair tooth, it's blood sacrifice.

But where's our fearsome leader? Either of them?

We need somebody to gather all this hectic energy, to link these pulsing organs into one powerful, unstoppable body.

What if that somebody were me?

Moving girl to girl, I start back-stroking, French-braiding, tiger-balming, offering rallying words, *C'mon girls, let's show them what we got.*

I even talk, for the first time ever, to that poor yellow peep JV, the one who will have to fly tonight if Beth doesn't show, the one shivering like a downy chick.

I know I can lift her, I can.

She's not a girl but a butterfly resting on my fingertips.

But then there's a clatter from the backdoors, and a flurry of whoops and bratty squeals and, baby lamb JV tucked under my arm, I turn and know I will see her.

Beth.

Leaping up on the locker-room bench, eyelids scorched with blue glitter, she heaves her throaty voice to the drop ceiling.

"Hella bitches," she bellows, rocking her feet on the bench so it shudders. "Our scout, I can feel her out there, waiting. And, bitches, she is so ready to be fucked."

The gasp from us is loud and exultant.

"I've just trawled through that gym to check out the Celt squad and I've never seen anything so appalling. Ana girls with accordion ribs, a coupla dykey ringers with treebark legs and Charlie Brown faces. And those Celt ballers, skidding and squeaking, tossing that baby's ball around like they're kings of the world? Pathetic."

Everyone, so eager, twirling near her, just like the old days when she'd preen and twist and flash her blue Eagles tatts and we'd clamor, *Give it to us, Captain, rise up, rise up!* . . .

"You know who the stars are? We are. Why? Because we

don't throw around a fucking rubber ball. You know what *we* throw around? Live girls. Do you know who flies? We do. You know what we hurl to the rafters? Each other."

I hear Emily's tender gasp behind me, her boot brace clacking, and the muffled squeal of the JV Flyer.

"Tonight, you've got to spill their blood," she says, her raised arm, her temples, her neck pulsing, "or I promise you they will spill yours."

There's a dark roiling on Beth and it's starting to sweep through us. We are letting it, all of us.

"Brace those arms. Bolt those knees. Look at that crowd like you're about to give them the best piece of ass they ever had. Sell it."

The feelings charging through the room, they're complicated and incendiary and none of us, not even me, can name them all. Everything in Beth, in her dark energy, so captivating and so repulsive—

"Bases, eyes on your Flyer, she is yours. You lock her to your heart. You lose her, blood on the mat. She is yours. Make her."

All the swirling ponytails nod in unison, as if they know, as if any of us know what Beth, veins tight on her upstretched arms, meant or could ever mean.

"JV," Beth says, pointing her witching finger at the yearling under my arm, and because none of us really know her name, "you fail, you fail all of us. So you will not fail."

The JV shakes her head back and forth, looking like she might cry.

"Girlie, you've been a chick long enough. I need you to show me that egg tooth," she says, slipping her fingers under the JV's tank top, heaving her up on the bench with her. "Tonight's the night, you're gonna pip through the shell."

Beth tugs the girl under her own bronzed arm, stares her down and nearly laps her face. "So stiffen the sinews, summon up the blood. We've come to bury them. We've come to plow their bones by the final bell."

She pounds her pumas until that bench rattles, our bodies shake.

"It's harvest day, girlies," she says, her voice like crackling lightning. "Get busy when the corn is ripe."

I almost fall for it, for Beth's hoodoo grandiosity.

Our captain, like Beth from before, our noble, proud, heart-strong Beth, and this Beth too, a warrior nearly vanquished but not quite, never quite.

We few, we happy few, she might say, *we band of sistuhs, for she today that sheds her blood with me, shall be my sistuh always.*

Couldn't I just let that be enough for these two hours?

But then Tacy sputters in, late, her face still bruise-dappled and her eyes lightless, damned.

And I'm reminded of everything.

Including the feel of my foot pressed against her face, what she made me do.

This feeling, this high, it's not real. It's that Jesus-love flooding through me, by which I mean the adderall and the pro-clinical hydroxycut with green tea extract and the eating-nothing-but-hoodia-lollipops-all-day.

And most of all the high that comes from Beth's dark supply.

I don't want it.

Ten minutes to game time, and no Coach to stop the squad, everyone's breaking rules and whirring through the back bleachers, scout-spotting.

Back in the locker room, I sit, trying to get my game head on.

3 row frm top, lft — lady w. cap + mirror shades! RiRi texts.

I hear a rustling one row over and there's Beth, hands in her locker, tugging off her rows of friendship bracelets, tightening her pin-straight ponytail. Eyes on herself in her stick-on mirror, face blue and frightening.

Were it not for the angle of her locker door, the way the parking lot lights slanted through the high windows, I might never have seen it.

But I did.

The hot glow of an evil eye, creeping between a pile of hair ties and toe socks.

A hamsa bracelet. Coach's hamsa bracelet. My hamsa bracelet.

Hands to her slick shea-buttered arms, I catch her by surprise, flipping her around.

"What, did you think I wouldn't show?" she says, and her blood all up in her cheeks and temples. "I'd never let the squad down."

My chest lurching, I grab the bracelet with one hand and, with the other, shove her into the shower stalls.

"You did it. You took it. You lied about all of it," I shout raggedly, my voice echoing to the slimy ceiling of the showers. "It was never in Will's apartment, was it?"

"No," she says, with a strange stuttering laugh, "of course not."

"Why did you tell me the police found it?"

"I wanted you to see," she says. "She was hiding everything from you. She never cared about you."

"But you stole it. You were going to try to plant it, something," I say, squeezing her so hard I feel one of my nails start to give. "My god, Beth."

"Oh, Addy," she says, still laughing, her head shaking back and forth. "I took it a long time ago. That time we slept at her house."

I think of it now. That long-ago night after the Comfort Inn, Beth, the wounded kitty. Those hours I'd abandoned her to Coach's sofa, left her free to prowl the house, her viper's crawl. Shadows flitting by all night.

"But that was before everything," I say. "Why?"

"She didn't deserve it," Beth says, her voice rising, throaty, the laughing gone. "She'd tossed it on the kitchen window ledge, like an old sponge. She didn't deserve it."

Wrestling from me, she shoves hard, her face a blue smear.

"And now her time is up," she says, husky-voiced and deadly grave. "Now she'll see what I can do."

Face so close, painted shooting stars slashing up her temples, she's heated up on her own words. But I can smell something sweated and musky on her, like she has been clawing hard through loamy earth. Like she has very little left.

Which means it's my time.

"You're not going to the cops," I say, voice as cold and hard as I can manage. "You never were. You don't want them to find out what you did."

Maybe I thought I'd never see surprise on her face again, but there it is. It almost frightens me.

"What *I* did?" she says. "I gave you your goddamned day, and you used it to let her spit more venom in your ear. When I think of the yogi-hold that cheer bitch has over you, I wanna puke."

"Beth, I know it all now," I say, pushing myself close to her, towering over her. "You used Tacy to send that picture of you and Will to Matt French. Tacy told me everything."

A stitch of panic rises over that high brow, her back rustling against the vinyl curtain, and here I am, I suddenly realize, four inches taller than the little shrub, the little Napoleon, I just never felt it before.

"Slaussen. I should've guessed it," she says, grinning wryly. "I never saw a fox eat a rabbit before. I'd like to. How did she taste?"

"Did you hope Matt French would look at the picture and think you were Coach?"

"I didn't care what he thought," she says, chin jutting high, graveling her voice, "all I cared about was getting her out. She buried us in all her ugliness and someone had to get us out—"

Somehow my hand has a hold of the bottom of her pony-tail, fingers slapping against her scarred ear.

It's like how it sometimes is with me and Beth, the closeness that comes from being hand to hand, arm to arm, body to body, and always spotting each other. I know her body and the way it turns, the way it moves, and what makes her shake.

"You started all this," I say, fingers gripping tight. "It was you."

Snaking her fingers between mine, she foists my hand from her hair and rolls her eyes with comic-book magnitude.

"For fuck's sake, fuck me if Coach's husband mistakenly thought his wife was fucking the National Guard recruiter. Oh wait," she says, "she *was*."

"You set it all in motion," I say. Then, wielding another hidden card, "You knew Coach was with Sarge that night. Prine told me everything."

She doesn't say anything, just stares at me, the angry blue warpaint blaring.

"If you wanted me to believe Coach killed Will," I say, "why didn't you tell me she was there?"

And then I realize it. "You were afraid I'd tell Coach. Warn her."

"I wasn't *afraid* you would warn her," she snarls. "I *knew* you would. You're just her little pussy, and always were."

I shove her shoulder, and she laughs, an aching laugh, a laugh I remember most from the worst times for Beth, the scariest times after bad nights with boys or her mother, and I'd try to say tender things and she would laugh, which was her way of crying.

"Prine's gonna do what I say, Addy," she says, curling her hand on top of mine, pressing it into her own sharp shoulder. "He thinks I might statutory him, or worse."

"You knew all along," I say, feeling her veins pulsing under my clamped hand. "All your lies—"

"My lies?" she says. "All you've done is lie to me. All you've ever done. But you've always been the fox. Stone cold."

"I'm telling everything, Beth," I say.

Like there's a fever in my brain, or Jesus in my heart, my hands are on her again, hurling both her shoulders back against the shower tiles, her eyes flashing and her mouth a tight grin.

She's trying to smile, yes, but there's a horror in it. *Push harder, push harder. Ride that bitch.*

"What can you tell? All you have is Slaussen," she says. "You think I can't win back that rabbitheart of hers? I have my two front teeth sunk in it. I have things I can tell about her, about Coach, about you—"

My hand whips across her face so fast I gasp.

But she doesn't flinch. Instead, eyes darkening, she slides back against the wall, tilting her face so it smears against the damp tiles, her spangled mask blurring blue.

She doesn't say anything for a second and the silence feels heavy, epic. I don't know what to do with myself except listen to my own breathing.

"He said he was sick with himself over it," she says, quietly, darkly.

It takes me a second to realize she's talking about Will.

"Like I was this dirty thing he'd done," she says.

She puts a hand to the back of her head, rubbing it with an eerie softness, like she's in slow motion. "Who is he to call me dirty?" she asks, her eyelashes slipping glitter.

I'm thinking of the snapshot of the two of them, the look on his face.

"You should've seen how he looked at me after," she says. "Like you're looking at me now."

I don't know what to say to this.

"Then I saw him and Coach together," she says, "the way they just gloated in their fucking. So freaking enthralled with themselves, and you just so enthralled with them. With her."

There is the secret song in me of an old Beth, schoolyard Beth, playground and sleeping bag and bikes with streamers Beth. The Beth who never wanted me to sleep over at Katie Lerner's house, and would always wait in front of my house the night I got back from summer vacation. The Beth who always, chin to my shoulder, looked out for me, and I for her. Our bodies interlocked.

"But Beth, you can stop now," I say, shaking my head. "You can stop all this."

Something stirs in her face and she's looking down at my clenched, glitter-crusted hands on her arms.

"I did it for all of us," she says. "I did it for you, Addy. Somebody had to. And it's always been me."

I let my hands go, staring, not sure what to do or what she means.

"The funny thing is, Addy, it turns out you were the dangerous one," she says, voice steadying now, drawing strength.

She walks past me and, her palm clasped over her scarred

left ear, adds, "You were the tough one, the cruel one. The fox. You just couldn't admit it. You've always done whatever you wanted. It was always you."

And she's gone.

I hear her whistling through the locker room, and her voice, mournful but resonant now.

"Arrow in the quiver," she sings. "At daggers drawn."

31.

We are phalanx-spread four deep across the floor. Oh, the roaring, if you only knew. Like being crest deep in a wave and all the pounding to go through you.

We are assembled soldiers. My eyes flashing past us, it's like looking at fifteen duplicates of one shiny-eyed girl, midnight-blue halters and silver-lined minis, spoking legs and bleached white sneaks, hair slicked back into uniform ponys, shimmer-blue foiled bows.

We all have our eyes on the woman in the red hat and mirrored shades, high up on the left flank. Whether she's the scout or not, we're giving everything to her.

RiRi, superstitious, singing softly, *Jesus on my necklace, glitter on my eyes*, knuckles rapping against mine.

The pounding of our thirty assembled feet, pounding so it thunders all through us, as we undulate into a V.

There is Beth at the diamond tip, her face streaked indigo and, from afar, never looking more like the savage princess she is, like she might have a necklace of human tongues.

"Split the 'V,' " she shouts, and forking her fingers at her hips, "Dot the 'I,' " and sliding her finger down low, shimmying, legs vibrating, "Rock that C-T-O-R-Y!"

Seeing her like that. Seeing her, bright white sneaks on the gym floor, legs and arms together, chin up proud to the crowd, their howling and foot-thundering frenzy, I feel all kinds of things I can't name.

Her face is so lovely, a perfect spritely smile carved there, lightning bolt tattoo streaked across one high cheekbone.

And on her wrist, the hamsa, plucked from the shower stall floor.

Marching in formation, our heads snapping, feet thumping, four-five-six across, the diamond splitting.

"Beat those Celts, slaughter that ball

"We will die for you above all."

"That's not how it goes," mewls Brinnie Cox, as if Beth has just flubbed the line.

"We will die for you above all," Beth repeats.

Those words, I know them, but I don't know how and there's no time.

RiRi, Paige, and I darting to the mat's far corners to spring across with our tumbling passes, everyone whipping past me and the noise like an ocean in my ear.

And I land it and Beth is there and I am spotting, Mindy and Cori popping her into the air, ticktocking one leg to the other, her feet in their hands, her arms V'd.

And Beth is shouting, and I am looking up at her, her chin trembling, her neck pulsing.

She is crying, but only I can see that. I can see because I've never seen it but once or twice, and it's like something precious split in two. A diamond cracked, a web spreading.

"It's Coach," comes Tacy's squealing shout. "It's Coach."

My head whipping to my side, I can't believe it, but I see her there, soft hoodie and hemp yoga pants, and her hair knotted tight on her head.

Coach.

Oh, my Coach.

And she is saying something, or she isn't saying anything at all, but we know what to do and we do our back tucks in perfect unison, symmetric soldiers all in a line, then the whistle blows and the bounding boys come and we run to her.

We run to her.

And I see Beth, and her broken face, and I can't help her at all.

I can't.

It's all a heady blur, the floor board-pounding mayhem of the game, and Coach there, placing her hand gently on the backs of our heads, pulling even, so un-Coach-like, on Mindy's golden braids, and by the time the half-time horn thunders, I've lost Beth entirely.

In the locker room, the air clear from the tall windows lifted open by Coach with that long iron stick.

We are not actually on our knees, but it feels that way. It feels as if we're on our knees, like prayerful Southern football players.

We are all bowing inside, to her.

Coach, you've not forsaken us.

"I'm glad to be here right now," she says, and she's speaking so low but somehow even amid the bumptious din coming from the gym we can hear her, hear every beat.

"I'm lucky to be in your company. And I'm talking about all of you. You mighty women."

Something catches in my throat. *Coach.*

I feel a hand twist around my arm, and it's RiRi, her curls shaking, and beside her Emily, half leaning, still casted, against the lockers, and all of us standing, craning our necks, huddling toward Coach's clear eyes, clear face, clear voice.

How could the things we would laugh at out there, scoff and eye roll and dismiss, move us so much in here? Because it is Coach.

"For all kinds of reasons," she says, her voice wobbling so slightly I feel sure only I can hear, "we're all going to remember tonight."

All of us circling forward, wanting to warm our hands, our bodies to it.

"It's the last game of the season, after all these months of sweat and blood. And, after all this, I want you to be able to speak proudly, to strip your sleeves and show your scars, and talk about what you did tonight."

Her words are vibrating through me, touching my very center.

"After the night's over," she says, her voice lifting higher, "after you graduate, and you're off to college or wherever you girls go—ten years from now, your little girl's going to pull your dusty Eagles yearbook off the shelf and ask what you were like in high school.

"You won't have to cough, look the other way and say,

'Well, sweetie, your mom was in the French club and sang in the choir.' You won't even have to say, 'Your mom waved pom-poms and shook her ass.' Because you will know what you were, what you are forever.

"Squad, *take this moment*, seal it over your heart."

The quiet among us, the devotional silence starts to break apart as we feel ourselves, lifted, feelings and gasps and eager squeaks and throatier yeas and rustling and rumbling and most of all the sense of greatness rising from within us and hoisted high.

"You're going to look your girl straight in the eye and say, 'Baby, your mom rode to the rafters. Your mom lifted three girls in her hands, grinning all the way,' " she says, our voices rising to a baying now, all together.

" 'Your mom built pyramids and flew high in the sky, and back in Sutton Grove, they're still talking about the wonders they saw that night, still talking about how they watched us all reach to the heavens.'

"Don't you want to be able to say that?"

Our innermost selves, in some magnificent ascent, and a clattering as some girls leap onto the benches, crying out, overtaken.

But not me—me who wants to bathe in the moment's sacredness forever.

"You may have the bodies of young girls," she says, her voice deep and holy, "but you have the hearts of warriors. Tonight, show me your warrior hearts.

"That's all."

—

And she turns and pushes through the locker-room doors into the brightly lit hallway.

But instead of turning into the clanging gym, its frenzy pitched to madness, she walks straight out the loading dock doors, into the starred night.

It's like when a fever breaks, and you don't know what's happened, or what all those voices in your head meant, but the Celts squad does their half-time routine and all I see is flying bodies and cries and the greater and greater sense of a battlefield of fallen enemies on which we will march.

And I realize, Beth gone again, I don't even know who top girl is.

"It's gotta be the JV, right?" whispers RiRi. "We're tossing her up, right?"

But there is no time, and there we are, running out on that gym floor, and I feel my body flipping into my handspring, and Brinnie Cox's legs spiraling next to me, and suddenly we're twenty seconds in and I can hear myself shouting:

. . . said shah shah shah shah booty
Got that rhythm feelin' tight
Let your body rock *snap snap*
Let your hips show some might *stomp stomp stomp*
shah shah shah shah booty

I'm looking for the JV Flyer, but I don't see her.
We don't need no music
We don't need no bands.
All we need are Eagles fans jammin' in the stands!

Oh wait, stop a minute, WAIT
shah shah shah shah booty

I feel her before I see her.

Dark hair shimmering, the thunderbolt seared to her face.

Beth, in the JV's place. Lining up in the top Flyer spot for the 2-2-1.

And if you could understand how time can stop, it did for me.

Mindy has her hands on my waist, my hands gripping soft shoulders, my toe slipping into the pocket of her bent knee, pushing off with my right foot and lifting my other knee as high as I can, planting it on her shoulder, front-spotting Paige below, propelling up my other foot.

RiRi and I face each other, feet fixed on Mindy and Cori's shoulders, their hands tight on our ankles.

"Who's counting?" I shout.

shah shah shah shah booty

Emily, swinging her boot brace across the front row, her eyes avid, her fear gone.

"I'll do it," she cries. "I'll count. No one knows better than me. No one knows—"

We are now ten and a half feet high, my eyes fixed on RiRi's wild green ones, her face cobalt brushed, ecstatic, mouthing, *"B-E-T-H!"*

shah shah shah shah booty

"One-two, three-four," Emily's fierce counting like a pulse in my brain, like a hammer over my heart.

The whole pyramid sponging, rubber-banding as it should, the living thing, the beating heart.

Below I see Beth's black hair, and she flings her head back, her eyes squeezed shut.

I will die only for you above all.

That's what she'd said, and I remembered it now, from long ago. Age nine or ten, poring over a Time-Life book in my dad's library, an old picture of a Japanese pilot tying his headband, eyes determined, jaw set.

And the caption: "I will die only for you above all."

Beth loved that picture and tore the page out and pasted it in her locker with rubber cement and at year's end we tried to claw it free, but it came off in shreds and there was nothing she could do.

I will die only for you above all.

Six hands on her and she's propelled up between RiRi and me. Lying flat, her arms outstretched and we pop her up, so she is standing.

And—blocking out Emily's dire warnings of what it's like from out there, from the stands, as they see all of us spring-loaded into the air, defying gravity, logic, the laws of physics itself, because all I need to think of is Beth's wrist in my tight-clawed—

One

shah shah shah shah booty

and loading her forward, slingshotting her back to life, pitching her higher, locking her in place, holding her wide-spread arms like pinpoints on a cross,

Two

shah shah shah shah booty

I can feel, fingers to Beth's wrist, the veins pulsing, the beat slower than it should be, and I think—

Three

you ain't got

—her pumas balancing on the gathered hands below, a pinched tightrope and she is cheering, oh, is she cheering.

Waiting for Emily to count EIGHT, then *DEADMAN*, we drop her wrists, she falls backward, limbs outspread, into the waiting arms below . . . that is what she is to—

Four

you ain't got it, you ain't got it, ain't got it

She is so high, fifteen feet, sixteen, seventeen, a thousand—and the whole gym shaking victorious, her body still like a fierce arrow—when I feel her suddenly yank her wrist from my clasp.

My body pitches forward, but terror-eyed Mindy has hold of me, and RiRi clambers to keep hold of Beth's other wrist.

I have my eyes on Beth, I think I am calling out to her, her name choked in my chest, but she won't turn, she couldn't or she'd—

Five

. . . and I know and I'm not going to stop her, there is no stopping her.

This is what she wants, after all.

Six-and—and two beats too soon, she propels herself backward with such force

The gasp from the bleachers lashes through the air.

The power with which she thrusts her body backward.

The force with which she twists her body, spinning it, and then kicking backward

RiRi and I teetering on our Bases, nearly falling forward toward each other—

—and all our hands grabbing for her, and the will with which Beth pitches her body, legs kicking so far back, so far back.

All the way back.

The air sucked from me, the sounds gone from the world.

The way, for a second, her body seems to lift, dance to the rafters, then the way everything shifts, all our bodies tilting in space as I feel myself falling, as I feel Beth falling.

It's like she doesn't weigh anything at all, and she might never hit the floor, until she does.

Then the sickening crack and seeing her head click backward, like a doll's.

But you must see:

She never really wanted anything but this.

The Abyss, Addy, it gazes back into you.

32.

Monday Night

I'm sitting in the hospital's east corridor, the waiting-room light soft to prepare you for the end of light, of all things.

That's how it feels.

Beth's mom appears in the doorway just past nine, flinging her camel Coach bag onto the sofa and bursting into inky tears that seem to come in gaping spurts for hours.

She talks mournfully of her failures, her weaknesses, and most of all the harshness of life for pretty girls who never know how good they have it.

Finally, she cries herself into a stuttering sleep, sinking into her coat like a slumbering bat.

I move three seats away.

The TV, pitched high in a corner, scrolls footage of Beth being wheeled out on the gurney, one arm dangling limply.

Then, the on-camera interviews, and there's Tacy Slaussen's lapine face.

"I just want everyone to know that our stunts usually hit," she says, tightening her ponytail and showing all her teeth. "But let's face it. Cheer can be dangerous. I got injured just the other day. It was supposed to be me out there."

Behind her, Emily sobbing in the background, "I didn't mess up the count, I didn't."

I reach up and switch the channel, but Tacy's on WXON too.

"But Beth always told us, life is about taking risks, and you can die at any moment," she says with those pointy teeth of hers, forehead shining.

"It's what we sign up for."

And then Brinnie Cox, crying just as she cried a few hours before when she flunked a Chemistry quiz, and a few hours before that, when Greg Lurie called her Bitty Titty.

"She is such a talented girl," she wails, raccoon-eyed, "and we all feed off her positiveness."

Not long after, I see the news of the arrest.

The closed caption reads: *Cheerleading coach husband to be charged in slaying.*

Which is such a simple way to say what is anything but simple.

The snapshot they show on the news seems to be from some other world I don't know, Coach and Matt French, faces giddy, a great custardy wedding veil whipping around her.

I think of him out there in the backyard the other day, his stillness. But wasn't he always so still, a shadow drifting past all our antic energy? So strange to think how much was roiling in him. The thing we mistook for blankness, for boringness, for a Big Nothing, turned out to be everything. A beating heart, a raging one.

"What is this, the all-cheerleading network?" brays a tired

expectant father in the chair next to me, until he sees my uniform, the sequins matted to my leg.

Later, Beth's mom comes back from talking to the doctor and smoking twelve cigarettes in the back parking lot.

She says it's a skull fracture in three places.

"I was waiting for her." That's what Beth kept saying, lying on the gym floor, her eyes black. "Where did she go?"

All the way out, like on some continuous loop. "When will she come back? I was waiting for her."

Waiting, there seems no point, so I drive to the police station at two a.m. and sit.

It's an hour before I see Coach, holed up in the back lot with a pack of Kools—these are not times for clove cigarettes—her breath making dragony swirls.

"Hey," she says, when she spots me.

We sit in my car, her eyes darting over and over to the back door, like she's waiting for the cops to realize she shouldn't be out here alone.

I don't tell her about Beth, don't ask if she knows.

It's her time to talk, and she does.

That night, like any other night, she tells me Matt was working late and she still had no car.

Will wants to see her, needs to, really.

Says he'll drive her back and forth if she'll come. He never wants to be alone.

No one ever needed her half as much, not even her daughter. She is sure of it.

At his apartment, like it often does lately, everything feels different, it's all too much, and even scary, the way he holds her hard enough to hurt, talking the whole time in broken whispers about how she is all that keeps him from the way he feels, like his heart is pumping water and drowning him to death.

These are the ways he talks lately, and the only thing to do is to hold on to him. Some nights she's held him so hard, she has bruises on the heels of each hand.

They are in the bedroom a long time, and nothing is made better for more than one tight minute. The look on his face after frightens her.

She takes a long shower to give him time to pull himself together, to shake off the night horrors of his dark room.

But when she turns off the faucet she hears a man talking loudly. Saying something over and over. At first she thinks it's Will, but it isn't Will.

Over and over, the same rhythm and the same feeling of panicky anger, like her dad after things started to go wrong for him, at work, with her mom, with the world, and sometimes it was like he would tear the whole house down with him, raze it, incinerate it.

She guesses she is hearing it through the ceiling, the floor. Doesn't that happen in apartments, where nothing was private or secret?

For a few seconds, she doesn't even call out to Will, figures she is being silly, all the noises that rattle through these big buildings, the way sound carries in the gorges.

But then the sound flies up fast and is newly familiar to her, feels close enough to touch. That's when she pulls on her T-shirt, her body still so wet it fuses to her in an instant, and starts walking out of the bathroom.

"Will," she says. "Will."

And she is shaking the water from her hair. Her head is down and so she doesn't see how it started.

"Listen, please, calm down and—"

Will, towel wrapped around him, is talking to someone in the tone she sometimes uses with Caitlin when Caitlin scares herself at night, seeing ghosts slipping under her closet door.

And another voice, one she knows:

"—think you can do whatever you want. Another man's wife—"

And it is Matt, and how can Matt be here? She wonders if she is still asleep and this is like a soap opera when you walk out of the shower and learn everything has been a dream.

Matt.

At first she thinks it's his phone in his hand, that black curve always like a dark beetle in his palm.

She remembers hearing Will say, "How did you get my gun—"

Will had shown her the gun the week before. He'd taken the gun from his top bureau drawer and said, *Is this what life is supposed to be about?*

He'd held it in his lap as he told her he hated the Guard, hated everything except her.

Because that's how he talks now, which isn't a way she wanted anyone to talk, not after Dad.

In bed with him, it was all she could think about.

When he was sleeping, she opened the bureau drawer again, took the gun and put it in her purse.

She hid it in her file cabinet at home, far in the back behind the hundreds and hundreds of Xeroxed cheer routines. She tried not to think about it. But it was there and, trying to sleep at night, she could think of nothing else.

But now her husband has the gun, holding it funny, like it's this thing in his hand he doesn't recognize.

It happens so fast, Will saying to Matt, "Do you think I care? Do you think I'd stop you?"

And Will grabbing for the gun, and Matt's eyes seizing on her at last, spotting her standing there, and abruptly gaining focus, gaining balance.

Matt, suddenly realizing, but not fast enough to stop it.

The two men pressed together, almost like they are embracing. It is as though they are embracing.

And then suddenly the gun is shoved up between their faces, and Will tipping back, the gun tilting—like the way you'd feed a bottle to a baby.

"This is it," he says. Will says.

She'll always remember that.

And the pop.

The flash from Will's mouth.

Like a cherry bomb.

Like Will's face lit from within.

Candescent.

And Will sliding to the floor.

It is so graceful, like a dance.

If it hadn't been what it was, it would've been beautiful.

After that, she loses time.

Mostly, she remembers the high, sharp whistling sound that she finally realizes is coming from her.

And Matt crying. She'd never ever seen him cry, except when Caitlin was born and he'd sat in the chair next to her hospital bed and told her that he had never been so happy and nothing could ever be bad again, he wouldn't let it be.

After that, everything is a red blur, Matt was smearing the gun on the sofa cushions, smearing his fingerprints away.

She remembers thinking, *How does he know to do that?* And then thinking, *Everyone in the world would know to do that.*

She remembers him holding her in his arms and telling her things, and the red-wrung way of his face, and how she felt sorry for him, she just did.

She remembers how she looked down and his shirt cuffs were misted red.

He tried to get her to leave with him, but she refused. Maybe he tried. That part she doesn't really remember.

She remembers sitting on the leather sofa for a minute, staring out the big windows, night-blackened.

She couldn't have, but she thinks she heard Matt driving away, twenty-seven floors down.

She doesn't remember calling me.

She never looked down at the floor.

When she finishes telling me, we're sitting on a back curb and it's so cold but neither of us wants to go inside.

"After, I remember shouting, 'How could you do this to me?' " she says with almost a wry laugh. "But which one of them was I saying it to?"

How could you do this to me? I wonder if she knows she's still saying it in her sleep.

"When I came home that night, all the drawers were open, the file cabinet dumped on the floor. He'd gone through everything," Coach says. "But I don't know what started it."

I don't say anything.

"I don't think he ever meant to use that gun at all," she says. "That's not how he is."

"But if Matt explains how it was, if you both do," I say, my voice rising up. "Maybe they'll let him go."

She looks at me wearily, as if to say, *And then what, Addy? Then what?*

"I saw his face right before," she says. "Will's face. I saw the way he was looking at Matt."

She turns to me.

"He never looked at me at all."

Picturing Will, I think I finally see what it was. I could never name it before, the way his eyes were always drifting, never connecting. There was the feeling with him always of a room everybody had left.

"Tonight, just before they came to arrest him," she says, "Matt said, 'What they'll never believe is that he wanted to die.' He said, 'Colette, it doesn't seem fair that I get to know that. That I get that. But it's true.' "

She looks at me, smiling sadly. "But you know what? He's right. It really isn't fair that he gets to know that."

Her smile turning grim. "Because that doesn't help me."

We sit quietly for a long time.

"Coach," I say, my voice surprising me. Then I ask something because I have the feeling it's my last chance to ever ask it. "I never knew why you love it. Cheer. How you came to love it."

She runs a finger along her upper lip. "I never loved it," she says, shaking her head. "It was just a thing. I never cared about it at all."

I don't believe her.

"What happens now?" I say, because I can't think of anything else.

She looks at me and laughs.

A few days later, I'm watching the news, my new habit, when I see the latest report.

"The break came when a witness identified Matthew French as the man he had seen running from The Towers apartment building the night of the murder. Sources say that the witness reported that, under the parking lot lights, it looked like French's clothes were covered in blood."

You can't keep secrets long and it's RiRi who tells me who the witness was.

Jordy Brennan, crooked nose and high tops.

One of his late-night runs, he made it nearly all the way to Wick Park. Spotting the bright lights of The Towers parking lot, he stopped to look for just the right song for the run home.

I wonder what it must have been like to see Matt French tearing through those doors. If Jordy was really close enough to see any blood. If he was close enough to see the expression on Matt French's face. Sometimes I feel like I can.

Jordy Brennan. I picture him up there, taking long, dragging breaths in the frosted air, during the moments before he saw Matt French. Just a few hundred yards from the spot he once kissed me messily for a half-hour or more, those vacant eyes of his shut tight. Believing something was beginning.

Those moments he stood up there, catching his breath, looking for his song, I wonder if he thought about me.

I visit Beth in the hospital once. It's very late and past visiting hours, but I don't want to see her mom again or all the squad girls teeming there, as if on death watch and then as if on a healing prayer vigil. Oh, to see them and to watch their paroxysms, like Salem witches tearing their hair out, rolling their tongues.

Then, when the reaper no longer lurked and there was no more talk of intracranial bleeding and cognitive impairment, they turned to epic poems on the We Miss You Beth! Facebook page where everyone wishes their ♥ ♥ and *get well soon, sistuhs!,* and to hourly deliveries, cookie bouquets, pluming gift baskets stuffed with smiley-face cupcakes, teddy bears donning nurse's hats. Everything Beth would just love.

So I come late, the hospital blue and lonesome.

I stand at her bed, my hands on the side rails.

There's a start in my chest when I see she's awake, her eyes bright in the moonlight, as if waiting for me.

She tells me she didn't think I'd come, that everyone has come but me.

"Even my dad," she says, smiling faintly. "He wants to talk about a lawsuit. Can you figure?"

I tell her Coach has left town, has taken Caitlin to her mother's, will only come back for the trial.

But she doesn't say anything and it's a while before she talks again.

When she does, she starts in the dreamy middle of something, her words caught in her lips.

"I'll never forget seeing it. How she came in one day and I saw her wearing it," she says, her voice wool-thick and plaintive. "I couldn't believe it when I saw it. It was the worst part, worse than anything."

I don't know what she means, and wonder about the things happening in her brain.

"I couldn't believe it," she said, "you gave it to her, the very same one, the very same."

She keeps looking at me, a barely banked fire there, hovering behind her eyes.

"How could you give her that bracelet, Addy?" she asks.

The bracelet. I can't believe we're back on the hamsa bracelet after everything that's happened. The fluid pressing on Beth's skull, that's what it is, like when it happened, the black blood pooling in her ear.

I shake my head. "It was just a bracelet, Beth. I don't even remember where I got it—"

"I mean, that was the worst part," she says. "It really was."

That's when I remember.

A present for you, Beth had said when she gave it to me a year ago, or more. *Wear it forever*. Which I think is the same thing I'd hoped for Coach.

"I forgot," I say. Which must be a lie, but it's part of the pieces I don't look at. Like Beth says, I choose what to look at. I choose what to remember. Beth is my memory, remembering for me.

"You've given me lots of bracelets. We all do that," I say. "It's what we do."

It's a terrible thing to say, but I'm ashamed.

"I shouldn't have kept it," she says. "I should have thrown it down the gorge. Down at the bottom of the gorge with the Apache maidens."

"I can't believe I forgot," I say, softer now.

Her eyes glassing, she turns away.

"It was you and me, Addy," she says.

Something plucks inside of me, something deep and near forgotten.

"Addy, are we going to pretend forever? I know you remember," she says, her back to me.

But of course I remember. I know precisely what she is holding tight.

A year ago, early spring, drunken sky-searching at midnight

up on the ridge, cold enough to see our breath, but Beth, stripped to streaky-white, and the way I leapt after her, foot sliding in wet leaves, and my hand on her back, hot to the touch.

Collapsing to mossy soil, our backs sinking into it, our faces pitched up to the sky. Just back from two weeks with her mother in Baja, she has something for me, and asks me to lay my hand across her belly and close my eyes. The feeling of the soft leather on my wrist, the cold amulet, the Hand of Fatima charm.

And she told me the story of Fatima, how she was stirring a pot when her husband came home with a new wife. Brokenhearted, she let the ladle slip from her fingers and continued stirring with her own hand, not noticing the pain.

"The hand protects you," she said. "Nothing can hurt it now. Nothing can touch us now."

We raised our arms in the air and let our wrists touch, the beam from its silver hand, its promise of protection.

Wearing it, it made me feel strong and safe. Powerful. It made me feel like her.

Lying there, our shorts riding up, we compared the plummy bruises that marked both our right hips, matching thumbprints from where Mindy, Cori, and other girls would press hard to spin into their stunts.

She pushed at mine and I poked hers, and, wincing, we kept pushing on each other's, the pain mysterious and soothing and strange.

How did it happen, us tangled upon each other.

My breath on her neck, my mouth on her ear. I started it, but I don't even remember why or how. We never tugged our shorts all the way off, and we never did what things we might do, but, if I let myself, I can still feel my cheek on her knee bone, still feel the pressure of her hands on my thighs. My mouth on her mouth, her laughing.

We never talked about it, and things were maybe different after. Maybe I felt different.

Then the season ended and there was a boy or another boy, and cheer camp and I bunked with Casey Jaye and wore the love knot Casey gave me, and things got bad and were never the same again. And when she saw Casey and me, legs swinging from the upper bunk, laughing—the look on her face, and the look on mine. I can guess what mine looked like.

No, I don't think about it ever, that night with Beth up high on the ridge.

There was a wonder in it, and who needs to talk of such wonders? We nestle them away, deep in the fury at the center of us, where things can be held tightly, protected and secretly cherished as a special notion we once held, then had to stow away.

"You never could look at yourself, Addy," she says. "What you wanted, what you'd do to get it. But here you are."

Here I am.

"You wanted it. It's yours now," she says. "It was always you."

33.

August Cheerleader Tryouts

"The one shining thing about high school for me has been Cheer."

Pacing in front of the fifteen soon-to-be JV girls in the epicly hot gym, first day of summer cheer camp, that's me, offering it up. The words, true and real.

"There are people who say it isn't cool," I say, "who make fun of it, but I've never cared. I know they don't have what I have."

Sitting on the long mats, their fluffy faces, eyes cartoon-wide, they gaze up at me as though I were passing along all the wisdom of the world, which I am.

"Cheering has given me a purpose. It has given me a hard body and a strong mind. And I've made friends for life."

RiRi at my side, I walk the length of the mat, back straight, chin high.

"Don't you want to be able to say that?" I say. "If you do, you have to hang tight and tough with your girls."

They all nod, soundless.

"If you don't trust each other," I say, "this mat becomes your gangplank."

The hush falls even greater now. I'm swinging my whistle and all you can hear is the faint scratch of it as it brushes against my sweats.

Emily marches up beside me, her wounded leg back in fighting form, her mind swept clean of her Cassandra-like horrors. She is finished with all that. I know. I showed her how.

Lifting her elbow, she rests it on my shoulder, jaw up. She and RiRi, my deputies, my bad lieutenants.

"We've got five weeks before the new coach begins," I say, "but I choose not to waste those weeks. Do you?"

Clicking jaws, flipping ponytails, rocking in their Indian-style poses, their jelly legs waiting to be molded. Rescued from mediocrity. Saved.

"I choose to excel, not compete—do you?

"I choose to make changes, not excuses—do you?

"To be motivated, not manipulated.

"To be useful, not used."

Beth could come back this fall, couldn't she? Emily says. *She's at home, she took her finals, I even saw her in her car.*

But I know she never will. She never will and I took something from her and I won't even look at it. I won't—

"I choose to live by choice," I say, "not by chance—do you?"

Their fingers twisting into each other's linking hands, looking up at me, at RiRi and her magnificent body, and Emily and her beatific grin. All of us.

"Cheer taught me to trust my girls to catch me when I fall," I say, *and it's Beth's face I see when I gaze past them, into the empty stands, not Coach's. It's Beth's face, all the darkness and mischief and mayhem and, beneath it, that beating heart.*

Turning from the stands, facing my girls, I gather everything in my chest. I hold it there. I have to hold it tight. These things I've learned—

"It showed me," I say, pulling in my breath, "how to be a leader."

tarmės plote atsirado acc. pl. f. formos *baltúosius* 'baltąsias', *túos* 'tas', plg. *bált's* 'baltus' ir 'baltas'.

Naujadarinė dviskaitos galūnė -*ʊ*, kaip jau buvo nurodyta, šalia savęs vietomis turi variantą -*u*, kuris gali būti dedamas visų kamienų moteriškosios giminės vardažodžiams. Galimas daiktas, kad galūnę -*u* palaiko tokių instr. sing. formų, kaip *pelù* 'pele' (su *ā* kamieno galūne vietoj senesnės -*ʊ*), buvimas šalia nom.–acc. du. tipo *dvì pelù* (prie varianto *dvì pelʊ*), juoba kad rytų Lietuvoje *ā* ir *lė* paradigmų sąveika labai stipri, plg. acc. sing. tipą *pẽlų* 'pelę' (-*ų* iš -*ą*), instr. sing. *pelù* 'pele' (-*u* iš *-ą̃*), debeikiškių loc. sing. *žolõj* 'žolėje', ill. sing. *žolõn* 'žolėn', instr. pl. *žolõm* 'žolėmis', loc. pl. *žolos* 'žolėse' arba įvairiose šnektose paplitusias *lė*-kamienes kai kurių *lā* kamieno daiktavardžių formas (*balẽ* 'bala', *ganyklẽ* 'ganykla', *ylẽ* 'yla', *mokyklẽ* 'mokykla' ir kt.)[6].

Dėl tokios sąveikos, suprantamas daiktas, vienur kitur pagal nom.–acc. du. gretimines formas *dvì pelù* ‖ *pelʊ* galėjo ir šalia *dvì šakù* atsirasti variantas *dvì šakʊ*. Vieną tokį pavyzdį nurodo D. Gargasaitė iš Truskavõs apylinkių: *dvi lóvʊ* (*lŏ́vʊ*)[7]. Tačiau tokios formos, matyt, iš tikrųjų yra nepaprastai retos.

Išnašos

1. D. Gargasaitė, „Lietuvių kalbos diaktavardžio dviskaita". *Lietuvių kalbos morfologinė sandara ir jos raida* (= LKK VII), Vilnius, 1964, 136.

2. Plg. *Lietuvių dainos ir giesmės šiaur-rytinėje Lietuvoje* Dr. A. R. Niemi ir kun. A. Sabaliausko surinktos (Annales Academiae scientiarum Fennicae. Ser. B. Tom. VI, 1911) Nr. 346 (Vabalninkas), Nr. 1058 (Biržai).

3. P. Arumaa, *Untersuchungen zur Geschichte der litauischen Personalpronomina*, Tartu, 1933, 72.

4. Žr. Z. Zinkevičius, *Lietuvių dialektologija*, Vilnius, 1966, 159, 162.

5. Apie dat. sing. galūnės -*um* paplitimą bei vartojimą ypatybes žr. Z. Zinkevičius, min. veik., p. 248 (§ 374).

6. Daugiau pavyzdžių žr. Z. Zinkevičius, min. veik., 228–229.

7. D. Gargasaitė, min. veik., 135.

Concerning an Inflection of Dual in Eastern Lithuanian

In some eastern dialects of Lithuanian the Nom. and Acc. Du. inflection is -*ʊ*, instead of the expected phonetically regular -*i* in the *ē*-stem-nouns, in which -*ė*- is preceded by *l*, e.g.: *dvì avełʊ, kiaułʊ, pelʊ*. The ending -*ʊ* cannot be derived from -*i*.

The analysis of the dialectal paradigm shows that conditions for the appearance of -ъ were created by the merger of the Instr. Sg. form with those of Nom. and Acc. Du., cf. *su katì* (Standard Lith. *su katè*) and *dvì katì*. The Instr. Sg. ending of the *pelẽ*-type nouns (with *l*) developed into -ъ in the dialect, e.g.: *su pelừ*. When the relationship

Instr. Sg.		Nom. and Acc. Du.
(*su*) *katì*	:	(*dvì*) *katì*
(*su*) *pelừ*	:	(*dvì*) *pelì*

arose, (*dvì*) *pelì* was ousted by (*dvì*) *pelừ* to regularize the paradigm.

The article also deals with some other cases of paradigmatic interdependence of the *katẽ*-and-*pelẽ*-type nouns and the dialectal variant forms *dvì šakừ* and *dvì šakъ*.

РУССКАЯ РУЛЕТКА

RUSSIAN ROULETTE
ANTHONY HOROWITZ

WALKER
BOOKS

First published 2013 by Walker Books Ltd
87 Vauxhall Walk, London SE11 5HJ

2 4 6 8 10 9 7 5 3 1

Text © 2013 Stormbreaker Productions Ltd
Cover design by Walker Books Ltd
Trademarks Alex Rider™; Boy with Torch Logo™
© 2013 Stormbreaker Productions Ltd

This book has been typeset in Officina Sans

Printed and bound in Great Britain by Clays Ltd, St Ives plc

British Library Cataloguing in Publication Data:
a catalogue record for this book
is available from the British Library

ISBN 978-1-4063-5050-0

www.walker.co.uk

For J, N & C – but not L.
Full circle.

CONTENTS

BEFORE THE KILL

He had chosen the hotel room very carefully.

As he crossed the reception area towards the lifts, he was aware of everyone around him. Two receptionists, one on the phone. A Japanese guest checking in ... from his accent, obviously from Miyazaki in the south. A concierge printing a map for a couple of tourists. A security man, Eastern European, bored, standing by the door. He saw everything. If the lights had suddenly gone out, or if he had closed his eyes, he would have been able to continue forward at exactly the same pace.

Nobody noticed him. It was actually a skill, something he had learned, the art of not being seen. Even the clothes he wore – expensive jeans, a grey cashmere jersey and a loose coat – had been chosen because it made no statement at all. They were well-known brands but he had cut out the labels. In the unlikely event that he was stopped by the police, it would be very difficult for them to know where the outfit had been bought.

He was in his thirties but looked younger. He had fair hair, cut short, and ice-cold eyes with just the faintest trace of blue. He was not large or well built but there was a sort of sleekness about him. He moved like an athlete – perhaps a sprinter approaching the starting blocks – but there was a sense of danger about him, a feeling that you should leave well alone. He carried three credit cards and a driving licence, issued in Swansea, all with the name Matthew Reddy. A police check would have established that he was a personal trainer, that he worked in a London gym and lived in Brixton. None of this was true. His real name was Yassen Gregorovich. He had been a professional assassin for almost half his life.

The hotel was in King's Cross, an area of London with no attractive shops, few decent restaurants and where nobody really stays any longer than they have to. It was called The Traveller and it was part of a chain; comfortable but not too expensive. It was the sort of place that had no regular clients. Most of the guests were passing through on business and it would be their companies that paid the bill. They drank in the bar. They ate the "full English breakfast" in the brightly lit Beefeater restaurant. But they were too busy to socialize and it was unlikely they would return. Yassen preferred it that way. He could have stayed in central London, in the

Ritz or the Dorchester, but he knew that the receptionists there were trained to remember the faces of the people who passed through the revolving doors. Such personal attention was the last thing he wanted.

A CCTV camera watched him as he approached the lifts. He was aware of it, blinking over his left shoulder. The camera was annoying but inevitable. London has more of these devices than any city in Europe, and the police and secret service have access to all of them. Yassen made sure he didn't look up. If you look at a camera, that is when it sees you. He reached the lifts but ignored them, slipping through a fire door that led to the stairs. He would never think of confining himself in a small space, a metal box with doors that he couldn't open, surrounded by strangers. That would be madness. He would have walked fifteen storeys if it had been necessary – and when he reached the top he wouldn't even have been out of breath. Yassen kept himself in superb condition, spending two hours in the gym every day when that luxury was available to him, working out on his own when it wasn't.

His room was on the second floor. He had thoroughly checked the hotel on the Internet before he made his reservation and number 217 was one of just four rooms that exactly met his demands. It was too high up to be reached from the street but low enough for him to jump out of the window if he had to – after shooting out the glass. It was not overlooked. There were other buildings around but any form of surveillance would be difficult. When Yassen went to bed, he never closed the curtains. He liked to see out, to watch for any movement in the street. Every city has a natural rhythm and anything that breaks it – a man lingering on a corner or a car passing the same way twice – might warn him that it was time to leave at once. And he never slept for more than four hours, not even in the most comfortable bed.

A DO NOT DISTURB sign hung in front of him as he turned the corner and approached the door. Had it been obeyed? Yassen reached into his trouser pocket and took out a small silver device, about the same size and shape as a pen. He pressed one end, covering the handle with a thin spray of diazafluoren – a simple chemical reagent. Quickly, he spun the pen round and pressed the other end, activating a fluorescent light. There were no fingerprints. If anyone had been into the room since he had left, they had wiped the handle clean. He put the pen away, then knelt down and checked the bottom of the door. Earlier in the day, he had placed a single hair across the crack. It was one of the oldest warning signals in the book but that didn't stop it being effective. The hair was still in place. Yassen straightened up and, using his electronic pass key, went in.

It took him less than a minute to ascertain that

everything was exactly as he had left it. His brief-case was 4.6 centimetres from the edge of the desk. His suitcase was positioned at a 95 degree angle from the wall. There were no fingerprints on either of the locks. He removed the digital tape recorder that had been clipped magnetically to the side of his service fridge and glanced at the dial. Nothing had been recorded. Nobody had been in. Many people would have found all these precau-tions annoying and time-consuming but for Yassen they were as much a part of his daily routine as tying his shoelaces or cleaning his teeth.

It was twelve minutes past six when he sat down at the desk and opened his computer, an ordinary Apple MacBook. His password had seventeen digits and he changed it every month. He took off his watch and laid it on the surface beside him. Then he went to eBay, left-clicked on Collectibles and scrolled through Coins. He soon found what he was looking for: a gold coin show-ing the head of the emperor Caligula with the date AD11. There had been no bids for this par-ticular coin because, as any collector would know, it did not in fact exist. In AD11, the mad Roman emperor, Caligula, had not even been born. The entire website was a fake and looked it. The name of the coin dealer – Mintomatic – had been specially chosen to put off any casual purchaser. Mintomatic was supposedly based in Shanghai and did not have Top-rated Seller status. All the coins it advertised were either fake or valueless.

Yassen sat quietly until a quarter past six. At exactly the moment that the second hand passed over the twelve on his watch, he pressed the button to place a bid, then entered his User ID – false, of course – and password. Finally, he entered a bid of £2,518.15. The figures were based on the day's date and the exact time. He pressed ENTER and a window opened that had nothing to do with eBay or with Roman coins. Nobody else could have seen it. It would have been impossible to discover where it had originated. The message had been bounced around a dozen countries, travelling through an anonymity network, before it had reached him. This is known as onion routing because of its many layers. It had also passed through an encrypted tunnel, a secure shell, that ensured that only Yassen could read what had been written. If someone had managed to arrive at the same screen by accident, they would have seen only nonsense and within three seconds a virus would have entered their computer and obliterated the motherboard. The Apple computer, however, had been authorized to receive the message and Yassen saw three words:

KILL ALEX RIDER

They were exactly what he had expected.

Yassen had known all along that his employers would insist on punishing the agent who had been involved in the disaster that the Stormbreaker operation had become. He even wondered if he himself might not be made to retire ... permanently, of course. It was simple common sense. If people failed, they were eliminated. There were no second chances. Yassen was lucky in that he had been employed as a subcontractor. He didn't have overall responsibility for what had happened and at the end of the day he couldn't be blamed. On the other hand, they would have to make an example of Alex Rider. It didn't matter that he was just fourteen years old. Tomorrow he would have to die.

Yassen looked at the screen for a few seconds more, then closed the computer. He had never killed a child before but the thought did not particularly trouble him. Alex Rider had made his own choices. He should have been at school, but instead, for whatever reason, he had allowed the Special Operations Division of MI6 to recruit him. From schoolboy to spy. It was certainly unusual – but the truth was, he had been remarkably successful. Beginner's luck, maybe, but he had brought an end to an operation that had been several years in the planning. He was responsible for the deaths of two operatives. He had annoyed some extremely powerful people. He very much deserved the death that was coming his way.

And yet...

Yassen sat where he was with the computer in front of him. Nothing had changed in his expression but there was, perhaps, something flickering deep in his eyes. Outside, the sun was beginning to set, the evening sky turning a hard, unforgiving grey. The streets were full of commuters hurrying home. They weren't just on the other side of a hotel window. They were in another world. Yassen knew that he would never be one of them. Briefly, he closed his eyes. He was thinking about what had happened. About Stormbreaker. How had it gone so wrong?

From Yassen's point of view, it had been a fairly routine assignment. A Lebanese businessman by the name of Herod Sayle had wanted to buy two hundred litres of a deadly smallpox virus called R5 and he had approached the one organization that might be able to supply it in such huge quantities. That organization was Scorpia. The letters of the name stood for sabotage, corruption, intelligence and assassination, which were its main activities. R5 was a Chinese product, manufactured illegally in a facility near Guiyang, and by chance one of the members of the executive board of Scorpia was Chinese. Dr Three had extensive contacts in East Asia and had used his influence to organize the purchase. It had been Yassen's job to oversee delivery to the UK.

Six weeks ago, he had flown to Hong Kong a few days ahead of the R5, which had been transported in a private plane, a turboprop Xian MA60, from Guiyang. The plan was to load it into a container ship to Rotterdam – disguised as part of a shipment of Luck of the Dragon Chinese beer. Special barrels had been constructed at a warehouse in Kowloon, with reinforced glass containers holding the R5 suspended inside the liquid. There are more than five thousand container ships at sea at any one time and around seventeen million deliveries are made every year. There isn't a customs service in the world that can keep its eye on every cargo and Yassen was confident that the journey would be trouble-free. He'd been given a false passport and papers that identified him as Erik Olsen, a merchant seaman from Copenhagen, and he would travel with the R5 until it reached its destination.

But, as is so often the way, things had not gone as planned. A few days before the barrels were due to leave, Yassen had become aware that the warehouse was under surveillance. He had been lucky. A cigarette being lit behind a window in a building that should have been empty told him all he needed to know. Slipping through Kowloon under cover of darkness, he had identified a team of three agents of the AIVD – the Algemene Inlichtingen en Veiligheidsdienst – the Dutch secret service. There must have been a tip-off. The agents did not know what they were looking for but they were aware that something was on its way to their country and Yassen had been forced to kill all three of them with a silenced Beretta 92, a pistol he particularly favoured because of its accuracy and reliability. Clearly, the R5 could not leave in a container ship after all. A fallback had to be found.

As it happened, there was a Chinese Han class nuclear submarine in Hong Kong going through final repairs before leaving for exercises in the Northern Atlantic. Yassen met the captain in a private club overlooking the harbour and offered him a bribe of two million American dollars to carry the R5 with him when he left. He had informed Scorpia of this decision and they knew that it would dig into their operational profit but there were at least some advantages. Moving the R5 from Rotterdam to the UK would have been difficult and dangerous. Herod Sayle was based in Cornwall with direct access to the coast, so the new approach would make for a much more secure delivery.

Two weeks later, on a crisp, cloudless night in April, the submarine surfaced off the Cornish coast. Yassen, still using the identity of Erik Olsen, had travelled with it. He had quite enjoyed the experience of cruising silently through the depths of the ocean, sealed in a metal tube. The Chinese crew had been ordered not to speak to him on any account and that suited him too. It was only when he climbed onto dry land that he once again took command, overseeing the transfer of the virus and other supplies that Herod Sayle had ordered. The work had to be done swiftly. The captain of the submarine had insisted that he would wait no more than thirty minutes. He might have two million dollars in a Swiss bank account but he had no wish to provoke an international incident ... which would certainly have been followed by his own court martial and execution.

Thirty guards had helped carry the various boxes to the waiting trucks, scrambling along the shoreline in the light of a perfect half-moon, the submarine looking somehow fantastic and out of place, half submerged in the slate-grey water of the English Channel. And almost from the start, Yassen had known something was wrong. He was being watched. He was sure of it. Some might call it a sort of animal instinct but for Yassen it was simpler than that. He had been active in the field for many years. During that time, he had been in danger almost constantly. It had been necessary to fine-tune all his senses simply to survive. And although he hadn't seen or heard anything, a silent voice was screaming at him that there was someone hiding about twenty metres away, behind a cluster of boulders on the edge of the beach.

He had been on the point of investigating when one of Sayle's men, standing on the wooden jetty, had dropped one of the boxes. The sound of metal hitting wood shattered the calm of the night and Yassen spun on his heel, everything else forgotten. There was limited space on the submarine and so the R5 had been transferred from the beer barrels to less-protective aluminium boxes. Yassen knew that if the glass vial inside had been shattered, if the rubber seal had been compromised, everyone on the beach would be dead before the sun had risen.

He sprinted forward, crouching down to inspect the damage. There was a slight dent in one side of the box. But the seal had held.

The guard looked at him with a sickly smile. He was quite a lot older than Yassen, probably an ex-convict recruited from a local prison. And he was scared. He tried to make light of it. "I won't do that again!" he said.

"No," Yassen replied. "You won't." The Beretta was already in his hand. He shot the man in the chest, propelling him backwards into the darkness and the sea below. It had been necessary to set an example. There would be no further clumsiness that night.

Sitting in the hotel with the computer in front of him, Yassen remembered the moment. He was almost certain now that it had been Alex Rider behind the boulder and if it hadn't been for the accident, he would have been discovered there and then. Alex had infiltrated Sayle Enterprises, pretending to be the winner of a magazine competition. Somehow he had slipped out of his room, evading the guards and the searchlights, and had joined the convoy making its way down to the beach. There could be no other explanation. Later on, Alex had followed Herod Sayle to London. He had already been responsible for the deaths of two of Sayle's associates – Nadia Vole and the disfigured servant Mr Grin – despite little training and no experience. This was his first mission. Even so, he had single-handedly smashed the Stormbreaker operation. Sayle had been lucky to escape, a few steps ahead of the police.

KILL ALEX RIDER

It was what he deserved. Alex had interfered with a Scorpia assignment and he would have cost the organization at least five million pounds ... the final payment owed by Herod Sayle. Worse than that, he would have damaged their international reputation. The lesson had to be learnt.

There was a knock at the door. Yassen had ordered room service. It wasn't just easier to eat inside the hotel, it was safer. Why make himself a target when he didn't need to?

"Leave it outside," he called out. He spoke English with no trace of a Russian accent. He spoke French, German and Arabic equally well.

The room was almost dark now. Yassen's dinner sat on a tray in the corridor, rapidly getting cold. But still he did not move away from the desk and the computer in front of him. He would kill Alex Rider tomorrow morning. There was no question of his disobeying orders. It didn't matter that the two of them were linked, that they were connected in a way Alex couldn't possibly know.

John Rider. Alex's father.

Their code names. Hunter and Cossack.

Yassen couldn't help himself. He reached into his pocket and took out a car key, the sort that had two remote control buttons to open and close the doors. But this key did not belong to any car. Yassen pressed the OPEN button twice and the CLOSE button three times and a concealed memory stick sprang out onto the palm of his hand. He glanced at it briefly. He knew that it was madness to carry it. He had been tempted to destroy it many times. But every man has his weakness and this was his. He opened the computer again and inserted it.

The file required another password. He keyed it in. And there it was on the screen in front of him, not in English letters but in Cyrillic, the Russian alphabet.

His personal diary. The story of his life.

He sat back and began to read.

ДОМА

"Yasha! We've run out of water. Go to the well!"

I can still hear my mother calling to me and it is strange to think of myself as a fourteen-year-old boy, a single child, growing up in a village six hundred miles from Moscow. I can see myself, stick-thin with long, fair hair and blue eyes that always look a little startled. Everyone tells me that I am small for my age and they urge me to eat more protein ... as if I can ever get my hands on anything that resembles fresh meat or fish. I have not yet spent many hundreds of hours working out and my muscles are undeveloped. I am sprawled out in the living room, watching the only television we have in the house. It's a huge, ugly box with a picture that often wavers and trembles and there are hardly any channels to choose from. To make things worse, the electricity supply is unreliable and you can be fairly sure that the moment you get interested in a film or a news programme, the image will suddenly flicker and die and you'll be left alone, sitting in the dark. But whenever I can, I tune into a documentary, which I devour. It is my only window onto the outside world.

I am describing Russia – about ten years before the end of the twentieth century. It is not so long ago and yet it is already somewhere that no longer exists. The changes that began in the main cities became a tsunami that engulfed the entire country, although they took their time reaching the village where I lived. There was no running water in any of the houses and so, three times a day, I had to make my way down to the well with a wooden harness over my shoulders and two metal buckets dragging down my arms. I sound like a peasant and a lot of the time I must have looked like one, dressed in a baggy shirt with no collar and a waistcoat. As a matter of fact, I had one pair of American jeans, which had been sent to me as a present from a relative in Moscow, and I can still remember everyone staring at me when I put them on. Jeans! They were like something from a distant planet. And my name was Yasha, not Yassen. Quite by accident, it got changed.

If I am going to explain what happened to me and what I became, then I must begin here, in Estrov. Nobody speaks of it any more. It is not on the map. According to the Russian authorities, it never existed. But I remember it well; a village of about eighty wooden houses surrounded by farmland with a church, a shop, a police station, a bathhouse and a river that was bright blue in the summer but freezing all year round. A single road ran through the middle of the village but it was hardly needed, as there were very few cars. Our neighbour, Mr Vladimov, had a tractor which often rumbled past, billowing oily, black smoke, but I was more used to being woken up by the sound of horses' hooves. The village was wedged between thick forest in the north and hills to the south and west so that the view never really changed. Sometimes I would see planes flying overhead and I thought of the people inside them, travelling to the other side of the world. If I was working in the garden, I would stand still and watch them – the wings blinking, the sunlight glinting on their metal skin – until they had gone out of sight, leaving only the echo of their engines behind. They reminded of me who and what I was. Estrov was my world and I certainly didn't need an aeroplane to get from one side to the other.

My own home, where I lived with my parents, was small and simple, made of painted wooden boards with shutters on either side of the windows and a weather vane that squeaked all night if there was too much wind. It was quite close to the church, set back from the main road with similar houses on either side. Flowers and brambles grew right beside the walls and were slowly creeping towards the roof. There were just four rooms. My parents slept upstairs. I had a room at the back but I had to share it whenever anyone came to stay. My grandmother, who lived with us, had the room next to mine but she preferred to sleep in a sort of hole in the wall, above the stove, in the kitchen. She was a very small, dark brown woman and when I was young, I used to think that she had been cooked by the flames.

There was no railway station in Estrov. It was not considered important enough. Nor was there a bus service or anything like that. I went to school in a slightly larger village that liked to think of itself as a town, two miles away down a track that was dusty and full of potholes in the summer, and thick with mud or covered in snow during the winter. The town was called Rosna. I walked there every day, no matter what the weather, and I was beaten if I was late. My school was a big, square, brick building on three floors. All the classrooms were the same size. There were about five hundred children in all, boys and girls. Some of them travelled in by train, pouring out onto the platform with eyes that were still half-closed with sleep. Rosna did have a railway station and they were very proud of it, decking it with flowers on public holidays. But actually it was a mean, run-down little place and nine out of ten trains didn't even bother to stop there.

We students were all very smart. The girls wore black dresses with green aprons and had their hair tied back with ribbons. The boys looked like little soldiers, with grey uniforms and red scarves tied around our neck, and if we did well with our studies, we were given badges with slogans – "For Active Work", "School Leader", that sort of thing. I don't really remember much of what I learned at school. Who does? History was important ... the history of Russia, of course. We were always learning poems by heart and had to recite them, standing to attention beside our desks. There was maths and science. Most of the teachers were women but our headmaster was a man called Lavrov and he had a furious temper. He was short but he had huge shoulders and long arms, and I would often see him pick up a boy by the throat and pin him against the wall.

"You're not doing well, Leo Tretyakov!" he would boom. "I'm sick of the sight of you. Buck up your ideas or get out of here!"

Even the teachers were terrified of him. But actually, he was a good man at heart. In Russia, we were brought up to respect our teachers and it never occurred to me that his titanic rages were anything unusual.

I was very happy at school and I did well. We had a star system – every two weeks the teachers gave us a grade – and I was always a five-star student, what we called a *pyatiorka*. My best subjects were physics and maths, and these were very important to the Russian authorities. Nobody ever let you forget that we were the country that had sent the first man – Yuri Gargarin – into space. There was even a photograph of him in the front entrance and you were supposed to salute him as you came in. I was also good at sport and I remember how the girls in my class used to come along and cheer me when I scored a goal. I wasn't all that interested in girls at this time, which is to say I was happy to chat to them but I didn't particularly want to hang out with them after school. My best friend was the Leo that I just mentioned and the two of us were inseparable.

Leo Tretyakov was short and skinny with jutting out ears, freckles and ginger hair. He used to joke that he was the ugliest boy in the district and I found it hard to disagree. He was also far from bright. He was a two-star student, a dismal *dvoyka* and he was always getting into trouble with the teachers. In the end they actually gave up punishing him because it didn't seem to make any difference and he just sat there quietly daydreaming at the back of the class. But at the same time he was the star of our NVP – military training – classes which were compulsory throughout the school. Leo could strip down an AK47 automatic machine gun in twelve seconds and reassemble it in fifteen. He was a great shot. And twice a year there were military games, when we had to compete with other schools using a map and a compass to find our way through the woods. Leo was always in charge. And we always won.

I liked Leo because he was afraid of nothing and he always made me laugh. We did everything together. We would eat our sandwiches in the yard, washed down with a gulp of vodka that he had stolen from home and brought to school in one of his mother's old perfume bottles. We smoked cigarettes in the woodland close to the main building, coughing horribly because the tobacco was so rough. Our school toilets had no compartments and we often sat next to each other doing what we had to do, which may sound disgusting but that was the way it was. You were meant to bring your own toilet paper too, but Leo always forgot and I would watch him guiltily tearing pages out of his exercise books. He was always losing his homework that way. But with Leo's homework – and he'd have been the first to admit it – that was probably all it was worth.

The best time we had together was in the summer, when we would go for endless bicycle rides, rattling along the country roads, shooting down hills and pedalling backwards furiously, which was the only way to stop. Everyone had exactly the same model of bicycle and they were all death traps with no suspension, no lights and no brakes. We had nowhere to go but in a way that was the fun of it. We used our imagination to create a world of wolves and vampires, ghosts and Cossack warriors – and we chased each other right through the middle of them. When we finally got back to the village, we would swim in the river, even though there were parasites in the water that could make you sick, and we always went to the bathhouse together, thrashing each other with birch leaves in the steam room which was meant to be good for your skin.

Leo's parents worked in the same factory as mine, although my father, who had once studied at Moscow State University, was the more senior of the two. The factory employed about two hundred people, who were collected by coaches from Estrov, Rosna and lots of other places. I have to say, the place was a source of constant puzzlement to me. Why was it tucked away in the middle of nowhere? Why had I never seen it? There was a barbed wire fence surrounding it and armed militia standing at the gate, and that didn't make sense either. All it produced was pesticides and other chemicals used by farmers. But when I asked my parents about it, they always changed the subject. Leo's father was the transportation manager, in charge of the coaches. My father was a research chemist. My mother worked in the main office doing paperwork. That was about as much as I knew.

At the end of a summer afternoon, Leo and I would often sit close to the river and we would talk about our future. The truth was that just about everyone wanted to leave Estrov. Outside work, there was nothing to do and half the people who lived there were perpetually drunk. I'm not making it up. During the winter months, they weren't allowed to open the village shop before ten o'clock in the morning or people would rush in as soon as it was light to buy their vodka; and during December and January, it wasn't unusual to see some of the local farmers flat on their backs, half covered with snow and probably half dead too after downing a whole bottle. We were all being left behind in a fast-changing world. Why my parents had ever chosen to come here was another mystery.

Leo didn't care if he ended up working in the factory like everyone else but I had other ambitions. For reasons that I couldn't explain, I'd always thought that I was different from everyone else. Maybe it was the fact that my father had once been a professor in a big university and that he had himself experienced life outside the village. But when I was watching those planes disappear into the distance, I always thought they were trying to tell me something. I could be on one of them. There was a whole life outside Estrov that I might one day explore.

Although I had never told anyone else except Leo, I dreamt of becoming a helicopter pilot – maybe in the army but if not, in air-sea rescue. I had seen a programme about it on television and for some reason it had caught hold of my imagination. I devoured everything I could about helicopters. I borrowed books from the school library. I cut out articles in magazines. By the time I was thirteen, I knew the name of almost every moving part of a helicopter. I knew how it used all the different forces and controls, working in opposition to each other to fly. The only thing I had never done was sit in one.

"Do you think you'll ever leave?" Leo asked me one evening, the two of us sprawled out in the long grass, sharing a cigarette. "Go and live in a city with your own flat and a car?"

"How am I supposed to do that?"

"You're clever. You can go to Moscow. Learn how to become a pilot."

I shook my head. Leo was my best friend. Whatever I might secretly think, I would never talk about the two of us being apart. "I don't think my parents would let me. Anyway, why would I want to leave? This is my home."

"Estrov is a dump."

"No, it's not." I looked at the river, the fast-flowing water chasing over the rocks, the surrounding woodland, the muddy track that led through the centre of the village. In the distance, I could see the steeple of St Nicholas. The village had no priest. The church was closed; but its shadow stretched out almost to our front door and I had always thought of it as part of my childhood. Maybe Leo was right. There wasn't very much to the place, but even so, it was my home. "I'm happy here," I said and at that moment I believed it.

"It's not such a bad place."

I remember saying those words. I can still smell the smoke coming from a bonfire somewhere on the other side of the village. I can hear the water rippling. I see Leo, twirling a piece of grass between his fingers. Our bicycles are lying, one on top of the other. There are a few puffs of cloud in the sky, floating lazily past. A fish suddenly breaks the surface of the river and I see its scales glimmer silver in the sunlight. It is a warm afternoon at the start of October. And in twenty-four hours everything will have changed. Estrov will no longer exist.

When I got home, my mother was already making the dinner. Food was a constant subject of conversation in our village because there was so little of it and everyone grew their own. We were lucky. As well as a vegetable patch, we had a dozen chickens, which were all good layers so (unless the neighbours crept in and stole them) we always had plenty of eggs. She was making a stew with potatoes, turnips and tinned tomatoes that had turned up the week before in the shop and that had sold out instantly. It was exactly the same meal as we'd had the night before. She would serve it with slabs of black bread and, of course, small tumblers of vodka. I had been drinking vodka since I was nine years old.

My mother was a slender woman with bright blue eyes and hair which must have once been as blond as mine but which was already grey, even though she was only in her thirties. She wore it tied back so that I could see the curve of her neck. She was always pleased to see me and she always took my side. There was that time, for example, when Leo and I were almost arrested for letting off bombs outside the police station. We had got up at first light and dug holes in the ground which we'd filled up with drawing pins and the gunpowder stripped from about five hundred matches. Then we'd sneaked behind the wall of the churchyard and watched. It was two hours before the first police car drove over our booby trap and set it off. There was a bang. The front tyre was shredded and the car lost control and drove through a bush. The two of us nearly died laughing, but I wasn't so happy when I got home and found Yelchin, the police chief, in my front room. He asked me where I'd been and when I said I'd been running an errand for my mother, she backed me up, even though she knew I was lying. Later on, she scolded me but I know that she was secretly amused.

In our household, my mother and my grand-mother did most of the talking. My father was a very thoughtful man who looked exactly like the scientist that he was, with greying hair, a serious sort of face and glasses. He lived in Estrov but his heart was still in Moscow. He kept all his old books around him and when letters came from the city, he would disappear to read them and at dinner he would be miles away. Why did I never question him more? I ask myself that now but I suppose nobody ever does. When you are young, you accept your parents for what they are and you believe the stories they tell you.

Conversation at dinner was often difficult because my parents didn't like to discuss their work at the factory and there was only so much I could tell them about my day at school. As for my grandmother, she had somehow got stuck in the past, twenty years ago, and much of what she said didn't connect with reality at all. But that night was different. Apparently there had been an accident, a fire at the factory ... nothing serious. My father was worried and for once he spoke his mind.

"It's these new investors," he said. "All they think about is money. They want to increase production and to hell with safety measures. Today it was just the generator plant. But suppose it had been one of the laboratories?"

"You should talk to them," my mother said.

"They won't listen to me. They're pulling the strings from Moscow and they've got no idea." He threw back his vodka and swallowed it in one gulp. "That's the new Russia for you, Eva. We all get wiped out and as long as they get their cheque, they don't give a damn."

This all struck me as insane. There couldn't be any real danger, not here in Estrov. How could the production of fertilizers and pesticides do anyone any harm?

My mother seemed to agree. "You worry too much," she said.

"We should never have gone along with this. We should never have been part of it." My father refilled his glass. He didn't drink as much as a lot of the people in the village but, like them, he used vodka to draw down the shutters between him and the rest of the world. "The sooner we get out of here, the better. We've been here long enough."

"The swans are back," my grandmother said. "They're so beautiful at this time of the year."

There were no swans in the village. As far as I knew, there never had been.

"Are we really going to leave?" I asked. "Can we go and live in Moscow?"

My mother reached out and put her hand on mine. "Maybe one day, Yasha. And you can go to university, just like your father. But you have to work hard..."

The next day was a Sunday and I had no school. On the other hand, the factory never closed and both my parents had drawn the weekend shift, working until four and leaving me to clean the house and take my grandmother her lunch. Leo looked in after breakfast but we both had a lot of homework, so we agreed to meet down at the river at six and perhaps kick a ball around with some other boys. Just before midday I was lying on my bed, trying to plough my way through a chapter of *Crime and Punishment*, which was this huge Russian masterpiece we were all supposed to read. As Leo had said to me, none of us knew what our crime was, but reading the book was certainly a punishment. The story had begun with a murder but since then nothing had happened and there were about six hundred pages to go.

Anyway, I was lying there with my head close to the window, allowing the sun to slant in onto the pages. It was a very quiet morning. Even the chickens seemed to have abandoned their usual clucking and I was aware of only the ticks of the watch on my left wrist. It was a Pobeda with black numerals on a white face and fifteen jewels that had been made just after the Second World War and that had once belonged to my grandfather. I never took it off and over the years it had become part of me. I glanced at it and noticed the time: five minutes past twelve. And that was when I heard the explosion. Actually, I wasn't even sure it was an explosion. It sounded more like a paper bag being crumpled somewhere out of sight. I climbed off the bed and went and looked out of the open window. A few people were walking across the fields but otherwise there was nothing to see. I returned to the book. How could I have so quickly forgotten my parents' conversation from the night before?

I read another thirty pages. I suppose half an hour must have passed. And then I heard another sound – soft and far away but unmistakable all the same. It was gunfire, the sound of an automatic weapon being emptied. That was impossible. People went hunting in the woods sometimes, but not with machine guns, and there had never been any army exercises in the area. I looked out of the window a second time and saw smoke rising into the air on the other side of the hills to the south of Estrov. That was when I knew that none of this was my imagination. Something had happened. The smoke was coming from the factory.

I leapt off the bed, dropping the book, and ran down the stairs and out of the house. The village was completely deserted. Our chickens were strutting around on the front lawn of our house, pecking at the grass. There was a dog barking somewhere. Everything was ridiculously normal. But then I heard footsteps and looked up. Mr Vladimov, our neighbour, was running down from his front door, wiping his hands on a cloth.

"Mr Vladimov!" I called out to him. "What's happened?"

"I don't know," he wheezed back. He had probably been working on his tractor. He was covered in oil. "They've all gone to see. I'm going with them."

"What do you mean ... all of them?"

"The whole village! There's been some sort of accident!"

Before I could ask any more, he had disappeared down the muddy track.

He had no sooner gone than the alarm went off. It was extraordinary, deafening, like nothing I had ever heard before. It couldn't have been more urgent if war had broken out. And as the noise of it resounded in my head, I realized that it had to be coming from the factory, more than a mile away! How could it be so loud? Even the fire alarm at school had been nothing like this. It was a high-pitched siren that seemed to spread out from a single point until it was everywhere – behind the forest, over the hills, in the sky – and yet at the same time it was right next to me, in front of my house. I knew now that there had been another accident. I had heard it, of course, the explosion. But that had been half an hour ago. Why had they been so slow to raise the alarm?

The siren stopped. And in the sudden silence, the countryside, the village where I had spent my entire life, seemed to have become photographs of themselves and it was as if I was on the outside looking in. There was nobody around me. The dog had stopped barking. The chickens had scattered.

I heard the sound of an engine. A car came hurtling towards me, bumping over the track. The first thing I registered was that it was a black Lada. Then I took in the bullet holes all over the bodywork and the fact that the front windscreen was shattered. But it was only when it stopped that I saw the shocking truth.

My father was in the front seat. My mother was behind the wheel.

КРОКОДИЛЫ

CROCODILES

I didn't even know my mother could drive. We hardly ever saw any cars in Estrov because nobody could afford to buy one, and anyway, there wasn't anywhere to go. The black Lada probably belonged to one of the senior managers.

Not that I was thinking about these things just then. The driver's door opened and my mother got out. Straight away, I saw the fear in her eyes. She raised a hand in my direction, urging me to stay where I was, then ran round to the other side and helped my father out. He was wearing a loose white coat that flapped over his normal clothes, and I saw with a sense of horror that was like a pool of black water, sucking me in, that he had been hurt. The fabric was covered with his blood. His left arm hung limp. He was clutching his chest with his right hand. His face looked thin and pale and his eyes were empty, clouded by pain. My mother had her arm around him, helping him to walk. She at least had not been hurt but she still looked like someone who had escaped from a war zone. There were streaks running down her face. Her hair was wild. No boy should ever see his parents in this way. It is not natural. Everything I had always believed and taken for granted was instantly smashed.

The two of them reached me. My father could go no further and sank to the ground, resting his back against our garden fence. And all the time I had said nothing. There were a million questions I wanted to ask but the words simply would not reach my lips. Time seemed to have fragmented. The first explosion, the gunfire and the smoke, going downstairs, seeing the car ... they were like four separate incidents that could have taken place years apart. I needed them to explain it for me. Somehow, perhaps, they could make it all make sense.

"Yasha!" My father was the first to speak and it didn't sound like him at all. The pain was distorting his voice.

"What's happened? What is it? Who hurt you? You've been shot!" Once I had begun to speak I could barely stop, but I was making little sense.

My father reached out and grabbed hold of my arm. "I am so glad you're here. I was afraid you'd be out of the house. But you have to listen to us very carefully, Yasha. We have very little time."

"Yasha, my dear boy..." It was my mother who had spoken and suddenly there were tears coursing down her cheeks. It didn't matter what had happened at the factory. It was seeing me that had made her cry.

"I will try to explain to you," my father said. "But you can't argue with me. Do you understand that? You have to leave the village immediately."

"What? I'm not leaving! I'm not going anywhere."

"You have no choice. If you stay here, they'll kill you." His grip on me tightened. "They're already on their way. Do you understand? They'll be here. Very soon."

"Who? Why?"

My father was too weak, in too much pain to say anything more, so my mother took over.

"We never told you about the factory," she said. "We weren't allowed to. But it wasn't just that. We didn't want you to know. We were ashamed." She wiped her eyes, pulling herself together. "We were making chemicals and pesticides for farmers, like we always said. But we were also making other things. For the military."

"Weapons," my father said. "Chemical weapons. Do you understand what I mean?" I said nothing so he went on. "We had no choice, Yasha. Your mother and I got into trouble with the authorities a long time ago, when we were in Moscow, and we were sent out here. That was before you were born. It was all my fault. They stopped us from teaching. They threatened us. We had to earn a living and there was no other way."

The words were like a stampede of horses galloping through my head. I wanted them to stop, to slow down. Surely all that mattered was to get help for my father. The nearest hospital was miles away but there was a doctor in Rosna. It seemed to me that my father was getting weaker and that the blood was spreading.

But still they went on. "This morning there was an accident in the main laboratory," my mother explained. "And something was released into the air. We had already warned them it might happen. You heard us talking about it only last night. But they wouldn't listen. Making a profit was all that mattered to them. Well, it's over now. The whole village has been contaminated. We have been contaminated. We brought it with us in that car. Not that it would have made any difference. It's in the air. It's everywhere."

"What is? What are you talking about?"

"A form of anthrax." My mother spat out the words. "It's a sort of bacterium but it's been modified so that it's very contagious and acts very quickly. It could wipe out an army! And maybe we deserve this. We were responsible. We helped to make it..."

"Do it!" my father said. "Do it now!" With his free hand, he fumbled in his pocket and took out a metal box, about fifteen centimetres long. It was the sort of thing that might contain a pen.

My mother took it. Her eyes were still fixed on me. "As soon as we knew what had happened, our

43

first thoughts were for you," she said. "Nobody was allowed to leave the factory. That was the protocol. They had to keep us there, to contain us. But your father and I had already made plans ... just in case. We stole a car and we smashed through the perimeter fence. We had to reach you."

"The siren...?"

"That was nothing to do with the accident. They set it off afterwards. They saw we were trying to escape." She drew a breath. "The guards fired machine guns at us and they sounded the alarm. Your father was hit. We were so frightened we wouldn't be able to find you, that you wouldn't be at the house..."

"Thank God you're here!" my father said. He was still holding onto me. He was breathing with difficulty.

My mother opened the box. I didn't know what would be inside or why it was so important but when I looked down, I saw that it contained the last thing I had expected. There was some grey velvet padding and in the middle of that, a hypodermic syringe.

"For every weapon there has to be a defence," my mother went on. "We made a poison but we were also working on an antidote. This is it, Yasha. There was only a tiny amount of it but we stole it and we brought it to you. It will protect you..."

"No. I don't want it! You have it!"

"There isn't enough for us. This is all we have." My father's hand had tightened on my arm, pinning me down. He was using the very last of his strength. "Do it, Eva," he insisted.

My mother was holding the syringe up to the light, tapping it with her finger, examining the glass vial. She pressed the plunger with her thumb so that a bead of liquid appeared at the end of the needle. I began to struggle. I couldn't believe that she was about to inject me.

My father wouldn't let me move. As weak as he was, he kept me still while my mother closed in on me. It must be every child's nightmare to be attacked by his own parents and at that moment I forgot that everything they were doing was for my own good. They were saving me, not killing me, but that wasn't how it seemed to me. I can still see my mother's face, the cold determination as she brought the needle plunging down. She didn't even bother to roll up my shirt sleeve. The point went through the material and into my arm. It hurt. I think I actually felt the liquid, the antidote, coursing into my bloodstream. She pulled out the needle and dropped the empty hypodermic onto the ground. I looked down and saw more blood, my own, forming a circle on my sleeve.

My father let go of me. My mother closed her eyes for a moment. When she opened them again, she was smiling. "Yasha, my dearest," she said. "We don't mind what happens to us. Can you understand that? Right now, you're all we care about. You're all that matters."

The three of us stood there for a moment. We were like actors in a play who had run out of lines. We were breathless, shocked by the violence of what had taken place. It was like being in some sort of waking dream. We were surrounded by silence. Smoke was still rising slowly above the hills. And the village was still completely empty. There was nobody in sight.

It was my father who began again. "You have to go into the house," he said. "You need to take some clothes with you and any food you can find. Look in the kitchen cupboard and put it all in your backpack. Get a torch and a compass. But, most important of all, there is a metal box in the kitchen. You know where it is ... beside the fire. Bring it out to me." I hesitated so he went on, putting all his authority into his voice. "If you are not out of the village in five minutes, Yasha, you will die with us. Even with the antidote. The government will not allow anyone to tell what has happened here. They will hunt you down and they will kill you. If you want to live, you must do as we say."

Did I want to live? Right then, I wasn't even sure. But I knew that I couldn't let my parents down, not after everything they had done to reach me. Not daring to speak, my mother silently implored me. I could feel my throat burning – I reeled away and staggered into the house. My father was still sitting on the ground with his legs stretched out in front of him. Looking back, I saw my mother go over and kneel beside him.

Almost tripping over myself, I ran across the garden and through the front door. I went straight up to my bedroom and, in a daze, pulled out the uniform I had worn on camping trips with the Young Pioneers, our Russian scouting organization. I had been given a dark green anorak and waterproof trousers. I wasn't sure whether to carry them or to wear them, but in the end I pulled them on over my ordinary clothes. I quickly put on my leather boots, which were still covered in dried mud and took my backpack, a torch and a compass from under the bed. I looked around me, at the pictures on the wall – a football club, various helicopters, a photograph of the world taken from outer space. The book that I had been reading was on the floor. My school clothes were folded on a chair. I could not accept that I was leaving all this behind, that I would never see any of it again.

I went downstairs. Every house in the village had its own special hiding place and ours was in the wall beside the stove. There were two loose bricks and I pulled them out to reveal a hollow opening with a tin box inside. I grabbed it and took it with me. As I straightened up, I noticed my grandmother, still standing at the sink, peeling potatoes, with her apron tied tightly around her waist.

She beamed at me. "I can't remember when there's been a better harvest," she said. She had absolutely no idea what was going on.

I went over to a cupboard and shoved some tins, tea, sugar, a box of matches and two bars of chocolate into my backpack. I filled a glass with water I had taken from the well. Finally, I kissed my grandmother quickly on the side of the head and hurried out, leaving her to her work.

The sky had darkened while I was in the house. How could that have happened? It had only been a few minutes, surely? But now it looked as though it was going to rain, perhaps one of those violent downpours we often had during the months leading up to winter. My father was sitting where I had left him and seemed to be asleep. His hand was clutched across the wound in his chest. I wanted to carry the tin box over to him but my mother moved round and stood in my way. I held out the glass of water.

"I got this. For Father."

"That's good of you, Yasha. But he doesn't need it."

"But..."

"No, Yasha. Try to understand."

It took a few moments for the significance of what she was saying to sink in and at once a trap-door opened and I plunged through it, into a world of pain.

My mother took the box and lifted the lid. Inside there was a roll of banknotes – a hundred rubles, more money than I had ever seen. My parents must have been saving it from their salaries, planning for the day when they returned to Moscow. But that wasn't going to happen, not now. She gave it all to me along with my internal passport, a document that everyone in Russia was required to own, even if you didn't travel. Finally she took out a small, black velvet bag and handed it to me too.

"That is everything, Yasha," she said. "You have to go."

"Mother..." I began. I felt huge tears swell up in my eyes and the burning in my throat was worse than ever.

"You heard what your father said. Now, listen very carefully. You have to go to Moscow. I know it's a long way away and you've never travelled on your own but you can make it. You can take the train. Not from Rosna. They'll be checking everyone at the station. Go to Kirsk. You can reach it through the forest. That's the safest way. Find the new highway and follow it. Do you understand?"

I nodded, miserably.

"You remember Kirsk. You've been there a few times. There's a station with trains every day to Moscow ... one in the morning, one in the evening. Take the evening train, when it's dark. If anyone asks you, say you're visiting an uncle. Never tell anyone you came from Estrov. Never use that word again. Promise me that."

"Where will I go in Moscow?" I asked. I didn't want to leave. I wanted to stay with her.

She reached out and took me in her arms, hugging me against her. "Don't be scared, Yasha. We have a good friend in Moscow. He's a biology professor. He worked with your father and you'll find him at the university. His name is Misha Dementyev. I'll try to telephone him but I expect they'll have cut the lines. It doesn't matter. When you tell him who you are, he'll look after you."

Misha Dementyev. I clung onto the two words, my only lifeline.

My mother was still embracing me. I was looking at the curve of her neck, smelling her scent for the last time. "Why can't you come with me?" I sobbed.

"It would do no good. I'm infected. I want to stay with your father. But it's not so bad, knowing you've got away." She moved me away from her, still holding me, looking straight into my eyes. "Now, you have to be brave. You have to leave. Don't look back. Don't let anyone stop you."

"Mother..."

"I love you, my dear son. Now go!"

If I'd spoken to her again, I wouldn't have been able to leave her. I knew that. We both did. I broke away. I ran.

The forest was on the other side of the house, to the north and spreading to the east of Estrov. It stretched on for about thirty miles, mainly pine trees but also linden, birch and spruce. It was a dark, tangled place and none of us ever went into it, partly because we were afraid of getting lost but also because there were rumoured to be wolves around, particularly in the winter. But somewhere inside me I knew my mother was right. If there were police or soldiers in the area, they would concentrate on the main road. I would be safer out of sight. The highway that she'd mentioned cut through the forest and they were laying a new water pipe alongside it.

To begin with, I followed the track that wound through the gardens, trying to keep out of sight, although there was nobody around. In the distance, I saw a boy I knew, cycling past with a bundle under his arm, but he was alone. I passed the village shop. It was closed. I continued through the allotments where the villagers grew their own food and stole everyone else's. I was already hot, wearing a double set of clothes, and the air was suddenly warm and thick. The clouds were grey and swollen, rolling in from every side. It was definitely going to rain.

I still wasn't sure I was going to do what my mother had told me. Did she really think I could so easily run off and leave her on her own with my father lying dead beside the fence? No matter what had happened at the factory, and whatever she had said, I couldn't just abandon her. I would wait a few hours in the forest and see what happened. And then, once it was dark, I would return. She had talked about a weapon – anthrax. She had said the whole village was contaminated. But I refused to believe her. I was even angry with her for telling me these things. In truth, I do not think I was actually in my right mind.

And then I saw someone ahead of me, crouching down with their bottom in the air, pulling vegetables out of the ground. Even from this angle, I recognized him at once. It was Leo. He had been working on his family's vegetable patch, probably as a punishment for doing something wrong. He had two younger brothers and whenever any of them fought, their father would take a belt to them and they would end up either mending fences or gardening. He was covered in mud with a bunch of very wrinkled carrots dangling from his hand, but seeing me approach, he broke into a grin.

"Hey, Yasha!" he called out. He did a double take, noticing my Pioneers clothes. "What are you doing?"

"Leo..." I was so glad to see him but I didn't know what to say. How could I explain what had just happened?

"Did you hear the siren?" he said. "And there was shooting. I think something's happened over at the factory."

"Where are your parents?" I asked.

"Dad's working. Mum's at home."

"Leo, you have to come with me." The words came rushing out. I hadn't planned to ask him along but suddenly it was the most important thing in the world. I couldn't leave without him.

"Where are you going?" He lowered the carrots and stood there with his legs slightly apart, one hand on his hip, his boots reaching up to his thighs. For a moment he looked like one of those old posters, the sort they had printed to get the peasants to work in the fields. He gave me a crooked smile. "What's the matter, Yasha? What's wrong?"

"My dad's dead," I said.

"What?"

Hadn't he understood anything? Hadn't he realized that something was wrong? But that was Leo for you. Explosions, gun shots, alarms ... and he would just carry on weeding.

"He's been shot," I said. "That was what the siren was about. It was him. They tried to stop him leaving. But he told me I have to go away and hide. Something terrible has happened at the factory." I was pleading with him. "Please, Leo. Come with me."

"I can't..."

He was going to argue. No matter what I told him, he would never have abandoned his family. But just then we became aware of a sound, something that neither of us had ever heard before. At the same time, we felt a slight pulsing in the air, beating against our skin. We looked round and saw five black dots in the sky, swooping low over the hills, heading towards the village. They were military helicopters, just like the ones in the pictures in my room. They were still too far away to see properly but they were lined up in precise battle formation. It was that exactness that made them so menacing. Somehow I was certain that they weren't going to land. They weren't going to disgorge doctors and technicians who had come to help us. My parents had warned me that people were coming to Estrov to kill me and I had no doubt at all that they had arrived.

"Leo! Come on! Now!"

There must have been something in my voice, or perhaps it was the sight of the helicopters themselves, but this time Leo dropped his carrots and obeyed. Together, without a single thought, we began to run up the slope, away from the village. The edge of the forest, an endless line of thick trunks, branches, pine needles and shadows, stretched out before us. We were still about fifty metres away and now I found that my legs wouldn't work, that the soft mud was deliberately dragging me down. Behind me, the sound of the helicopters was getting louder. I didn't dare turn round but I could feel them getting closer and closer. And then – another shock – the bells of St Nicholas began to ring, the sound echoing over the rooftops. The church was empty. I had never heard the bells before.

I was sweating. My whole body felt as if it were trapped inside an oven. Something hit me on the shoulder and for a crazy moment I thought one of the helicopters had fired a bullet. But it was nothing more than a fat raindrop. The storm was about to break.

"Yasha!"

We stopped at the very edge of the forest and turned round just in time to see the helicopters deliver their first payload. They fired five missiles, one after the other. But they didn't hit anything ... not like in an old war film. The pilots hadn't actually been aiming at any particular buildings. The missiles exploded randomly – in lanes, in peoples' gardens – but the destruction was much, much worse than anything I could have imagined. Huge fireballs erupted at the point of impact, spreading out instantly so that they joined up with one another, wiping out everything they touched. The flames were a brilliant orange; fiercer and more intense than any fire I had ever seen. They devoured my entire world, burning up the houses, the walls, the trees, the roads, the very soil. Nothing that touched those flames could possibly survive. The first five missiles wiped out almost the entire village but they were followed by five more and then another five. We could feel the heat reaching out to us, so intense that even though we were some distance from it, our eyes watered and we had to look away. I put up my hand to protect my face and felt the back of my fingers burn. In seconds, Estrov, the village where I had spent my entire life, was turned into hell. My father was already dead but I had no doubt at all that my mother had now joined him. And my grandmother. And Leo's mother and his brothers. It was impossible to see his house through the curtain of fire but by now it would be nothing more than ash.

The helicopters were continuing, heading towards us. Now that they were closer, I recognized them at once. They were Mil Mi-24s, sometimes known as Crocodiles, developed for the Russian military for both missile support and troop movements. Each one could carry eight men at speeds of over three hundred and fifty miles per hour. As well as the main and the tail rotors, the Mil had two wings stretching out of the main fuselage, each one equipped with a missile launcher that dangled beneath it. I had never seen anything that looked more deadly, more like a giant bird with claws outstretched, swooping out of the sky to snatch me up. They were getting closer and closer. I could actually see the nearest pilot, very low down in the glass bubble that was the cockpit window. Where had he come from? Had he once been a boy like me, dreaming of flying? How could he sit there and be responsible for so much killing? And yet he was without mercy. There could be no doubt at all that he was aiming the next salvo at me. I swear I saw him gazing straight at me as he fired. I saw the spurt of flame as the missiles were fired.

Fortunately, they fell short. A wall of flame

erupted about thirty metres behind me. Even so, the heat was so intense that Leo screamed. I could smell the air burning. A cloud of chemicals and smoke poured over us. It was only later that I realized it must have briefly shielded us from the pilot. Otherwise he would have fired again.

Leo and I plunged into the forest. The light was cut out behind us. Instantly we were surrounded by green, with leaves and branches everywhere and soft moss beneath our feet. We had reached the top of the hill. The forest sloped down on the other side and this proved our salvation. We lost our footing and tumbled down, rolling over roots and mud. It was already raining harder. Water was dripping down and maybe that helped us too. We were invisible. We were away from the flames. As I fell, through the trees I caught a glimpse of the red and black horror that I had left behind. I heard the roar of helicopter blades. Branches were whipping and shaking all around me. Then I was at the very bottom of the hollow. Leo was next to me, staring helplessly, completely terrified. But we were protected by the forest and by the earth. The helicopters could not reach us.

Well, perhaps the pilots could have tried again. Maybe they had exhausted their missile supply. Maybe they didn't think it was worth wasting more of their ammunition on two small boys. But even as I lay there I knew that this wasn't over. They had seen us and they would radio ahead. Others would come to finish the work. It wasn't enough that the village had been destroyed. If anybody had managed to survive, they would have to be killed. There must be nobody left to tell what had happened.

"Yasha..." Leo gasped. He was crying. His face was a mess of mud and tears.

"We have to go," I said.

We struggled to our feet and dropped into the safety of the forest. Behind us, the sky was red, the helicopters hovering as Estrov continued to burn.

ЛЕС

THE FOREST

When I was a small boy, I had feared the forest with its ghosts and its demons. It had given me nightmares. My own parents had come from the city and didn't believe such things but Leo's mother used to tell me stories about it, the same stories that her mother had doubtless told her. Every child in the village knew them and stayed away. But now I wanted it to draw me in, to swallow me up and never let me go. The deeper I went, the safer I felt, surrounded by huge, solid trunks that blotted out the sky and everything silent except for the drip of the rain on the canopy of leaves. The real nightmare was behind me. It was almost impossible to think of my village and the people who had lived there. Mr Vladimov smoking his cigarettes until the stubs burnt his fingers. Mrs Bek who ran the village shop and put up with everyone's complaints when there was nothing on the shelves. The twins, Irina and Olga, so alike that we could never tell them apart but always arguing and at each other's throats. My grandmother. My parents. My friends. They had all gone as if they had never existed and nothing would remain of them, not even their names.

Never tell anyone you came from Estrov. Never use that word again.

My mother's warning to me. And of course she was right. The place of my birth had now become a sentence of death.

I was in shock. So much had happened and it had happened so quickly that my brain simply wasn't able to cope with it all. I had seen very few American films, and computer games hadn't arrived in my corner of Russia yet – so the sort of violence I had just experienced was completely alien to me. Perhaps it was for the best. If I had really considered my situation, I might easily have gone mad. I was fourteen years old and suddenly I had nothing except a hundred rubles, the clothes I was wearing and the name of a man I had never met in a city I had never visited. My best friend was with me but it was as if his soul had flown out of him, leaving nothing but a shell behind. He was no longer crying but he was walking like a zombie. For the last hour, he had said nothing. We had been walking in silence with only the sound of our own footsteps and the rain hitting the leaves.

It wasn't over yet. We were both waiting for the next attack. Maybe the helicopters would return and bomb the forest. Maybe they would use poison gas next time. They knew we were here and they wouldn't let us get away.

"What was it all about, Yasha Gregorovich?" Leo asked. He used my full name in the formal way that we Russians do sometimes – when we want to make a point or when we are afraid. His face was puffy and I could see that his eyes were bright with tears, although he was trying hard not to cry in front of me.

"I don't know," I said. But that wasn't true. I knew only too well. "There was an accident at the factory," I went on. "Our parents lied to us. They weren't just making chemicals for farmers. They were also making weapons. Something went wrong and they had to close it down very quickly."

"The helicopters..."

"I suppose they didn't want to tell anyone what had happened. It's like that place we learnt about. You know... Chernobyl."

We all knew about Chernobyl in Ukraine. Not so long ago, when Russia was still part of the Soviet Union, there had been a huge explosion at a nuclear reactor. The whole area had been covered with clouds of radioactive dust – they had even reached parts of Europe. But at the time, the authorities had done everything they could to cover up what had happened. Even now it was uncertain how many people had actually died. That was the way the Russian government worked back then. If they had admitted there had been a catastrophe, it would have shown they were weak. So it was easy to imagine what they would do following an accident at a secret facility creating biological weapons. If a hundred or even five hundred people were murdered, what would it matter so long as things were kept quiet?

Leo was still trying to take it all in. It hurt me seeing him like this. This was a boy who had been afraid of nothing, who had been rude to all the teachers and who had never complained when he was beaten or sent on forced marches. But it was as if he had become five years younger. He was lost. "They killed everyone," he said.

"They had to keep it a secret, Leo. My mother and father managed to get out of the factory. They told me to run away because they knew what was going to happen." My voice cracked. "They're both dead."

"I'm sorry, Yasha."

"Me too, Leo."

He was my best friend. He was all that I had left in the world. But I still wasn't telling him the whole truth. My arm was throbbing painfully and I was sure that he must have noticed the bloodstain on my sleeve but I hadn't mentioned the syringe. My mother had inoculated me with the antidote against whatever had escaped into the air. She had said it would protect me. No one had done the same for Leo. Did that mean he was carrying the anthrax spores on him even now? Was he dying? I didn't want to think about it and, coward that I was, I certainly couldn't bring myself to talk to him about it.

We were still walking. The rain was getting heavier. Now it was making its way through the leaves and splashing down all around us. It was early in the afternoon but most of the light had gone. I had taken out my compass and given it to Leo. I could have used it myself of course but I thought it would be better for him to have his mind occupied – and anyway, he was better at finding directions than me. Not that the compass really helped. Every time we came to a particularly nasty knot of brambles or found a tangle of undergrowth blocking our path, we had to go another way. It was as if the forest itself was guiding us. Where? If it was feeling merciful, it would lead us to safety. But it might be just as likely to deliver us into our enemies' hands.

The forest began to slope upwards, gently at first, then more steeply, and we found our feet kept slipping and we tripped over the roots. Leo looked dreadful, his clothes plastered across him, his face deadly white, his hair soaking wet now, hanging lifelessly over his eyes. I felt guilty in my waterproof clothes but it was too late to hand them over. Ahead of us, the trees began to thin out. This was doubly bad news. First, it meant that we were even less protected from the rain. It would also be easier to spot us from the air if the helicopters returned.

"Over there!" I said.

I had seen an electricity pylon not too far away, poking out above the trees, part of the new construction. They had been laying all three together – the new highway, the water pipe and electricity – all part of the modernization of the area, before the work had ground to a halt. But even without tarmac or lighting, the road would lead us straight to Kirsk. At least we knew which way to go.

I had very little memory of Kirsk. The last time I had been there had been about a year ago, on a school trip. Getting out of Estrov had been exciting enough but when we had got there we had spent half the time in a museum, and by the afternoon I was bored stiff. When I was twelve, I had spent a week in Kirsk Hospital after I'd broken my leg. I had been taken there by bus and had no idea how to get around. But surely the station wouldn't be too difficult to find and at least I would have enough money to buy two tickets for the train. A hundred rubles was worth a great deal. It was more than a month's salary for one of my teachers.

We trudged forward, making better progress. We were beginning to think that we had got away after all, that nobody was interested in us any more. Of course it is just when you begin to think like that, when you relax your guard, that the worst happens. If I had been in the same situation now, I would have gone anywhere except towards the new highway. When you are in danger, you must always opt for what is least expected. Predictability kills.

We reached the first evidence of the construction; abandoned spools of wire, cement slabs, great piles of plastic tubing. Ahead of us, a brown ribbon of dug-up earth stretched out into the gloom. The town of Kirsk and the railway to Moscow lay at the other end.

"How far is it?" Leo asked.

"I don't know," I said. "About twenty miles, I think. Are you OK?"

Leo nodded but the misery in his face told another story.

"We can do it," I said. "Five or six hours. And it can't rain for ever."

It felt as if it was going to do just that. We could actually see the raindrops now, fat and relentless, slanting down in front of us and splattering on the ground. It was like a curtain hanging between the trees and we could barely make out the road on the other side. There were more pipes scattered on both sides and after a short while we came to a deep ditch which must have been cut as part of the water project. Was it really possible for an entire community to near the end of the twentieth century without running water? I had carried enough buckets down to the well to know the answer to that.

We walked for another ten minutes, neither of us speaking, our feet splashing in the puddles, and then we saw them. They were ahead of us, a long line of soldiers, spread out across the forest, making steady progress towards us ... like detectives looking for clues after a murder. They were spaced so that nobody would be able to pass through the line without being seen. They had no faces. They were dressed in pale silver anti-chemical and biological uniforms with hoods and gas masks, and they carried semi-automatic machine guns. They had dogs with them, scrawny Alsatians, straining at the end of metal leashes. It was as if they had walked out of my worst nightmare. They didn't look human at all.

It should have been obvious from the start that whoever had sent the helicopters would follow them up with an infantry backup. First, destroy the village, then put a noose around the place to make sure there are no survivors who can spread the virus. The line of militia men, if that's what they were, would have formed a huge circle around Estrov. They would close in from all sides. And they would have been told to shoot any stragglers – Leo and me – on sight. Nobody could be allowed to tell what had happened. And, above all, the anthrax virus that we might be carrying must not break free.

They would have seen us at once but for the rain. And the dogs too would have smelt us if everything hadn't been so wet. In the darkness of the forest, the pale colour of their protective gear stood out, but for a few precious seconds we were invisible. I reached out and grabbed Leo's arm. We turned and ran the way we had come.

It was the worst thing to do. Since that time, long ago now, I have been taught survival techniques for exactly such situations. You do not break your pace. You do not panic. It is the very rhythm of your movement that will alert your enemy. We should have melted to one side, found cover and then retreated as quickly but as steadily as we could. Instead, the sound of our shoes stamping on the wet ground signalled that we were there. One of the dogs began to bark ferociously, followed immediately by the rest of them. Somebody shouted. An instant later there was the deafening clamour of machine-gun fire, weapons spraying bullets that sliced through the trees and the leaves, sending pieces of debris showering over our heads. We had been seen. The line began to move forward more urgently. We were perhaps thirty or forty metres ahead of them but we were already close to exhaustion, drenched, unarmed. We were children. We had no chance at all.

More machine-gun fire. I saw mud splattering up inches from my feet. Leo was slightly ahead of me. His legs were shorter than mine and he had been more tired than me but I was determined to keep him in front of me, not to leave him behind. If one went down, we both went down. The dogs were making a hideous sound. They had seen their prey. They wanted to be released.

And we stayed on the half-built highway! That was a killing ground if ever there was one, wide and exposed ... an easy matter for a sniper to pick us off. I suppose we thought we could run faster with a flat surface beneath our feet. But every step I took, I was waiting for the bullet that would come smashing between my shoulders. I could hear the dogs, the guns, the blast of the whistles. I didn't look back but I could actually feel the men closing in behind me.

Still, we had the advantage of distance. The line of soldiers would move more slowly than us. They wouldn't want to break rank and risk the chance of our doubling back and slipping through. I had perhaps one minute to work out some sort of scheme before they caught up with us. Climb a tree? No, it would take too long, and anyway,the dogs would sniff us out. Continue back down the hill? Pointless. There were probably more soldiers coming up the other side. I was still running, my heart pounding in my chest, the breath harsh in my throat. And then I saw it ... the ditch we had passed with the plastic tubes scattered about.

"This way, Leo!" I shouted.

At the same time, I threw myself off the road, skidding down the deep bank and landing in a stream of water that rose over my ankles.

"Yasha, what are you...?" Leo began but he was sensible enough not to hesitate, turning back and following me down, almost landing on top of me.

And so there we were, below the level of the road, and I was already making my way back, heading *towards* the line of soldiers, looking for what I prayed must be there.

Hundreds of metres of the water pipe had already been laid. The opening was in front of us: a perfect black circle, like the entrance to some futuristic cave. It was small. If I hadn't been so thin and Leo hadn't been so slight, neither of us would have fitted into it and it was unlikely that many of the soldiers would have been able to follow – certainly not in their gas masks and protective gear. They would have been mad to try. Would they really have been prepared to bury themselves alive, plunging into utter darkness with tons of damp earth above their heads?

That was what we did. On our hands and knees, we threw ourselves forward, our shoulders scraping against the curve of the pipe. At least it was dry inside the tunnel. But it was also pitch-black. When I looked back to see if Leo was behind me, I caught a glimmer of soft light a few metres away. But when I looked ahead ... there was nothing! I brought my hand up and touched my nose but I couldn't see my fingers. For a moment, I found it difficult to breathe. I had to fight off the claustrophobia, the sense of being suffocated, of being squeezed to death. I wondered if it would be a good idea to go any further. We could have stayed where we were and used the tunnel as a hiding place until everyone had gone – but that wasn't good enough for me. I could imagine a burst of machine-gun fire killing me or, worse still, paralysing me and leaving me to die slowly in the darkness. I could feel the Alsatians, sent after us, snapping and snarling their way down the tunnel and then tearing ferociously at our legs and thighs. I had to let the tunnel carry me away and it didn't matter where it took me. So I kept going with Leo behind me, the two of us burrowing ever further beneath the wood.

To the soldiers it must have seemed as if we had disappeared by magic. They would have passed the ditch but it's quite likely that they didn't see the pipeline – or, if they did, refused to believe that we could actually fit into it. Once again, the rain covered our tracks. The dogs failed to pick up our scent. Any footprints were washed away. And the soldiers were completely unaware that, as they moved forward, we were right underneath them, crawling like insects through the mud. When I looked back again, the entrance was no longer there. It was as if a shutter had come down, sealing us in. I could hear Leo very close to me, his breath sobbing. But any sound in the tunnel was strange and muted. I felt the weight above me, pressing down.

We had swapped one hell for another.

We could only go forward. There wasn't enough room to turn round. I suppose we could have shuffled backwards until we reached the tunnel entrance, but what was the point of that? The soldiers would be looking for us and once we emerged the dogs would be onto us instantly. On the other hand, the further we went forward, the worse our situation became. Suppose the tunnel simply ended? Suppose we ran out of air? Every inch that we continued was another inch into the grave and it took all my willpower to force myself on. I think Leo only followed because he didn't want to be left on his own. I was getting warmer. Once more, I was sweating inside my clothes. I could feel the sweat mixed with rainwater under my armpits and in the palms of my hands. My knees were already hurting. Occasionally, I passed rivets, where one section of the pipe had been fastened into the next, and I felt them tugging at my anorak, scratching across my back. And I was blind. It really was as if someone had switched off my eyes. The blackness was very physical. It was like a surgical operation.

"Yasha...?" Leo's whispered voice came out of nowhere.

"It's all right, Leo," I said. My own voice didn't sound like me at all. "Not much further."

But we continued for what felt like an eternity. We were moving like robots with no sense of direction, no choice of where to go. We were simply functioning – one hand forward, then the next, knees following behind, utterly alone. There was nothing to hear apart from ourselves. Suppose the tunnel went all the way to Kirsk? Would we have the strength to travel as far as twenty miles underground? Of course not. Between us, we had half a litre of water. We hadn't eaten for hours. I had to stop myself imagining what might happen. If I wasn't careful, I would scare myself to death.

Hand and knee, hand and knee. Every part of me was hurting. I wanted to stand up, and the fact that I couldn't almost made me cry out with frustration. My shoulders hit the curve of the pipe again and again. My eyes were closed. What was the point of using them when I couldn't see? And then, quite suddenly, I was outside. I felt the breeze brush over my shoulders and the rain, lighter now, patter onto my head and the back of my neck. I opened my eyes. The workmen had constructed some sort of inspection hatch and they had left this part of the pipe open. I was crouching in a V-shaped ditch with pieces of wire and rusting metal bolts all around. I pulled back my sleeve and looked at my watch. Amazingly, it was five o'clock. I thought only an hour had passed but the whole day had gone.

Leo clambered out into the half-light and sat there, blinking. For a moment, neither of us dared speak but there were no sounds around us and it seemed fairly certain we were on our own.

"We're OK," I said. "We went under them. They don't know we're here."

"What next?" Leo asked.

"We can keep going ... follow the road to Kirsk."

"They'll be looking for us there."

"I know. We can worry about that when we get there."

And just for one moment, I thought we were going to make it. We had escaped from the helicopters. We had outwitted the soldiers. I had a hundred rubles in my pocket. I would get us to Moscow and we would tell the whole world what had happened and we would be heroes. Right then, I really did think that, despite what we had been through and all that we had lost, we might actually be all right.

But then Leo spoke.

"Yasha," he said. "I don't feel well."

НОЧЬ

NIGHT

We couldn't stay where we were. I was afraid that the soldiers would see the entrance to the pipeline and realize how we had managed to slip past them – in which case they would double back and find us. We had to put more distance between us and them while we still had the strength. But at the same time I saw that Leo couldn't go much further. He had a headache and he was finding it difficult to breathe. Was it too much to hope that he had simply caught a cold, that he was in shock? It didn't have to be contamination by the chemicals from the factory. I tried to convince myself that, like me, he was exhausted and if he could just get a night's rest he would be well again.

Even so, I knew I had to find him somewhere warm to shelter. He needed food. Somehow I had to dry his clothes. As I looked around me, at the spindly trees that rose up into an ever darkening sky, I felt a sense of complete helplessness. How could I possibly manage on my own? I wanted my parents and I had to remind myself that they weren't going to come, that I was never going to see them again. I was sick with grief – but something inside me told me that I couldn't give in. Leo and I hadn't escaped from Estrov simply to die out here, a few miles away, in the middle of a forest.

We walked together for another hour, still following the road. They'd been able to afford asphalt for this section, which at least made it easier to find our way in the dark. I knew it was dangerous, that we had more chance of being spotted, but I didn't dare lose myself among the trees.

And in the end it was the right decision. We stumbled upon it quite by chance, a wooden hut which must have been built for the construction team and abandoned only recently. The door was padlocked but I managed to kick it in, and once we were inside I was surprised to find two bunks, a table, cupboards and even an iron stove. I checked the cupboards. There was no food or medicine but the almost empty shelves did offer me a few rewards. Using my torch, I found some old newspapers, saucepans, tin mugs and a fork. I was glad now that I had thought to take a box of matches from my kitchen and that my waterproof clothes had managed to keep them dry. There was no coal or firewood so I tore off some of the cupboard doors and smashed them up with my foot, and ten minutes later I had a good fire blazing.

I wasn't worried about the smoke being seen. It was too dark and I kept the door and the shutters closed to stop the light escaping.

I helped Leo out of his wet clothes and laid them on the floor to dry. He stretched himself out on the nearest bunk and I covered him with newspaper and a rug from the floor. It might not have been too clean but at least it would help to keep him warm. I had the food that I had brought from my home and I took it out. Leo and I had drunk all our water but that wasn't a problem. I carried a saucepan outside and filled it from the gutter that ran round the side of the building. After the rain, it was full to overflowing and boiling the water in the flames would get rid of any germs. I added the tea and the sugar, and balanced the pan on the stove. I broke the chocolate bars into pieces and examined the tins. There were three of them and they all contained herring but, fool that I was, I had forgotten to bring a tin opener.

While Leo drifted in and out of sleep, I spent the next half-hour desperately trying to open the tins. In a way, it did me good to have to focus on a problem that was so small and so stupid. Forget the fact that you are alone, in hiding, that there are soldiers who want to kill you, that your best friend is ill, that everything has been taken from you. Open the tin! In the end, I managed it with the fork that I had found, hammering at it with a heavy stone and piercing the lid so many times that eventually I was able to peel it away. The herring was grey and oily. I'm not sure that anyone eats it any more, but it had always been a special treat when I was growing up. My mother would serve it with slabs of dry black bread or sometimes potatoes. When I smelt the fish, I thought of her and I felt all the pain welling up once more, even though I was doing everything I could to block out what had happened.

I tried to feed some to Leo but, after all my efforts, he was too tired to eat and it was all I could manage to force him to sip some tea. I was suddenly very hungry myself and gobbled down one of the tins, leaving the other two for him. I was still hopeful that he would be feeling better in the morning. It seemed to me that now that he was resting, he was breathing a little easier. Maybe all the rain would have washed away the anthrax spores. His clothes were still drying in front of the fire. Sitting there, watching his chest rise and fall beneath the covers, I tried to persuade myself that everything would be all right.

It was the beginning of the longest night of my life. I took off my outer clothes and lay down on the second bunk but I couldn't sleep. I was frightened that the fire would go out. I was frightened that the soldiers would find the hut and burst in. Actually, I was so filled with fears of one sort or another that I didn't need to define them. For hours I listened to the crackle of the flames and the rasp of Leo's breath in his throat. From time to time, I drifted into a state where I was floating, although still fully conscious. Several times, I got up and fed more of the furniture into the stove, doing my best to break the wood without making too much noise. Once, I went outside to urinate. It was no longer raining but a few drops of water were still falling from the trees. I could hear them but I couldn't see them. The sky was totally black. As I stood there, I heard the howl of a wolf. I had been holding the torch but at that moment I almost dropped it into the undergrowth. So the wolves weren't just a bit of village gossip! This one could have been far away, but it seemed to be right next to me, the sound starting impossibly low then rising higher and higher as if the creature had somehow flown into the air. I buttoned myself up and ran back inside, determined that nothing would get me out again until it was light.

My own clothes were still damp. I took them off and knelt in front of the fire. If anything got me through that night it was that stove. It kept me warm and without its glow I wouldn't have been able to see, which would have made all my imaginings even worse. I took out the roll of ten-ruble notes that had been in the tin and at the same time I found the little black bag my mother had given me. I opened it. Inside, there was a pair of earrings, a necklace and a ring. I had never seen them before and wondered where she had got them from. Were they valuable? I made an oath to myself that whatever happened, I would never sell them. They were the only remains of my past life. They were all I had left. I wrapped them up again and climbed onto the other bunk. Almost naked and lying uncomfortably on the hard mattress, I dozed off again. When I next opened my eyes, the fire was almost out and when I pulled back the shutters, the very first streaks of pink were visible outside.

The sun seemed to take for ever to rise. They call them the small hours, that time from four o'clock onwards, and I know from experience that they are always the most miserable of the day. That is when you feel most vulnerable and alone. Leo was sound asleep. The hut was even more desolate than before – I had fed almost anything that was made of wood into the fire. The world outside was wet, cold and threatening. As I got dressed again, I remembered that in a few hours I should have been going to school.

Wake up, Yasha. Come on! Get your things together...

I had to force my mother's voice out of my head. She wasn't there for me any more. Nobody was. From now on, if I was to survive, I had to look after myself.

The two remaining tins of fish were still waiting, uneaten, on a shelf beside the fire. I was tempted to wolf them down myself, as I was really hungry, but I was keeping them for Leo. I made some more tea and ate a little chocolate, then I went back outside. The sky was now a dirty off-white, and the trees were more skeletal than ever. But at least there was nobody around. The soldiers hadn't come back. Walking around, I came across a shrub of bright red lingonberries. They were past their best but I knew they would be edible. We used to make them into a dish called *kissel*, a sort of jelly, and I stuffed some of them into my mouth. They were slightly sour but I thought they would keep me going and I placed several more in my pockets.

"Yasha...?"

As I returned to the hut, I heard Leo call my name. He had woken up. I was delighted to hear his voice and hurried over to him. "How are you feeling, Leo?" I asked.

"Where are we?"

"We found a shed. After the tunnel. Don't you remember?"

"I'm very cold, Yasha."

He looked terrible. As much as I wanted to, I couldn't pretend otherwise. There was no colour at all in his face, and his eyes were burning, out of focus. I didn't know why he was cold. The one thing I had managed to do was to keep the hut reasonably warm and I had put plenty of makeshift covers on the bed.

"Maybe you should eat something," I said.

I brought the open tin of herring over but he recoiled at the smell. "I don't want it," he said. His voice rattled in his chest. He sounded like an old man.

"All right. But you must have some tea."

I took the mug over and forced him to sip from it. As he strained his neck towards me, I noticed a red mark under his chin and, very slowly, trying not to let him know what I was doing, I folded back the covers to see what was going on. I was shocked by what I saw. The whole of Leo's neck and chest was covered in dreadful, diamond-shaped sores. His skin looked as if it had been burned in a fire. I could easily imagine that his whole body was like this and I didn't want to see any more. His face was the only part of him that had been spared. Underneath the covers he was a rotting corpse.

I knew that if it hadn't been for my parents, I would be exactly the same as Leo. They had injected me with something that protected me from the biochemical weapon that they had helped to build. They had said it acted quickly and here was the living – or perhaps the dying – proof. No wonder the authorities had been so quick to quarantine the area. If the anthrax had managed to do this to Leo in just a few hours, imagine what it would do to the rest of Russia as it spread.

"I'm sorry, Yasha," Leo whispered.

"There's nothing to be sorry about," I said. I was casting about me, trying to find something to do. The fire, untended, had almost gone out. But there was no more wood to put in it anyway.

"I can't come with you," Leo said.

"Yes, you can. We're just going to have to wait. That's all. You'll feel better when the sun comes up."

He shook his head. He knew I was lying for his sake. "I don't mind. I'm glad you looked after me. I always liked being with you, Yasha."

He rested his head back. Despite the marks on his body, he didn't seem to be in pain. I sat beside him, and after a few minutes he began to mutter something. I leant closer. He wasn't saying anything. He was singing. I recognized the words. *"Close the door after me ... I'm going."* Everyone at school would have known the song. It was by a rock singer called Viktor Tsoi and it had been the rage throughout the summer.

Perhaps Leo didn't even want to live – not without his family, not without the village. He got to the end of the line and he died. And the truth is that, apart from the silence, there wasn't a great deal of difference between Leo alive and Leo dead. He simply stopped. I closed his eyes. I drew the covers over his face. And then I began to cry. Is it shocking that I felt Leo's death even more than that of my own parents? Maybe it was because they had been snatched from me so suddenly. I hadn't even been given a chance to react. But it had taken

Leo the whole of that long night to die and I was sitting with him even now, remembering everything he had been to me. I had been close to my parents but much closer to Leo. And he was so young ... the same age as me.

In a way, I think I am writing this for Leo.

I have decided to keep a record of my life because I suspect my life will be short. I do not particularly want to be remembered. Being unknown has been essential to my work. But I sometimes think of him and I would like him to understand what it was that made me what I am. After all, living as a boy of fourteen in a Russian village, it had never been my intention to become a contract killer.

Leo's death may have been one step on my journey. It was not a major step. It did not change me. That happened much later.

I set fire to the hut with Leo still inside it. I remembered the helicopters and knew that the flames might attract their attention, but it was the only way I could think of to prevent the disease spreading. And if the soldiers were drawn here, perhaps it wasn't such a bad thing. They had their gas masks and protective suits. They would know how to decontaminate the area.

But that didn't mean I was going to hang around waiting for them to come. With the smoke billowing behind me, carrying Leo out of this world, I hurried away, along the road to Kirsk.

КИРСК

KIRSK

I entered Kirsk on legs that were tired and feet that were sore and remembered that the last time I had been there, it had been on a school trip to the museum.

Lenin had once visited Kirsk. The great Soviet leader had stopped briefly in the town on his way to somewhere more important because there was a problem with his train. He made a short speech on the station platform, then went to the local café for a cup of tea and, happening to glance in the mirror, decided that his beard and moustache needed a trim. Not surprisingly, the local barber almost had a heart attack when the most powerful man in the Soviet Union walked into his shop. The cup that he drank from and the clippings of black hair were still on display in the History and Folklore Museum of Kirsk.

It was a large, reddish-brown building with rooms

that were filled with objects and after only an hour my head had already been pounding. From the outside, it looked like a railway station. Curiously, Kirsk railway station looked quite like a museum, with wide stairs, pillars and huge bronze doors that should have opened onto something more important than ticket offices, platforms and waiting rooms. I had seen it on that last trip but I couldn't remember where it was. When you've been taken to a place in a coach and marched around shoulder to shoulder in a long line with no talking allowed, you don't really look where you're going. That hadn't been my only visit. My father had taken me to the cinema here once. And then there had been my visit to the hospital. But all these places could have been on different planets. I had no idea where they were in relation to one another.

After Estrov, the place felt enormous. I had forgotten how many buildings there were, how many shops, how many cars and buses racing up and down the wide, cobbled streets. Everywhere seemed to have electricity. There were wires zigzagging from pole to pole, crossing each other like a disastrous cat's cradle. But I'm not suggesting that Kirsk was anything special. I'd spent my whole life in a tiny village so I was easily impressed. I didn't notice the crumbling plaster on the buildings, the empty construction sites, the pits in the road and the dirty water running through the gutters.

It was late afternoon when I arrived and the light

was already fading. My mother had said there were two trains a day to Moscow and I hoped I was in time to catch the evening one. I had never spent a night in a hotel before and even though I had money in my pocket, the idea of finding one and booking a room filled me with fear. How much would I have to pay? Would they even give a room to a boy on his own? I had been walking non-stop, leaving the forest behind me just after midday. I was starving hungry. Since I had left the shed, all I'd had to eat were the lingonberries I'd collected. I still had a handful of them in my pocket but I couldn't eat any more because they were giving me stomach cramps. My feet were aching and soaking wet. I was wearing my leather boots, which had suddenly decided to leak. I felt filthy and wondered if they would let me onto the train. And what if they didn't? I had only one plan – to get to Moscow – and even that seemed daunting. I had seen pictures of the city at school, of course, but I had no real idea what it would be like.

Finding the station wasn't so difficult in the end. Somehow I stumbled across the centre of the town ... I suppose every road led there if you walked enough. It was a spacious area with an empty fountain and a Second World War monument, a slab of granite shaped like a slice of cake with the inscription: WE SALUTE THE GLORIOUS DEAD OF KIRSK. I had always been brought up to respect all those who had lost their lives in the war, but I know now that there is nothing glorious about being dead. The monument was surrounded by statues of generals and soldiers, many of them on horseback. Was that how they had set off to face the German tanks?

The station was right in front of me, at the end of a wide, very straight boulevard with trees on both sides. I recognized it at once. It was surrounded by stalls selling everything from suit-cases, blankets and cushions to all sorts of food and drink. I could smell *shashlyk* – skewers of meat – cooking on charcoal fires and it made my mouth water. I was desperate to buy something but that was when I realized I had a problem. Although I had a lot of money in my pocket, it was all in large notes. I had no coins. If I were to hand over a ten-ruble note for a snack that would cost no more than a few kopecks, I would only draw attention to myself. The stallholder would assume I was a thief. Better to wait until I'd bought my train ticket. At least then I would have change.

With these thoughts in my mind, I walked towards the main entrance of the station. I was so relieved to have got here and so anxious to be on my way that I was careless. I was keeping my head down, trying not to catch anyone's eye. I should have been looking all around me. In fact, if I had been sensible, I would have tried to enter the station from a completely different direction ... around the side or the back. As it was, I hadn't taken more than five or six steps before I found that my way was blocked. I glanced up and saw two policemen standing in front of me, dressed in long grey coats with insignia around their collars and military caps. They were both young, in their twenties. They had revolvers hanging from their belts.

"Where are you going?" one of them asked. He had bad skin, very raw, as if he had only started shaving recently and had used a blunt razor.

"To the station." I pointed, trying to sound casual.

"Why?"

"I work there. After school. I help clean the platforms." I was making things up as I went along.

"Where have you come from?"

"Over there..." I pointed to one of the apartment blocks I had passed on my way into the town.

"Your name?"

"Leo Tretyakov." My poor dead friend. Why had I chosen him?

The two policemen hesitated and for a moment I thought they were going to let me pass. Surely there was no reason to stop me. I was just a boy, doing odd jobs after school. But then the second policeman spoke. "Your identity papers," he demanded. His eyes were cold.

I had used a false name because I was afraid the authorities would know who I was. After all, it had been my parents, Anton and Eva Gregorovich, who had escaped from the factory. But now I was trapped. The moment they looked at my passport, they would know I had lied to them. I should have been watching out for them from the start. Now that I looked around me, I realized that the station was crawling with policemen. Obviously. The police would know what had happened at Estrov. They would have been told that two boys had escaped. They had been warned to keep an eye out for us at every station in the area ... and I had simply walked into their arms.

"I don't have them," I stammered. I put a stupid look on my face, as if I didn't realize how serious it was to be out without ID. "They're at home."

It might have worked. I was only fourteen and looked young for my age. But maybe the policemen had been given my description. Maybe one of the helicopter pilots had managed to take my photograph as he flew overhead. Either way, they knew. I could see it in their eyes, the way they glanced at each other. They were only at the start of their careers, and this was a huge moment for them. It could lead to promotion, a pay rise, their names in the newspaper. They had just scored big time. They had me.

"You will come with us," the first policeman said.

"But I've done nothing wrong. My mother will be worried." Why was I even bothering? Neither of them believed me.

"No arguments," the second man snapped.

I had no choice. If I argued, if I tried to run, they would grab me and call for backup. I would be bundled into a police van before I could blink. It was better, for the moment, to stick with them. If they were determined to bring me into the police station themselves, there might still be an opportunity for me to get away. The building could be on the other side of town. By going with them, I would at least buy myself a little time to plan a way out of this.

We walked slowly and all the time I was thinking, my eyes darting about, adding up the possibilities. There were plenty of people around. The working day was coming to an end and they were on their way home. But they wouldn't help me. They wouldn't want to get involved. I glanced back at the two policemen who were walking about two steps behind me. What was it that I had noticed about them? They had clearly been pleased they had caught me, no question of that – but at the same time they were nervous. Well, that was understandable. This was a big deal for them.

But there was something else. They were nervous for another reason. I saw it now. They were walking very carefully, close enough to grab me if I tried to escape but not so close that they could actually touch me. Why the distance between me and them? Why hadn't they put handcuffs on me? Why were they giving me even the smallest chance to run away? It made no sense.

Unless they knew.

That was it. It had to be.

I had supposedly been infected with a virus so deadly that it had forced the authorities to wipe out my village. It had killed Leo in less than twenty-four hours. The soldiers in the forest had all been dressed in biochemical protective gear. The police in Kirsk – and in Rosna, for that matter – must have been told that I was dangerous, infected. None of them could have guessed that my parents had risked everything to inoculate me. They probably didn't know that an antidote existed at all. There was nothing to protect the young officers who had arrested me. As far as they were concerned, I was a walking time bomb. They wanted to bring me in. But they weren't going to come too close.

We continued walking, away from the station. A few people passed us but said nothing and looked the other way. The policemen were still hanging back and now I knew why. Although it didn't look like it, I had the upper hand. They were afraid of me! And I could use that.

Casually, I slipped my hand into my pocket. Because the two men were behind me, they didn't see the movement. I took it out and wiped my mouth. I sensed that we were drawing close to the police station from the police cars parked ahead.

"Down there...!" one of the policemen snapped. We were going to enter the police station the back way, down a wide alleyway and across a deserted car park with overflowing dustbins lined up along a rusting fence. We turned off and suddenly we were on our own. It was exactly what I wanted.

I stumbled slightly and let out a groan, clutching hold of my stomach. Neither of the policemen spoke. I stopped. One of them prodded me in the back. Just one finger. No contact with my skin.

"Keep moving," he commanded.

"I can't," I said, putting as much pain as I could manage into my voice.

I twisted round. At the same time, I began to cough, making horrible retching noises as if my lungs were tearing themselves apart. I sucked in, gasping for air, still holding my stomach. The policemen stared at me in horror. There was bright blood all around my lips, trickling down my chin. I coughed again and drops of blood splattered in their direction. I watched them fall back as if they had come face to face with a poisonous snake. And as far as they knew, my blood *was* poison. If any of it touched them, they would end up like me.

But it wasn't blood.

Just a minute ago, I had slipped some of the lingonberries from the forest into my mouth and chewed them up. What I was spitting was red berry juice mixed with my own saliva.

"Please help me," I said. "I'm not well."

The two policemen had come to a dead halt, caught between two conflicting desires: one to hold onto me, the other to be as far away from me as possible. I was overacting like crazy, grimacing and staggering about like a drunk, but it didn't matter. Just as I'd suspected, they'd been told how dangerous I was. They knew the stakes. Their imagination was doing half the work for me.

"Everyone died," I went on. "They all died. Please ... I don't want to be like them." I reached out imploringly. My hand was stained red. The two men stepped back. They weren't coming anywhere near. "So much pain!" I sobbed. I fell to my knees. The juice dripped onto my jacket.

The policemen made their decision. If they stayed where they were, if they tried to force me to my feet, it would kill them ... quickly and unpleasantly. Yes, they wanted their promotion. But their lives mattered more. Maybe it occurred to them that the very fact that they had come close to me meant they themselves would have to be eliminated. As far as they could see, I was dying anyway. I was lying on my side now, writhing on the ground, sobbing. My whole face was covered in blood. One of them spoke briefly to the other. I didn't hear what he said but his colleague must have agreed because a moment later they had gone, hurrying back the way they had come. I watched them turn a corner. I very much doubted that they would report what had just happened. After all, dereliction of duty would not be something they would wish to advertise. They would probably spend the rest of the day at the bathhouse, hoping that the steam and hot water would wash away the disease.

I waited until I was sure they had gone, then got to my feet and wiped my face with my sleeve. At least the encounter had given me an advance warning. There was no way I was going to walk into the railway station at Kirsk. The moment I tried to buy a train ticket, there would be someone there to arrest me and I very much doubted the same trick would work a second time. If I was going to get onto a train to Moscow, I was going to have to think of something else.

And I already had an idea.

There had been quite a few passengers arriving in taxis and coming off buses just before I had been arrested and that suggested that the evening train might be coming soon. At the same time, I'd seen a number of porters running forward to help them with their luggage. Some of them had been boys, dressed in loose-fitting grey jackets with red piping down the sleeves. I don't think they were employed officially. They were just trying to make a few kopecks on the side.

I made my way back towards the station – only this time I stayed behind the trees, close to the buildings, keeping an eye out for any policemen, mingling with the crowd. I soon found what I was looking for. One of the porters was sitting outside a café, smoking a cigarette. He was about my age, even if he was trying to disguise it with a beard and a moustache. They were both made of that horrible wispy hair that doesn't really belong on a face. His jacket was hanging open. His cap sat crookedly on his head.

I sidled up next to him and sat down. After a while, he noticed me and nodded in my direction without smiling. It was enough.

"When's the next train to Moscow?" I asked.

He glanced at his watch. "Twenty minutes."

I pretended to consider this piece of information. "How would you like to make five rubles?" I asked.

His eyes narrowed. Five rubles was probably as much as he earned in a week.

"I'll be honest with you, friend," I said. "I'm in trouble with the police. I was almost arrested just now. I need to get on that train and if you'll sell me your jacket and your cap, I'll give you the cash."

It was not such a big gamble. Somehow, I knew that this boy would be greedy. And anyway, most people in Russia would help you if you were trying to get away from the authorities. That was how we were.

"Why do the police want you?" he asked.

"I'm a thief."

He sucked lazily on his cigarette. "I will give you my jacket and cap," he said. "But it will cost you ten rubles."

"Agreed."

I took out the money, taking care not to show him how much I had, and handed over a single note. Tonight, this porter would drink himself into a stupor. He might invite his friends to join him. He handed me his coat and his cap – but I did not go straight to the station. I stopped at one of the stalls and used another four rubles to buy a pair of second-hand suitcases from an old man who had a whole pile of them. Quickly, I took off my outer clothes and slipped them into one of the cases. I put on the jacket and cap. Then, carrying the suit-cases, I made my way to the station.

It seemed now that the police were every-where. Was it possible that the ones who had arrested me had talked after all? They had thrown a ring around the entire building. They were in front of the ticket office, on the platform. But not one of them noticed me. I waited until a smart-looking couple – some sort of local govern-ment official and his wife – got out of a taxi and I followed them into the station. They did not look round. But to the police and to anyone else who glanced our way, it simply looked as if they had hired a porter and that the two almost empty cases I was carrying were theirs.

I had timed it perfectly. We had no sooner arrived at the platform than a train drew in. The evening train to Moscow. I followed my clients to their carriage and climbed in behind them. They were completely unaware of my presence and although I was out there, in plain sight, nobody challenged me.

This is something that has not changed to this day. People look at the clothes you are wearing without ever thinking about the person who is inside. A man with a back-to-front collar is a vicar. A woman in a white coat with a stethoscope around her neck is a doctor. It is as simple as that. You do not ask them for ID.

I stayed on the train and a few minutes later it left, very quickly picking up speed, carrying me into the darkness. I knew I would never return.

МОСКВА

MOSCOW

Kazansky Station. Moscow.

It is hard to remember my feelings as the train drew near to its final destination. On the one hand, I was elated. I had made it. I had travelled six hundred miles, leaving the police and all my other problems behind me. But what of this new world in which I was about to find myself? The train would stop. The doors would open. And what then?

Through the windows I had already seen apartment blocks, one after another, that must have been home to tens of thousands of people. How could they live like that, so many of them, piled up on top of each other? Then there were the churches and their golden domes, ten times the size of poor St Nicholas. The factories billowing smoke into a sky that was cloudless, sunless, a single sheet of grey. But all of these were dwarfed by the skyscrapers with their spires and glittering needles, thousands of windows, millions of bricks, rising up as if from some crazy dream. Of course I had been shown pictures of them at school. I knew they had been built by Stalin back in the 1940s and 1950s. But seeing them for myself was different. Somehow I was shocked that they did actually exist and that they really were here, scattered around the city, watching over it.

I had been fortunate on the train. There was an empty compartment right at the back with a bunk bed that folded down. That was where I slept – not on the bunk but underneath it on the floor, out of sight of the ticket collectors. The strange thing was that I managed to sleep at all, but then I suppose I was exhausted. I woke up once or twice in the night and listened to the train rumbling through the darkness and I could almost feel the memories slipping away ... Estrov, Leo, my parents, my school. I knew that by the time I arrived in Moscow, I would be little more than an empty shell, a fourteen-year-old boy with no past and perhaps no future. There was even a small part of me that wished I hadn't escaped from the police. At least, that way, I wouldn't have to make any decisions. I wouldn't be on my own.

One name stayed with me, turning over and over in my head. Misha Dementyev. He worked in the biology department of Moscow State University and my mother had insisted that he would look after me. Surely it wouldn't be so hard to find him. The worst of my troubles might already be over. That was what I tried to tell myself.

The station was jammed. I had never seen so many people in one place. As I stepped down from the train, I found myself on a platform that seemed to stretch on for ever, with passengers milling about everywhere, carrying suitcases, packages, bundles of clothes, some of them chewing on sandwiches, others emptying their hip-flasks. Everyone was tired and grimy. There were policemen too but I didn't think they were looking for me. I had taken off the porter's cap and jacket and abandoned the suitcases. Once again I was wearing my Young Pioneers outfit, although I thought of getting rid of that too. It was quite warm in Moscow. The air felt heavy and smelt of oil and smoke.

I allowed myself to be swept along, following the crowd through a vast ticket hall, larger than any room I had ever seen, and out into the street. I found myself standing on the edge of a square. Again, it was the size that struck me first. To my eyes, this one single space was as big as the whole of Kirsk. It had lanes of traffic and cars, buses, trams roaring past in every direction. Traffic – the very notion of a traffic jam – was a new experience for me and I was overwhelmed by the noise and the stench of the exhaust fumes. Even today it sometimes surprises me that people are willing to put up with it. The cars were every colour imaginable. I had seen official Chaikas and Ladas but it was as if these vehicles had driven here from every country in the world. Grey taxis with chessboard patterns on their hoods dodged in and out of the different lines. Subways had been built for pedestrians, which was just as well. Trying to cross on the surface would have been suicide.

There were three separate railway stations in the square, each one trying to outdo the other with soaring pillars, archways and towers. Travellers were arriving from different parts of Russia and as soon as they emerged they were greeted by all sorts of food stalls, mainly run by wrinkled old women in white aprons and hats. In fact people were selling everything ... meat, vegetables, Chinese jeans and padded jackets, electrical goods, their own furniture. Some of them must have come off the train for no other reason. Nobody had any money. This was where you had to start.

My own needs were simple and immediate. I was dizzy with hunger. I headed to the nearest food stall and started with a small pie filled with cabbage and meat. I followed it with a currant bun – we called them *kalerikas* and they were specially made to fill you up. Then I bought a drink from a machine that squirted syrup and fizzy water into a glass. It still wasn't enough. I had another and then a raspberry ice cream that I bought for seven kopecks. The lady beamed at me as she handed it over ... as if she knew it was something special. I remember the taste of it to this day.

It was as I finished the last spoonful that I realized I was being watched. There was a boy of about seventeen or eighteen leaning against a lamppost, examining me. He was the same height as me but more thickly set with muddy eyes and long, very straight, almost colourless hair. He would have been handsome but at some time his nose had been broken and it had set unevenly, giving his whole face an unnatural slant. He was wearing a black leather jacket which was much too big for him, the sleeves rolled back so that they wouldn't cover his hands. Perhaps he had stolen it. Nobody was coming anywhere near him. Even the travellers seemed to avoid him. From the way he was standing there, you would think he owned the pavement and perhaps half the city. I quite liked that, the way he had nothing but pretended otherwise.

As I gazed around me, I realized that there were quite a lot of children outside Kazansky station, most of them huddling together in groups close to the entrance without daring to go inside. These children looked much less well off than the boy in the leather jacket; emaciated with pale skin and hollow eyes. Some of them were trying to beg from the arriving passengers but they were doing it half-heartedly, as if they were nervous of being seen. I saw a couple of tiny boys who couldn't have been more than ten years old, homeless and half starved. I felt ashamed. What would they have been thinking as they watched me gorge myself? I was tempted to go over and give them a few kopecks but before I could move, the older boy suddenly walked forward and stood in front of me. There was something about his manner that unnerved me. He seemed to be smiling at some private joke. Did he know who I was, where I had come from? I got the feeing that he knew everything about me, even though we had never met.

"Hello, soldier," he said. He was referring, of course, to my Young Pioneers outfit. "Where have you come from?"

"From Kirsk," I said.

"Never heard of it. Nice place?"

"It's all right."

"First time in Moscow?"

"No. I've been here before."

I had a feeling he knew straight away that I was lying, like the policemen in Kirsk. But he just smiled in that odd way of his. "You got somewhere to stay?"

"I have a friend..."

"It's good to have a friend. We all need friends." He looked around the square. "But I don't see anyone."

"He's not here."

It reminded me of my first day at senior school. I was trying to sound confident but I was completely defenceless and he knew it. He examined me more closely, weighing up various possibilities, then suddenly he straightened up and stretched out a hand. "Relax, soldier," he said. "I don't want to give you any hassle. I'm Dimitry. You can call me Dima."

I took his hand. I couldn't really refuse it. "I'm Yasha," I said.

We shook.

"Welcome to Moscow," he said. "Welcome back, I should say. So when were you last here?"

"It was a while ago," I said. I knew that the more I spoke, the more I would give away. "It was with my parents," I added.

"But this time you're on your own."

"Yes."

The single word hung in the air.

It was hard to make out what Dima had in mind. On the one hand he seemed friendly enough, but on the other, I could sense him unravelling me. It was that broken nose of his. It made it very difficult to read his face. "This person I'm supposed to be meeting..." I said. "He's a friend of my parents. He works at the University of Moscow. I don't suppose you know how to get there?"

"The university? It's a long way from this part of town but it's quite easy. You can take the Metro." His hand slipped over my shoulder. Before I knew it, we were walking together. "The entrance is over here. There's a direct line that runs all the way there. The station you want is called Universitet. Do you have any money?"

"Not much," I said.

"It doesn't matter. The Metro's cheap. In fact, I'll tell you what..." He reached out and a coin appeared at his fingertips as if he had plucked it out of the air. "Here's five kopecks. It's all you need. And don't worry about paying me back. Always happy to help someone new to town."

We had arrived at a staircase leading underground and to my surprise he began to walk down with me. Was he going to come the whole way? His hand was still on my shoulder and as we went he was telling me about the journey.

"Nine stops, maybe ten. Just stay on the train and you'll be there in no time..."

As he spoke, a set of swing doors opened in front of us and two more boys appeared, coming up the steps. They were about the same age as Dima, one dark, the other fair. I expected them to move aside – but they didn't. They barged into me and for a moment I was sandwiched between them with Dima still behind to me. I thought they were going to attack me but they were gone as suddenly as they'd arrived.

"Watch out!" Dima shouted. He twisted round and called out after them. "Why don't you look where you're going?" He turned back to me. "That's how people are in this city. Always in a hurry and to hell with everyone else."

The boys had gone and we said no more about it. Dima took me as far as the barriers. "Good luck, soldier," he said. "I hope you find who you're looking for."

We shook hands again.

"Remember – Universitet." With a cheerful wave, he ambled away, leaving me on my own. I walked forward and stopped in front of the escalator.

I had never seen anything like it. Stairs that moved, that carried people up and down in an endless stream. They seemed to go on and on, and I couldn't believe that the railway lines had been laid so deep. Cautiously, I stepped onto it and found myself clinging onto the handrail, being carried down as if into the bowels of the earth. At the very bottom, there was a uniformed woman in a glass box. Her job was simply to watch the passengers, to make sure that nobody tripped over and hurt themselves. I couldn't imagine what it must be like to work here all day, buried underground, never seeing the sun.

The Moscow Metro was famous all over Russia. It had been built by workers from every part of the country and famous artists had been brought in to decorate it. Each station was spectacular in its own way. This one had gold-coloured pillars, a mosaic floor and glass spheres hanging from the ceiling blazing with light. To the thousands of passengers who used it, it was nothing – simply a way of getting around – but I was amazed. A train came roaring out of the tunnel almost immediately. I got on and a moment later the doors slammed shut. With a jolt, the train moved off.

I took a spare seat – and it was as I sat down that I knew that something was wrong. I reached back and patted my trouser pocket. It was empty. I had been robbed. All my money had gone apart from a few coins. I played back what had happened and realized that I had been set up from the start. Dima had seen me paying for the food. He knew I had cash. Somehow he must have signalled to the two other boys and sent them into the station through another entrance. He'd kept me talking just long enough and then he'd led me down the steps and straight into their arms. It was a professional job and one they had probably done a hundred times before. My anger was as black as the tunnel we'd plunged into. I had lost more than seventy rubles! My parents had saved that money. They had thought it would save me. But I had stupidly, blindly allowed it to be taken away from me. What a fool I was! I didn't deserve to survive.

But sitting there, being swept along beneath the city, I decided that perhaps it didn't matter after all. Even as the train was carrying me forward, I could put it all behind me. I was going to meet Misha Dementyev and he would look after me. I didn't actually need the money any more. Looking back now, I would say that this was one of the first valuable lessons I learnt, and one that would be useful in my future line of work. Sometimes things go wrong. It is inevitable. But it is a mistake to waste time and energy worrying about events that you cannot influence. Once they have happened, let them go.

What was I expecting the university to be like? In my mind, I had seen a single building like my school, only bigger. But instead, when I came out of the station, I found a city within the city, an entire neighbourhood devoted to learning. It was much more spacious and elegant than anything I had so far seen of Moscow. There were boulevards and parks, special buses to carry the students in and out, lawns and fountains, and not one building but dozens of them, evenly spaced, each one in its own domain. It was all dominated by one of Stalin's skyscrapers, and as I stood in front of it I saw how it had been designed to make you feel tiny, to remind you of the power and the majesty of the state. Standing in front of the steps that led to the front doors – hidden behind a row of columns – I felt like the world's worst sinner about to enter a church. But at the same time, the building had a magnetic attraction. I had no idea where the biology department was. But this was the heart of the university. I would find Misha Dementyev here. I climbed the steps and went in.

The inside of the building didn't seem to fit what I had seen outside. It was like stepping into a submarine or a ship with no windows, no views. The ceilings were low. It was too warm. Corridors led to more corridors. Doors opened onto other doors. Staircases sprouted in every direction. Students marched past me on all sides, carrying their books and their backpacks, and I forced myself to keep moving, knowing that if I stopped and looked lost it would be a sure way to get noticed. It seemed to me that if there was an administrative area, an office with the names of all the people working at the university, it would be somewhere close to the entrance. Surely the university wouldn't want casual visitors to plunge too far into the building or to take one of the lifts up to the fortieth or fiftieth floor? I tried a door. It was locked. The next one opened into a toilet. Next to it there was a bare room, occupied by a cleaner with a mop and a cigarette.

"What do you want?" she asked.

"The administration office."

She looked at me balefully. "That way. On the left. Room 1117."

The corridor went on for about a hundred metres but the door marked 1117 was only halfway down. I knocked and went in.

There were two more women sitting at desks which were far too small for the typewriters, piles of paper, files and ashtrays that covered them. One of the women was plugged into an old-fashioned telephone system, the sort with wires looping everywhere, but she glanced up as I came in.

"Yes?" she demanded.

"Can you help me?" I asked. "I'm looking for someone."

"You need the student office. That's room 1301."

"I'm not looking for a student. I need to speak to a professor. His name is Misha Dementyev."

"Room 2425 – the twenty-fourth floor. Take the lift at the end of the corridor."

I felt a surge of relief. He was here! He was in his office! At that moment, I saw the end of my journey and the start of a new life. This man had known my parents. Now he would help me.

I took the lift to the twenty-fourth floor, sharing it with different groups of students who all looked purposefully grubby and dishevelled. I had been in a lift before and this old-fashioned steel box, which shuddered and stopped at least a dozen times, had none of the wonders of the escalator on the Metro. Finally I arrived at the floor I wanted. I stepped out and followed a cream-coloured corridor that, like the ground floor, had no windows. At least the offices were clearly labelled and I found the one I wanted right at the corner. The door was open as I approached and I heard a man speaking on the telephone.

"Yes, of course, Mr Sharkovsky," he was saying. "Yes, sir. Thank you, sir."

I knocked on the door.

"Come in!"

I entered a small, cluttered room with a single, square window looking out over the main avenue and the steps that had first brought me into the building. There must have been five or six hundred books there, not just lined up along the shelves but stacked up on the floor and every available surface. They were fighting for space with a whole range of laboratory equipment, different-sized flasks, two microscopes, scales, Bunsen burners, and boxes that looked like miniature ovens or fridges. Most unnerving of all, a complete human skeleton stood in a frame in one corner as if it were here to guard all this paraphernalia while its owner was away.

The man was sitting at his desk. He had just put down the phone as I came in. My first impression was that he was about the same age as my father, with thick black hair that only emphasized the round bald patch in the middle of his head. The skin here was stretched tight and polished, reflecting the ceiling light. He had a heavy beard and moustache, and as he examined me from behind a pair of glasses, I saw small, anxious eyes blinking at me as if he had never seen a boy before – or had certainly never allowed one into his office.

Actually, I was wrong about this. He was nervous because he knew who I was. He spoke my name immediately. "Yasha?"

"Are you Mr Dementyev?" I asked.

"Professor Dementyev," he replied. "Please, come in. Close the door. Does anyone know you're here?"

"I asked in the administration room down-stairs," I said.

"You spoke to Anna?" I had no idea what the woman's name was. He didn't let me reply. "That's a great pity. It would have been much better if you had telephoned me before you came. How *did* you get here?"

"I came by train. My parents—"

"I know what has happened in Estrov." He was agitated. Suddenly there were beads of sweat on the crown of his head. I could see them glistening. "You cannot stay here, Yasha," he said. "It's too dangerous."

I couldn't believe what I was hearing. "My parents said you'd look after me!"

"And I will! Of course I will!" He tried to smile at me but he was full of nervous energy and he was allowing his different thought processes to tumble over each other. "Sit down, Yasha, please!" He pointed to a chair. "I'm sorry but you've taken me completely by surprise. Are you hungry? Are you thirsty? Can I get you something?" Before I could answer, he snatched up the telephone again. "There's somebody I know," he explained to me. "He's a friend. He can help you. I'm going to ask him to come."

He dialled a number and as I sat down facing him, uncomfortably close to the skeleton, he spoke quickly into the receiver.

"It's Dementyev. The boy is here. Yes ... here at

the university." He paused while the person at the other end spoke to him. "We haven't had a chance to speak yet. I thought I should let you know at once." He was answering a question I hadn't heard. "He seems all right. Unharmed, yes. We'll wait for you here."

He put the phone down and it seemed to me that he was suddenly less agitated than he had been when I had arrived – as if he had done what was expected of him. For some reason, I was feeling uneasy. By the look of it, Professor Dementyev wasn't pleased to see me. I was a danger to him. This was my parents' closest friend but I was beginning to wonder how much that friendship was worth.

"How did you know who I was?" I asked.

"I've been expecting you, ever since I heard about what happened. And I recognized you, Yasha. You look very much like your mother. I saw the two of you together a few times when you were very young. You won't remember me. It was before your parents left Moscow."

"Why did they leave? What happened? You worked with them."

"I worked with your father. Yes."

"Do you know that he's dead?"

"I didn't know for certain. I'm sorry to hear it. He and I were friends."

"So tell me—"

"Are you sure I can't get you something?"

I had eaten and drunk everything I needed at Kazansky Station. What I really wanted was to be away from here. I have to say that I was disappointed by Misha Dementyev. I'm not sure what I'd been expecting, but maybe he could have been more affectionate, like a long-lost uncle or something? He hadn't even come out from behind his desk.

"What happened?" I asked again. "Why was my father sent to work in Estrov?"

"I can't go through all that now." He was flustered again. "Later..."

"Please, Professor Dementyev!"

"All right. All right." He looked at me as if he was wondering if he could trust me. Then he began. "Your father was a genius. He and I worked here together in this department. We were young students; idealists, excited. We were researching endospores ... and one in particular. Anthrax. I don't suppose you know very much about that."

"I know about anthrax," I said.

"We thought we could change the world ... your father especially. He was looking at ways to prevent the infection of sheep and cattle. But there was an accident. Working in the laboratory together, we created a form of anthrax that was much faster and deadlier than anything anyone had ever known. It had no cure. Antibiotics were useless against it."

"It was a weapon?"

"That wasn't our intention. That wasn't what we

wanted. But – yes. It was the perfect biological weapon. And of course the government found out about it. Everything that happens in this place they know about. It was true then. It's true now. They heard about our work here and they came to us and ordered us to develop it for military use." Dementyev took out a handkerchief and used it to polish the lenses of his glasses. He put them back on. "Your father refused. It was the last thing he wanted. So they started to put the pressure on. They threatened him. And that was when he did something incredibly brave ... or incredibly stupid. He went to a journalist and tried to get the story into the newspapers.

"He was arrested at once. I was here, in the laboratory, when they marched him away. They arrested your mother too."

"How old was I?" I asked.

"You were two. And – I'm sorry, Yasha – they used you to get at your parents. That was how they worked. It was very simple. If your parents didn't do what they were told, they would never see you again. What choice did they have? They were sent to Estrov, to work in the factory. They were forced to produce the new anthrax. That was the deal. Stay silent. And live."

So everything – my parents' life or their non-life as prisoners in a remote village, the little house, the boredom and the poverty – had been for me. I wasn't sure how that made me feel. Was I to blame for everything that had happened? Was I the one who had destroyed their lives?

"Yasha..." Dementyev stood up and came over to me. He was much taller than I had expected now that he was on his feet. He loomed over me. "Were you inoculated?" he asked.

I nodded. "My parents were shot at when they escaped. But they stole a syringe. They injected me."

"I knew your father had been working on an antidote. Thank God! But I guessed it the moment I saw you. Otherwise you would have been dead a long time ago."

"My best friend died," I said.

"I'm so sorry. Anton and Eva – your parents – were my friends too."

We fell silent. He was still standing there, one hand on the back of my chair.

"What will happen to me?" I asked.

"You don't need to worry any more, Yasha. You'll be well looked after."

"Who was that you called?"

"It was a friend. Someone we can trust. He'll be here very soon."

There was something wrong. Things that he'd told me just didn't add up. I was about to speak when I heard the sound of sirens, police cars approaching, still far away but drawing nearer. And I knew instantly that there was no friend, that Dementyev had called them. It wasn't detective work. I could have asked him why my parents had been sent to live in Estrov while he had been allowed to stay here. I could have played back the conversation he'd had on the telephone, how he had referred to me simply as "the boy". Not Yasha. Not Anton's son. The people at the other end knew who I was because they'd been expecting me to show up, waiting for me. I could have worked it out but I didn't need to. I saw it all in his eyes.

"Why?" I asked.

He didn't even try to deny it. "I'm sorry, Yasha," he said. "But nobody can know. We have to keep it secret."

We. The factory managers. The helicopter pilots. The militia. The government. And Dementyev. They were all in it together.

I scrabbled to my feet – or tried to. But Dementyev was ahead of me. He pounced down, his hands on my shoulders, using his weight to pin me to the seat. For a moment his face was close to mine, the eyes staring at me through the thick lenses.

"There's nowhere you can go!" he hissed. "I promise you ... they won't treat you badly."

"They'll kill me!" I shouted back. "They killed everyone!"

"I'll talk to them. They'll take you somewhere safe..."

Yes. I saw it already. A prison or a mental asylum, somewhere I'd never be seen again.

I couldn't move. Dementyev was too strong for

me. And the police cars were getting closer. We were twenty-four floors up but I could hear the sirens cutting through the air. And then I had an idea. I forced myself to relax.

"You can't do this!" I exclaimed. "My father gave me something for you. He said it was very valuable. He said if I gave it to you, you'd have to help me."

"What is it?"

"I don't know. It's in a bag. It's in my pocket!"

"Show me."

He let go of one of my shoulders ... but only one of them. I still couldn't wrench myself free. I was sitting down. He was standing over me and he was twice my size.

"Take it out," he said.

The police must have turned into the main university drive. I heard car doors slam shut.

Using my one free arm, I drew out the black bag that my mother had given me. At least Dima and his friends hadn't stolen it when they took my money. I placed it on the desk. And it worked just as I'd hoped. Dementyev still didn't let go of me but his grip loosened as he reached out and opened the bag. I saw his face change as he tipped out the contents.

"What...?" he began.

I jerked myself free, throwing the chair backwards. As it toppled over, I managed to get to my feet. Dementyev swung round but he was too late to stop me lashing out with my fist. I knocked the glasses off his face. He fell back against the desk but then recovered and seized hold of me again. I needed a weapon and there was only one that I could see. I reached out and grabbed the arm of the skeleton, wrenching it free from the shoulder. The hand and the wrist dangled down but I hung onto the upper bone – the humerus – and used it as a club, smashing it against Dementyev's head again and again until, with a howl, he fell back. I twisted away. Dementyev had crumpled over the desk. There was blood streaming down his face.

"It's too late..." he stammered. "You won't get away."

I snatched back the jewellery and tumbled out of the office. There was nobody outside. Surely someone must have heard what had happened? I didn't want to know. I ran to the lift. It was already on the way up and it took me a few seconds to work out that the police were almost certainly inside, travelling towards me. And I might have been caught standing there, waiting for them! I continued down the corridor and found a fire exit – leading to twenty-four flights of stairs. I didn't stop until I reached the bottom and it was only then that I realized I was still carrying the skeleton's arm. I found a dustbin, picked up some loose papers and dropped the arm in.

As I walked down the steps at the front door, I saw three police cars parked there with their lights flashing. I pretended to be immersed in the papers I had taken. If there were any policemen outside, I would look like one more of the countless students coming in and out.

But nobody stopped me. I hurried back to the station with just one thought in my head. I was alone in Moscow with no money.

ТВЕРСКАЯ

TVERSKAYA

I went back to Kazansky Station.

In a way, it was a mad decision. The police knew I was in Moscow and they would certainly be watching all the major stations – just as they had in Rosna and Kirsk. But I wasn't leaving. The truth was that in the whole of Russia, I had nowhere to go and no one to look after me. I couldn't go back to Estrov, obviously, and although I remembered my mother once telling me that she had relations in a city called Kazan, I had no idea where it was or how to get there.

No, it was much better to stay in Moscow, but first of all I would need to change my appearance. That was easy enough. I stripped off my Pioneer uniform and dumped it in a bin. Then I got my hair cut short. Although the bulk of my money had gone, I had managed to find eighteen kopecks scattered through my pockets and I used nine of them at a barber's shop, a dank little place in a backstreet with old hair strewn over the floor. As I stepped out again, feeling the unfamiliar cool of the breeze on my head and the back of my neck, a police car rushed past – but I wasn't worried. Even today, I am aware of how little you need to change to lose yourself in a city. A haircut, different clothes, perhaps a pair of sunglasses ... it is enough.

I still had enough kopecks for the return journey and as I sat once again in the Metro, I tried to work out some sort of plan. The most immediate problem was accommodation. Where would I sleep when night came? If I stayed out on the street, I would be at my most vulnerable. And then there was the question of food. Without money, I couldn't eat. Of course, I could steal but the one thing I most dreaded was falling back into the hands of the police. If they recognized me, I was finished. And even if they didn't, I had heard enough stories about the prison camps all over Russia, built specially for children. Did I want to end up with the rest of my hair shaved off, stuck behind barbed wire in the middle of nowhere? There were thousands of Russian boys whose lives were exactly that.

This time I barely even noticed the stations, no matter how superbly they were decorated. I was utterly miserable. My parents had believed in Misha Dementyev and they had sent me to him, even though it had cost them their lives. But the moment I had walked into his office, he had thought only of saving his own skin. It seemed to me that there was nobody in the world I could trust. Even Dima, the boy I had met when I got off the train, had only been interested in robbing me.

But perhaps Dima was the answer.

The more I thought about it, the more I decided he might not be all bad. Certainly, when we had met, he had been pleasant enough, smiling and friendly, even if he was simply setting me up for his friends. But maybe I was partly to blame for what had happened, coming off the train and flashing my money around all the different stalls. Dima was living on the street. He had to survive. I'd made myself an obvious target and he'd done what he had to.

At the same time, I remembered what he'd said to me. *It's good to have a friend. We all need friends.* Could it be possible that he actually meant it? He was, after all, only a few years older than me and we were both in the same situation. Part of me knew that I was fooling myself. Dima was probably miles away by now, laughing at me for being such a fool. But at the end of the day, he was the only person in the city I actually knew. If I could find him again, perhaps I could persuade him to help me.

And there was something else. I still had my mother's jewels.

Half an hour later, I climbed up to street level and found myself back where I had begun. The women were still there at their food stalls but they almost seemed to be taunting me. Before, they had been welcoming. Now, all their pies and ice creams were beyond my reach. I found a bench and sat down, watching the crowds around me. Stations are strange places. When you pass through them, travelling somewhere, you barely notice them. They simply help you on your way. But stand outside with nowhere to go and they make you feel worthless. You should not be here, they shout at you. If you are not a passenger, you do not belong here.

To start with, I did nothing at all. I just sat there, staring at the traffic, letting people stream past me on all sides. The children I had seen were still dotted around and I wondered what they would do with themselves when night fell. That could only be a few hours away. The light was barely changing, the sun trapped behind unbroken cloud, but there were already commuters arriving at the station, on their way home. There was no sign of Dima. In the end, I went over to a couple of boys, the ten-year-olds that I had seen before.

"Excuse me," I said.

Two pairs of very sly and malevolent eyes turned on me. One of the children had snot running out of his nose. Both of them looked worn out, unhealthy.

"I'm looking for someone I was talking to earlier," I went on. "He was wearing a black leather jacket. His name is Dima."

The boys glanced at each other. "You got any money?" one of them asked.

"No."

"Then get lost!" Those weren't his actual words. This little boy, whose voice hadn't even broken, used the filthiest language I'd ever heard. I saw that he had terrible teeth with gaps where half of them had fallen out. His friend hissed at me like an animal and at that moment the two of them weren't children at all. They were like horrible old men, not even human. I was glad to leave them on their own.

I tried to ask some of the other street kids the same question but as I approached them, they moved away. It was as if they all knew that I was from out of town, that I wasn't one of them, and for that reason they would have nothing to do with me. And now the light really was beginning to disappear. I was starting to feel the threat of nightfall and knew that I couldn't stay here for much longer. I would have to find a doorway – or perhaps I could sleep in one of the subways beneath the streets. I had four kopecks left in my pocket. Barely enough for a cup of hot tea.

And then, quite unexpectedly, I saw him. Dima – with his oversized leather jacket and his half-handsome, half-ugly face – had turned the corner, smoking a cigarette, flicking away the match. There was another boy with him and I recognized him too. He had been one of the two who had robbed me. Dima said something and they laughed. It looked as if they were heading for the Metro, presumably on their way home.

I didn't hesitate. It was now or never. I crossed the concourse in front of the station and stood in their path.

Dima saw me first and stopped with the cigarette halfway to his lips. I had taken him by surprise and he thought I was going to make trouble. I could see it at once. He was tense, wary. But I was completely relaxed. I'd already worked it out. He'd tricked me. He'd robbed me. But I had to treat him as my friend.

"Hi, Dima." I greeted him as if the three of us had arranged to meet here for coffee.

He smiled a little but he was still suspicious. And there was something else. I wasn't quite sure what it was but he was looking at me almost as if he had expected me to come back, as if there was something he knew that I didn't. "Soldier!" he exclaimed. "How are you doing? What happened to your hair?"

"I got it cut."

"Did you meet your friend?"

"No. He wasn't there. It seems he's left Moscow."

"That's too bad."

I nodded. "In fact, I've got a real problem. He was going to put me up but now I don't have anywhere to go."

I was hoping he might offer to help. That was the idea, anyway. Why not? He was seventy rubles richer than me. Thanks to him, I had nothing. He could at least have offered me a bed for the night. But he didn't speak and I realized I was wasting my time. He was street-hardened, the sort of person who would have never helped anyone in his life. His friend muttered something and pushed past me, disappearing into the Metro, but I stood my ground. "Can you help me?" I said. "I just need somewhere to stay for a few nights." And then – my last chance. "I can pay you."

"You've got money?" That surprised him. He thought he'd taken it all already.

"Not any more," I said. I shrugged as if to let him know that it didn't matter, that I'd already forgotten about it. "But I've got this." I went on. I took out the black velvet bag that my mother had given me and that I'd used to trick Dementyev. I opened it and poured the contents – the necklace, the ring and the earrings – into my hand. "There must be a pawnshop somewhere. I'll sell them and then I can pay you for a room."

Dima examined the jewellery, the brightly coloured stones in their silver and gold settings, and I could already see the light stirring in his eyes as he made the calculations. How much were they worth and how was he going to separate them from me? He dropped his cigarette and reached out, picking up one of the earrings. He let it hang from his finger and thumb. "This won't get you much," he said. "It's cheap."

Right then, I thought of my mother and I could feel the anger rising in my blood. I wanted to punch him but still I forced myself to stay calm. "I was told they were valuable," I said. "That's gold. And those stones are emeralds. Take me to a pawnshop and we can find out."

"I don't know..." He was pretending otherwise but he knew that the jewels were worth more than the money he had already stolen. "Give me the stuff and I'll take it to a pawnbroker for you. But I don't think you'll get more than five rubles."

He'd get fifty. I'd get five ... if I was lucky. I could see how his mind worked. I held out my hand and, reluctantly, he gave me the earring back. "I can find a pawnbroker on my own," I said.

"There's no need to be like that, soldier! I'm only trying to help." He gave me a crooked smile, made all the more crooked by his broken nose. "Listen, I've got a room and you're welcome to stay with me. You know ... we're all friends, here in Moscow, right? But you'll have to pay rent."

"How much rent?"

"Two rubles a week."

I pretended to consider. "I'll have to see it first."

"Whatever you say. We can go there now if you like."

"Sure. Why not?"

He took me back down into the Metro. He even

paid my fare again. I knew I was taking a risk. He could lead me to some faraway corner of the city, take me into an alleyway, put a knife into me and steal the jewels. But I had a feeling that wasn't the way he worked. Dima was a hustler, a thief – but at the end of the day, he just didn't have the look of someone who was ready to kill. He would get the jewellery in the end anyway. I would pay it to him as rent or he would steal it from me while I slept. My plan was simply to make myself useful to him, to become part of his gang. If I could do this quickly enough, he might let me stay with him, even when I had nothing more to give. That was my hope.

He took me to a place just off Tverskaya Street, one of the main thoroughfares in Moscow, which leads all the way down to the Kremlin and Red Square. Today, there is a hotel on that same corner – the nine-storey Marriott Grand, where American tourists stay in total luxury. But when I came there, following Dima and still wondering if I wasn't making another bad mistake, it was very different. Moscow has changed so much, so quickly. It was another world back then.

Dima lived in what had once been a block of flats but which had long been abandoned and left to rot. All the colour had faded from the brickwork, which was damp and mouldy, and covered with graffiti – not artwork but political slogans, swear words, and the names of city football teams. The windows were so dirty that they looked more like rusting metal than glass. The building rose up twelve floors, three more than the hotel that would one day replace it, and whole thing seemed to be sagging in on itself, hardly bothering to stay upright. It was surrounded by other blocks that were similar ... they looked like old men standing out in the cold, having a last cigarette together before they died. The streets here were very narrow; more like alleyways, twisting together in the darkness, covered with rubbish and mud. The block of flats had shops on the ground floor – an empty grocery store, a chemist and a massage parlour – but the further up you went, the more desolate it became. It had no lifts, of course. Just a concrete staircase that had been used as a toilet so many times that it stank. By the time you got to the top, there was no electricity, no proper heating. The only water came dribbling, cold, out of the taps.

We climbed up together. I noticed that Dima was wheezing when we got to the top and I wondered if he was ill – although it could just have been all those cigarettes. On the way, we passed a couple of people, a man and a woman, lying on top of each other, unconscious. I couldn't even be sure they were actually alive. Dima just stepped over them and I did the same, wondering what I was getting myself into. My village had been a place of poverty and hardship but it was somehow more shocking here, in the middle of a city.

Dima's room was on the eighth floor. Since there was no lighting, he had taken out a torch and used it to find the way. We went down a corridor that was missing its carpet with gaping holes showing the pipework and wiring. There were doors on either side, most of them locked, one or two reinforced with metal plating. Somewhere, I could hear a baby crying. A man shouted out a swear word. Another laughed. The sounds that echoed around me only added to the nightmare, the sense that I was being sucked into a dark and alien world.

"This is me," Dima said.

We'd come to a door marked with a number 83. Somebody had added DIMA'S PLACE in bright red letters but the paint hadn't been allowed to dry and it had trickled down like blood. Perhaps the effect was deliberate. There was a hole where the lock should have been but Dima used a padlock and a chain to keep the place secure. At the moment, it was hanging open. His friends had arrived ahead of us.

"Welcome home!" he said to me. "This is my place. Come in and meet my mates..."

He pushed the door open. We went in.

The flat was tiny. Most of it was in a single room, which he shared with the two boys who had robbed me. On the floor were three mattresses and some filthy pillows on a carpet which was mouldy and colourless. The place was lit by candles and my first thought was that if one of them toppled over in the night, we would all burn to death. A single table and four chairs stood on one side. Otherwise there was no furniture of any description. A few bits of the kitchen were still in place but I could tell at a glance that the sink hadn't been used for years and without electricity the fridge was no more than an oversized cupboard. The smell in the room was unpleasant; a mixture of human sweat, unwashed clothes, dirt and decay.

Dima waved me over to the table. "This is Yasha," he announced. "He's going to be staying with us for a while." His two friends were already sitting there playing Snap with a deck that was so worn that the cards hung limp in their hands. They didn't look pleased as I joined them. "He's going to pay," Dima added. "Two rubles a week."

Dima opened the fridge and took out a bottle of vodka and some black bread. He found some dirty glasses in the sink and poured drinks for us all. He lit a cigarette for himself, then offered me one, which I accepted gratefully. It wasn't just that I wanted to smoke. It was a gesture of friendship and that was what I most needed.

Dima introduced the two boys. "This is Roman. That's Grigory." Roman was tall and thin. He looked as if he had been deliberately stretched. Grigory was round-faced, pock-marked with oily, black hair. All three of them looked not just adult but old, as if they had forgotten their true age ...

which was about seventeen. Roman collected the cards and put them away. It was obvious who was the leader here. So long as Dima said I could stay, they weren't going to argue.

"Tell us about yourself, soldier," Dima said. "I'd like to know what brought you to Moscow." He winked at me. "And I'd particularly like to know why the police are so interested in you."

"What?"

So I'd been right. When I'd got back to the station I'd thought the children had been behaving strangely and now I knew why. The police had been there, looking for me.

"That's right. Tell him, Grig." Grigory said nothing so Dima went on. "They're looking for someone new to town. Someone who might have come into Kazansky Station, dressed up like a Young Pioneer. They've been asking everyone." He tapped ash. "They're offering a reward for information."

My heart sank. I wondered if I had walked into another trap. Had Dima invited me here to have me arrested? But there was no sound coming from outside; no footsteps in the corridor, no sirens in the street.

"Don't worry, soldier! No one's going to turn you in. Not even for the money. They never pay up anyway.

"I hate the p–p–p–police." Roman had a stutter. I watched his face contort as he tried to spit out the last word.

"What do they want with you?" Grigory asked. He sounded hostile. Maybe he was afraid that I was bringing more trouble into his life. He probably had enough already.

I wasn't sure how to answer. I didn't want to lie but I was afraid of telling the truth. In the end, I kept it as short as I could. "They killed my parents," I said. "My dad knew something he wasn't meant to know. They wanted to kill me too. I escaped."

"What about your friend at the university?" Dima asked.

"He wasn't my friend." I was on safer ground here. I told them everything that had happened in Misha Dementyev's office. When I described how I had beaten Dementyev off using the arm of the skeleton, Dima laughed out loud. "I wish I'd seen that," he said. "You certainly gave him the elbow!"

It was a weak joke but we all laughed. Dima refilled our glasses and once again we drank the Russian way, throwing the liquid back in a single gulp. It didn't take us long to finish the bottle and about an hour later we all went to bed ... if you can call bed a square of carpet with a pile of old clothes as a pillow. I was just glad to have a roof over my head and, helped by the vodka, I was asleep almost at once.

The next morning, Dima took me to the pawnbroker he had mentioned. It was a tiny shop with a cracked front window and an old, half-shaven man sitting behind a counter that was stacked with watches and jewellery. I handed across my mother's earrings and stood there, watching him examine them briefly through an eyeglass which he screwed into his face as if it was part of him. Right then, a little part of me died. It had been a pawnbroker that the hero had murdered in *Crime and Punishment*, the book I had been forced to read at school. I could almost have done the same.

He wanted to give me eight rubles for the earrings but Dima talked him up to twelve. The two of them knew each other well.

"You're a crook, Reznik," Dima scowled.

"And you're a thief, Dima," Reznik replied.

"One day someone will stick a knife in you."

"I don't mind. So long as they buy it from me first."

Dima took the money and we went back out into the sunlight. He gave me three rubles, keeping nine for himself, and when I looked down reproachfully at the crumpled notes he clapped me on the back. "That's three weeks' rent, soldier," he said.

"What about the other three rubles?"

"That's my commission. If you hadn't had me with you, that old crook would have ripped you off."

I'd been ripped off anyway but I didn't complain. Dima had said I could stay with him for three weeks. It was exactly what I wanted to hear.

"Let's get some breakfast!" he said.

We ate breakfast in the smallest, grimiest restaurant it would be possible to imagine. Somehow, I ended up paying for that too.

So began my stay in Moscow. I adapted very quickly to the way of life. The truth is that nobody did anything very much. They stole, they ate, they survived. I spent long hours outside the station with Dima, Roman and Grigory. The two boys didn't warm to me but gradually they began to accept that I was there. At the same time, Dima had made me his special project. I wondered if he might have had a younger brother at some time. He never spoke about his past life but that was how he treated me. When I write about him now, I still see him with the sleeves of his precious leather jacket falling over his hands, his smile, the way he swaggered along the street, and I wonder if he is alive or dead. Dead most probably. Homeless kids in Moscow never survived long.

Dima taught me how to beg. You had to be careful because if the police saw you they would pick you up and throw you into jail. But my fair hair, and the fact that I looked so young, helped. If I stood outside the Bolshoi Theatre at night, I could earn as much as five rubles from the rich people coming out. There were tourists in Red Square and I would position myself outside St Basil's Cathedral with its towers and twisting, multicoloured domes. I didn't even have to speak. Once, an American gave me five dollars, which I passed on to Dima. He gave me fifty kopecks back but that was his own special exchange rate. I knew it was worth a lot more.

I got used to the city. Streets that had seemed huge and threatening became familiar. I could find my way around on the Metro. I visited Lenin, lying dead in his tomb, although Dima told me that most of the body was made of wax. I also saw the grave of Yuri Gagarin, the first man in space. Not that he meant anything to me now. I went to the big shops – GUM department store and Yeliseev's Food Hall and stared at all the amazing food I would never be able to afford. Just once, I visited a bathhouse near the Bolshoi and enjoyed the total luxury of sitting in the steam, breathing in the scent of eucalyptus leaves and feeling warm and clean.

And I stole.

We needed to buy food, cigarettes and – most importantly – vodka. It sometimes seemed that it was impossible to live in Tverskaya without alcohol and every night there were terrible arguments when somebody's bottle was finished. We would hear the screams and the knife fights, and the next day there would often be fresh blood on the stairs. Those who couldn't afford vodka got high on shoe polish. I'm not lying. They would spread it on bread and place it on a hot pipe, then breathe in the fumes.

No matter how much time I spent begging, we never had enough money and I wasn't surprised to find myself back at Reznik's, the pawnshop. With Dima's help, I got fifteen rubles for my mother's necklace; more than the earrings but less than I'd hoped. I was determined not to part with her ring. It was the only memory of her that I had left.

And so, inevitably, I turned to crime. One of Dima's favourite tricks was to hang around outside an expensive shop, watching as the customers came out with their groceries. He would wait while they loaded up their car, then either Roman or Grigory would distract them while he snatched as much as he could out of the boot and then ran for it. I watched the operation a couple of times before Dima let me play the part of the decoy. Because I was so much younger than the other two boys, people were more sympathetic – and less suspicious. I would go up to them and pretend to be lost while Dima sneaked up to the back of their car.

The first three times, it worked perfectly and we found ourselves eating all sorts of things that we'd never tasted before. Roman and Grigory were getting used to me now. We'd begun playing cards together – a game that every Russian knows, called *Durak* or Fool. They'd even found a mattress for me. It wasn't a lot softer than the floor and it was infested with insects, but I still appreciated the gesture.

The fourth time, however, was almost a disaster. And it changed everything.

It was the usual set-up. We were outside a shop in a quiet street. It was an area we hadn't been to before. Our target was a chauffeur, obviously working for some big businessman who could afford to entertain. His car was a Daimler and there was enough food in the back to keep us going for a month. As usual, I went up to the man and, looking as innocent as possible, tried to engage him in conversation.

"Can you help me? I'm looking for Pushkin Square..."

Out of the corner of my eye, I saw Dima scurry up the pavement and disappear behind the raised door of the boot.

The chauffeur glared at me. "Get lost!"

"I am lost! I need to get to Pushkin Square..."

All I had to do was keep up the conversation for about thirty seconds. By the end of that time, Dima would have gone and two or three bags would have gone with him. But suddenly I heard him cry out and I saw, with complete horror, that a policeman had appeared out of nowhere. To this day I don't know where he had come from because we always checked the immediate area first, but I can only assume that he'd been expecting us, that the police must have decided to crack down on this sort of street theft and that he had been lying in wait all along. He was a huge man with the neck and the shoulders of a professional weightlifter. Dima was squirming in his jacket but he was like a fish caught in a net.

I saw the chauffeur making a grab for me but I ducked under his arms and ran round the back of the car. There was nothing I could do for Dima. The only sensible thing was to run away and leave him and just be thankful I'd had a lucky escape. But I couldn't do it. Despite everything, I was grateful to him. I had been with him for six weeks now and he had protected me. I couldn't have survived without him. I owed him something.

I threw myself at the policeman, who reacted in astonishment. I was honestly less than half his size and I barely even knocked him off balance. He didn't let go of Dima ... if anything he tightened his grip, bellowing at the chauffeur to come and join in. Dima lashed out with a fist but the policeman didn't feel it. With his spare hand, he grabbed hold of my shirt so that we were both held captive and, seeing us unarmed and helpless, the chauffeur lumbered forward to help.

We would certainly have been taken prisoner and that would have been the end of my Moscow adventure. Indeed, if I were recognized, it might be the end of my life. But as I struggled, I saw that one of the shopping bags had fallen over, spilling out its contents. There was a plastic bag of red powder on the top. I snatched it up, split it open and hurled it into the policeman's face, all in a single movement.

It was chilli powder. The policeman was instantly blinded and howled in pain, both hands rushing to cover his eyes. Dima was forgotten. In fact everything was forgotten. The policeman's head was covered in red powder. He was spinning round on his feet. I grabbed Dima and the two of us began to run. At the same moment, a police car appeared at the far end of the street, speeding towards us, its lights blazing. We ran across the pavement and down a narrow alleyway between two shops. It was a cul-de-sac, blocked at the far end by a wall. We didn't let it stop us, not for a second. We simply sprinted up the brickwork and over the top, crashing down onto an assortment of dustbins and cardboard boxes on the other side. Dima rolled over then got back on his feet. We could hear the siren behind us and knew that the police were only seconds away. We kept running – down another alleyway and across a main road with six lanes of traffic and cars, trucks, motorbikes and buses bearing down on us from every direction. It's a miracle we weren't killed. As it was, one car swerved out of our way and there was a screech and a crumpling of metal as a second car crashed into it. We didn't slow down. We didn't look back. We must have run half a mile across Moscow, ducking into side roads, chasing behind buildings, doing everything we could to keep out of sight. Eventually we came to a Metro entrance and darted into it, disappearing underground.

There was a train waiting at the platform. We didn't care where it was going. We dived in and sank, exhausted, into two seats.

Neither of us spoke again until we got back to our own station and climbed back up to our familiar streets. We didn't go to the flat straight away. Dima took me to a coffee house and we bought a couple of glasses of *kvass*, a sweet, watery drink made from bread.

We sat next to the window. We were both still out of breath. I could hear Dima's lungs rattling. Climbing the stairs was enough exercise for him and he had just run a marathon.

"Thank you, soldier," he said eventually.

"We were unlucky," I said.

"I was lucky you were there. You could have just left me."

I didn't say anything.

"I hate this stupid city," Dima said. "I never wanted to come here."

"Why did you?"

"I don't know." He shrugged, then pointed to his broken nose. "My dad did this to me when I was six years old. He threw me out when I was seven. I ended up in an orphanage in Yaroslav and that was a horrible place ... horrible. You don't want to know." He took out a cigarette and lit it. "They used to tie the kids down to the beds, the troublemakers. They left them there until they were covered in their own dirt. And the noise! The screaming, the crying... It never stopped. I think half of them were mad."

"Were you adopted?" I asked.

"Nobody wanted me. Not the way I looked. I ran away. Got out of Yaroslav and ended up on a train to Moscow ... just like you."

He fell silent.

"There's something I want you to know," he said. "That first day we met, at Kazansky Station." He took a drag on his cigarette and exhaled blue smoke. "We took your money. It was Roman, Grig and me. We set you up."

"I know," I said.

He looked at me. "I thought you must have. But now I'm admitting it ... OK?"

"It doesn't matter," I went on. "I'd have done the same."

"I don't think so, soldier. You're not the same as us."

"I like being with you," I said. "But there's something I want to ask."

"Go ahead."

"Do you mind not calling me 'soldier'?"

He nodded. "Whatever you say, Yasha."

He patted me on the shoulder. We finished our drinks, stood up and went home. And it seemed to me that I'd actually done what I'd set out to do. The two of us were friends.

ФОРТОЧНИК

FORTOCHNIK

For the next few days, we barely left the flat. Dima was worried the police would be looking for us and I also had my concerns. Forget Estrov. I was now wanted for theft and for assaulting a police officer. It was better for us not to show our faces in the street and so we ate, drank, played cards ... and we were bored. We were also running out of cash. I never asked Dima what he had done with the rubles he had taken from me and it wasn't as if we were spending a lot of money but somehow there was never enough for our basic needs. Roman and Grigory brought in a few rubles now and then but the truth is that they were too unattractive to have much success begging and Roman's stutter made it hard for him to ask for money.

Even so, it was Roman who suggested it one night. "We should try b–b–b–burglary."

We were sitting around the table with vodka and cards. All we had eaten that day was a couple of slices of black bread. The four of us were looking ill. We needed proper food and sunlight. I had got used to the smell in the room by now – in fact I was part of it. But the place was looking grimier than ever and we longed to be outside.

"Who are we going to b–b–burgle?" Dima asked.

Roman shrugged.

"It's a good idea," Grigory said. He slapped down an attack card – we were having another bout of *Durak*. "Yasha is small enough. He could be our *fortochnik*."

"What's a *fortochnik*?" I asked.

Dima rolled his eyes. "It's someone who breaks in through a *fortochka*," he explained.

That, at least, I understood. A *fortochka* was a type of window. Many apartments in Moscow had them before air conditioning took over. There would be a large window and then a much smaller one set inside it, a bit like a cat flap. In the summer months, people would open the *fortochkas* to let in the breeze and, of course, they were an invitation for thieves ... provided they were small enough. Grigory was right. He was too fat and Roman was too ungainly to crawl through, but I could make it easily. I was small for my age – and I'd lost so much weight that I was stick-thin.

"It is a good idea," Dima agreed. "But we need an address. There's no point just breaking in anywhere, and anyway, it's too dangerous. His eyes brightened. "We can talk to Fagin!"

Fagin was an old soldier who lived three floors down in a room on his own. He had been in Afghanistan and had lost one eye and half his left arm – in action, he claimed, although there was a rumour he had been run over by a trolleybus while he was home on leave. Fagin wasn't his real name, of course but everyone called him that after a character in an English book, *Oliver Twist*. And the thing about Fagin was that he knew everything about everything. I never found out how he got his information but if a bank was about to move a load of money or a diamond merchant was about to visit a smart hotel, somehow Fagin would catch wind of it and he would pass the information on – at a price. Everyone in the block respected him. I had seen him a couple of times, a short, plump man with a huge beard bristling around his chin, shuffling along the corridors in a dirty coat, and I had thought he looked more like a tramp than a master criminal.

But now that Dima had thought of him, the decision had been made and the following day we gathered in his flat, which was the same size as ours but at least furnished with a sofa and a few pictures on the wall. He had electricity too. Fagin himself was a disgusting old man. The way he looked at us, you didn't really want to think about what was going on in his head. If Santa Claus had taken a dive into a sewer he would have come up looking much the same.

"You want to be *fortochniks*?" he asked, smiling to himself. "Then you want to do it soon before the winter comes and all the windows are closed! But you need an address. That's what you need, my boys. Somewhere worth the pickings!" He produced a leather notebook with old bus tickets and receipts sticking out of the pages. He opened it and began to thumb through.

"How much is your share?" Dima asked.

"Always straight to the point, Dimitry. That's what I like about you." Fagin smiled. "Whatever you take, you bring to me. No lying! I know a lie when I hear one and, believe me, I'll cut out your tongue." He leered at us, showing the yellow slabs that were his teeth. "Sixty per cent for me, forty for you. Please don't argue with me, Dimitry, dear boy. You won't get better anywhere else. And I have the addresses. I know all the places where you won't have any difficulty. Nice, slim boys, slipping in at night..."

"Fifty-fifty," Dima said.

"Fagin doesn't negotiate." He found a page in his notebook. "Now here's an address off Lubyanka Square. Ground-floor flat." He looked up. "Shall I go on?"

Dima nodded. He had accepted the deal. "Where is it?"

"Mashkova Street. Number seven. It's owned by a rich banker. He collects stamps. Many of them valuable." He flicked the page over. "Maybe you'd prefer a house in the Old Arbat. Lots of antiques.

Mind you, it was done over last spring and I'd say it was a bit early for a return visit." Another page. "Ah yes. I've had my eye on this place for a while. It's near Gorky Park ... fourth floor and quite an easy climb. Mind you, it's owned by Vladimir Sharkovsky. Might be too much of a risk. How about Ilinka Street? Ah yes! That's perfect. Nice and easy. Number sixteen. Plenty of cash, jewellery..."

"Tell me about the flat in Gorky Park," I said.

Dima turned to me, surprised. But it was the name that had done it. Sharkovsky. I had heard it before. I remembered the time when I entered Dementyev's office at Moscow State University. I had heard him talking on the telephone.

Yes, of course, Mr Sharkovsky. Yes, sir. Thank you, sir.

"Who is Sharkovsky?" I asked.

"He's a businessman," Fagin said. "But rich. Very, very rich. And quite dangerous, so I'm told. Not the sort of man you'd want to meet on a dark night and certainly not if you were stealing from him."

"I want to go there," I said.

"Why?" Dima asked.

"Because I know him. At least ... I heard his name."

At that moment, it seemed almost like a gift. Misha Dementyev was my enemy. He had tried to hand me over to the police. He had lied to my parents. And it sounded as if he was working for this man, Sharkovsky – assuming it was the same Sharkovsky. So robbing his flat made perfect sense. It was like a miniature revenge.

Fagin snapped the notebook shut. We had made our decision and it didn't matter which address we chose. "It won't be so difficult," he muttered. "Fourth floor. Quiet street. Sharkovsky doesn't actually live there. He keeps the place for a friend, an actress." He leered at us in a way that suggested she was much more than a friend. "She's away a lot. It could be empty. I'll check."

Fagin was as good as his word. The following day he provided us with the information we needed. The actress was performing in a play called *The Cherry Orchard* and wouldn't be back in Moscow until the end of the month. The flat was deserted but the *fortochka* was open.

"Go for the things you can carry," he suggested. "Jewellery. Furs. Mink and sable are easy to shift. TVs and stuff like that ... leave them behind."

We set off that same night, skirting round the walls of the Kremlin and crossing the river on the Krymsky Bridge. I thought I would be nervous. This was my first real crime – very different from the antics that Leo and I had got up to during the summer, setting off schoolboy bombs outside the police station or pinching cigarettes. Even stealing from the back of parked cars wasn't in the same league. But the strange thing was that

I was completely calm. It struck me that I might have found my destiny. If I could learn to survive in Moscow by being a thief, that was the way it would have to be.

Gorky Park is a huge area on the edge of the Moscow River. With a fairground, boating lakes and even an open-air theatre, it's always been a favourite place for the people in the city. Anyone who had a flat here would have to be rich. The air was cleaner and if you were high enough you'd get views across the trees and over to the river, where barges and pleasure boats cruised slowly past, and the Ministry of Foreign Affairs, another Stalin sky-scraper, in the far distance. The flat that Fagin had identified was right next to the park in a quiet street that hardly seemed to belong to the city at all. It was too elegant. Too expensive.

We got there just before midnight but all the street lamps were lit and I was able to make out a very attractive building, made of cream-coloured stone, with arched doorways and windows and lots of decoration over the walls. It was smaller and neater than our apartment block, just four storeys high, with a slanting orange-tiled roof.

"That's the window – up there."

Dima pointed. The flat was on the top floor, just as Fagin had said, and sure enough I could make out the *fortochka*, which was actually slightly ajar. The woman who lived there might have thought she was safe, being so high up, but I saw at once that it would be possible to climb in, using the building's adornments as footholds. There were ledges, windowsills, carved pillars and even a drainpipe that would act as one side of a ladder. It wouldn't be easy for me but once I was inside I would go back down and open the front door. I'd let the others in and the whole place would be ours.

There were no lights on inside the building. The other residents must have been asleep. Nor was there anyone in the street. We crossed as quickly as we could and grouped ourselves in the shadows, right up against the wall.

"What do you think, Yasha?" Dima asked.

I looked up and nodded. "I can do it." But still I hesitated. "Are you sure she's away?"

"Everyone says Fagin is reliable."

"OK."

"We'll be waiting for you at the door. Make sure you don't make any noise coming down the stairs."

"Right. Good luck."

Dima cupped his hands to help me climb up to the first level and as I raised my foot, our eyes met and he smiled at me. But at that moment I suddenly felt troubled. This might be my destiny but what would my parents have said if they could have seen me now? They were honest people. That was the way I'd been brought up. I was amazed at how quickly I'd become a burglar, a thief. And if I stayed in Moscow much longer? I wondered what I might become next.

I began the climb. The three boys scattered. We'd agreed that if a policeman happened to come along on patrol, Grigory would warn me by hooting like an owl. But right now we were alone and at first it was easy. I had the drainpipe on one side and there were plenty of bricks and swirling plasterwork to give me a foothold. The architect or the artist who had built this place might have had plenty of ideas about style and elegance but he had been less brilliant when it came to security.

Even so, the higher I went, the more dangerous it became. The pipe was quite loose. If I put too much weight onto it, I risked tearing it out of the wall. Some of the decorations were damp and had begun to rot. I rested my foot briefly on a diamond-shaped brick, part of a running pattern, and to my horror it crumbled away. First, there was the sound of loose plaster hitting the pavement. Then I found myself scrabbling against the face of the building, desperately trying to stop myself plunging down. If I'd fallen from the first floor, I'd have broken an ankle. From this height it was more likely to be my neck. Somehow I managed to steady myself. I looked down and saw Dima standing underneath one of the street lamps. He had seen what had happened and waved a hand – either spurring me on or warning me to be more careful.

I took a deep breath to steady my nerves, then continued up – past the third floor and up to the fourth. At one stage I was right next to a window and, peeping in, I saw the vague shape of two people lying in bed under a fur cover. I was lucky they were heavy sleepers. I pulled myself up as quickly as possible and finally reached the ledge that ran along the whole building just below the top floor. It was no more than fifteen centimetres wide and I had to squeeze flat against the wall, shuffling along with my toes touching the brickwork and my heels hanging in the air. If I had leaned back even slightly I would have lost my balance and fallen. But I had come this far without killing myself. I was determined to see it through.

I got to the window with the smaller window set inside it and now I saw that I had two more problems. It was going to be an even tighter fit than I had imagined. And it was going to be awkward too. Somehow I had to lever myself up and in, but that would mean putting all my weight on the main sheet of glass. The windows were only separated by a narrow frame and unless I was careful there was a real chance they would shatter beneath me and I would end up being cut in half. Once again I looked for Dima but this time there was no sign of him.

I reached out and held onto the edge with one hand. The *fortochka* was definitely unlocked. The room on the other side was dark but seemed to be a lounge with a dining area and a kitchen attached. I grabbed the glass with my other hand. I saw now that I was going to have to go in head first. It just wasn't possible to lever up my leg. Using my forehead, I pushed the little window open. I leant forward, pushing my head inside. Now the glass was resting against the back of my neck, making me think of a prisoner in the old days, about to be decapitated by guillotine. Trying to keep as much of my weight off the glass as I could, I arched forward and in. The fit was very tight. The opening was barely more than forty centimetres square ... a cat flap indeed. My shoulders only just passed through and I felt the loose end of the glass scraping against my back. I pushed harder and found myself wedged with the lower rim of the *fortochka* pressing into my back just above my buttocks. Suddenly I was trapped! I couldn't move in either direction and I had a nightmare vision of being stuck there all night, waiting for someone to discover me and call the police in the morning. The glass was creaking underneath me. I was sure it was going to break. I pushed again. It was like giving birth to myself. The edge cut into me but then, somehow, gravity took over. I plunged forward into the darkness and hit the floor. I was in!

If it hadn't been for the carpet, I would have definitely broken my nose and ended up looking like Dima. If there was anyone in the flat, they would certainly have heard me and I lay there for a moment, waiting for the door to open and the lights to go on. It didn't happen. I remembered the people I had seen beneath their fur cover in the flat below. Surely they would have heard the thump and wondered what it was. But there was no sound from below either. I waited another minute. My arm was sticking out at a strange angle and I was worried that I had dislocated my shoulder, but when I shifted my weight and got back into a sensible position, it seemed all right. Dima and the others would have seen me go in. They would be waiting for me to come down and open the front door. It was time to move.

First I examined my surroundings. As my eyes got used to the half-light, I saw that I was in the main living area and that the owner must have been as wealthy as Fagin had said. I had never been anywhere like this. The furniture was modern and looked brand new. Living in a wooden house in a village, I had never seen – I had never even imagined – glass and silver tables, leather sofas, and beautiful cabinets with rings hanging off the drawers. Everything I had ever sat on or slept in had been old and shabby. There was a gorgeous rug in front of a fireplace and even to steal that would make this adventure worthwhile. How much more comfortable I would be lying on a luxurious rug than on the lumpy mattress back at the Tverskaya Street apartment!

Paintings in gold frames hung on the walls. I didn't really understand them. They seemed to be splashes of paint with no subject matter at all.

There had been a few framed photographs in my house, a tapestry hanging in my parents' bedroom, pictures cut out of magazines, but nothing like this. Next to the sitting area there was a dining-room table – an oval of wood, partly covered by a lace cloth, with four chairs – and beyond it a kitchen that was so clean it had surely never been used. I ran my eye over the electric oven, the sink with its gleaming taps. No need to run down to any wells if you lived here. There was a fridge in one corner. I opened the door and found myself bathed in electric light, staring at shelves stacked with ham, cheese, fruit, salad, pickled mushrooms and the little pancakes that we called *blinis*. I'm afraid I couldn't help myself. I reached in and stuffed as much food into my mouth as I could, not caring if it was salty or sweet.

And that was how I was, standing in the kitchen with food in my hands and in my mouth, when there was the rattle of a key in the lock and the main door of the flat opened and the lights came on.

Fagin had got it wrong after all.

A man stood staring at me. I saw his eyes turn instantly from surprise to understanding and then to dark, seething fury. He was wearing a black fur coat, black gloves and the sort of hat you might see on an American gangster. A white silk scarf hung around his shoulders. He was not a huge man but he was solid and well built and he had a presence about him, a sense of power. I could see it in his extraordinarily intense eyes, heavy-lidded with thick, black eyebrows. His flesh had the colour and the vitality of a man lying dead in his coffin and standing there, framed in the doorway, he had that same, heavy stillness. His face was unlined, his mouth a narrow gash. I could make out the edges of a tattoo on the side of his neck: red flames. It suggested that the whole of his body, underneath his shirt, was on fire. Without knowing anything about him, I knew I was in terrible trouble. If I had met the devil I could not have been more afraid.

"Who is it, Vlad?" There was a woman standing behind him. I glimpsed a mink collar and blonde hair.

"There is someone in the flat," he said. "A boy."

His eyes briefly left me, darting across the room to the window. He didn't need to ask any questions. He knew how I had got in. He knew that I was alone.

"Do you want me to call the police?"

"No. There's no need for that."

His words were measured, uttered with a sort of dull certainty. And they told me the worst thing possible. If he wasn't calling the police it was because he had decided to deal with me himself, and he wasn't going to shake my hand and thank me for coming. He was going to kill me. Perhaps there was a gun in his coat pocket. Perhaps he would tear me apart with his bare hands. I had no doubt at all that he could do it.

I didn't know how to react. My one desire was to get out of the flat, back into the street. I wondered if Dima, Roman and Grigory had seen what had happened but I knew that even if they had, there was nothing they could do. The front door would be locked. If they were sensible, they would probably be halfway back to Tverskaya Street. I tried to collect my thoughts. All I had to do was to get past this man and out into the corridor. The woman wouldn't try to stop me. I looked around me and did perhaps the most stupid thing I could have done. There was a bread knife on the counter. I picked it up.

The man didn't move. He didn't speak. He glanced at the blade with outrage. How could I dare to pick up *his* property and threaten him in *his* home? That was what he said without actually saying anything. Holding the knife didn't make me feel any stronger. In fact all the strength drained out of me the moment I had it in my hand and the silver, jagged blade filled me with horror.

"I don't want any trouble," I said and my voice didn't sound like my own. "Just let me go and nobody will be hurt."

He had no intention of doing that. He moved towards me and I jabbed out with the knife without thinking, not meaning to stab him, not really knowing what I was doing. He stopped. I saw the face of the girl behind him, frozen in shock. The man looked down. I followed his eyes and saw that the point of the blade had gone through his coat, into his chest. I was even more horrified. I stepped back, dropping the knife. It clattered to the floor.

The man didn't seem to have felt any pain. He brought up a hand and examined the gash in his coat as if it mattered more to him than the flesh underneath. When he brought his hand away, there was blood on the tips of his glove.

He gazed at me. I was unarmed now, trapped by those terrible eyes.

"What have you done?" he demanded.

"I..." I didn't know what to say.

He took one step forward and punched me in the face. I had never been struck so hard. I didn't even know it was possible for one human to hurt another human so much. It was like being hit by a rod of steel and I felt something break. I heard the girl cry out. I was already falling but as I went down he hit me again with the other fist so that my head snapped back and my body collapsed in two directions at once. I remember a bolt of white light that seemed to be my own death. I was unconscious before I reached the floor.

РУССКАЯ РУЛЕТКА

RUSSIAN ROULETTE

I woke up in total darkness, lying in a cramped space with my legs hunched up, a gag in my mouth and my hands tied. My first thought was that I was locked inside a box, that I had been buried alive – and for the next sixty seconds I was screaming without making any sound, my heart racing, my muscles straining against the ropes around my wrists, barely able to catch breath. Somehow I got myself under control. It wasn't a box. I was in the boot of a car. We had been standing stationary a moment ago but now I heard the throb of the engine and felt us move off. That still wasn't good. I was being allowed to live – but for how long?

I was in a bad way. My head was pounding – and by that I mean all of it, inside and out. The whole side of my face was swollen. It hurt me to move my mouth and I couldn't close one of my eyes. The man's fist had broken my cheekbone.

I had no idea what I looked like but what did that matter? I did not expect to live.

I presumed the man was Vladimir Sharkovsky. Fagin had warned me that he was dangerous but that was only half the story. I had seen enough of him in the flat to know that he was a psychopath. No ordinary person had eyes like that. He had been utterly cold when I had attacked him but when his temper flared up it had been like a demon leaping out of the craters of hell. *He hadn't called the police.* That was the worst of it. He was taking me somewhere and when he got there he could do whatever he wanted to me. I dreaded to think what that might be. Was he planning to torture me as a punishment for what I had done? I had heard that many hundreds of children went missing from the streets of Moscow every year. It might well be my fate to become one of them.

I cannot say how long the journey took. I couldn't see my watch with my hands tied behind me and after a while, I dozed off. I didn't sleep exactly. I simply drifted out of consciousness. It would have been nice to have dreamt of my parents and of my life in Estrov, to have spent my last hours on this planet reliving happier times, but I was in too much pain. Every few minutes, my eyes would blink open and I would once again find myself struggling for breath in that almost airtight compartment, desperately wanting to straighten up, to go to the toilet, to be anywhere but there.

The car just rumbled on.

Eventually, we arrived. I felt us slowing down. Then we stopped and I heard a man's voice, a command being given, followed by what sounded like the click of a metal gate. When we set off again, there was a different surface – gravel – beneath the tyres. The car stopped and the engine was turned off. The driver's door opened and shut and I heard footsteps on the gravel. I tensed myself, waiting for the car boot to be released, but it didn't happen. The footsteps disappeared into the distance and when, a long time later, they hadn't come back, I began to think that I was going to be left here all night, like a piece of baggage nobody needed.

And so it was. I was left in the dark, in silence, with no idea how long it was going to last or what would happen when I was released. It was being done on purpose, of course, to break my spirit, to make me suffer. I was the victim of my own worst imaginings. I had nothing to do except to count every single painful minute. Unable to move, to stretch myself, my whole body was in torment. My only option was to try to sleep, fighting back all the dread that came from being tied up and left in this small space. It was a long, hideous night. By the time the boot was opened, I was no longer afraid of death. I think I would have welcomed it. A short tunnel of horrors followed by release. It would be worth the journey.

There was a man leaning over me; not the one from the Moscow flat. He was quite simply massive – with oversized shoulders and a thick neck – and dressed in a cheap grey suit, a white shirt and a black tie. His hair was blond and thickly oiled so that it stood up in spikes. He was wearing dark glasses and there was a radio transmitter behind his ear that had a wire curling down to a throat mike. His skin was utterly white and it occurred to me that he might have been in a prison or some other institution all his life. He didn't look as if he had ever spent any time in the sun.

He reached down and with a single movement dragged me out of the boot, then stood me up so that I was balanced against the back of the car. I would have fallen otherwise. There was no strength in my legs. He looked at me with hardly any expression apart from disgust and I couldn't blame him for that. I stank. My clothes were crumpled. My face was caked with blood. He reached into his jacket pocket and I winced as he produced a knife. I was quite ready for him to plunge it into my chest but he just leant over me and cut the cords of my wrists. My hands fell free. They looked horrible. The flesh of my wrists was blue, covered in welts. I couldn't move my fingers but I felt the pins and needles as the blood supply was restored.

"You are to come with us," he said. He had a deep, gravelly voice. He spoke without emotion, as if he didn't actually enjoy speaking.

Us? I glanced round and saw a second man standing at the side of the car. For a moment, I thought my brain was playing tricks on me after my long captivity. This second man was identical to the first – the same height, the same looks, the same clothes. They were twins ... just like the two girls I had once known in Estrov. But it was almost as if these two had trained themselves to be indistinguishable. They had the same haircut, the same sunglasses. They even moved at exactly the same time, like mirror images.

The first twin hadn't bothered to find out my name. He didn't want to know anything about me.

"Where are we?" I asked. The words came out clumsily because of the damage to my face.

"No questions. Do as you are told."

He gestured. I began to walk and for the first time I was able to take in my surroundings. I was in what looked like a large and very beautiful park with pathways, neatly cut grass and trees. The park was surrounded by a brick wall, several metres high with razor wire around the top, and I could make out the tips of more trees on the other side. The car that I had been in was a black Lexus. It had been parked quite close to an arched gateway with a barrier that rose and fell, the only way out, I suspected. A guardhouse stood next to it. This was a wooden construction with a large glass window and I could see a man in uniform, watching us as we walked together. My first thought was that

I had been brought to some sort of prison. There were arc lamps and CCTV cameras set at intervals along the wall.

We were heading towards a cluster of eight wooden houses that had been tucked out of sight behind some fir trees, about fifty metres from the gates. They were new-looking, completely featureless and almost identical. In the West, they would be called portakabins, although they were a little larger and they'd been built two high with external staircases connecting them. I noticed that there were no bars on any of the windows. These weren't cells. I guessed they provided accommodation for the people who worked here. A larger, brick building stood nearby perhaps with a dining room attached.

I glanced behind me. And although I hadn't been given permission, I came to a stumbling halt. Where the hell was I? I had never seen anything like this.

A gravel drive with lamps and flower beds on each side led from the entrance through the parkland and up to a monumental white house. Not a house. A palace ... and not one that had come out of any fairy tale. It was a modern building, newly built, pure white, with two wings stretching out from a central block which alone must have contained about fifty rooms. There were terraces with white balustrades, white columns with triple-height doorways opening behind, walkways and balconies, and above it all a white dome like that of a planetarium or perhaps a cathedral. Half a dozen satellite dishes had been mounted on the roof along with television aerials and a radio tower. A man stood there, watching me through binoculars. He was wearing the same uniform as the man at the gate – but with a difference. Even at this distance I could see that he had a machine gun strapped to his shoulder.

Closer to the house, the gardens became more ornamental with statues on plinths, marble benches, beautifully tended walkways and arbours, bushes cut into fantastic shapes, more flower beds laid out in intricate patterns. An army of gardeners would have to work the whole year round to keep it all looking like this and even as I stood there I saw some of them pushing wheelbarrows or on their knees weeding. The drive broke into two as it reached the front door, sweeping round a white marble fountain that had gods and mermaids all tangled together and water splashing down. I saw two Rolls Royces, a Bentley and a Ferrari parked outside. But the owner didn't just have cars. His private helicopter was parked on a concrete square, discreetly located next to a summer house. It was under canvas with the blades tied down.

"Why are you waiting?" one of the twins demanded.

"Who lives here?" I asked.

His answer was a jab in the side of my stomach.

It had been aimed around my kidney and it hurt. "I told you. No questions."

I was very quickly learning the rules of this place. I was worth nothing. Anyone could do anything to me. I swallowed a grunt of pain and continued to the smallest cabin, right on the edge of the complex. The door was open and I looked into a room with a narrow metal bed, a table and a chair. There was no carpet, no curtains, nothing in the way of decoration. A second door led into a toilet and shower.

"You have five minutes," the man said. "Throw those clothes away. You will not need them. Wash yourself and make yourself presentable. Do not leave this room. If you do, the guards will shoot you down."

He left me on my own. I stripped off my clothes and went into the bathroom. I used the toilet, then I had a shower. I knew I was in danger. It was quite likely that I would soon be dead. But that shower was still a wonderful experience. The water was hot and there was enough pressure to soak me completely. There was even a bar of soap. It had been three weeks since I had last washed – that had been in the *banya*, the bathhouse in Moscow – and black dirt seemed to ooze out of my body, disappearing down the plughole. Thinking of the bathhouse reminded me of Dima. What would he be doing now? Had he seen me being bundled into the car by Sharkovsky and, if so, might he come looking for me? At least that was something to give me hope.

My face still hurt though, and when I examined myself in the mirror, it was as bad as I had feared. I barely recognized myself. One eye was half closed. There was a huge bruise all around it. My cheek looked like a rotting fruit with a gash where the man's fist had caught me. I was lucky I still had all my teeth. Looking at the damage, I was reminded of what lay ahead. I hadn't been brought here for my own comfort. I was being prepared for something. My punishment was still to come.

I went back into the bedroom. My own clothes had been taken away while I was washing and, with a jolt, I realized that the last of my mother's jewellery had gone with them. Her ring had been in my back pocket. I knew at once that there would be no point in asking for it back and I had to hold down a great wave of sadness, the sense that I had nothing left. She had worn that ring and touching it, I had felt I was touching her. Now that it had been taken from me, it was as if I had finally been separated from the boy I had once been.

I had been supplied with a black tracksuit, black socks and black slip-on shoes. I dried myself, using a towel that had been hanging in the bathroom, and got dressed. The clothes fitted me very well.

"Are you ready?" The twins were standing outside, calling to me. I left the cabin and joined them. They glanced at me, both of them still showing a complete lack of interest.

"Come with us," one of them said. They appeared to have a fairly limited vocabulary too.

We walked up the drive all the way to the big house. As we went, we passed another security guard, this one with an Alsatian dog on a leash. A television camera mounted above the front door watched our approach. But we didn't go in that way. The twins took me in through a side door next to the dustbin area and along a corridor. Here the walls were plain and the floor black and white tiles. The servants' entrance. We passed a laundry room, a boot room and a pantry next to a kitchen. I glimpsed a woman in a black dress and a white apron, polishing silver. She didn't notice me or, if she did, she pretended not to. My feet, in the soft shoes, made no sound as we continued through. I was feeling queasy and I knew why. I was afraid.

We passed through a hallway; this was the main entrance to the house. A magnificent staircase swept down to the front door with a marble pillar on each side. The hallway itself was huge. You could have parked a dozen cars there. A bowl of flowers stood on a table – it must have emptied a flower shop. The central light was a chandelier, hundreds of crystals twinkling brilliantly like a firework display. It made the lights I had seen in the Moscow Metro look cheap and gaudy. There were more doors on every side. It was all too much for me to take in. If a spaceship had grabbed me and deposited me on the moon, I would have felt as much at home.

"In here..."

One of the twins knocked on an oak door and, without waiting for a reply, opened it. I went in.

The man from the Moscow apartment was sitting behind an oversized antique desk. There were bookshelves behind him and on one side a globe that looked so old that quite a few of the countries were probably missing ... yet to be discovered. He was framed by two windows with red velvet curtains and a view out to the fountain and the drive. The room was very warm. One wall contained a stone fireplace – two crouching imps or demons supporting the mantelpiece on their shoulders – and a Dalmatian, lay stretched out in front of it. The walls were covered with paintings. The largest was a portrait of the man I was facing and I have to say that the painted version was the more welcoming of the two. He had not looked up from his work. He was reading a document, making notes in the margins with a black fountain pen.

There was a gun on the desk in front of him.

As I stood there, waiting to be told what to do, I found myself staring at it. It was a revolver, a very old-fashioned model with a stainless steel barrel, five inches long, and a black, enamel grip. It wasn't like an automatic or a self-loading pistol where you feed the bullets into a clip. This one had a cylinder and six chambers. A single bullet lay beside it.

"Sit down," he said, pointing to an empty chair in front of him.

I stepped forward, although it felt more as if I was floating, and sat down. The door clicked shut behind me. Without being instructed, the twins had left.

I waited for the master of the house to speak. He was wearing a suit now and somehow I knew that it was expensive and that it hadn't been made in Russia. The material was too luxurious and it fitted too well. He had a pale blue shirt and a brown tie. Now that he wasn't wearing his coat, I could see that he was very muscular. He must have spent hundreds of hours in the gym. He had also removed the hat and I saw that he was completely bald. He had not lost his hair. He had shaved it off, leaving a dark shadow that made him more death-like than ever. I waited in dread for his heavy, ugly eyes to settle on me. My face was hurting badly and I wanted to go to the toilet again. But I didn't dare say anything. I didn't move.

At length he stopped and lay the pen down. "What is your name?" he asked.

"Yasha Gregorovich."

"Yassen?" He had misheard me. The side of my face was so swollen that I had mispronounced my own name. It would be very unusual to be called Yassen.

It is Russian for ash tree. But I did not correct him. I had decided it would be better not to speak unless I had to. "How old are you?" he asked.

"I'm fourteen."

"Where are you from?"

I remembered my mother's warning. "A town called Kirsk," I said. "It's a long way away. You won't have heard of it."

The man thought for a moment, then he got up, walked round the desk and stood next to me. He took his time, considering the situation, then suddenly and without warning slapped me across the face. The blow wasn't a particularly hard one, certainly not as hard as the night before, but nor did it need to be. My cheekbone was already broken and the fresh pain almost knocked me off the chair. Black spots appeared in front of my eyes. I thought I was going to be sick.

By the time I had recovered, the man was back in his chair. "Never make assumptions," he said. "Never assume anything about me. And when you speak to me, call me 'sir'. Do you understand?"

"Yes, sir."

He nodded. "Do you have parents?"

"No, sir. They're both dead."

"And last night, when you broke into my flat, were you alone?"

I had already decided that I wasn't going to tell him about Dima, Roman and Grigory. If I told him their names, I had no doubt he would send his men round to Tverskaya to kill them. I still thought he was going to kill me. "Yes, sir," I replied. "I was on my own."

"How did you come to choose that flat – as opposed to any other?"

"I was walking past. I saw that the window was open and the lights were out. I didn't even think about it. I just went in."

The answer seemed to satisfy him. He took out a gold cigarette case. I noticed the initials V.S. on the cover. He removed a cigarette and lit it, then lay the case on the desk, close to the gun. "Vladimir Sharkovsky," he said. "That is my name."

I didn't tell him that I knew. I simply sat there and watched as he smoked in silence. I would have liked a cigarette but I needed the toilet more. My insides were churning.

"You must be wondering why you are still alive," he continued. "In fact, you should not be. Last night, as I drove over the bridge, I thought of dropping you in the Moscow River. I would have quite enjoyed watching you drown. When I drove you here, my intention was to give you to Josef and Karl to be punished and then killed. Even now, I am undecided if you will live or if you will die." His eyes rested briefly on the revolver. "The fact that you are sitting in this room, talking to me, is down to one reason only. It is a question of timing. Perhaps you have been lucky. A week ago it would have been different. But right now..."

He trailed off, then took another drag on the cigarette, the blue smoke curling into the air. A log snapped in the fireplace and the dog stirred briefly, then went back to sleep. So far, Vladimir Sharkovsky had shown no emotion whatsoever. His voice was flat, entirely disinterested. If machines had ever learned to speak, they would speak like him.

"I am a careful man," he went on. "One of the reasons why I have prospered is that I have always used everything that has been given to me. I never miss an opportunity. It may be an investment in a company, the chance to buy my way into a bank, the weakness of a government official who is open to bribery. Or it may be the chance appearance of a worthless thief and guttersnipe like yourself. But if it can be used, then I will use it. That is how I live.

"There is something you need to understand about me. I am extremely successful. Right now, Russia is changing. The old ways are being left behind. For those of us with the vision to see what is possible, the rewards are limitless. You have nothing. You steal because you are hungry and all you think about is your next pathetic meal. I have the world and everything in it. And now, Yassen Gregorovich, I have you.

"A large number of people work for me in this house. Because of the nature of my work and who

I am, I have to be careful. Josef and Karl, the two men who brought you here, are my personal body-guards. They are standing outside and I should perhaps warn you that there is a communication button underneath this desk. If you were to try anything, if you were to threaten me again, they would be in here in an instant. Be glad they were not with me in Moscow. That was the private apartment of a friend of mine. The moment you picked up that knife, your own life would have been over.

"I will not kill you – yet – because I think I can use you. As it happens, a position has arisen here, a vacancy which it would not normally be easy to fill. You are, as I said, very fortunate with the timing. I have no doubt that you are stupid and uneducated. But even so, you might be acceptable."

He paused and it took me a few seconds to realize that he was waiting for me to reply. I couldn't believe what he had just told me. He wasn't going to kill me. He was offering me a job!

"I'd be very happy to work for you, sir," I said.

His eyes settled on me, full of contempt. "Happy?" He repeated the word with a sneer. "You say stupid things without thinking. It is not my intention to make you happy. Quite the opposite. You broke into my apartment. You attempted to hurt me and in doing so you ruined a perfectly good overcoat, a jacket and a shirt. You even cut my flesh. For this, you must pay. You must be punished. If you decide to accept my proposal, you will spend every hour of the rest of your life wishing that the two of us had never met. I am not offering to pay you. I will own you. I will use you. From this moment on, I will expect your total obedience. You will do whatever I tell you. You will not hesitate." He gestured at the fireplace. "You see the dog? That is what you are now. That's all you mean to me."

He stubbed out the cigarette. I could see that he was bored with the interview, that he wanted it to be over.

"What do you want me to do?" I asked. "What sort of work?"

I had no choice. I had to survive. Let him employ me in whatever capacity and somehow I would find a way out of this place. In the back of a car, over the wall ... I would escape.

"You will clean. You will carry messages. You will sweep floors. You will help in the garden. But that's just part of it. The main reason that I need you is something quite different." He paused. "You will be my food taster."

"Your...?" I almost laughed out loud and if I had, I am sure he would have shot me there and then. But it was ridiculous. At school, we had been taught about the Roman emperors – Julius Caesar and the others – who had employed slaves to taste everything they ate. But this was Russia in the twentieth century. He couldn't possibly mean what he had just said.

"It is unfortunately the case that I have many enemies," Sharkovsky explained. He was completely serious. "Some of them fear me. Some are jealous of me. All of them would benefit if I was no longer here. In the last year, there have been three attempts on my life. That is how things are now. Several of my associates have been less fortunate – which is to say, they have been less careful than me. And they have died.

"Apart from my wife and my children, I can trust no one and even my immediate family might one day be bribed to do me harm. I employ a great many people to protect me and I have to employ more people to watch over them. I trust none of them." His dark eyes bore into me. "Can I trust you?"

I was trying to make sense of all this. Was that really to be my fate? Sitting at his dining table, digging my fork into his *blinis* and caviar?

"I'll do whatever you want," I said.

"Will you?"

"Yes, sir."

"Anything?"

"Yes..." This time I was uneasy.

It was what he had been waiting for. It was the very worst thing I could have said.

"We will see." He reached out and took the gun. He jerked open the cylinder and showed me that it was empty. Then he picked up the bullet – a little cylinder of gleaming silver – and held it between his finger and thumb like a scientist giving a demonstration. I watched silently. I didn't know what was about to happen but I could feel my heart pounding. He slid the bullet into one of the chambers and snapped the cylinder shut. Then he spun it several times so that the metal became a blur and it was impossible for either of us to tell where the bullet had lodged.

"You say you will do anything for me," he said. "So do this. The gun has six chambers. As you have seen, one of them now contains a live bullet. You do not know where the bullet is. Nor do I." He placed the gun back on the desk, right in front of me. "Put the gun into your mouth and pull the trigger."

I stared at him. "I don't understand."

"It's simple enough!" he said. "Point the gun at the back of your mouth and shoot."

"But why...?"

"Because you said to me five seconds ago that you would do anything I wanted and now I am asking you to prove it. I need to know that I can rely on you. Either you will pull the trigger or you will not. But let us consider the options, Yassen Gregorovich. If you will not do what I ask, then you have lied to me and I cannot use you after all. In that case, I can assure you that your death is certain. If you do as I have asked, then there are two possibilities that lie ahead of you. It is quite possible that you will kill yourself, that in a few minutes' time, my cleaners will be wiping your brains off my carpet.

That will be annoying. But there is also a very good chance that you will live and from that moment on you will serve me. It is your decision and you must make it now. I don't have all day."

He was torturing me after all. He was asking me to play this horrific game to prove beyond any doubt that he had complete power over me. I would never argue with him. I would never refuse an order. If I did this, I would be accepting that my own life no longer belonged to me. That in every respect I was his.

What could I do? What choice did I have?

I picked up the gun. It was much heavier than I had expected but at the same time, I had no strength at all. Nothing below my shoulder seemed to be working properly – not my wrist, not my hand, not my fingers. I could feel my pulse racing and I had to struggle even to breathe. What this man was demanding was horrific ... beyond imagination. Six chambers. One containing a bullet. A one in six chance. When I pulled the trigger, nothing might happen. Or I might send a piece of metal travelling at two hundred miles per hour into my own head. If I didn't do it, he would kill me. That was what it came down to. I felt hot tears brimming over my cheeks. It seemed impossible that my life could have come to this.

"Don't cry like a baby," Sharkovsky said. "Get on with it."

My arm and wrist were aching. I could feel the

blood pumping through my veins. Almost involuntarily, my finger had curled around the trigger. The grip was pressed against the palm of my hand. For a crazy moment, I thought of firing at Sharkovsky, of emptying the chamber in his direction. But what good would that do me? He probably had a second gun concealed somewhere and if I didn't find the bullet at the first attempt he would have plenty of time to shoot me where I sat.

"Please, sir..." I whispered.

"I am not interested in your tears or your pleading," he snapped. "I am interested only in your obedience."

"But..."

"Do it now!"

I touched the muzzle of the gun against the side of my head.

"In your mouth!"

I will never forget his insistence, that one obscene detail. I pushed the barrel of the gun between my teeth, feeling the muzzle grazing the roof of my mouth. I could taste the metal, cold and bitter. I was aware of the black hole, the muzzle, pointing at my throat with, perhaps, a bullet resting behind it, waiting to begin its short journey. Sharkovsky was gloating. I don't think he cared one way or the other what the outcome would be. I couldn't breathe. The contents of my stomach were rising up. I pressed with my finger but I couldn't make it work. In my mind I already heard the explosion. I felt the scorching heat and saw the darkness falling like a blade as my life was snatched away.

"Do it!" he snarled.

One chance in six.

I squeezed the trigger.

The hammer drew back. How far would it travel before it fell? I was certain that these were the last seconds of my life. And yet everything was happening horribly slowly. They seemed to stretch on for ever.

I felt the mechanism release itself in my hand. The hammer fell with a heavy, thunderous click.

Nothing.

There had been no explosion. The chamber was empty.

Relief rushed through me but it did not feel good. It was as if I was being emptied, as if my entire life and all the good things I had ever experienced were being taken from me. From this moment on, I belonged to Sharkovksy. That was what he had demonstrated. I dropped the gun. It fell heavily against the surface of the desk and lay there between us. The muzzle was wet with my saliva.

"You can leave now," he said.

He must have pressed the communication button under his desk because although I hadn't heard them, the men who had brought me here had returned. Perhaps the twins had been present and had seen what had just happened. I didn't know.

I stood up. My whole body felt foreign to me. I might not have killed myself but even so, something inside me had died.

"Yassen Gregorovich is working for me now," Sharvovsky continued. "Take him downstairs and show him."

The two men led me out of the study and back into the corridor we had come through together. But this time we took a staircase down into a basement area. There was an oversized fridge door that led into a cold storage room and I watched as one twin opened it and the other went inside. He wheeled out a trolley. There was a dead body on it, covered by a sheet. He lifted it up and I saw a naked man. He couldn't have been more than ten years older than me when he died. It had happened very recently. His face was distorted with pain. His hands seemed to be scrabbling at his throat.

I understood without being told. The old food taster.

A position has arisen here. That was what Vladimir Sharkovsky had said to me. Now I knew why.

СЕРЕБРЯНЫЙ БОР

SILVER FOREST

I made my first escape attempt that same day.

I knew I couldn't stay there. I wasn't going to play any more of Sharkovsky's sadistic games and I certainly wasn't going to swallow his food ... not when there was a real chance of my ending up on a metal slab. I had been left alone for the rest of the day. Perhaps they thought I needed time to recover from my ordeal and they were certainly right. The moment I got back to my room, I was sick. After that, I slept for about three hours. One of the twins visited me during the afternoon. He brought more clothes with him: overalls, boots, an apron, a suit. Each piece of clothing related to a different task I would be expected to perform. I left them on the floor. I wasn't going to be part of this. I was out.

As soon as night had come, I left my room and set out to explore the grounds, now empty of gardeners although there were still guards patrolling close to the wall. It was clear to me that the wall completely surrounded the complex and there was no possibility of my climbing it. It was too high, and anyway, the razor wire would cut me to shreds. The simple truth was that the archway was the only way in and out – but at least that meant I could focus my attention on that one avenue. And looking at it, I wasn't sure that it was as secure as it seemed. Three uniformed guards sat inside the wooden cabin with a glass window that allowed them to look out over the driveway. They had television monitors too. There was a red and white pole, which they had to raise, and they searched every vehicle that came in, one of them looking underneath with a flat mirror on wheels while another checked the driver's ID. But when there were no cars, they did nothing. One of them read a newspaper. The others simply sat back looking bored. I could just slip out. It wouldn't be difficult at all.

That was my plan. It was about seven o'clock and I assumed everyone was eating. I'd had no food all day but I was in no mood to eat. Still wearing the black tracksuit – the colour would help to conceal me in the darkness – I slipped outside. When I was sure there was nobody around, I sprinted to the edge of the cabin and then crept round, crouching underneath the window and keeping close to the wall. The road back to Moscow lay in front of me. I couldn't believe it was this easy.

It wasn't. I only found out about the infrared

sensors when I passed through one of them, immediately setting off a deafening alarm. At once the whole area exploded into brilliant light as arc lamps sliced into me and I found myself trapped between the beams. There was no point in running – I would have been shot before I had taken ten steps – and I could only stand there looking foolish as the guards seized hold of me and dragged me back.

Punishment was immediate and hideous. I was given to the twins, who simply beat me up as if I were a punchbag in a gym. It wasn't just the pain that left its mark on me. It was their complete indifference. I know they were being paid by Sharkovsky. They were following his orders. But what sort of man can do this to a child and live with himself the next day? They were careful not to break any more bones, but by the time they dragged me back to my room, I was barely conscious. They threw me onto my bed and left me. I had passed out before they closed the door.

I made my second escape attempt as soon as I was able to move again, the next day. It was certainly foolish but it seemed to me that it was the last thing they would expect and so they might briefly lower their guard. They thought I was broken, exhausted. Both of these things were true but I was also determined. This time, a delivery truck provided the opportunity. I'd eaten breakfast in my room – one of the twins had brought it on a tray – but after I'd finished I was sent up to the house to help unload about fifty crates of wine and champagne that Sharkovsky had ordered. It didn't matter that I could feel my shirt sticking to my open wounds and that every movement caused me pain. While the driver waited, I carried the crates in through the back door and down the steps that led to the cold storage room. There was a wine cellar next to it, a cavernous space that housed hundreds of bottles, facing each other in purpose-built racks. It took me about two hours to carry them all down and when I'd finished I noticed that there were a lot of empty boxes in the back of the van. It seemed easy enough to hide myself behind a pile of them. Surely they wouldn't bother searching the van on the way out?

The driver closed the door. Crouching behind the boxes, I heard him start the engine. We drove back down the drive and slowed down. I waited for the moment of truth, the acceleration that meant we had passed through the barrier and were outside the compound. It never came. The door was thrown open again and a voice called me.

"Get out!"

Again, it was one of the twins. I don't know how he'd been so certain that I was there. Maybe I'd been caught by one of the CCTV cameras. Maybe he had been expecting it all along. I felt a weakness in my stomach as I stood up and showed myself. I wasn't sure I could take another beating. But even as I climbed down, I wouldn't let him see I was scared. I wasn't going to give in.

"Come with me," he instructed.

His face gave nothing away. I followed him back to the house but this time he took me round the back. There was a conservatory on the other side, although actually it was more like a pavilion, constructed mainly out of glass with white wooden panels, at least fifty metres long. It had a series of folding doors so that in the full heat of the summer the whole thing could be opened out, but this was late October and they were all closed. The twins opened a single door and led me inside. I found myself in front of an enormous blue-tiled swimming pool, almost Olympic-sized. The water was heated. I could see the steam rising over the surface. Sunloungers had been arranged around the edge and there was a well-stocked bar with a mirrored counter and leather stools.

Sharkovsky was doing lengths. We stood there, watching, while he went from one end to the other and back again, performing a steady, rhythmic butterfly stroke. I counted eighteen lengths and he never stopped once. Nor did he look my way. This was how he liked to keep himself fit, and as he continued I couldn't help but notice the extraordinarily well-developed muscles in his back and shoulders. I also saw his tattoos. There was a Jewish Star of David in the centre of his back – but it wasn't a religious symbol. On the contrary, it was on fire with the words DEATH TO ZIONISM engraved below.

These were the flames that I had seen reaching up to his neck in his Moscow apartment. When he finally finished swimming and climbed out, I saw a huge eagle with outstretched wings, perched on a Nazi swastika tattooed across his chest. He had a slight paunch, but even this was solid rather than flabby. There was a plaster underneath one of his nipples and I realized that this was where I must have cut him with the knife. He was wearing tiny swimming trunks. His whole appearance was somehow very grotesque.

At last he noticed me. He picked up a towel and walked over. I was trembling. I couldn't stop myself. I was expecting the worst.

"Yassen Gregorovich," he said. "I understand that you tried to leave this place last night. You were punished for this but it didn't prevent you from making a second attempt today. Is that right?"

"Yes, sir." There was no point in denying it.

"It is understandable. It shows spirit. At the same time, it goes against the contract that you and I made between us in my study yesterday. You agreed to work for me. You agreed you were mine. Have you forgotten so soon?"

"No, sir."

"Very well. Then hear this. You cannot escape from here. It is not possible. Should you try again, there will be no further discussion, no punishment. I will simply have you killed. Do you understand?"

"Yes, sir."

He turned to the twins. "Josef, take Yassen away. Give him another beating – this time use a cane – and then lock him up on his own without food. Let me know when he has recovered enough to start work. That's all."

But we didn't leave. The twin wouldn't let me. And Sharkovsky was waiting for me to say something.

"Thank you, sir," I said.

Sharkovsky smiled. "That's alright, Yassen. It's my pleasure."

I was to spend the next three years with Vladimir Sharkovsky.

I could not risk another escape attempt – not unless I was prepared to commit suicide. It took me a week to recover from the beating I received that day. I will not say that it broke my spirit. But by the end of it I knew that when I had picked up that gun and placed it in my mouth, I had signed a deal with the devil. I was not just his servant. I was his possession. You might even say I was his slave.

The place where I found myself, the huge white house, was his *dacha* – his second home outside Moscow. It was in Serebryany Bor – Silver Forest – not that many miles from the centre. This was an area well suited to wealthy families. The air was cleaner in the forest. It was quieter and more private. There were lakes and wooded walkways outside the complex where you could exercise the dogs or go hunting and fishing ... not that these activities were available to me because, of course, I was never once allowed outside. I was restricted to the same few faces, the same menial tasks. My life was to have no rewards and no prospect of advancement or release. It was a terrible thing to do to anyone – even worse when you consider that I was so young.

And yet slowly, inevitably perhaps, I accepted my destiny. The injury to my face healed and fortunately it left no mark. I began to get used to my new life.

I worked all the time at the *dacha* ... fifteen hours a day, seven days a week. I never had a holiday and, as Sharkovsky had promised, I didn't receive one kopeck. The fact that I was being allowed to live was payment enough. Christmas, Easter, Victory Day, Spring and Labour Day, my birthdays – all these simply disappeared into each other.

Sharkovsky had told me I would be his food taster but he had also made it clear to me that this was only a part of my work. He was true to his word. I chopped and carried firewood. I cleaned bathrooms and toilets. I helped in the laundry and the kitchen. I washed dishes. I painted walls. I looked after the dog, picking up after it when it fouled. I lifted suitcases. I unblocked drains. I washed cars. I polished shoes. But I never complained. I understood that there was no point in complaining. The work never stopped.

Sharkovsky lived in the big house with his wife, Maya, and his two children, Ivan and Svetlana. Maya had very little to do with me. She spent most of her time reading magazines and paperbacks – she liked romances – or shopping in Moscow. She had once been a model and she was still attractive, but life with Sharkovsky was beginning to take its toll and I would sometimes catch her looking anxiously in the mirror, tracking a finger along a wrinkle or a wisp of grey hair. I wondered if she knew about the flat in Gorky Park and the actress who lived there. In a way, she was as much a prisoner as I was and maybe that was why she avoided me. I reminded her of herself.

The family were seldom together. Sharkovsky had business interests all over the world. As well as the helicopter, he kept a private jet at Moscow airport. It was on permanent standby, ready to take him to London, New York, Hong Kong or wherever. I once glimpsed him on television, standing next to the President of the United States. He took his holidays in the Bahamas or the South of France, where he kept a hundred and fifty metre yacht with twenty-one guest cabins, two swimming pools and its own submarine. His son, Ivan, was at Harrow School, in London. If there was one thing that all wealthy Russians wanted, it was an English public school education for their children. Svetlana was only seven when I arrived but she was kept busy too. There were always private tutors coming to

191

the house to teach dance, piano, horse riding, tennis (they had their own tennis court), foreign languages, poetry... When they were small, each child had had two nannies; one for the day, one for the night. Now they had two full-time house-keepers ... and me.

Sixteen members of staff lived full-time on the estate. They all slept in wooden cabins, similar to mine, apart from Josef and Karl, who lived in the big house. There were the two housekeepers – bossy women who were always in a hurry, permanently scowling. One of them was called Nina and she had it in for me from the start. She used to carry a wooden spoon in her apron and whenever she got the chance she would clout me over the head with it. She didn't seem to have noticed that we were both servants, on the same level, but I didn't dare complain. I have a feeling that she hated working for Sharkovsky as much as I did. The only trouble was, she'd decided to take it out on me.

Then there was Pavel, about fifty years old, short, twitchy, always dressed in whites. He was very important to me because he was the chef and it was his cooking that I would be tasting. I'll say this for him, he was good at his job. All the food he prepared was delicious and I was given things I hadn't even known existed. Until I came to the *dacha*, I had never eaten salmon, pheasant, veal, asparagus, French cheese ... or even such a thing as a chocolate éclair. Pavel only used the very best and the freshest ingredients, which were flown in from all over the world. I remember a cake he made for Maya's birthday. It was shaped like a Russian cathedral, complete with gold-leaf icing on the domes. Heaven knows how much he was given to spend.

I never got to know Pavel very well, even though he slept in the cabin next to me. He was hard of hearing so he didn't talk much. He was unmarried. He had no children. All he cared about was his work.

The staff included a personal trainer and two chauffeurs. Sharkovsky had a huge fleet of cars and he was always buying more. Six armed guards patrolled the grounds and took turns manning the gatehouse. There was a general maintenance man, who was always smoking, always coughing. He looked after the tennis court and the heated swimming pool in the conservatory. I will not waste time describing these people ... or the gardeners, who turned up every morning and worked ten hours a day. They are not really part of my story. They were simply there.

But I must mention the helicopter pilot, a very quiet man in his forties, with silver hair cut short in a military style. His name was Arkady Zelin and he had once flown with the VVS – the Soviet Air Force. He neither drank nor smoked. Sharkovsky would never have put his life in the hands of a man who was not utterly dependable. He was always on standby in case his master needed to get somewhere in a hurry, so he might spend weeks at the *dacha* between flights, and once the helicopter had been tied down there was little for him to do. Just like Maya, he read books. He also kept himself fit, doing press-ups and running around the grounds. Sharkovsky had a gymnasium as well as the pool but Zelin wasn't allowed to use either of them.

Zelin was one of the few people who bothered to introduce himself to me and I was quick to let him know about my old love of helicopters. He piloted a two-bladed Bell 206 JetRanger with seating for four passengers – Sharkovsky had ordered it from Canada – and although I wasn't allowed near it, I often found myself gazing at it across the lawn. Escape was too dangerous to consider, but even so, in my wilder moments, it sometimes occurred to me that the helicopter might be my only way out. I couldn't hide in it. I'd have been spotted at once unless I crawled into the luggage compartment and that was always kept locked. But maybe, one day, I would be able to persuade Zelin to take me with him – if he was flying alone. It was a foolish thought but I had to keep some sort of hope alive in my head or I'd go mad. And so I stayed close to him. The two of us would play *Durak* together, the same game that I had played with Dima, Roman and Grigory. Sometimes I wondered what had happened to them. But as time went on, I thought about them less and less.

One other member of the staff was important to me. His name was Nigel Brown and he was English, a thin, elderly man with straggly ginger hair and a pinched face. He had once been the headmaster of a prep school in Norfolk and still dressed as if he worked there, with corduroy trousers and, every day, the same tweed jacket with leather patches on the elbows. Zelin told me there had been some sort of scandal at the school and he had been forced to take early retirement. It was certainly true that Mr Brown never talked about his time there. Sharkovsky had hired him as a private tutor, to help Ivan and Svetlana pass their exams. Other tutors came and went but he lived at the *dacha* permanently.

All the staff met every evening. Just as I had thought, the brick building which I had seen beside the cabins was a recreation room with a kitchen and dining area, where we ate our meals. There were a few battered sofas and chairs, a snooker table, a television, a coffee machine and a public telephone – although all calls were monitored and I wasn't allowed to use it at all. After dinner, the guards who weren't on duty, the chauffeurs and sometimes the chef would sit and smoke. Mr Brown had nothing to say to any of them but perhaps because I was so young, he took an interest in me and decided for no good reason to teach me English. It soon became a personal project and he took delight in my progress. It turned out that I had a natural aptitude for languages and after a while he began to teach me French and German too. Most of the languages I speak today, I owe to him.

While he taught me, he drank. Maybe this was what had led to his downfall in Norfolk, but at the start of each lesson he would open a bottle of vodka and by the end of it I could hardly work out what he was saying, no matter what the language. By midnight he was usually unconscious and there were many occasions when I had to carry him back to his room. There was, however, one aspect of his drinking habit that was useful to me. He was not a cautious man and under the influence of alcohol he didn't care what he said.

It was Nigel Brown who told me what little I knew about Sharkovsky.

"How did he make all his money?" I once asked. It was a warm evening about six months after I had arrived. There was no breeze and the mosquitoes were whining beneath the electric lights.

"Ah, well, that's all politics," he replied. We had been talking in English but now he slipped back into Russian, which he spoke fluently. "The end of Communism in your country created a sort of vacuum. A few men stepped in and he was one of them. They've sucked all the money out of your country, every last ruble. Some of them have made billions! Mr Sharkovsky invested in companies. Scrap metal, chemicals, cars... He bought and he sold and the money flowed in."

"But why does he need so much protection?"

"Because he's an evil bastard." He smiled as if was surprised by what he had just said but decided to continue anyway. "Mr Sharkovsky is connected with the police. He's connected with the politicians. He's connected with the mafia. He's a very dangerous man. God knows how many people he's killed to get to where he is. But the trouble is, you can't go on like that without making enemies. He really is a *shark*." He repeated the last word in English. "Do you know the word 'shark', Yassen? It's a big fish. A dangerous fish. It will gobble you up. Now, let's get back to these irregular verbs, past tense. *I buy, you bought. I see, you saw. I speak, you spoke*..."

Sharkovsky must have had plenty of enemies. We lived our life under siege at the *dacha*, and as I had discovered, painfully, there was no way in or out. There were X-ray machines and metal detectors at the main gates – just like at a modern airport – and nobody was allowed in or out without being searched. The gardeners arrived empty-handed and were expected to leave their tools behind when they finished work. The tutors, the drivers, the housekeepers ... each person's background had been checked except for mine, but then my background didn't matter. Josef and Karl always stayed close to their boss. The CCTV cameras were on at all times. Everyone watched everyone else. Other businessmen in Russia were careful but none of them went to these extremes. Sharkovsky was paranoid but, as I had seen for myself in that basement refrigerator, he had good reason to be.

He was extremely careful about what he ate and drank. For example, he only accepted mineral water from bottles that he had opened himself after checking that the seal had not been broken. The bottles always had to be glass. His enemies might be able to contaminate a plastic one using a hypodermic syringe. He sometimes ate food straight from the packet or the tin, pronging it into his mouth with no sign of pleasure, but if it arrived on a plate, I would have to taste it first.

Most times, I would report to the kitchen before the meals were sent out and I would eat straight out of the pans, with Josef or Karl watching over me and Pavel standing nervously to one side. It's hard to describe how I felt about this. On one level, I have to admit that there was a part of me that enjoyed it. As I have said, the food was superb. But at the same time, it was still an unpleasant experience. First of all, one mouthful was all I was allowed and I was always aware that one mouthful might be enough to kill me. In a way, every tasting session was the same as the Russian roulette I had been forced to play on my first night. I learned to attune my senses to look out for the acrid taste of poison or simply the suspicion that something might not be right. The trouble was, by the time I detected it, it might well have killed me.

After a while, I put the whole thing out of my

mind. I simply did what I was told, robotically, without complaining. You might say that I had a very strange relationship with death. The two of us were constantly together, side by side. And yet we ignored each other. In this way, we were able to get by.

What I most dreaded were the formal dinners that I was forced to attend in the huge dining room with its brilliant chandeliers, gold and white curtains, antique French table and chairs, and countless flickering candles. Sharkovsky often invited business associates and friends ... people he knew well. To begin with, I was worried that Misha Dementyev, the professor from Moscow State University, might show up. He knew Sharkovsky. Indeed he – along with my own stupidity – was the reason I was here. What would happen if he recognized me? Would it make my situation worse? But he never did appear and it occurred to me that he was probably a minor employee in Sharkovsky's empire and that it was very unlikely that he would receive an invitation. Nearly all the guests arrived in expensive cars. Some even came in their own helicopters. They were as rich and as vicious as Sharkovsky himself.

I had been given a grey suit with a white shirt and a black tie for these events – the same uniform as his bodyguards – and I would stand behind him as I had been instructed, looking down at the floor with my hands held behind my back. I was not allowed to speak. As each course was served, I would step forward and, using my own cutlery, would take a sample directly from his plate, eat it, nod and step back again. There was no doubt that Sharkovsky was afraid for his life but at the same time he was enjoying himself. He loved playing the Roman emperor, showing me off to his other guests, deliberately humiliating me in front of them.

But if the father was bad, his son was much, much worse. Ivan Sharkovsky first became aware of me at one of those dinners and although I wasn't supposed to look at the guests, I noticed him examining me out of the corner of my eye. Ivan, a year older than me, resembled his father in many ways. He had the same dark qualities but they had been distributed differently – in his curly black hair, his heavy jowls, his down-turned mouth. He seemed to be constantly brooding about something. His father was solid and muscular. He was fat with puffy cheeks, thick lips and eyelids that were slightly too large for his eyes. Sitting hunched over the table, spooning food into his mouth, he had something brutish about him.

"Papa?" he asked. "Where did you get him from?"

"Who?" Sharkovsky was at the head of the table with Maya sitting next to him. She was wearing a huge diamond necklace that sparkled in the light. Whenever there were guests, he insisted that she smothered herself in jewellery.

"The food taster!"

"From Moscow." Sharkovsky dismissed the question as if he had simply picked me up in a shop.

"Can he taste my food?"

Shakovsky leant forward and jabbed a fork in the direction of his son. He had been drinking heavily – champagne and vodka – and although he wasn't drunk, there was a looseness about the way he spoke. "You don't need a food taster. You're not important. Nobody would want to kill you."

The other guests all took this as a joke and laughed uproariously, but Ivan scowled and I knew that I would be hearing from him soon.

And the very next day, he came outside and found me. It was a cold afternoon. I was washing one of his father's cars, spraying it with a hose. As soon as I saw him coming, I stopped my work and looked down. This was what I had been taught. We had to treat the whole family as if they were royalty. Part of me hoped he would simply walk on, but I could see it wasn't going to happen. I knew straight away that I was in trouble.

"What is your name?" he asked, although of course he knew.

"Yassen Gregorovich," I answered. That was the name I always used now.

"I'm Ivan."

"Yes," I said. "I know."

He looked at me questioningly and I could feel the sense of menace hanging in the air. "But you don't call me that, do you?"

"No ... sir." It made me sick having to say the words but I knew that was what he wanted.

He glanced at the car. "How long has it taken you to clean that? he asked.

"An hour," I said. It was true. The car was the Bentley and it had been filthy. When I had finished with it, it would have to look as if it had just come out of the showroom.

"Let me help you."

He gestured for the hose, which was still spouting water onto the ground, and, dreading what was to come, I handed it to him. First he pointed it at the car. He placed his thumb over the end so that the water rushed out in a jet. It poured over the windscreen and down over the doors. Then he turned it on me ... my head, my chest, my arms, my legs. I could only stand there uselessly as he soaked me. Had this happened in my village, I would have knocked him to the ground. Right then I had to use all my self-restraint to stop myself punching him in the face. But that was exactly what he was showing me. He had complete power over me. He could do anything to me that he wanted.

When he had finished, he smirked and handed the hose back to me. Finally, he noticed the bucket of muddy water beside the car. He kicked out, sending the contents spraying over the bodywork.

"Bad luck, Yassen," he said. "You're going to have to start again."

I stood there, dripping wet, as he turned and walked away.

After that, he tormented me all the time. His father must have known what was happening – Ivan would have never acted in this way without his authority – but he allowed it to carry on. And so I would get an order, usually transmitted by Josef, Karl or one of the housekeepers. It didn't matter if it was morning or the middle of the night. I would go up to the big house and there he would be with football boots that needed cleaning, suitcases that needed carrying or even crumpled clothes that needed ironing. He liked me to see his room, spacious and comfortable, filled with so many nice things, because he knew I lived in a small wooden cabin with nothing. And despite what Sharkovsky had said, he sometimes got me to taste his food for him, watching with delight as I leant over his plate. Often, he would play tricks with me. I would discover that he had deliberately filled the food with salt or chilli powder so that it would make me sick. I used to long for the day he would return to his school in England and I would finally be left alone.

Three years...

I grew taller and stronger. I learned to speak different languages. But otherwise I might as well have been dead. I saw nothing of the world except what was shown on the television news. The horror of my situation was not the drudgery of my work and the daily humiliations I received. It was in the dawning realization that I might be here for the rest of my life, that even as an old man I might be cleaning toilets and corridors and, worse still, that I might be grateful. Already, I could feel part of myself accepting what I had turned into. I no longer thought about escaping. I didn't even think about what might exist on the other side of the wall. Once, I found myself looking in the mirror because there was a stain on my shirt. There was to be a dinner that night and I was genuinely embarrassed, afraid I would let my master down. At that moment I was disgusted with myself. I saw, quite clearly, what I was becoming ... perhaps what I had already become.

I never thought of Estrov. It was as if my parents had not existed. Even my time in Moscow seemed far behind me. It was obvious that Dima would never find me and even if he did I would be out of his reach. All I could think about was the work I would do the next day. This was Sharkovsky's revenge. He had allowed me to keep my life but he had taken away my humanity.

And so it might have continued.

But things changed quite suddenly in the early summer of my third year of captivity. Ivan had just finished his last year at Harrow and was due back any time. Svetlana was staying with friends near the Black Sea. Sharkovsky was having another dinner party and I had been told to report to the dining room to help with the preparations.

For some reason, I arrived early. As I walked up to the house, a car passed me and stopped at the front door. A man got out, rang the bell and hurried inside. I had seen him before. His name was Brodsky and he was one of Sharkovsky's business associates from Moscow. The two of them owned several companies together and they were connected in other ways it was probably best not to know. I went into the kitchen and a few moments later, the telephone rang. Mr Brodsky wanted tea. Pavel was busy preparing the dinner – a broiled Atlantic salmon, which he was decorating with red and black caviar. The housekeepers were laying the table. I was there and in my suit so I made the tea and carried it up.

I crossed the hallway, which was now so familiar to me that I could have made my way blindfolded. The sweeping staircase, the marble pillars, the huge bowl of flowers and the chandelier no longer meant anything to me. I had seen them too often. The door to the study was half open as I approached and normally I would have knocked and entered, set the tray down on a table and left as quickly as I could. But this time, just as I drew close, I heard a single word that stopped me in my tracks and rooted me to the floor.

"They're asking questions about it again. Estrov. We're going to have to do something before the situation gets out of hand..."

Estrov.

My village.

It had been Brodsky who had spoken. Estrov. What could he possibly know about Estrov? Hardly daring to breathe, I waited for Sharkovsky to reply.

"You can deal with it, Mikhail."

"It's not as easy as that, Vladimir. These are Western journalists, working in London. If they connect you with what happened..."

"Why should they?"

"They're not stupid. They've already discovered you were a shareholder."

"So what?" Sharkovsky didn't sound concerned. "There were lots of shareholders. What exactly am I supposed to have done?"

"You wanted them to raise productivity. You wanted more profit. You ordered them to change the safety procedures."

"Are you accusing me, Mikhail?"

"No. Of course not. I'm your closest advisor and your friend and why should I care if a few peasants got killed? But these people smell a story. And it would be seriously damaging to us if the name of Estrov were to be mentioned in the British press or anywhere else."

"It was all taken care of at the time," Sharkovsky replied. "There was no evidence left. Our friends in the ministry made sure of that. It never happened! Let these stupid journalists sniff around and ask questions. They won't find anything. And if I do come to believe that they are dangerous to me or to my business, then I'll deal with them. Even in London there are car accidents. Now stop worrying and have a drink."

"I ordered tea."

"It should be here. I'll call down."

It was a miracle I hadn't been caught listening outside. If Karl or Josef had come down the stairs and seen me, I would have been beaten. But I couldn't go in quite yet. I had to wait for the echoes of the conversation to die away. I counted to ten, then knocked on the door and entered. I kept my face blank. It was vital that they should not know that I had heard them talking. But as I crossed the carpet to where the visitor was sitting, the cup and the saucer rattled on the silver tray and I'm sure there can't have been any colour in my face.

Sharkovsky barely glanced at me. "What took you so long, Yassen?" he asked.

"I'm sorry, sir," I said. "I had to wait for the kettle to boil."

"Very well. Get out."

I bowed and left as quickly as I could.

I was shaking by the time I returned to the hall. It was as if all the pain and misery I had suffered in the last three years had been bundled together and then slammed into me, delivering one final, knock-out blow. It wasn't enough that Vladimir Sharkovsky had been endlessly cruel to me. It wasn't enough that he had reduced me to the role of his mindless slave. He was also directly implicated in the deaths of my mother and father, of Leo and of everyone else in the village.

Was it really such a surprise? When I had first heard his name, it had been at the university in Moscow. He had been talking to Misha Dementyev on the telephone and Dementyev had been implicated in what had happened. Nigel Brown had warned me too. He had told me that Sharkovsky invested in chemicals. I should have made the connection. And yet how could I have? It was almost beyond belief.

That night, as I stood at the table watching him tear apart the salmon that I had just tasted in front of all the other guests, I swore that I would kill him. It was surely the reason why fate had brought me here and it no longer mattered if I lived or died.

I would kill him. I swore it to myself.

I would kill him.

I would kill.

МЕХАНИК

THE MECHANIC

I barely slept that night. Every time I closed my eyes, my thoughts turned to guns, to kitchen knives, to the forks and spades that were used in the garden, to hammers and fire axes. The truth was that I was surrounded by weapons. Sharkovsky was used to having me around. I could reach him and have my revenge for Estrov before anyone knew what had happened.

But what good would it do? Josef and Karl – of course I knew which was which by now – were always nearby and even assuming I could get to Sharkovsky before they stopped me, they would deal with me immediately afterwards. Lying in my simple wooden bed, in my empty room, looking at the cold light of day, I saw that any action on my part would only lead to my own death. There had to be another way.

I felt sick and unhappy. I remembered Fagin with his leather notebook, reading out the different names and addresses in Moscow. Why had I made this choice?

Once again, and for the first time in a very long while, I thought about escape. I knew what the stakes were. If I tried and failed, I would die. But one way or another, this had to end.

I had just one advantage. By now I knew everything about the *dacha* and that included all the security arrangements. I took out one of the exercise books that Nigel Brown had given me – it was full of English vocabulary – and turned to an empty page at the back. Then, using a pencil, I drew a sketch of the compound and, resting it on my knees, I began to consider the best way out.

There wasn't one.

CCTV cameras covered every inch of the gardens. Climbing the wall was impossible. Quite apart from the razor wire, there were sensors buried under the lawn and they would register my footfall before I got close. Could I approach one of the guards? No. They were all far too afraid of Sharkovsky. What about his wife, Maya? Could I somehow persuade her to take me on one of her shopping trips to Moscow? It was a ridiculous idea. She had no reason to help me.

Even if I did miraculously make it to the other side, what was I to do next? I was surrounded by countryside – the Silver Forest – with no idea of how near I was to the nearest bus stop or station. If I made it to Moscow, I could go back to

Tverskaya Street. I had no doubt that Dima would hide me ... assuming he was still there. But Sharkovsky would use all his police and underworld contacts to hunt me down. It wouldn't bother him that he had been keeping me a prisoner for three years and he had treated me in a way that was certainly illegal. It was just that we had made a deal and he would make sure I kept it. I worked for him or I was dead.

For the next few weeks, everything went on as before. I cleaned, I washed, I bowed, I scraped. But for me, nothing was the same. I could hardly bear to be in the same room as Sharkovsky. Tasting his food made me physically sick. This was the man responsible for what had happened to Estrov, the unnamed investor my parents had been complaining about the night before they died. If I couldn't escape from him, I would go mad. I would kill him or I would kill myself. I simply couldn't stay here any more.

I had hidden the exercise book under my mattress and every night I took it out and jotted down my thoughts. Slowly, I realized that I had been right from the very start. There was only one way out of this place – and that was the Bell JetRanger helicopter. I turned to a new page and wrote down the name of the pilot, Arkady Zelin, then underlined it twice. What did I know about him? How could I persuade him to take me out of here? Did he have any weaknesses, anything I could exploit?

We had known each other for three years but I wouldn't say we were friends. Zelin was a very solitary person, often preferring to eat alone. Even so, it was impossible to live in such close confinement without giving things away and the fact was that we did talk to each other, particularly when we were playing cards. Zelin liked the fact that I was interested in helicopters. He'd even let me examine the workings of the engine once or twice, when he was stripping it down for general maintenance, although he had drawn the line at allowing me to sit in the cockpit. The security guards wouldn't have been happy about that. And then there was Nigel Brown. He knew a bit about Zelin too and when he'd had a few drinks he would share it with me.

> Arkady Zelin
> Soviet Air Force. Gambling?
> Saratov.
> Wife? Son.
> Skiing... France/Switzerland. Retire?

This was about the total knowledge that I had of the man who might fly me out of the *dacha*. I wrote it down in my exercise book and stared at the useless words, sitting there on the empty page.

What did they add up to?

Zelin had been in the Soviet Air Force but he'd

been caught stealing money from a friend. There had been a court martial and he had been forced to leave. He was still bitter about the whole thing and claimed that he was innocent, that he had been set up, but the truth was he was always broke. It was possible that he was addicted to gambling. I often saw him looking at the racing pages in the newspapers and once or twice I heard him making bets over the phone.

Zelin owned a crummy flat in the city of Saratov, on the Volga River, but he hardly ever went there. He had three weeks' holiday a year – he often complained it wasn't enough – and he liked to travel abroad, to Switzerland or France in the winter. He loved skiing. He once told me that he would like to work in a ski resort and had talked briefly about heli-skiing – flying rich people to the top of glaciers and watching them ski down. He had been married and he carried a photograph in his wallet ... a boy who was about eleven or twelve years old, presumably his son. I remembered the day when I had come into the recreation room with a huge bruise on my face. I'd made a bad job of polishing the silver and Josef had lost control and almost knocked me out. Zelin had seen me and although he had said nothing, I could tell he was shocked. Perhaps I could appeal to him as a father? On the other hand, he never spoke about his son ... or his wife, for that matter. He never saw either of them; perhaps they had cut him out of their life. He was quite lonely. He was the sort of person who looks after number one simply because there is nobody else.

I could have scribbled until I had filled the entire exercise book but it wasn't going to help very much. Sharkovsky had a number of trips abroad that summer and each time he left in the helicopter, I would stop whatever I was doing and watch the machine rise from the launch pad and hover over the trees before disappearing into the sky. I had nothing I could offer – no money, no bribe. I knew that there was no way Zelin was going to fall out with his employer. In the end I forgot about him and began to think of other plans.

We came to the end of another summer and I swore to myself that it would be my last at the *dacha*, that by Christmas I would be gone. And yet August bled into September and nothing changed. I was feeling sick and angry with myself. No only had I not escaped, I hadn't even tried. Worse still, Ivan Sharkovsky had returned. He had left Harrow by now and was on his way to Oxford University. Presumably his father had offered to pay for a new library or a swimming pool because I'm not sure there was any other way he'd have got in.

I was in the garden when I first saw him, pushing a wheelbarrow full of leaves, taking it down to the compost heap. Suddenly he was standing there in front of me, blocking my path. Age had not improved him. He was still overweight. We were both about the same height but he was much heavier than me. I stopped at once and bowed my head.

"Yassen!" he said, spitting out the two syllables in a sing-song voice. "Are you glad to see me?"

"Yes, sir," I lied.

"Still slaving for my dad?"

"Yes, sir."

He smirked at me. Then he reached down and picked up a handful of filthy leaves from the wheelbarrow. I was wearing a tracksuit and, very deliberately, he shoved the leaves down the front of my chest. Then he laughed and walked away.

From that moment on, there was a new, very disturbing edge to his behaviour. His attacks on me became more physical. If he was angry with me, he would slap me or punch me, which was something he had never done before. Once, at the dinner table, I spilt some of his wine and he picked up a fork and jabbed it into my thigh. His father saw this but said nothing. In a way, the two of them were equally mad. I was afraid that Ivan wouldn't be satisfied until I was dead.

That was the month that Nigel Brown was fired. He wasn't particularly surprised. He was no longer tutoring Ivan, and his sister, Svetlana, had been accepted into Cheltenham Ladies' College in England so there was nothing left for him to do. Mr. Brown was sixty by now and his teaching days were over. He talked about going back to Norfolk but he didn't seem to have any fondness for the place. It's often interested me how some people can follow a single path through life that takes them to somewhere they don't want to be. It was hard to believe that this crumpled old man with his vodka and his tweed jacket had once been a child, full of hopes and dreams. Was this what he had been born to be?

I was having dinner with him one evening, shortly before he left. Arkady Zelin had joined us. He had returned from Moscow that morning with Sharkovsky, who had flown in from the United States. Mr Brown hadn't begun drinking yet – at least he'd only had a couple of glasses – and he was in a reflective mood.

"You're going to have to keep up your languages, Yassen, once I'm gone," he was saying. "Maybe they'll let me send you books. There are very good tapes these days."

He was being kind but I knew he didn't really mean what he was saying. Once he was gone, I would never hear from him again.

"What about you, Arkady?" he went on. "Are you going to stay working here?"

"I have no reason to leave," Zelin said.

"No. I can see you're doing well for yourself. Nice new watch!"

It was typical of my teacher to notice a detail like that. When we were doing exercises together, he could instantly spot a single misspelt word in the middle of a whole page. I glanced at Zelin's wrist just in time to see him draw it away, covering it with his sleeve.

"It was given to me," he said. "It's nothing."

"A Rolex?"

"Why do you interest yourself in things that don't concern you? Why don't you mind your own business?"

For the rest of the meal, Zelin barely spoke – and when he had finished eating he left the room, even though we'd agreed to play cards. I did an hour's German with Mr Brown but my heart wasn't in it and in the end he gave up, dragged the bottle off the table and plonked himself in an armchair in the corner. I was left on my own, thinking. It was a small detail. A new Rolex. But it was strange the way Zelin had tried to conceal it, and why had it made him so angry?

I might have forgotten all about it but the next day something else happened which brought it back to my mind. Sharkovsky was leaving for Leningrad at the end of the week. It was an important visit and he much preferred to fly than go by road. During the course of the morning, I saw Zelin working on the helicopter, carrying out a routine inspection. There was nothing unusual about that. But just before lunch, he presented himself at the house. I happened to be close by, cleaning the ground-floor windows, and I heard every word that was said.

"I'm very sorry, sir," he said. "We can't use the helicopter."

Sharkovsky had come to the front door, dressed in riding gear. He had taken up riding the year before and had bought two horses – one for himself, one for his wife. He'd also built a stable close to the tennis court and employed one of the gardeners as a groom. Zelin was standing in his overalls, wiping his hands on a white handkerchief that was smeared with oil.

"What's wrong with it?" Sharkovsky snapped. He had been very short-tempered recently. There was a rumour that things hadn't been going too well with his business. Maybe that was why he had been travelling so much.

"There's been a servo actuator malfunction, sir," Zelin said. "One of the piston rods shows signs of cracking. It's going to have to be replaced."

"Can you do it?"

"No, sir. Not really. Anyway, we have to order the part..."

Sharkovsky was in a hurry. "Well, why don't you call in the mechanic ... what's his name ... Borodin?"

"I called his office just now. It's annoying but he's ill." He paused. "They can send someone else."

"Reliable?"

"Yes, sir. His name is Rykov. I've worked with him."

"All right. See to it."

Maya was waiting for him. He stormed off without saying another word.

I didn't know for certain that Zelin was lying but I had a feeling that something was wrong. Every day at the *dacha* was the same. When I say that life went like clockwork, I mean it had that same dull, mechanical quality. But now there were three coincidences and they had all happened at the same time. The helicopter had been fine the day before but suddenly it was broken. The usual mechanic – a brisk, talkative man who turned up every couple of months – was mysteriously ill. And then there was that new watch, and the strange way that Zelin had behaved.

There was something else. It occurred to me that it really wasn't so difficult to replace a piston rod. I had been reading helicopter magazines all my life and knew almost as much as if I'd actually been flying myself. I was sure that Zelin would have a spare and should have been able to fix it himself.

So what was he up to? I said nothing, but for the rest of the day I kept my eye on him and when the new mechanic arrived that same afternoon, I made sure I was there.

He came in a green van marked MVZ Helicopters and I saw him step out to have his passport and employment papers checked by the guards. He was a short, plump man with a mop of grey hair that sprawled over his head and several folds of fat around his chin. He was dressed in green overalls with the same initials, MVZ, on the top pocket. He had to wait while the guards searched his van – for once, their metal detectors weren't going to help them. The back was jammed with spare parts. He didn't seem to mind though. He stood there smoking a cigarette and when they finally let him through he gave them a friendly wave and drove straight across to the helicopter pad. Arkady Zelin was waiting for him there and they spent the rest of the day working together, stripping down the engine and doing whatever it was they had to do.

It was a warm afternoon, and at four o'clock one of the housekeepers sent me over to the helicopter with a tray of lemonade and sandwiches. The mechanic – Rykov – came strutting towards me with a smile on his face.

"Who are you?" he demanded.

"My name is Yassen, sir."

"And what's in these sandwiches?" He prised one open with a grimy thumb. "Ham and cheese. Thanks, Yassen. That's very nice of you." He was already eating, talking with his mouth full. Then he signalled to Zelin and the two of them went back to work.

I saw him a second time when I came back to pick up the tray. Once again he was pleased to see me but I thought that Zelin was more restrained. He was quieter than I had ever known him and this was a man I knew fairly well. You cannot play cards with someone and not get a sense of the way they think. I would have said he was nervous. I wondered why he wasn't wearing his new watch today. By now, the helicopter was almost completely reassembled. I lingered with the two men, waiting to take back the tray. And it seemed only natural to chat.

"Do you fly these?" I asked the mechanic.

"Not me," he said. "I just take them apart and put them back together."

"Is it difficult?"

"You have to know what you're doing."

"Wouldn't you like to fly?"

He shook his head. "Not really." He took out a cigarette and lit it. "I wouldn't know what to do with a joystick between my legs. I prefer to keep my feet safely on the ground."

"That's enough, Yassen," Zelin growled. "Don't you have work to do? Go and do it."

"Yes, Mr Zelin."

I picked up the tray with the dirty glasses and carried it back to the house. But I'd already discovered everything I needed to know. The mechanic knew nothing about helicopters. Even I could have told him that a Bell helicopter doesn't have a joystick. It has a cyclic control which transmits instructions to the rotor blades. And it's not in front of you. It's to one side. Zelin had lied about the malfunction just as he had lied about the usual mechanic, Borodin, being sick. I was sure of it.

From that moment, I didn't let them out of my

sight. I knew I would get into trouble. There were ten pairs of shoes I was meant to polish and a whole pile of crates to be broken up in the cellar. But there was no way I was going to disappear inside. Zelin was planning something. If Rykov wasn't a helicopter mechanic, what was he? A thief? A spy? It didn't matter. Zelin had brought him into the compound and had to be part of it. This was the opportunity I'd been waiting for. I could blackmail him. Suddenly I saw him with his hand on the cyclic. He could fly me out.

My biggest worry was that Ivan would return to the *dacha*. He'd gone into Moscow for the day, driving the new Mercedes sports car that his father had bought him for his birthday, but if he came back and saw me, the chances were that he would find some task for me to do. At five o'clock there was still no sign of him but Sharkovsky and his wife returned from a ride and I helped them down from the saddle and walked the horses back to the stable. All the gardeners had gone. There were just the usual guards, walking in pairs, unaware that anything unusual was going on.

As I got back to the house, I heard the helicopter start up, the whine of the engine rising as the rotors picked up speed. There was no sign of Rykov but the van with the MVZ logo was still parked close by so I knew he couldn't have left. I pretended to walk into the house but at the last minute I hurried forward and ducked behind one of the cars. It was actually the Lexus that had first brought me here. If anyone found me there, I would pretend I was cleaning it.

I could see Arkady Zelin inside the cockpit, checking the controls, and suddenly the mechanic emerged from the other side of the helicopter and began to walk towards me, towards the house, carrying a sheaf of papers. If the guards had seen him, it would have looked completely natural. He had finished the job and he needed someone to sign the documentation. But he was being careful. He kept to the shadows. Nobody except me saw him go in through the side door.

I followed. I didn't know what I was going to do because I still hadn't worked out what was happening. All I knew was, it wasn't what it seemed.

I crept down the corridor past the service rooms – the laundry and the boot room, where I had spent so many hundreds of hours, day and night, in mindless drudgery. There was nobody around and that was very unusual. The mechanic couldn't have just walked into the house. One of the housekeepers would have challenged him and then made him wait while she went to fetch Josef or Karl. Rykov had only entered a few seconds ahead of me. He should have been here now. I felt the silence all around me. None of the lights were on. I glanced into the kitchen. There was a pot of soup or stew bubbling away on top of the stove but no sign of Pavel.

I was tempted to call out but something told me to stay quiet. I continued past the pantry. The door was ajar and that too was strange, as it was always kept locked in case the dog went in. I pushed it open and at that moment everything made sense. It should have been obvious from the start. How could I have been so slow not to see it?

The housekeeper was there, lying on the floor. I had lost count of the number of times that Nina had snapped at me, scolding me for being too slow or too clumsy, hitting me on the head whenever she got the chance. I could see the wooden spoon still tucked into her apron but she wasn't going to be using it. She had been shot at close range, obviously with a silencer because I hadn't heard the sound of the gun. She was on her back with her hands spread out, as if in surprise. There was a pool of blood around her shoulders.

Arkady Zelin had been bribed. There was no other explanation. He never had any money but suddenly he had an expensive new watch. Rykov was an assassin who had come here to kill Sharkovsky. The safest way to smuggle a gun into the compound – perhaps the only way to get past the metal detectors and X-ray machines – was to bring it in a truck packed with metal equipment. It would have been easy enough to dismantle it and scatter the separate parts among the other machinery. And the fastest way out after he had done his work was the helicopter, which was waiting even now, with the rotors at full velocity.

My mouth was dry. My every instinct was to turn and run. If Rykov saw me, he would kill me without even thinking about it, just as he had killed Nina. But I didn't leave. I couldn't. This was the only chance I would ever get and I had to take it. There was a small axe hanging in the pantry. I had used it until there were blisters all over my hands, chopping kindling for the fire in Sharkovsky's study. Making as little noise as possible and doing my best not to look at the dead woman, I unhooked it. An axe would be little use against a gun, but even so, I felt safer having some sort of weapon. I continued to the door that led into the main hall. It was half open. Hardly daring to breathe, I looked through.

I had arrived just in time for the endgame.

The hall was in shadow. The sun was setting behind the house and its last rays were too low to reach the windows. The lights were out. I could hear the shrill whine of the helicopter outside in the distance but a curtain of silence seemed to have fallen on the house. Josef was lying on the stairs, where he had been gunned down. Rykov was standing in front of me, edging forward, an automatic pistol with a silencer in his hand.

He was making his way towards the study, his feet making no sound on the thick carpet. But even as I watched, the door of the study opened and Vladimir Sharkovsky came out, dressed in a suit and tie but with his jacket off. He must have heard the disturbance, the body tumbling down the stairs, and had come out to see what was happening.

"What...?" he began.

Rykov didn't say anything. He stepped forward and shot my employer three times, the bullets thudding into his chest and stomach so quietly that I barely heard them. The effect was catastrophic. Sharkovsky was thrown backwards ... off his feet. His head hit the carpet first. If the bullets hadn't killed him, he would surely have broken his neck. His legs jerked then became still.

What did I feel at that moment? Nothing. Of course I wasn't going to waste any tears on Sharkovsky. I was glad he was dead. But I couldn't find it in myself to celebrate the death of another human being. I was frightened. I was still wondering how I could turn this to my advantage. Everything was happening so quickly that I didn't have time to work out my emotions. I suppose I was in a state of shock.

And then a voice came floating out of the darkness.

"Don't turn round. Put the gun down!"

Rykov twisted his head but saw nothing. I was hiding behind the door, out of sight. It was Karl. He had come up from the cellar. Maybe he had been looking for me, wondering why I hadn't broken up those crates. He was behind Rykov and over to one side, edging into the hall with a gun clasped in both hands, holding it at the same level as his head.

Rykov froze. He was still holding the gun he had used to kill Sharkovsky and I wondered if he'd had time to reload. He had fired at least five bullets. Rykov couldn't see where the order had come from but he remained completely calm. "I will pay you one hundred thousand rubles to let me leave here," he said. He sounded very different from the mechanic I had spoken to. His voice was younger, more cultivated.

"Who sent you?"

"Scorpia."

The word meant nothing to me. Nor did it seem to have any significance for Karl. "Lower your gun very slowly," he said. "Put it on the carpet where I can see it … in front of you."

There was nothing Rykov could do. If he couldn't see the bodyguard, he couldn't kill him. He lowered the gun to the floor.

"Kick it away."

"If it hadn't been me, it would have been someone else," Rykov said. "Do yourself a favour. You're out of a job. Take the money and go."

Silence. Rykov knew he had to do what he was told. He kicked the gun across the carpet. It came to a halt a few inches away from the dead man.

Karl stepped further into the hall, still holding his gun in both hands. It was aimed at the back of Rykov's neck. He glanced to the right and saw Josef lying spreadeagled on the stairs. Something flickered across his face and I had no doubt that he was going to shoot down the man who had been responsible for the death of his brother. As he moved forward, his path took him in front of the door where I was standing and suddenly I was behind him.

"One hundred and fifty thousand rubles," Rykov said. "More money than you will ever see in your life."

"You have killed my brother."

Rykov understood. There was no point in arguing. In Russia, blood ties, particularly between brothers, are strong.

Karl was very close to him now and without really thinking about it, I made the decision – probably the most momentous of my life. I slipped through the door and, raising the axe, took three steps into the hall. The bodyguard heard me at the very last moment but it was too late. Using the blunt end, I brought the axe swinging down and hit him on the back of the head. He collapsed in front of me, his arms, his legs, his entire body suddenly limp. The mechanic moved incredibly fast. He didn't know what had happened but he dived forward, reaching out for the gun he had just kicked away. But I was faster. Before he could grab it, I had dropped the axe and swept up Karl's gun and already I was aiming it straight at him, doing my best to stop my hand shaking.

Rykov saw me and stared. He was unarmed. He

couldn't believe what had just happened. "You!" he exclaimed.

"Listen to me," I said. "I could shoot you now. If I fire a single shot, everyone will come. You'll never get away."

"What do you want?" he demanded.

"I want to get out of here."

"I can't do that."

"Yes, you can. You have to help me!" I scrabbled for words. "I knew you weren't really a mechanic. I knew you and Zelin were working together. But I didn't say anything. It's thanks to me that you managed to do what you came for." I nodded at the body of Vladimir Sharkovsky.

"I will give you money…"

"I don't want money. I want you to take me with you. I never chose to come here. I'm a prisoner. I'm their slave. All I'm asking is for you to take me as far away as you can and then to leave me. I don't care about you or who you're working for. I'm glad he's dead. Do you understand? Is it a deal?"

He pretended to think … but only very briefly. The helicopter was still whining outside and very soon one of the guards might ask what was happening. Arkady Zelin might panic and take off without him. Rykov didn't have any time. "Let me get my gun," he said. He stretched out his hand.

"No!" I tightened my grip. "We'll leave together. It'll be better for you that way. The guards know me and they're less likely to ask questions." He still seemed to be hesitating, so I added, "You do it my way or you never leave."

He nodded, once. "Very well. Let's go."

We left together, back down the corridor, past the room with the dead woman. I was terrified. I was with a man who had just killed three people without even blinking and I knew that he would make me the fourth if I gave him the slightest chance. I made sure I didn't get too close to him. If he hit out at me or tried to grab me, I would fire the gun. This one wasn't silenced. The sound of the explosion would act as a general alarm.

Rykov didn't seem at all concerned. He didn't speak as we left the house and walked through the half-darkness together, skirting the fountain and making our way across the lawn towards the helicopter. And it had been true, what I had told him. One of the guards saw us but did nothing. The fact that I was walking with him meant that everything had to be OK.

But Zelin was shocked when he saw the two of us together. "What is he doing?" he shouted.

I could barely hear a word he said but the meaning was obvious. I was struggling to keep the gun steady, feeling the wind from the rotors buffeting my arms. I knew that this was the most dangerous part. As we climbed in, the mechanic could wrench the gun away and kill me with it. He could probably kill me with his bare hands. I wasn't sure if I should go in first or second.

What if he had another gun hidden under one of the seats?

I made my decision. "I'm getting in first!" I shouted. "You follow!"

As I climbed into the back seat, I kept the gun pointed at Zelin, not the mechanic. I knew that he couldn't fly. If he tried anything, I would shoot the pilot and we would both be stuck. I think he understood my strategy. There was actually something close to a smile as he climbed into the seat next to the pilot.

Zelin shouted something else. The mechanic leant forward and shouted back into his ear. Again, it was impossible to hear. For all I knew, he was sentencing me to death. I might have the advantage now but their moment would come while we were flying or perhaps when we landed. I wouldn't be able to keep them both covered and one of them would get me.

An alarm went off in the house, even louder than the scream of the helicopter. At once, the arc lamps all exploded into life. Two of the guards started running towards us, lifting their weapons. At the same time, a jeep appeared from the gatehouse, its headlamps blazing, tearing across the grass. The mechanic slammed the door and Zelin hit the controls. The muzzles of the automatic machine guns were flashing in the darkness. Machine-gun bullets were strafing past. One of them hit the cockpit but ricocheted away uselessly and I realized that, of course, it must be armoured glass.

The helicopter rose. It turned. It rocked above the lawn as if anchored there, unable to lift off. Bullets filled the air like fireflies.

And then Zelin jerked the cyclic. The helicopter twisted round one last time and, carrying me with it, soared away, over the wall, over the forest and into the darkening sky.

БОЛТИНО

BOLTINO

I had done it. For the first time in three long years I was outside the compound. Even if I hadn't been sitting in a helicopter, I would have felt as if I was flying.

Sharkovsky was dead. It was nothing less than he deserved and I was glad that he would not be able to come after me. Would I be blamed for his death? The guards had seen me leave with Rykov. They knew I was part of what had happened. But I had not been the one who had invited the mechanic into the house. That had been Zelin. With a bit of luck, Sharkovsky's people would concentrate on the two of them and they would forget about me.

I was not safe yet. Far from it.

Both Zelin and Rykov had put on headphones and although the blast of the rotors made conversation impossible for me, they were able to talk freely. What were they planning? I knew Zelin had been angry to see me but he was not the one in charge. Everything depended on Rykov. It might well be that he had already radioed ahead. There could be people waiting for me when we landed. I could be dragged out of my seat and shot. I knew already that human life meant nothing to the so-called mechanic. He had killed Nina, Josef and Sharkovsky without batting an eyelid. It would make no difference to him if he added an unknown teenager to the score.

But I didn't care. I hated myself at the *dacha*. I was eighteen years old, still cleaning toilets and sweeping corridors, kneeling in front of Ivan to polish his shoes or, worse, performing like a trained monkey at his father's dinner parties. It had been necessary to do these things to live but what was the point of a life so debased? If I were to die now, at least it would be on my own terms. I had grabbed hold of the opportunity. I had escaped. I had proved to myself that I was not beaten after all.

And there were so many other things I was experiencing for the first time. I had never flown before. Even to sit in the luxurious leather seat of the Bell JetRanger was extraordinary. It had once been my dream to fly helicopters and here I was, gazing over Zelin's shoulder, watching him as he manipulated the controls. I wished I could see more of the countryside but it was already dark and the outskirts of Moscow were little more than a scattering of electric lights. I didn't mind if I was being taken to my death. I was happy! Sharkovsky was finished. I had got away. I was flying.

After about ten minutes, Rykov turned round with a plastic bottle of water in his hand. He was offering it to me. I shook my head. At the same time, I retreated into the furthest corner, once again raising the gun. I was afraid of a trick. Rykov shrugged as if to say that I was making a mistake, but he understood and turned back again. We continued for another half-hour, then began to descend. It was only the pressure in my ears that warned me. Looking out of the window, everything seemed to be black and I got the idea we must be above water. Gently we touched down. Zelin hit the controls and the engine stopped, the rotors slowing down.

Rykov took off his headphones and hung them up. Then he turned to me. "What now?" he asked.

"Where are we?" I demanded.

"On the edge of a town called Boltino. To the north of Moscow." He unfastened his seat belt. "You have your wish, Yassen. You have escaped from Vladimir Sharkovsky. I'm sure we all agree that the world is a better place without him. As for Arkady and me, we have a plane waiting to take us on the next leg of our journey. I'm afraid we have to say goodbye."

Ignoring the gun, almost forgetting I was there,

Rykov opened the door and let himself out of the helicopter.

Arkady Zelin faced me. "You shouldn't have done this," he hissed. "You don't know these people..."

"Who are they?" I asked. I remembered the name I had heard. "Scorpia..."

"They will kill you." He undid his own belt and scrambled out, following the mechanic.

Suddenly I didn't want to be left on my own. I went after them. Looking around me, I had no idea why we had landed here. The helicopter was resting on a strip of mud that was so light-coloured that on second thoughts I realized it must be sand. An expanse of water stretched out next to it with about thirty sailing boats and cruisers moored to a jetty. There were trees on either side of us and what looked like wooden hangars or warehouses behind. The mechanic had been doing something to himself as I climbed down and by the time I reached him I was astonished to see that he had completely changed his appearance. The tangled grey hair was a wig. His hair was the same colour as mine, short and neatly cut. There had been something in his mouth, which had changed the shape of his face, and the folds of flesh around his chin had gone. He was suddenly slimmer and younger. He stripped out of his oily overalls. Underneath he was wearing a black T-shirt and jeans. The man who had come to the *dacha* in a green van marked MVZ Helicopters had disappeared. Nobody would ever see him again.

"Where are you going?" I asked.

"We are leaving the country."

"In a boat?"

"In a plane, Yassen." I looked around me, confused. How could a plane possibly land here? "A seaplane," he went on. "Don't you see it?"

And there it was, sitting flat on the water with a pilot already in the cockpit, waiting to fly them to their next destination. The seaplane was white. It had two propellers perched high up on the wings and a tail that was higher still so that even without moving it looked as if it was trying to lift itself into the air.

"Take me with you," I said.

The mechanic who was no longer a mechanic smiled once again. "Why should I do that?"

I still had the gun. I could have forced him to take me ... or tried to. But I knew that was a bad idea, that it would only end up getting me killed. Instead, I had to make a gesture, to show them I could be trusted. It was a terrible risk but I knew there was no other way. I turned the gun round in my hand and gave it to him. He looked genuinely surprised. He could shoot me where I stood and no one would be any the wiser. Apart from Zelin and the waiting pilot, there was nobody near.

"I saved your life," I said. "Back at the *dacha* ... Karl would have shot you. And I don't know why you killed Sharkovsky but you couldn't have hated him more than I did. We're on the same side."

He weighed the gun. Zelin watched the two of us, his face pale.

"I'm not on any side. I was paid to kill him," Rykov said.

"Then take me with you. It doesn't matter where you're going. Maybe I can work for you. I can be useful to you. I'll do anything you tell me. I speak three languages. I..." My voice trailed away.

Rykov was still holding the gun. Perhaps he was amused. Perhaps he was wondering where to fire the next bullet. It was impossible to tell what was going on in his head. Eventually he spoke – but not to me. "What do you think, Arkady?" asked.

"I think we should leave," Zelin said.

"With or without our extra passenger?"

There was a pause and I knew my life was hanging in the balance. Arkady Zelin had known me for three years. He had played cards with me. I had never been a threat to him. Surely he wouldn't abandon me now.

At last he made up his mind. "With him, if you like. He's not so bad. And they treated him like a dog."

"Very well." Rykov slid the gun into his waistband. "It may well be that my employers have a use for you. They can make the final decision. But until then, you do exactly as you're told."

"Yes, sir."

"There's no need to call me that."

He was already walking down the jetty to the plane. The pilot saw him and flicked on the engine. It sounded like one of the petrol lawnmowers at the *dacha* and, looking at the tiny propellers, the ungainly wings, I wondered how it could possibly separate itself from the water and fly. Arkady Zelin was carrying a travel bag, which he had brought from the helicopter. It occurred to me that everything he owned must be inside it. He was leaving Russia and, if he was wise, he would never come back. Sharkovsky's people might leave me alone but they would certainly be looking for him. It was impossible to say how much Zelin had been paid for his part in all this but I hoped the price included a completely new identity.

We got into the plane, a four-seater. I was lucky there was room for me. The new pilot ignored me. He knew better than to ask unnecessary questions.

But I had to know. "Where are we going?" I asked for a second time.

"To Venice," Rykov said.

"And to Scorpia," he might have added. The most dangerous criminal organization in the world. And I was about to walk right into its arms.

ВЕНЕЦИЯ

VENICE

It was night-time when we landed.

Once again we came plunging out of the darkness with only the sound of the engine and the rising feeling in my stomach to tell me we had reached the end of our journey. The seaplane hit the water, bounced, then skimmed along the surface before finally coming to rest. The pilot turned off the engine and we were suddenly sitting in complete silence, rocking gently on the water. Looking out of the window, I could make out a few lights twinkling in the distance. I glanced at Rykov, his face illuminated by the glow of the control panels, trying to work out what was going on in his mind. I was still afraid he would turn round and shoot me. He gave nothing away.

What next?

Although I didn't know it at the time, Venice was a perfect destination for those travelling by seaplane, particularly if they wished to arrive without being seen. It is possible, of course, that the Italian police and air traffic control had been bribed but nobody seemed to have noticed that we had landed. For about two minutes, no one spoke. Then I heard the deep throb of an engine and, with my face pressed against the window, I saw a motor launch slip out of the darkness and draw up next to us. The pilot opened the door and we climbed out.

The motor launch was about thirty feet long, made of wood, with a cabin at the front and leather seats behind. There were two men on board, a captain and a deckhand who helped us climb down. If they were surprised to find themselves with an extra passenger, they didn't show it. They said nothing. Rykov gestured and I sat out in the open at the back of the launch, even though the night was chilly. Zelin sat opposite me. He was clutching his travel bag, deep in thought.

We set off and as we went I heard the seaplane start up and take off again. I was already impressed. Everything about this operation had been well planned and executed down to the last detail. There had been only one mistake ... and that was me. It took us about ten minutes to make the crossing, pulling into a ramshackle wooden jetty with striped poles slanting in different directions. Rykov stepped out and waited for me to follow but Zelin stayed where he was and I realized he was not coming with us.

I held out a hand to the helicopter pilot. "Thank you," I said. "Thank you for letting me come with you."

"That place was horrible and Sharkovsky was beneath contempt," Zelin replied. "All those things they did to you... I'm sorry I didn't help."

"It's over now."

"For both of us." He shook my hand. "I hope it works out for you, Yassen. Take care."

I climbed onto the jetty and the boat pulled away. Moments later it had disappeared over the lagoon.

Rykov and I continued on foot. He took me to a flat in an area near the old dockyards where we had disembarked. Why do I call him Rykov? As I was soon to discover, it was not his name. He was not a mechanic. I'm not even sure that he was Russian, although he spoke my language fluently. He told me nothing about himself in the time I was with him and I was wise enough not to ask. When you are in his sort of business – now my business – you are not defined by who you are but who you are not. If you want to stay ahead of the police and the investigation agencies, you must never leave a trace of yourself behind.

We reached a doorway between two shops in an anonymous street. Rykov unlocked it and we entered a hallway with a narrow, twisting staircase leading up. His flat was on the fourth floor. He unlocked a second door and turned on the light. I found myself in a square, whitewashed room with a high ceiling and exposed beams. It had very little personality and I guessed it was merely somewhere he stayed when he was in Venice rather than a home.

The furniture looked new. There was a sofa facing a television, a dining table with four chairs, and a small kitchen. The pictures on the wall were views of the city, probably the same views you could see if you opened the shutters. It did not feel as if anyone had been here for some time.

"Are you hungry?" Rykov asked.

I shook my head. "No. I'm OK."

"There are some tins in the cupboard if you want."

I was hungry. But I was tired too. In fact, I was exhausted as all the suffering of the last three years suddenly drained out of me. It had ended so quickly. I still couldn't quite accept it. "What happens now?" I asked.

Rykov pointed at a door which I hadn't noticed, next to the fridge. "There's only one bedroom here," he said. "You can sleep on the couch. I have to go out but I'll be back later. Don't try to leave here. Do you understand me? You're to stay in this room. And don't use the telephone either. If you do, I'll know."

"I don't have anyone to call," I said. "And I don't have anywhere to go."

He nodded. "Good. I'll get you some blankets before I leave. Help yourself to anything you need."

A short while later, he left. I drank some water, then made up a bed on the couch and lay down without getting undressed. I was asleep instantly.

It was the first time I had slept outside my small wooden cabin in three years.

I didn't hear Rykov come back but I was woken up by him the following morning as he folded back the shutters and let in the sun. He had changed once again and it took me a few moments to remember who he was. He was wearing a suit and sunglasses. There was a gold chain around his neck. He looked slim and very fit, ten years younger than the mechanic who had come to mend the Bell JetRanger.

"It's nine o'clock," he said. "I can't believe Sharkovsky let you sleep this long. Is that when you started work?"

"No," I replied. At the *dacha*, I'd woken at six every morning.

"You can use my shower. I've left you a fresh shirt. I think it's your size. Don't take too long. I want to get some breakfast."

Ten minutes later, I was washed and dried, wearing a pale blue T-shirt that fitted me well. Rykov took me out and for the first time I saw Venice in the light of an autumn day.

There is simply nowhere in the world like it. Even today, when I am not working, this is somewhere I will come to unwind. I love to sit outside while the sun sets, watching the seagulls circling and the traffic crossing back and forth across the lagoon ... the water taxis, the water ambulances, the classic speedboats, the *vaporettos* and, of course, the gondolas. I can walk for hours through the streets and alleyways that seem to play cat and mouse with the canals, suddenly bringing you to a church, a fountain, a statue, a tiny humpback bridge ... or perhaps depositing you in a great square with bands playing, waiters circling and tourists all around. Every corner has another surprise. Every street is a work of art. I am glad I have never killed anyone there.

Rykov took me to a café around the corner from his flat, an old-fashioned place with a tiled floor, a long counter and a giant-sized coffee machine that blew out clouds of steam. We sat together at a little antique table and he ordered cappuccinos, orange juice and *tramezzini* – little sandwiches, made out of soft bread with smoked ham and cheese. I hadn't eaten for about twenty hours and this was my first taste of Italian food. I wolfed them down and didn't complain when he ordered a second plate. There was a canal running past outside and I was fascinated to see the different boats passing so close to the window.

"So your name is Yassen Gregorovich," he said. He had been speaking in English ever since we had arrived in Venice. Perhaps he was testing me – although it was more likely that he had decided to leave the Russian language behind ... along with the rest of the character he had been. "How old are you?"

I thought for a moment. "Eighteen," I said.

"Sharkovsky kidnapped you in Moscow. He kept

you his prisoner for three years. You were his food taster. Is that true?"

"Yes."

"You're lucky. We tried to poison him once and we were considering a second attempt. Your parents are dead?"

"Yes."

"Arkady Zelin told me about you in the helicopter. And about Sharkovsky. I don't know why you put up with it so long. Why didn't you just put a knife into the bastard?"

"Because I wanted to live," I said. "Karl or Josef would have killed me if I'd tried."

"You were prepared to spend the rest of your life working for him?"

"I did what I had to to survive. Now he's dead and I'm here."

"That's true."

Rykov took out a cigarette and lit it. He did not offer me one but nor did I want it. This was the one good thing that had come out of my time at the *dacha*. I had not been allowed to have cigarettes and so I had been forced to give up smoking. I have never smoked since.

"Who are you?" I asked. "And who are Scorpia? Did they pay you to kill Sharkovsky?"

"I'll give you a piece of advice, Yassen. Don't ask questions and never mention that name again. Certainly not in public."

"I'd like to know why I'm here. It would have

been easier for you to kill me when we were in Boltino."

"Don't think I wasn't tempted. As it is, it may be that I've made a bad mistake. We'll see." He drew on the cigarette. "The only reason I didn't kill you is because I owed you. It was stupid of me not to see the second bodyguard. I don't usually make mistakes and I'd be dead if it wasn't for you. But before you get any fancy ideas, we're quits. The debt is cancelled. From now on, you're nothing to me. You're not going to work for me. And I don't really care whatever happens to you."

"So why am I here?"

"Because the people I work for want to see you. We're going there now."

"There?"

"The Widow's Palace. We'll get a boat."

From the name, I expected somewhere sombre, an old, dark building with black curtains drawn across the windows. But in fact the Widow's Palace was an astonishing place, like something out of the story books I had read as a child, built out of pink and white bricks with dozens of windows glittering in the sun. There was a covered walkway on the level of the first floor, stretching from one end to the other, held up by slender pillars with archways below. And the palace wasn't standing beside the canal. It was actually sinking into it. The water was lapping at the front door with the white marble steps disappearing below the murky surface.

We pulled in and stepped off the boat. There was a man standing at the entrance with thick shoulders and folded arms, wearing a white shirt and a black suit. He examined us briefly, then nodded for us to continue forward. Already I was regretting this. As I passed from the sunlight to the shadows of the interior, I was thinking of what Zelin had said as he left the helicopter. *You don't know these people. They will kill you.* Maybe three long years of taking orders from Vladimir Sharkovsky had clouded my judgement. I was no longer used to making decisions.

It would have been better if I had run away before breakfast. I could have sneaked on a train to another city. I could have gone to the police for help. I remembered something my grandmother used to say when she was cooking: out of the *latki*, into the fire.

A massive spiral staircase – white marble with wrought-iron banisters – rose up, twisting over itself. Rykov went first and I followed a few steps behind, neither of us speaking. I was nervous but he was completely at ease, one hand in his trouser pocket, taking his time. We came to a corridor lined with paintings: portraits of men and women who must have died centuries before. They stood in their gold frames, watching us pass. We walked down to a pair of doors and before he opened them, Rykov turned and spoke briefly, quietly.

"Say nothing until you are spoken to. Tell the truth. She will know if you're lying."

She? The widow?

He knocked and without waiting for an answer opened the doors and went through.

The woman who was waiting for us was surely too young to have married and lost a husband. She couldn't have been more than twenty-six or twenty-seven and my first thought was that she was very beautiful. My second was that she was dangerous. She was quite short, with long, black hair, tied back. It contrasted with the paleness of her skin. She wore no make-up apart from a smear of crimson lipstick that was so bright it was almost cruel. She was dressed in a black silk shirt, open at the neck. A simple gold necklace twisted around her neck. She could have been a model or an actress but there was something that danced in her eyes and told me she was neither.

She was sitting behind a very elegant, ornate table with a line of windows behind her, looking out over the Grand Canal. Two chairs had been placed in front of her and we took our places without waiting to be told. She had not been doing anything when we came in. It was clear that she had simply been waiting for us.

"Mr Grant," she said, and it took me a moment to realize she was talking to Rykov. "How did it go?" Her voice was very young. She spoke English with a strange accent which I couldn't place.

"There was no problem, Mrs Rothman," Rykov – or Grant – replied.

"You killed Sharkovsky?"

"Three bullets. I got into the compound, thanks to the helicopter pilot. He flew me out again. Everything went according to plan."

"Not quite." She smiled and her eyes were bright but I knew something bad was coming and I was right. Slowly she turned to face me as if noticing me for the first time. Her eyes lingered on me. I couldn't tell what was in her mind. "I do not remember asking you to bring me a Russian boy."

Grant shrugged. "He helped me and I brought him here because it seemed the easiest thing to do. It occurred to me that he might be useful to you ... and to Scorpia. He has no background, no family, no identity. He's shown himself to have a certain amount of courage. But if you don't need him, I'll get rid of him for you. And of course there'll be no extra charge."

I had been struggling to follow all this. My teacher, Nigel Brown, had done a good job – my English was very advanced. But still, it was the first time I had heard it spoken by other people, and there were one or two words I didn't understand. But nor did I need to. I fully understood the offer that Grant had just made and knew that once again my life was in the balance. The worst of it was that there was nothing I could do. I had nothing to say. I'd never be able to fight my way out of this house. I could only sit there and see what this woman decided.

She took her time. I felt her examining me and tried not to show how afraid I was. "That's very generous of you, Mr Grant," she said, at last. "But what gives you the idea that I can't deal with this myself?"

I hadn't seen her lower her hand beneath the surface of the table but when she raised it, she was holding a gun, a silver revolver that had been polished until it shone. She held it almost like a fashion accessory, a perfectly manicured finger curling around the trigger. It was pointing at me and I could see that she was deadly serious. She intended to use it.

I tried to speak. No words came out.

"It's rather a shame," Mrs Rothman went on. "I don't enjoy killing, but you know how it is. Scorpia will not accept a second-rate job." Her hand hadn't moved but her eyes slid back to Grant. "Sharkovsky isn't dead."

"What?" Grant was shocked.

Mrs Rothman moved her arm so that the gun was facing him. She pulled the trigger. Grant was killed instantly, propelled backwards in his chair, crashing onto the floor.

I stared. The noise of the explosion was ringing in my ears. She swung the gun back to me.

"What do you have to say for yourself?" she asked.

"Sharkovsky's dead!" I gasped. It was all I could think to say. "He was shot three times."

"That may well be true. Unfortunately, our intelligence is that he survived. He's in hospital in Moscow. He's critical. But the doctors say he'll pull through."

I didn't know how to react to this information. It seemed impossible. The shots had been fired at close range. I had seen him thrown off his feet. And yet I had always said he was the devil. Perhaps it would take more than bullets to end his life.

The gun was still pointing at me. I waited for Mrs Rothman to fire again. But suddenly she smiled as if nothing had happened, put the gun down and stood up.

"Would you like a glass of Coke?" she asked.

"I'm sorry?"

"Please don't ask me to repeat myself, Yassen. I find it very boring. We can't sit and talk here, with a dead body in the room. It isn't dignified. Let's go next door."

She slid out from behind the desk and I followed her through a door that I hadn't noticed before – it was part of a bookshelf covered with fake books so as not to spoil the pattern. There was a much larger living room behind the door with two plump sofas on either side of a glass table and a massive stone fireplace, though no fire. Fresh flowers had been arranged in a vase and the scent of them hung in the air. Drinks – Coke for me, iced tea for her – had already been served.

We sat down.

"Were you shocked by that, Yassen?" she asked.

I shook my head, not quite daring to speak yet.

"It was very unpleasant but I'm afraid you can't allow anyone too many chances in our line of work. It sends out the wrong message. This wasn't the first time Mr Grant had made mistakes. Even bringing you here and not disposing of you when you were in Boltino frankly made me question his judgement. But never mind that now. Here you are and I want to talk about you. I know a little about you but I'd like to hear the rest. Your parents are dead, I understand."

"Yes."

"Tell me how it happened. Tell me all of it. See if you can keep it brief, though. I'm only interested in the bare essentials. I have a long day..."

So I told her everything. Right then, I couldn't think of any reason not to. Estrov, the factory, Moscow, Dima, Demetyev, Sharkovsky ... even I was surprised how my whole life could boil down to so few words. She listened with what I can only describe as polite interest. You would have thought that some of the things that had happened to me would have caused an expression of concern or sympathy. She really didn't care.

"It's an interesting story," she said, when I had finished. "And you told it very well." She sipped her tea. I noticed that her lipstick left bright red marks on the glass. "The strange thing is that the late Mr Grant was quite right. You could be very useful to us."

"Who are you?" I asked. Then I added, "Scorpia..."

"Ah yes. Scorpia. I'm not entirely sure about the name if you want the truth. The letters stand for Sabotage, Corruption, Intelligence and Assassination, but that's only a few of the things we get up to. They could have added kidnapping, blackmail, terrorism, drug trafficking and vice, but that wouldn't make a word. Anyway, we've got to be called something and I suppose Scorpia has a nice ring to it.

"I'm on the executive board. Right now there are twelve of us. Please don't get the idea that we're monsters. We're not even criminals. In fact, quite a few of us used to work in the intelligence services ... England, France, Israel, Japan ... but it's a fast-changing world and we realized that we could do much better if we went into business for ourselves. You'd be amazed how many governments need to subcontract their dirty work. Think about it. Why risk your own people, spying on your enemies, when you can simply pay us to do it for you? Why start a war when you can pick up the phone and get someone to kill the head of state? It's cheaper. Fewer people get hurt. In a way, Scorpia has been quite helpful when it comes to world peace. We still work for virtually all the intelligence services and that must tell you something about us. A lot of the time we're doing exactly the same jobs that we were doing before. Just at a higher price."

"You were a spy?" I asked.

"Actually, Yassen, I wasn't. I'm from Wales. Do you know where that is? Believe it or not, I was brought up in a tiny mining community. My parents used to sing in the local choir. They're in jail now and I was in an orphanage when I was six years old. My life has been quite similar to yours in some ways. But as you can see, I've been rather more successful."

It was warm in the room. The sun was streaming in through the windows, dazzling me. I waited for her to continue.

"I'll get straight to the point," she said. "There's something quite special about you, Yassen, even if you probably don't appreciate yourself. Do you see what I'm getting at? You're a survivor, yes. But you're more than that. In your own way, you're unique!

"You see, pretty much everyone in the world is on a databank somewhere. The moment you're born, your details get put into a computer, and computers are getting more and more powerful by the day. Right now I could pick up the telephone and in half an hour I would know anything and everything about anyone you care to name. And it's not just names and that sort of thing. You break into a house and leave a fingerprint or one tiny little piece of DNA and the international police will track you down, no matter where in the world you are. A crime committed in Rio de Janeiro can be solved overnight at Scotland Yard – and, believe me, as the technology changes, it's going to get much, much worse.

"But you're different. The Russian authorities have done you a great favour. They've wiped you out. The village you were brought up in no longer exists. You have no parents. I would imagine that every last piece of information about you and anyone you ever knew in Estrov has been destroyed. And do you know what that's done? It's made you a non-person. From this moment on, you can be completely invisible. You can go anywhere and do anything and nobody will be able to find you."

She reached for her glass, turning it between her finger and her thumb. Her nails were long and sharp. She didn't drink.

"We are always on the lookout for assassins," she said. "Contract killers like Mr Grant. As you have seen, the price of failure in our organization is a high one, but so are the rewards of success. It is a very attractive life. You travel the world. You stay in the best hotels, eat in the best restaurants, shop in Paris and New York. You meet interesting people … and some of them you kill."

I must have looked alarmed because she raised a hand, stopping me.

"Let me finish. You were brought up by your parents who, I am sure, were good people. So were mine! You are thinking that you could never murder someone for money. You could never be like Mr Grant. But you're wrong. We will train you. We have a facility not very far from here, an island called Malagosto. We run a school there ... a very special school. If you go there, you will work harder than you have ever worked in your life – even harder than in that *dacha* where you were kept.

"You will be given training in weapons and martial arts. You will learn the techniques of poisoning, shooting, explosives and hand-to-hand combat. We will show you how to pick locks, how to disguise yourself, how to talk your way in and out of any given situation. We will teach you not only how to act like a killer but how to think like one. Every week there will be psychological and physical evaluations. There will also be formal schooling. You need to have maths and science. Your English is excellent but you still speak with a Russian accent. You must lose it. You should also learn Arabic, as we have many operations in the Middle East.

"I can promise you that you will be more exhausted than you would have thought possible but, if you last the course, you will be perfect. The perfect killer. And you will work for us.

"The alternative? You can leave here now. Believe it or not, I really mean it. I won't stop you. I'll even give you the money for the train fare if you like. You have nothing. You have nowhere to go. If you tell the police about me, they won't believe you. My guess is that you will end up back in Russia. Sharkovsky will be looking for you. Without our help, he will find you.

"So there you have it, Yassen. That's what it comes down to."

She smiled and finished her drink.

"What do you say?"

ОСТРОВ

THE ISLAND

They taught me how to kill.

In fact, during the time that I spent on the island of Malagosto, they taught me a great deal more than that. There was no school in the world that was anything like the Training and Assessment Centre that Scorpia had created. How do I begin to describe all the differences? It was, of course, highly secret. Nobody chose to go there ... they chose you. It was surely the only school in the world where there were more teachers than students. There were no holidays, no sports days, no uniforms, no punishments, no visitors, no prizes and no exams. And yet it was, in its own way, a school. You could call it the Eton of murder.

What was strange about Malagosto was how close it was to mainland Venice. Here was this city full of rich tourists drifting between jazz bars and restaurants, five-star hotels and gorgeous *palazzos* – and less than half a mile away, across a strip of dark water, there were activities going on that would have made their hair stand on end. The island had been a plague centre once. There was an old Venetian saying: "Sneeze in Venice and wipe your nose in Malagosto" – the last thing you could afford in a tightly packed medieval city, with its sweating crowds and stinking canals, was an outbreak of the plague. The rich merchants had built a monastery, a hospital, living quarters and a cemetery for the infected. They would house them, look after them, pray for them and bury them. But they would never have them back.

The island was small. I could walk around it in forty minutes. Even in the summer, the sand was a dirty yellow, covered with shingle, and the water was an unappealing grey. All the woodland was tangled together as if it had been hit by a violent storm. There was a clearing in the middle with a few gravestones, the names worn away by time, leaning together as if whispering the secrets of the past. The monastery had a bell tower made out of dark red bricks and it slanted at a strange angle … it looked sure to collapse at any moment. The whole building looked dilapidated, half the windows broken, the courtyards pitted with cracks, weeds everywhere.

But the actual truth was quite surprising. Scorpia hadn't just watched the place fall into disrepair, they had helped it on its way. They had removed anything that looked too attractive: fountains, statues, frescoes, stained-glass windows, ornamental doors. They had even gone so far as to insert a hydraulic arm into the tower, deliberately tilting it. The whole point was that Malagosto was not meant to be beautiful. It was off-limits anyway, but they didn't want a single tourist or archaeologist to feel it was worth hiring a boat and risking the crossing. The last time anyone had tried had been six years before, when a group of nuns had taken a ferry from Murano, following in the footsteps of some minor saint. They had still been singing when the ferry had inexplicably blown up. The cause was never found.

Inside, the buildings were much more modern and comfortable than anyone might have guessed. We had two classrooms, warm and soundproof with brand new furniture and banks of audio visual equipment that would have had my old teachers in Rosna staring in envy. All they'd had was chalk and blackboards. There were both indoor and outdoor shooting ranges, a superbly equipped gymnasium with an area devoted exclusively to fighting – judo, karate, kick-boxing and, above all, ninjutsu – and a swimming pool, although most of the time we used the sea. If the temperature was close to freezing, that only made the training more worthwhile. My own rooms, on the second floor of the accommodation block, were very comfortable. I had a bedroom, a living room and even my own bathroom with a huge marble bath that took only seconds to fill, the steaming hot water jetting out of a monster brass tap shaped like a lion's head. I had my own desk, my own TV, a private fridge that was always kept stocked up with bottled water and soft drinks. All this came at a price. Once I left the facility, I would be tied by a five-year contract working exclusively for Scorpia and the cost of my training would be taken from my salary. This was made clear to me from the start.

After I had met Mrs Rothman and accepted her offer, I was taken straight to the island in the back of a water ambulance. It seemed an odd choice of vessel but of course it would have been completely inconspicuous in the middle of all the other traffic and I did not travel alone. Mr Grant came with me, laid out on a stretcher. I have to say that I felt sorry for him. In his own way he had been kind to me. I turned my thoughts to Vladimir Sharkovsky, probably lying in a Moscow hospital, surrounded by fresh bodyguards watching over him just as the machines would be watching over his heart rate, his blood pressure – all his vital signs. Who would be tasting his food for him now?

It was midday when I arrived.

The water ambulance pulled up to a jetty that was much less dilapidated than it looked and I saw a young woman waiting for me. In fact, from a distance, I had mistaken her for a man. Her dark hair was cut short and she was wearing a loose white shirt, a waistcoat and jeans. But as we drew closer I saw that she was quite attractive, about two or three years older than me, and serious-looking. She wore no make-up. She reached out and gave me a hand off the boat and suddenly we were standing together, weighing each other up.

"I'm Colette," she said.

"I'm Yassen."

"Welcome to Malagosto. Do you have any luggage?"

I shook my head. I had brought nothing with me. Apart from what I was wearing, I had no possessions in the world.

"I've been asked to show you around. Mr Nye will want to see you later on."

"Mr Nye?"

"You could say he's the principal. He runs this place."

"Are you a teacher?"

She smiled. "No. I'm a student. The same as you. Come on – I'll start by showing you your rooms."

I spent the next two hours with Colette. There were only three students there at the time. I would be the fourth. The others were on the mainland, involved in some sort of exercise. As we stood on the beach, looking out across the water, Colette told me a little about them.

"There's Marat. He's from Poland. And Sam. He only got here a few weeks ago ... from Israel. Neither of them talks very much but Sam came out of the army. He was going to join Mossad – Israeli intelligence – but Scorpia made him a better offer."

"What about you?" I asked. "Where have you come from?"

"I'm French."

We had been speaking in English but I had been aware she had a slight accent. I waited for her to tell me more but she was silent. "Is that all?" I asked.

"What else is there?" You and me ... we're here. That's all that matters."

"How did you get chosen?"

"I didn't get chosen. I volunteered." She thought for a moment. "I wouldn't ask personal questions, if I were you. People can be a bit touchy around here."

"I just thought it was strange, that's all. A woman learning how to kill..."

She raised an eyebrow at that. "You are old-fashioned, aren't you, Yassen! And here's another piece of advice. Maybe you should keep your opinions to yourself." She looked at her watch, then drew a thin book out of her back pocket. "Now I'm afraid I'm going to have to leave you on your own. I've got to finish this."

I glanced at the cover: MODERN INTERROGATION TECHNIQUES BY DR THREE.

"You might get to meet him one day," Colette said. "And if you do, be careful what you say. You wouldn't want to end up as a chapter in his book."

I spent the rest of the day alone in my room, lying on my bed with all sorts of thoughts going through my head. Much later on, at about eight o'clock in the evening, I was summoned to the headmaster's office and it was there that I met the man who was in charge of all the training on Malagosto.

His name was Sefton Nye and my first thought was that he had the darkest skin I had ever seen. His glistening bald head showed off eyes that were extraordinarily large and animated. And he had brilliant white teeth, which he displayed often in an astonishing smile. He dressed very carefully – he liked well-cut blazers, obviously expensive – and his shoes were polished to perfection. He was originally from Somalia. His family were modern-day pirates, holding up luxury yachts, cruise ships and even, on one occasion, an oil tanker that had strayed too close to the shore. They were utterly ruthless... I saw framed newspaper articles in the office describing their exploits. Nye himself had a very loud voice. Everything about him was larger than life.

"Yassen Gregorovich!" he exclaimed, pointing me to a chair in the office, which was almost circular with an iron chandelier in the middle. There were floor to ceiling bookshelves, two windows looking out over woodland, and half a dozen clocks, each one showing a different time. A pair of solid iron filing cabinets stood against one wall. Mr Nye wore the key that opened them around his neck. "Welcome to Malagosto," he went on. "Welcome indeed. I always take the greatest pleasure in meeting the new recruits because, you see, when you leave here you will not be the same. We are going to turn you into something very special and when I meet you after that, it may well be that I do not want to. You will be dangerous. I will be afraid of you. Everyone who meets you, even without knowing why, will be afraid of you. I hope that thought does not distress you, Yassen, because if it does you should not be here. You are going to become a contract killer and although you will be rich and you will be comfortable, I am telling you now, it is a very lonely path."

There was a knock at the door and a second man appeared, barely half the height of the head-master, dressed in a linen suit and brown shoes, with a round face and a small beard. He seemed quite nervous of Mr Nye, his eyes blinking behind his tortoise-shell glasses. "You wanted to see me, headmaster?" he enquired. He had a French accent, much more distinct than Colette's.

"Ah yes, Oliver!" He gestured in my direction. "This is our newest recruit. His name is Yassen Gregorovich. Mrs Rothman sent him over from the Widow's Palace."

"Delighted." The little man nodded at me.

"This is Oliver d'Arc. He will be your personal tutor and he will also be taking many of your classes. If you're unhappy, if you have any prob-lems, you go to him."

"Thank you," I said, but I had already decided

that if I had any problems I would most certainly keep them to myself. This was the sort of place where any weakness would only be used against you.

"I am here for you any time you need me," d'Arc assured me.

I would spend a lot of time with Oliver d'Arc while I was on Malagosto but I never completely trusted him. I don't think I ever knew him. Everything about him – his appearance, the way he spoke, probably even his name – was an act put on for the students' benefit. Later on, after Nye was killed by one of his own students, d'Arc became the headmaster and, by all accounts, he was very good at the job.

"Do you have any questions, Yassen?" Mr Nye asked.

"No, sir," I said.

"That's good. But before you turn in for the night, there's something I want you to do for me, I hope you don't mind. It shouldn't take more than a couple of hours."

That was when I noticed that Oliver d'Arc was holding a spade.

My first job on Malagosto was to bury Mr Grant in the little cemetery in the woods. It was a final resting place that he would share with plague victims who had died four hundred years before him, although I had no doubt that there were other more recent arrivals too, men and women who had failed Scorpia just like him. It was an unpleasant, grisly task, digging on my own in the darkness. Even Sharkovsky had never asked me to do such a thing – but it's possible that it was meant to be a warning to me. Mrs Rothman had let me live. She had even recruited me. But this is what I could look forward to if I let her down.

As I dragged Mr Grant off the stretcher and tipped him into the hole which I had dug, I couldn't help but wonder if someone would do the same for me one day. For what it's worth, it is the only time I have ever had such thoughts. When your business is death, the only death you should never consider is your own. It had begun to rain slightly, a thin drizzle that only made my task more unpleasant. I filled in the grave, flattened it with the spade, then carried the stretcher back to the main complex. Oliver d'Arc was waiting for me with a brandy and a hot chocolate. He escorted me to my room and even insisted on running a bath for me, adding a good measure of "Floris of London" bath oil to the foaming water. I was glad when he finally left. I was afraid he was going to offer to scrub my back.

Five months...

No two days were ever exactly the same, although we were always woken at half past five in the morning for a one-hour run around the island followed by a forty-minute swim – out to a stump of rock and back again. Breakfast was at half past seven, served in a beautiful dining room with a sixteenth-century mosaic on the floor, wooden angels carved around the windows and a faded view of heaven painted on the domed ceiling above our heads. The food was always excellent. All four students ate together and I usually found myself sitting next to Colette. As she had warned me, Marat and Sam weren't exactly unfriendly but they hardly ever spoke to me. Sam was dark and very intense. Marat seemed more laid-back, sitting in class with his legs crossed and his hands behind his back. After they had graduated, they decided to work together as a team and were extremely successful but I never saw them again.

Morning lessons took place in the classrooms. We learned about guns and knives, how to create a booby trap, and how to make a bomb using seven different ingredients that you could find in any supermarket. There was one teacher – he was red-headed, scrawny and had tattoos all over his upper body – who brought in a different weapon for us to practice with every day: not just guns but knives, swords, throwing spikes, ninja fighting fans and even a medieval crossbow ... he actually insisted on firing an apple off Marat's head. His name was Gordon Ross and he came from a city called Glasgow, in Scotland. He had briefly been assistant to the Chief Armourer at MI6 until Scorpia had tempted him away at five times his original salary.

The first time we met, I impressed him by stripping down an AK-47 machine gun in eighteen seconds. My old friend Leo, of course, would have done it faster. Ross was actually a knife man. His two great heroes were William Fairbairn and Eric Sykes, who together had created the ultimate fighting knife for British commandos during the Second World War. Ross was an expert with throwing knives and he'd had a set specially designed and weighted for his hand. Put him twenty metres from a target and there wasn't a student on the island who could beat him for speed or accuracy, even when he was competing against guns.

Ross also had a fascination with gadgets. He didn't manufacture any himself but he had made a study of the secret weaponry provided by all the different intelligence services and he had managed to steal several items, which he brought in for us to examine. There was a credit card developed by the CIA. One edge was razor-sharp. The French had come up with a string of onions ... several of them were grenades. His own employers, MI6, had provided an antiseptic cream that could eat through metals, a fountain pen that fired a poisoned nib, and a Power Plus battery that concealed a radio transmitter. You simply gave the whole thing a half-twist and it would set off a beacon to summon immediate help. All these devices amused him but at the end of the day he dismissed them as toys. He preferred his knives.

Weapons and self-defence were only part of my training. I was surprised to find myself going back to school in the old-fashioned sense; I learned maths, English, Arabic, science – even classical music, art and cookery. Oliver d'Arc took some of these classes. However, I will not forget the day I was introduced to the unsmiling Italian woman who never told anyone her name but called herself the Countess. It may well be that she was a true aristocrat. She certainly behaved like one, insisting that we stand when she entered and always address her as "ma'am". She was about fifty, exquisitely dressed, with expensive jewellery and perfect manners. When she stood up, she expected us to do so too. The Countess took us shopping and to art galleries in Venice. She made us read newspapers and celebrity magazines and often talked about the people in the photographs. At first, I had absolutely no idea what she was doing on the island.

It was only later that I understood. A killer is not just someone who lies on a roof with a 12.7mm sniper rifle, waiting for his prey to walk out of a restaurant. Sometimes it is necessary to be inside that restaurant. To pin down your target, you have to get close to him. You have to wear the right clothes, walk in the right way, demand a good table in a restaurant, understand the food and the wine. How could a boy from a poor Russian village have been able to do any of these things if he had not been taught? I have been to art auctions, to operas, to fashion shows and to horse races. I have sipped champagne with bankers, professors, designers and multimillionaires. I have always felt comfortable and nobody has ever thought I was out of place. For this, I have the Countess to thank.

The toughest part of the day came after lunch. The afternoons were devoted to hand-to-hand combat and three-hour classes were taken either by the headmaster, Mr Nye, or a Japanese instructor, Hatsumi Saburo. We all called him HS and he was an extraordinary man. He must have been seventy years old but he moved faster than a teenager, certainly faster than me. If you weren't concentrating, he would knock you down so hard and so fast that you simply wouldn't be aware of what had happened until you were on the floor, and he would be standing above you, gazing at the ceiling, as if it had been nothing to do with him. Sefton Nye taught judo and karate but it was Hatsumi Saburo who introduced me to a third martial art, ninjutsu, and it is this that has always stayed with me.

Ninjutsu was the fighting method developed by the ninjas, the spies and the assassins who roamed across Japan in the fifteenth century. It was taught to them by the priests and the warriors who were in hiding in the mountains. What I learned from HS over the next five months was what I can only describe as a total fighting system that encompassed every part of my body including my feet, my knees, my elbows, my fists, my head, even my teeth. And it was more than that. He used to talk about *nagare*, the flow of technique ...

knowing when to move from one form of attack to the next. Ultimately, everything came down to mental attitude. "You cannot win if you do not believe you will win," he once said to me. He had a very heavy Japanese accent and barked like a dog. "You must control your emotions. You must control your feelings. If there is any fear or insecurity, you must destroy it before it destroys you. It is not the size or the strength of your opponent that matters. These can be measured. It is what cannot be measured ... courage, determination ... that count."

I felt great reverence for Hatsumi Saburo but I did not like him. Sometimes we would fight each other with wooden swords that were known as *bokken*. He never held back. When I went to bed, my whole body would be black and blue, while I would never so much as touch him. "You have too many emotions, Yas-sen!" he would crow, as he stood over me. "All that sadness. All that anger. It is the smoke that gets into your eyes. If you do not blow it away how can you hope to see?"

Was I sad about what had happened to me? Was I angry? I suppose Scorpia would know better than me because, just as Mrs Rothman had promised, I was given regular psychological examinations by a doctor called Karl Steiner who came from South Africa. I disliked him from the start; the way he looked at me, his eyes always boring into mine as if he suspected that everything I said was a lie. I don't think I ever heard Dr Steiner say anything that wasn't a question. He was a very neat man, always dressed in a suit with a carnation in his lapel. He would sit there with one leg crossed over the other, occasionally glancing at a gold pocket watch to check the time. His office was completely bare ... just a white space with two armchairs. It had a window that looked out over the firing range and I would sometimes hear the crack of the rifles outside as he fired his own questions my way.

I regretted now that I had told Mrs Rothman so much about myself. She had passed all the information to him and he wanted me to talk about my parents, my grandmother, my childhood in Estrov. The more we talked, the less I wanted to say. I felt empty, as if the life I was describing was something that no longer belonged to me. And the strange thing is, I think that was exactly what he wanted. In his own way he was just like Hatsumi Saburo. My old life was smoke. It had to be blown away.

We were given a couple of hours of rest before dinner but we were always expected to use the time productively. My tutor, Oliver d'Arc, insisted that I read books ... and in English, not Russian. Some evenings we had political discussions. I learned more about my own country while I was on the island than I had the whole time I was living there.

We also had guest lecturers. They were brought to Malagosto in blindfolds and many of them had been in prison but they were all experts in their own field. One was a pickpocket ... he shook hands with each one of us before he began and then started his lecture by returning our watches. Another showed us how to pick locks. There was one really brilliant lecture by an elderly Hungarian man with terrible scars down the side of his face. He had lost his sight in a car accident. He talked to us for two hours about disguise and false identities, and then revealed that he was actually a thirty-two-year-old Belgian woman and that she could see as well as any of us.

You never knew what was going to happen. The school loved to throw surprises our way. Sometimes, in the middle of the night, a whistle would blow and we would find ourselves called out to the assault course, crawling through the rain and the mud, climbing nets and swinging on ropes while Mr Ross fired live ammunition at our heels. Once, we were told to swim to the mainland, to steal clothes and money when we got there and then to make our own way back.

But Scorpia did not want us to become too cut off, too removed from the real world. As well as the expeditions with the Countess, they often gave us half a day off to visit Venice. Marat and Sam kept themselves to themselves so I usually found myself with Colette. We would go to the markets together and walk the streets. She was always stopping to take photographs. She loved little details ... an iron door handle, a gargoyle, a cat asleep on a windowsill. I had never been out with a girl before – I had never really had the chance – and I found myself being drawn to her in a way I could not completely understand. All the time, I was being taught to hide my feelings. When I was with her, I wanted to do the opposite.

She never told me much more about herself than she had that first time we had met and I was sensible enough not to ask. She let slip that she had once lived in Paris, that her father was something to do with the French government and that she hadn't spoken to him for years. She had left home when she was very young and had somehow survived on her own since then. She never explained how she had found out about Scorpia. But I did learn that her training would be over very soon. Like all recruits, she was going to be sent on her first solo kill – a real job with a real target.

"Do you ever think about it?" I asked her.

We were sitting outside a café on the Riva degli Schiavoni with a great expanse of water in front of us and hundreds of tourists streaming past. They gave us privacy.

"What?" she asked.

I lowered my voice. "Killing. Taking another person's life."

She looked at me over the top of her coffee. She was wearing sunglasses which hid her eyes but

I could tell she was annoyed. "You should ask Dr Steiner about that."

I held her gaze. "I'm asking you."

"Why do you even want to know?" she snapped. She stirred the coffee. It was very black, served in a tiny cup. "It's a job. There are all sorts of people who don't deserve to live. Rich people. Powerful people. Take one of them out, maybe you're doing the world a favour."

"What if they're married?"

"Who cares?"

"What if they have children?"

"If you think like that, you shouldn't be here. You shouldn't even be talking like this. If you were to say any of this to Marat or Sam, they'd go straight to Mr Nye."

"I wouldn't talk to them," I said. "They're not my friends."

"And you think I am?"

I still remember that moment. Colette was leaning towards me and she was wearing a jacket with a very soft, close-fitting jersey beneath. She took off her sunglasses and looked at me with brown eyes that, I'm sure, had more warmth in them than she intended. Right then, I wished that we could be just like all the other people strolling by us; a Russian boy and a French girl who had just happened to bump into each other in one of the most romantic places on the earth. But of course it couldn't be. It would never be.

"I'm not your friend," she said. "We'll never have friends, Yassen. Either of us."

She finished her coffee, stood up and walked away.

Colette left a few weeks later and after that there were just the three of us continuing with the training, day and night.

None of the instructors ever said as much but I knew I was doing well. I was the fastest across the assault course. On the shooting range, my targets always came whirring back with the bullets grouped neatly inside the head. I had mastered all sixteen body strikes – the so-called "secret fists" – that are essential to ninjutsu and during one memorable training session I even managed to land a blow on HS. I could see the old man was pleased ... although he flattened me half a second later. After hours in the gym, I was in peak physical condition. I could run six times around the island and I wouldn't be out of breath.

And yet I couldn't forget what I had talked about with Colette. When I fired at a target, I would always imagine a real human being and not the cut-out soldier with his fixed, snarling face in front of me. Instead of the quick snap, the little round hole that appeared in the paper as the bullet passed through, there would be the explosion of bone fragmenting, blood splashing out. The paper soldier's eyes ignored me. He felt nothing. But what would a man be thinking as he died? He would never see his family again. He would never feel the warmth of the sun. Everything that he had and everything he was would have been stolen away by me. Could I really do that to someone and not hate myself for ever?

I had not chosen this. There was a time when I'd thought I was going to work in a factory making pesticides. I was going to live in a village that nobody had ever heard of, dreaming of being a helicopter pilot, pinning pictures to the wall. Looking back, it felt as if some evil force had been manipulating me every inch of the way to bring me here. From the moment my parents had been killed, my own life had no longer been mine to control. And yet, it occurred to me, it was still not too late. Scorpia had taught me how to fight, how to change my identity, how to hide and how to survive. Once I left Malagosto, I could use these skills to escape from them. I could steal money and go anywhere in the world that I wanted, change my name, begin a new life. Lying in bed at night, I would think about this but at the same time I knew, with a sense of despair, that I was wrong. Scorpia was too powerful. No matter how far I ran, eventually they would find me and there was no escaping what the result would be. I would die young. But wasn't that better than becoming what they wanted? At least I would have stayed true to myself.

I was terrified of giving any of this away while with Dr Steiner. I always thought before I answered any of his questions and tried to tell him what he wanted to hear, not what I really thought. I was afraid that if he caught sight of my weakness, my training would be cancelled and the next recruit would end up burying me in the woods. The secret was to be completely emotionless. Sometimes he showed me horrible pictures – scenes of war and violence. I tried not to look at the dead and mutilated bodies, but then he would ask me questions about them and I would find myself having to describe everything in detail, trying to keep the quiver out of my voice. And yet I thought I was getting away with it. At the end of each session, he would take my hand – cupping it in both of his own – and purr at me, "Well done, Yassen. That was very, very good." As far as I could tell, he had no idea at all what was really going on in my head.

And then, at last, the day came when Oliver d'Arc called me to his study. As I entered, he was tuning the cello, which was an instrument he played occasionally. The room was a mess, with books everywhere and papers spilling out of drawers. It smelled of tobacco, although I never saw him smoke.

"Ah, Yassen!" he exclaimed. "I'm afraid you're going to miss evening training. Mrs Rothman is back in Venice. You're to have dinner with her. Make sure you wear your best clothes. A launch will pick you up at seven o'clock."

When I had first come to the island, I might

have asked why she wanted to see me but by now I knew that I would always be given all the information I needed, and to ask for more was only to show weakness.

"It looks like you're going to be leaving us," he went on.

"My training is finished?"

"Yes."

He plucked one of the strings. "You've done very well, my dear boy," he said. "And I must say, I've thoroughly enjoyed tutoring you. And now your moment has come. Good luck!"

From this, I understood that my final test had arrived ... the solo kill. My training was over. My life as an assassin was about to begin.

And that night, I met Mrs Rothman for the second time. She had sent her personal launch to collect me, a beautiful vessel that was all teak and chrome with a silver scorpion moulded into the bow. It carried me beneath the famous Bridge of Sighs – I hoped that was not an omen – and on to the Widow's Palace where we had first met. She was dressed, once again, in black; this time a very low-cut dress with a zip down one side, which I recognized at once as the work of the designer, Gianni Versace. We ate in her private dining room at a long table lit by candles and surrounded by paintings – Picasso, Cézanne, Van Gogh – all of them worth millions. We began with soup, then lobster, and finally a creamy custard mixed with wine that the Italians call *zabaglione*. The food was delicious but as I ate I was aware of her examining me, watching every mouthful, and I knew that I was still being tested.

"I'm very pleased with you, Yassen," she said as the coffee was poured. The whole meal had been served by two men in white jackets and black trousers, her personal waiters. "Do you think you're ready?"

"Yes, Mrs Rothman," I replied.

"You can stop calling me that now." She smiled at me and I was once again struck by her film-star looks. "I prefer Julia."

There was a file on the table beside her. It hadn't been there when we started. One of the waiters had brought it in with the coffee. She opened it. First she took out a printed report.

"You're naturally gifted ... an excellent marksman. Hatsumi Saburo speaks very highly of your abilities. I see also that you have learned from the Countess. Your manners are faultless. Six months ago you wouldn't have been able to sit at a table like this without giving yourself away, but you are very different from the street urchin I met back then."

I nodded but said nothing. Another lesson. Never show gratitude unless you hope to gain something from it.

"But now we must see if you can actually put into practice everything that we have taught you in theory." She took out a passport and slid it across the table. "This is yours," she said. "We have kept your family name. There was no reason not to, particularly as your first name had changed anyway. Yassen Gregorovich is what you are now and will always be ... unless of course we feel the need for you to travel under cover." An envelope followed. "You'll find the details of your bank account inside," she said. "You are a client of the European Finance Group. It's a private bank based in Geneva. There are fifty thousand American dollars, fifty thousand euros and fifty thousand pounds in the account, and no matter how much you spend, these figures will always remain the same. Of course, we will be watching your expenses."

She was enjoying this, sending me out for the first time, almost challenging me to show reluctance or any sign of fear. She took out a second envelope, thicker than the first. This one was sealed with a strip of black tape. There was a scorpion symbol stamped in the middle.

"This envelope contains a return air ticket to New York, which is where your first assignment will take place. There is another thousand dollars in here too ... petty cash to get you started. You are flying economy."

That didn't surprise me. I was young and I was entering the United States on my own. Travelling business or first class might draw attention to myself.

"You will be met at the airport and taken to your hotel. You will report back to me here in Venice in one week's time. Do you want to know who you are going to kill?"

"I'm sure you'll tell me when you want to," I said.

"That's right." She smiled. "You'll get all the information that you need once you arrive. A weapon will also be delivered to you. Is that all understood?"

"Yes," I said. Of course I had questions. Above all I wanted a name and a face somewhere; on the other side of the world, a man was going about his business with no knowledge that I was on my way. What had he done to anger Scorpia? Why did he have to lose his life? But I stayed silent. I was being very careful not to show any sign of weakness.

"Then I think our evening is almost over," Mrs Rothman said. She reached out and, just for a moment, her fingers brushed against the back of my hand. "You know, Yassen," she said, "you are incredibly good-looking. I thought that the moment I saw you and your five months on Malagosto have done nothing but improve you." She sighed and drew her hand away. "Russian boys aren't quite my thing," she continued. "Or else who knows what we might get up to? But it will certainly help you in your work. Death should always come smartly dressed."

She got up, as if about to leave. But then she had second thoughts and turned back to me. "You were fond of that girl, Colette, weren't you?"

"We spent a bit of time together," I said. "We came into Venice once or twice." Julia Rothman would know that, anyway.

"Yes," she murmured. "I had a feeling the two of you would hit it off."

She was daring me to ask. So I did.

"How is she?"

"She's dead." Mrs Rothman brushed some imaginary dust from the sleeve of her dress. "Her first assignment went very wrong. It wasn't entirely her fault. She took out the target but she was shot by the Argentinian police."

And that was when I knew what she had done to me. That was when I knew exactly what Scorpia had made me.

I felt nothing. I said nothing. If I was sad, I didn't show it. I simply watched impassively as she left the room.

НЬЮ-ЙОРК

NEW YORK

I had never spent so long in an aeroplane.

Nine hours in the air! I found the entire experience fascinating; the size of the plane, the number of people crammed together, the unpleasant food served in plastic trays, night and day refusing to behave as they should outside the small, round windows. I also experienced jet lag for the first time. It was a strange sensation, like being dragged backwards down a hill. But I was in excellent shape. I was full of excitement about my mission. I was able to fight it off.

I was entering the United States under my own name and with a cover story that Scorpia had supplied. I was a student on a scholarship from Moscow State University, studying American literature. I was here to attend a series of lectures on famous American writers being given at the New York Public Library. The lectures really were taking place. I carried with me a letter of introduction from my professor, a copy of my thesis and an NYPL programme. I would be staying with my uncle and aunt, a Mr and Mrs Kirov, who had an apartment in Brooklyn. I also had a letter from them.

I joined the long queue in the immigration hall and watched the uniformed men and women in their booths stamping the passports of the people in front of me. At last it was my turn. I was annoyed to feel my heart was thumping as I found myself facing a scowling black officer who seemed suspicious of me before I had even opened my mouth.

"What's your business in the United States?" he asked.

"I'm studying American literature. I'm here to attend some lectures."

"How long are you staying...?" He squinted at my name in the passport. "...Yassen?"

"One week."

I thought that would be it. I was waiting for him to pick up the stamp and allow me in. Instead, he suddenly asked, "So how do you like Scott Fitzgerald?"

I knew the name. F. Scott Fitzgerald had been one of the greatest American writers of the twentieth century. "I really enjoyed *The Great Gatsby*," I said. "I think it's his best book. Although his next one, *Tender is the Night*, was fantastic too."

He nodded. "Enjoy your stay."

The stamp came down. I was in.

I had one suitcase with me. Both the suitcase and all the clothes inside it had been purchased in Moscow. Of course I carried no weapon. It might have been possible to conceal a pistol somewhere in my luggage but it wasn't a risk worth taking. Thanks to America's absurd gun laws, it would be much easier to arm myself once I arrived. I waited by the luggage carousel until my case arrived. I knew at once that nobody had looked inside the case either at Rome Airport or here. If the police or airport authorities had opened one of the catches, they would have broken an electrical circuit which ran through the handle. There was a blue luggage tag attached and it would change colour, giving me advance warning of what had happened. The tag was still blue. I grabbed the case and went out.

My contact was waiting for me in the arrivals hall, holding up my name on a piece of white card. He looked like all the other limo drivers: tired and uninterested, dressed in a suit with a white shirt and sunglasses, even though it was early evening and there was little sign of the sun. He had misspelt my name. The card read: YASSEN GREGORIVICH. This was not a mistake. It was an agreed signal between the two of us. It told me that he was who he said he was and that it was safe for us to meet.

He did not tell me his name. Nor did I ask. I doubted that the two of us would meet again. We walked to the car park – or the parking garage as the Americans called it – without speaking. He had parked his car, a black Daimler, close to the exit and held the door open for me as I slid into the back seat. He climbed into the front, then handed me another envelope. This one was also marked with a scorpion.

"You'll find your instructions inside," he said. "You can read them in the car. The drive is about forty minutes. I'm taking you to the SoHo Plaza Hotel, where a room has been reserved in your name. You are to stay there this evening. There'll be a delivery at exactly ten o'clock. The man will knock three times and will introduce himself as Marcus. Do you understand?"

"Yes."

"Good. There's a bottle of water in the side pocket if you need it..."

He started the engine and a moment later, we set off.

Nothing quite prepares you for the view of New York as you come over the Brooklyn Bridge; the twinkling lights behind thousands and thousands of windows, the skyscrapers presenting them-selves to you like toys in a shop window, so much life crammed into so little space. The Empire State Building, the Chrysler Building, the Rockefeller Centre, the Beekman, the Waldorf-Astoria ... your eye travels from one to the other but all too soon you're overwhelmed. You cannot separate them. They merge together to become one island, one city. Every time you return you will be amazed. But the first time you will never forget.

I saw none of it. Of course I looked out as I was carried over the East River but I couldn't believe I was really there. It was as if I was sitting in some sort of prison and the tinted glass of the car window was a silent television screen that I was glimpsing out of the corner of my eye. If you had told me, a year ago, that I would one day arrive here in a chauffeur-driven car, I would have laughed in your face. But the view meant nothing. I had torn open the envelope. I had taken out a few sheets of paper and two photographs. I was looking at the face of the person I had come to kill. My first thoughts had been wrong. My target was not a man.

Her name was Kathryn Davis and she was a lawyer, a senior partner in a firm called Clarke Davenport based on Fifth Avenue. I suspected that the address was an expensive one. The first photograph was in black and white and had been taken as she stood beside a traffic light. She was a serious-looking woman with a square face and light brown hair cut in a fringe. I would have guessed she was in her mid-thirties. She was wearing glasses that only made her look more severe. There was something quite bullish about her. I could easily imagine her tearing someone apart in court. In the second photograph she was smiling. This one was in colour and generally she was more relaxed, waving at someone who was not in the shot. I wondered which Kathryn Davis I would meet. Which one would be easier to kill?

There was a newspaper article attached:

NY LAWYER THREATENED

In Red Knot Valley, Nevada, she's a heroine – but New York lawyer Kathryn Davis claims she has received death threats in Manhattan, where she lives and works.

Ms Davis represents two hundred and twelve residents of the Red Knot community, who have come together in a class action against the multinational Pacific Ridge Mining Company. They claim that millions of tonnes of mining waste have seeped into their ecosystem, killing their fish, poisoning their crops and causing widespread flooding. Pacific Ridge, which has denied the claim, owns several "open pit" gold mines in the area and when traces of arsenic were found in the food chain, local people were quick to cry foul. It has taken 37-year-old Kathryn Davis two years to gather her evidence but she believes that her clients will be awarded damages in excess of one billion dollars when the case comes to court next month.

"It's not been an easy journey," says

> mother-of-two Ms Davis. "My telephone has been bugged. I have been followed in the street. I have received hate mail that makes threats against me and which I have passed to the police. But I am not going to let myself be intimidated. What happened in Red Knot is a national scandal and I am determined to get to the truth."

I had also been supplied with the woman's home address – which was in West 85th Street – and a photograph of her house, a handsome building that looked out over a tree-lined street. According to her biography, she was married to a doctor. She had two children and a dog, a spaniel. She was a member of several clubs and a gym. There was a blank card at the bottom of the envelope. It contained just four words:

MUGGING. BEFORE THE WEEKEND.

It is embarrassing to remember this but I did not understand the word 'mugging' – I had simply never come across it – and I spent the rest of the journey worrying that the driver or Marcus would discover that I had no idea what I was meant to do. I looked up the word the next day in a bookshop and realized that Scorpia wanted this to look like a street crime. As well as killing her, I would steal money from her. That way there would be no connection with Scorpia or the gold mines at Pacific Ridge.

The driver barely spoke to me again. He pulled up in front of an old-fashioned hotel, where there were porters waiting to lift out my case and help carry it into reception. I showed my passport and handed over the credit card I had been given.

"You have a room for four nights, Mr Gregorovich," the receptionist confirmed. That would take me to Saturday. My plane back to Italy left John F. Kennedy Airport at eleven o'clock in the morning that day.

"Thank you," I said.

"You're in room 605 on the sixth floor. Have a nice day."

During my training, Oliver d'Arc had told me the story of an Israeli agent working under cover in Dubai. He had got into a lift with seven people. One of them had been his best friend. The others were an elderly French woman who was staying at the hotel, a blind man, a young honeymooning couple, a woman in a burka and a chambermaid. The lift doors had closed and that was the moment when he discovered that all of them – including his friend – were working for al-Qaeda. When the lift doors opened again, he was dead. I took the stairs to my floor and waited for my case to be brought up.

The room was small, clean, functional. I sat on the bed until the case came, tipped the porter and unpacked. Before I left Malagosto, Gordon Ross had supplied me with a couple of the items which he had shown us during our lessons and which he hoped would help me with my work. The first of these was a travelling alarm clock. I took it out of my suitcase and flicked a switch concealed in the back. It scanned the entire room, searching for electromagnetic signals ... in other words, bugs. There weren't any. The room was clean. Next, I took out a small tape recorder, which I stuck to the back of the fridge. When I left the room, it would record anyone who came in.

At ten o'clock exactly, there were three knocks on the door. I went over and opened it to find an elderly, grey-haired man, smartly dressed in a suit with a coat hanging open. He had a neat beard, also grey. If you had met him in the street you might have thought he was a professor or perhaps an official in a foreign embassy.

"Mr Gregorovich?" he asked.

It was all so strange. I was still getting used to being called "Mr". I nodded. "You're Marcus?"

He didn't answer that. "This is for you," he said, handing me a parcel, wrapped in brown paper. "I'll call back tomorrow night at the same time. By then, I hope, you'll have everything planned out. OK?"

"Right," I said.

"Nice meeting you."

He left. I took the parcel over to the bed and opened it. The size and weight had already told me what I was going to find inside and, sure enough, there it was – a Smith & Wesson 4546, an ugly but efficient semi-automatic pistol that looked old and well used. The serial number had been filed off, making it impossible to trace. I checked the clip. It had been delivered with six bullets. So there it was. I had the target. I had the weapon. And I had just four days to make the kill.

The following morning, I stood outside the offices of Clarke Davenport, which were located on the nineteenth floor of a skyscraper in Midtown Manhattan, quite close to the huge, white marble structure of St Patrick's Cathedral. This was quite useful to me. A church is one of the few places in a city where it is possible to linger without looking out of place. From the steps, I was able to examine the building opposite at leisure, watching the people streaming in and out of the three revolving doors, wondering if I might catch sight of Kathryn Davis among them. I was glad she did not appear. I was not sure if I was ready for this yet. Part of me was worried that I never would be.

The secret of a successful kill is to know your target. That was what I had been taught. You have to learn their movements, their daily routine, the restaurants where they eat, the friends they meet, their tastes, their weaknesses, their secrets. The more you know, the easier it will be to find a time and an opportunity and the less chance there will be of making a mistake. You might not think I would learn a great deal from staring at a building for five hours, but at the end of that time I felt myself connected to it. I had taken note of the CCTV cameras. I had counted how many policemen had walked past on patrol. I had seen the maintenance men go in and had noted which company they worked for.

At half past five that afternoon, just as the rush to get home had begun and when everyone would be at their most tired and impatient, I presented myself at the main reception desk, wearing the overalls of an engineer from Bedford (Long Island) Electricity. I had visited the company earlier that afternoon – it was actually in Brooklyn – pretending that I was looking for a job and it had been simple enough to steal a uniform and an assortment of documents. I had then returned to my hotel, where I had manufactured an ID tag using a square cut out from a company newsletter and a picture of myself, which I had taken in a photo booth. The whole thing was contained in a plastic holder, which I had deliberately scratched and made dirty so that it would be difficult to see. Maintaining a false identity is mainly about mental attitude. You simply have to believe you are who you say you are. You can show someone a travel card and they will accept it as police ID if you do it with enough authority. Another lesson from Malagosto.

The receptionist was a very plump woman with her eye already fixed on the oversized clock that was built into the wall opposite her. There was a security man, in uniform, standing nearby.

"BLI Electrics," I said. I spoke with a New York accent, which had taken me many hours, working with tapes, to acquire. "We've got a heating unit down..." I pretended to consult my worksheet. "Clarke Davenport."

"I don't think I've seen you before," the woman said.

"That's right, ma'am." I showed her my pass, at the same time holding her eye so she wouldn't look at it too closely. "It's my first week in the job. *And* it's my first job," I added proudly. "I only graduated this summer."

She smiled at me. I guessed that she had children of her own. "It's the nineteenth floor," she said.

The security man even called the lift for me.

I took it as far as the eighteenth floor, then got out and made my way to the stairwell. It was still too early and I had a feeling lawyers wouldn't keep normal office hours. I waited an hour, listening to the sounds in the building ... people saying goodbye to each other, the chimes of the lifts as the doors opened and shut. It was dark by now and with a bit of luck the building would be empty apart from the cleaners. I walked up one floor and found myself in the reception area of Clarke Davenport with two silver letters – C and D – on the wall. There was no one there. The lights were burning low. A pair of frosted glass doors opened onto a long corridor, a length of plush blue carpet leading clients past conference rooms with leather chairs and tables polished like mirrors. My feet made no sound as I made my way through an open-plan area filled with desks, computers and photocopying machines, but as I reached the far end I saw a movement out of the corner of my eye and suddenly I was being challenged.

"Can I help you?"

I hadn't seen the young, tired-looking woman who had been bending down beside a filing cabinet. She was wearing a coat and scarf, about to leave, but she hadn't gone yet and I had allowed her to see me. My heart sank at such carelessness. I could almost hear Sefton Nye shouting at me.

"The water cooler," I muttered, pointing down the corridor.

"Oh. Sure." She had found the file she was looking for and straightened up.

I continued walking. With a bit of luck, she wouldn't even remember we'd met.

All the offices at Clarke Davenport had the names of their occupants printed next to the doors. That was helpful. Kathryn Davis was at the far end. She must have been important to the company as she had been given a corner office with views over Fifth Avenue and the cathedral. The door was locked but that was no longer a problem for me. Using a pick and a tension wrench I had it open in five seconds and let myself into a typical lawyer's office with an antique desk, two chairs facing it, a shelf full of books, a leather sofa with a coffee table and various pictures of mountain scenery. I turned on her desk lamp. It might have been safer to use a torch but I didn't intend to stay here long and having proper light would make everything easier.

I went straight to the desk. There was a framed photograph of the woman with her two children, a girl and a boy, aged about fourteen and twelve. They were all wearing hiking gear. There was nothing of any interest in her drawers. I opened her diary. She had client meetings all week, lunches booked in the following day and on Friday some sort of evening engagement. The entry read:

MET 7.00 p.m.
D home

I quickly checked out the rest of the room. All the books were about law except for two on the coffee table which contained reproductions of famous paintings. She also had a catalogue from an auction house ... a sale of modern art. Briefly, I brushed my fingers over the sofa, trying to get a sense of the woman who might have sat on it. But the truth was that the office told me only so much about Kathryn Davis. It had been designed that way, to present a serious, professional image to the clients who came here but nothing more.

Even so, I had got what I had come for. I knew when and where the killing would take place.

I was back in my hotel room and at exactly ten o'clock there was a knock at the door. The man who called himself Marcus had returned. This time he came in.

"Well?" He waited for me to speak.

"Friday night," I said. "Central Park."

It hadn't taken me long to work out the diary entry, even without a detailed knowledge of the city. The art books on the table had been the clue. MET obviously meant the Metropolitan Museum of Art, a New York landmark. I had already telephoned them and discovered that there was indeed a private function at the museum that night for the American Bar Association ... Kathryn Davis would certainly be a member. The D in the diary was her husband, David. He was going to be home, babysitting. She would be there on her own.

I explained this to Marcus. His face gave nothing away but he seemed to approve of the idea. "You're going to shoot her in the park?" he asked. "How do you know she won't take a cab?"

"She likes walking," I said. The hiking gear and the mountain photographs had told me that. "And look at the map. She lives in West 85th Street. That's just a ten-minute stroll across the park."

"What if it's raining?"

"Then I'll have to do it when she comes out.

But I've looked at the forecast and it's going to be unusually warm and dry."

"You're lucky. This time last year it was snowing." Marcus nodded. "All right. It sounds as if you've got it all worked out. If things go according to plan, you won't see me again. Throw the gun into the Hudson. Make sure you're on that Saturday plane. Good luck."

You should never rely on luck. Nine times out of ten it will be your enemy and if you need it, it means you've been careless with your planning.

I was back outside St Patrick's Cathedral the next day and this time I did glimpse Kathryn Davis as she got out of a taxi and went into the building. She was shorter than I had guessed from her photographs. She was wearing a smart, beige-coloured overcoat and carried a leather briefcase so full of files that she wasn't able to close it. Seeing her jolted me in a strange way. I wasn't afraid. It seemed to me that Scorpia had deliberately chosen an easy target for my first assignment. But somehow the stakes had been raised. I began to think about what I was going to do, about taking the life of a person I had never met and who meant nothing to me. Today was Thursday. By the end of the week, my life would have changed and nothing would ever be the same again. I would be a killer. After that, there could be no going back.

The days passed in a blur. New York was such an amazing city with its soaring architecture, the noise and the traffic, the shop windows filled with treasures, the steam rising out of the streets ... I wish I could say I enjoyed my time there. But all I could think about was the job, the moment of truth that was getting closer and closer. I continued to make preparations. I examined the house in West 85th Street. I saw where the children went to school. I went to the Metropolitan Museum of Art and found the room where the private function would take place, checking out all the entrances and exits. I bought a silicone cloth and some degreaser, stripped the gun down and made sure it was in perfect working order. I meditated, using methods I had learned on Malagosto, keeping my stress levels down.

Friday evening was warm and dry, just as the weather office had predicted. I was standing outside the office on Fifth Avenue when Kathryn Davis left and I saw her hail a cab. That didn't surprise me. It was six forty-five and her destination was thirty blocks away. I hailed a second cab and followed. It took us twenty minutes to weave our way through the traffic, and when we arrived there were crowds of smartly dressed people making their way in through the front entrance of the museum. Somehow we had managed to overtake the taxi carrying Kathryn Davis and it took me a few anxious moments to find her again. She had just met a woman she knew and the two of them were kissing in the manner of two professionals rather than close friends, not actually touching each other.

As I stood watching, the two of them went in together. I very much hoped that the women would not leave together too. It had always been my assumption that Kathryn Davis would walk home alone. What if her friend offered to accompany her? What if there was a whole group of them? I could see now that I had made a mistake leaving the killing until my last evening in New York. I had to be on a plane at eleven o'clock the following morning. If anything went wrong tonight, there could be no backup. I wouldn't get a second chance.

It was too late to worry about that now. There was a long plaza in front of the museum with an ornamental pool and three sets of steps running up to the main door. I found a place in the shadows and waited there while more taxis and limousines arrived and the guests went in. I could hear piano music playing inside.

Nobody saw me. I was wearing a dark coat, which I had bought in a thrift shop and which was one size too large for me. I had chosen it for the pockets, which were big enough to conceal both the gun and my hand which was curved around it. It was an easy draw – I had already checked. I would get rid of the coat at the same time as the gun. I was very calm. I knew exactly what I was going to do. I had played out the scene in my mind. I didn't let it trouble me.

At nine-thirty, the guests began to leave. She was one of the first of them, talking to the same woman she had met when she had arrived. It seemed that they were going to set off together. Did it really matter, the death of two women instead of one? I was about to embark on a life where dozens, maybe hundreds of men and women would die because of me. There would always be innocent bystanders. There would be policemen – and policewomen – who might try to stop me. I could almost hear Oliver d'Arc talking to me.

The moment you start worrying about them, the moment you question what you are doing – goodbye, Yassen! You're dead!

I put my hand in my pocket and found the gun. One woman. Two women. It made no difference at all.

In fact, Kathryn Davis walked off on her own. She said something to her friend, then turned and left. Just as I had expected, she went round the side of the museum and into Central Park. I followed.

Almost at once we were on our own, cut off from the traffic on Fifth Avenue, the other guests searching for their cars and taxis. The way ahead was clear. Light was spilling out from a huge conservatory at the back of the museum, throwing dark green shadows between the shrubs and trees. We crossed a smaller road – this one closed to traffic – that ran through the park. Over to the left, a stone obelisk rose up in a clearing. It was called Cleopatra's Needle. I had stood in front of it that afternoon. A couple of joggers ran past, two young men in tracksuits, their Nike trainers hitting the track in unison. I turned away, making sure they didn't see my face. The moon had come out, pale and listless. It didn't add much light to the scene. It was more like a distant witness.

Kathryn Davis had taken one of the paths that circled the softball fields with a large pond on her left. She knew exactly where she was going, as if she had done this walk often. I was about ten paces behind her, slowly catching up, trying to pretend that I had nothing to do with her. We were already halfway across. I was beginning to hear the traffic noise on the other side. And then, quite suddenly, she turned round and looked at me. I would not say that she was scared but she was aggressive. She was using her body language to assert herself, to tell me that she wasn't afraid of me. There was an electric lamp nearby and it reflected in her glasses.

"Excuse me," she said. "Are you following me?"

The two of us were quite alone. The joggers had gone. There were no other walkers anywhere near. What she had done was really quite stupid. If she had become aware of me, which she clearly had, she would have done better to increase her pace, to reach the safety of the streets. Instead, she had signed her death warrant. I could shoot her here and now. We were less than ten paces apart.

"What do you want?" she demanded.

I was trying to take out the gun. But I couldn't. It was just like when I had played Russian roulette with Vladimir Sharkovsky. My hand wouldn't obey me. I felt sick. I had planned everything so carefully, every last detail. In the last four days, I had done nothing else. But all the time, I had ignored my own feelings and it was only now, here, that I realized the truth. I was not, after all, a killer. This woman was about the same age as my own mother. She had two children of her own. If I shot her down, simply for money, what sort of monster would that make me?

If you don't kill her, Scorpia will kill you, a voice whispered in my ear.

Let them, I replied. *It would be better to be dead than to become what they want.*

"Who are you?" Kathryn Davis asked.

"I'm no one," I said. I took my hands out of my coat pockets, showing that they were empty. "I was just walking."

She relaxed a little. "Well, maybe you should keep your distance."

"Sure. I'm sorry. I didn't mean to scare you."

"Yeah – OK."

She stood there, watching me, waiting for me to go. I quickly walked past her, then turned off in another direction.

I didn't look back. Inside, I felt glad. That was the simple truth. I was happy that she was still alive. I was aware of a sense of huge relief, as if I had just fought a battle with myself and won. I saw now that from the moment I had climbed into the helicopter with Rykov – or Mr Grant – I had been sinking into some sort of mental quicksand. Mrs Rothman in Venice. Sefton Nye, Hatsumi Saburo and Oliver d'Arc on Malagosto ... they had all been drawing me into it. They were like a disease. And I had come so close to being infected. I had been about to kill somebody! If Kathryn Davis had not turned and spoken to me, I might well have done what I had been told. I might have committed murder.

The sound of the gunshot was not loud but it was close and my first thought was that I had been targeted. But even as I dropped to one knee, drawing out the Smith & Wesson, I knew that the direction was wrong, that the bullet had not come close. At that moment I was helpless. I had lost my focus, the vital self-knowledge – who I am, where I am, what is around me – that Saburo had drummed into me a hundred times. Anyone could have picked me off.

Kathryn Davis was dead. I saw it at once. She had been shot in the back of the head and lay on a circle of dark grass, her arms and legs stretched out in the shape of a star. There was someone walking towards her, wearing a coat and black gloves, a gun in his hand. I recognized the neat beard, the unworried eyes. It was Marcus, the man who had met me at the hotel.

He checked the body, nodded to himself. Then he saw me. He had his gun. I had mine. But I saw instantly that there was no question of our firing at each other. He looked at me almost sadly.

"Make sure you're on that plane tomorrow," he said.

I wanted to talk to him. I wanted to explain what had happened, how I felt, but he had already turned his back on me and was walking away into the shadows. In the distance I heard the wail of a police siren. It might have nothing to do with what had happened here. Even if someone had heard the shot, they wouldn't know where it had come from. But it still warned me that it was time to go.

I walked out of the park and all the way to the Hudson River with the darkened mass of New Jersey in front of me. I took out the gun and weighed it in my hand, feeling nothing but loathing ... for it and for myself. At the same time, I was aware of the first stirrings of fear. I would pay for this.

I threw the gun into the river. Then I went back to the hotel.

The following day, I left for Venice.

ВТОРОЙ ШАНС

SECOND CHANCE

"I have to say, Yassen, we are extremely disappointed with you."

Sefton Nye was sitting behind the desk in his darkened office, his hands coming together in a peak in front of his face as if he were at prayer. A single light shone above his head, reflecting in the polished brass buttons on the sleeves of his blazer. His heavy, white eyes were fixed on me. He was surrounded by photographs of leering pirates, trapped in the headlines of the world news. His family. He was as ruthless as they were and I wondered why I was still alive. In Silver Forest, an assassin sent by Scorpia had made a mistake. He had emptied his gun into Vladimir Sharkovsky but had failed to finish him off and for that he had been executed right in front of my eyes. But I was still here. Oliver d'Arc was also in the room, his hands folded in his lap. He had chosen a chair close to the door, as if he wanted to keep as far away from me as possible.

"What do you have to say?" Nye asked.

I had prepared for this scene, on the plane to Rome, the train to Venice, the boat across the lagoon. But now that I was actually sitting here, now that it was happening, it was very hard to keep hold of everything I had rehearsed.

"You knew I wasn't ready," I said. I was careful to keep my voice very matter-of-fact. I didn't want them to think I was accusing them. The important thing was to defend myself without seeming to do so. That was my plan. If I tried to make excuses, it would all be over and Marat or Sam would spend the evening burying me in the woods. I was here for a reason. I still had to prove myself. "Your agent followed me," I went on. "There was no other reason for him to be in Central Park. And I was never needed. He would have done the job ... which is exactly what happened. I think you knew I would fail."

D'Arc twitched slightly. Nye said nothing. His eyes were still boring into me. "It is true that Dr Steiner was not satisfied with your progress," he intoned at last. "He warned us there was a seventy per cent probability that you would be unable to fulfil your assignment."

I suppose I shouldn't have been surprised. Dr Steiner had been hired because he knew what he was doing and, despite my attempts to fool him, he had read me like a book. "If I wasn't ready, why did you let me go?" I asked.

Very slowly, Nye nodded his head. "You have a point, Yassen. Part of the reason we sent you to New York was an experiment. We wanted to see how you would operate under pressure and, in some respects, you handled yourself quite well. You successfully broke into the offices of Clarke Davenport, although it might have been wise to change your appearance ... perhaps the colour of your hair. Also, you were seen by a secretary. That was careless. However, we can overlook that. You did well to work out the movements of your target and Central Park was a sensible choice."

"But you didn't kill her!" d'Arc muttered. He sounded angry, like an old lady who has been kept waiting for her afternoon tea.

"Why did you fail?" Nye asked me.

I thought for a moment. "I think it was because she spoke to me," I said. "I had seen her photograph. I had followed her from the office. But when she spoke to me ... suddenly everything changed."

"Do you think you will ever be able to do this work?"

"Of course. Next time will be different."

"What makes you think there will be a next time?"

Another silence. The two men were making me sweat but I didn't think they were going to kill me. I already had a sense of how Scorpia operated. If they had decided I was no use to them, they wouldn't have bothered bringing me back to the island. Marcus could have shot me down with the same gun he had used on Kathryn Davis. I could have been stabbed or strangled on the boat and dropped overboard. These were people who didn't waste their time.

Nye could see that I had worked it out. "All right," he said. "We will draw a line under this unfortunate event. You are very fortunate, Yassen, that Mrs Rothman has taken a personal liking to you. It's also to your advantage that you've had such excellent reports from your instructors. Even Dr Steiner believes there is something special about you. We think that you may one day become the very best in your profession – and whatever the reputation of our organization, we haven't forgotten that you are very young. Everyone deserves a second chance. Just be aware that there won't be a third."

I didn't thank him. It would only have annoyed him.

"We have decided to take your training up a notch. We are aware that you need to make a mental adjustment and so we want you to go back out into the field as soon as possible – but this time in the company of another agent, a new recruit. He is a man who has already killed for us on two occasions. By staying close to him, you will learn survival techniques, but more than that we hope he will be able to provide you with the edge that you seem to lack."

"He is a remarkable man," d'Arc added. "A British soldier who has seen action in Ireland and Africa.

I think the two of you will get on famously."

"You will have dinner with him tonight in Venice," Nye said. "And you will spend a few weeks training with him, here on the island. As soon as he agrees that you are ready, the two of you will leave together. First you will be going to South America, to Peru. He has a target there and we're just arranging the final details. Assuming that goes well, you will return to Europe and there will be a second assignment, in Paris. The more time you spend together, the better. There's only so much you can achieve in the classroom. I think you will find this experience to be invaluable."

"What's his name?" I asked.

"When you are travelling together, you will address each other using code names only," Nye replied. We have chosen a good one for you. You will be Cossack. There was a time when the Cossacks were famous soldiers. They were Russian, just like you, and they were much feared. I hope it will inspire you."

I nodded. "And his?"

A man stepped forward. He had been standing in the room, observing me all the time, lost in the shadows. It seemed incredible to me that I hadn't noticed him but at the same moment I understood that he must be a master in the ninja techniques taught by Hatsumi Saburo, that he was able to hide in plain sight. He was in his late twenties and still looked like a soldier in his physique, in the way he carried himself, in his close-cut brown hair. His eyes were also brown, watchful and serious, yet with just a hint of humour. He was wearing a sweatshirt and jeans. Even as he walked towards me, I saw that he was more relaxed than anyone I had met on the island. Both Nye and Oliver D'Arc seemed almost nervous of him. He was totally in control.

He reached out a hand. I shook it. He had a firm clasp.

"Hello, Yassen," he said. "I'm John Rider. The code name they've given me is Hunter."

ОХОТНИК

HUNTER

What is it about Alex Rider?

The Stormbreaker business may have been the first time we crossed paths, but it seems to me that our lives were like two mirrors placed opposite each other, reflecting endless possibilities. It's strange that when I met his father, Alex hadn't even been born. That was still a few months away. But those months, my time with John Rider, made a huge difference to me. He wasn't even ten years older than me but from the very start I knew that he had come from a completely different world and that we would never be on the same level. I would always look up to him.

We had dinner that night at a restaurant he knew near the Arsenale, a dark, quiet place run by a scowling woman who spoke no English and dressed in black. The food was excellent. Hunter had chosen a booth in the corner, tucked away behind a pillar, somewhere we would not be overheard. I call him that because it was the name he told me to use from the very start. He had good reason to hide his identity – there had been stories written about him in the British press – and there was less chance of my letting it slip out if it never once crossed my lips.

He ordered drinks – not alcohol but a red fruit syrup made from pomegranates called grenadine, which I had never tasted before. He spoke good Italian, though with an accent. And just as I had noted at our first meeting, he had an extraordinary ease about him, that quiet confidence. He was the sort of man you couldn't help liking. Even the elderly owner warmed up a little as she took the order.

"I want you to tell me about yourself," he said as the first course – pink slivers of prosciutto ham and chilled melon – was served. "I've read your file. I know what's happened to you. But I don't know you."

"I'm not sure where to start," I said.

"What was the best present anyone ever gave you?"

The question surprised me. It was the last thing anyone on Malagosto would have asked or would have wanted to know. I had to think for a moment. "I'm not sure," I said. "Maybe it was the bicycle I was given when I was eleven. It was important to me because everyone in the village had one. It put me on the same level as all the other boys and it set me free." I thought again. "No. It was this." I slid back the cuff of my jacket. I was still wearing my Pobeda watch. After the loss of my mother's jewels, it was the only part of my old life that had remained with me. In a way, it was quite extraordinary that I still had it, that I hadn't been forced to pawn it in Moscow or had it stolen from me by Ivan at the *dacha*. After everything I had been through, it was still working, ticking away and never losing a minute. "It was my grandfather's," I explained. "He'd given it to my father and my father passed it onto me after he died. I was nine years old. I was very proud that he thought I was ready for it, and now, when I look at it, it reminds me of him."

"Tell me about your grandfather."

"I don't really remember him. I only knew him when we were in Moscow and we left when I was two. He only came to Estrov a few times and he died when I was young." I thought of the wife he had left behind. My grandmother. The last time I had seen her, she had been at the sink, peeling potatoes. Almost certainly she would have been standing there when the flames engulfed the house. "My father said he was a great man," I recalled. "He was there at Stalingrad in 1943. He fought against the Nazis."

"You admire him for that?"

"Of course."

"What is your favourite food?"

I wondered if he was being serious. Was he playing psychological games with me, like Dr Steiner? "Caviar," I replied. I had tasted it at dinner parties at the *dacha*. Vladimir Sharkovsky used to eat mounds of it, washed down with iced vodka.

"Which shoelace do you tie first?"

"Why are you asking me these questions?" I snapped.

"Are you angry?"

I didn't deny it. "What does it matter which shoelace I tie first?" I said. I glanced briefly at my trainers. "My right foot. OK? I'm right-handed. Now are you going to explain exactly what that tells you about who I am?"

"Relax, Cossack." He smiled at me and although I was still puzzled, I found it difficult to be annoyed with him for very long. Perhaps he was playing with me but there didn't seem to be anything malicious about it. I waited to hear what he would ask next. Again, he took me by surprise. "Why do you think you were unable to kill that woman in New York?" he asked.

"You already know," I said. "You were in the study when I told Sefton Nye."

"You said it was because she spoke to you. But I don't think I believe you ... not completely. From what I understand, you could have gunned her down at any time. You could have done it when she turned the corner from the museum. You were certainly close enough to her when you were at Cleopatra's Needle."

"I couldn't do it then. There were two people running, joggers..."

"I know. I was one of them."

"What?" I was startled.

"Don't worry about it, Cossack. Sefton Nye asked me to take a look at you so I was there. We flew here on the same plane." He raised his glass as if he was toasting me and drank. "The fact is that you had plenty of opportunities. You know that. You waited until she turned round and talked to you. I think you wanted her to talk to you because it would give you an excuse. I think you'd already made up your mind."

He wasn't exactly accusing me. There was nothing in his face that suggested he was doing anything more than stating the obvious. But I found myself reddening. Although I would never have admitted it to Nye or d'Arc, it was possible he was right.

"I won't fail again," I said.

"I know," he replied. "And let's not talk about it any more. You're not being punished. I'm here to try and help. So tell me about Venice. I haven't had a chance to explore it yet. And I'd be interested to hear what you think about Julia Rothman. Quite a woman, wouldn't you say...?"

The second course arrived, a plate of home-made spaghetti with fresh sardines. In my time on Malagosto, I had come to love Italian food and I said so. Hunter smiled but I got the strange feeling that, once again, I had said the wrong thing.

For the next hour we talked together, avoiding anything to do with Malagosto, my training, Scorpia or anything else. He didn't tell me very much about himself but he mentioned that he lived in London and I asked him lots of questions about the city, which I had always hoped to visit. The one thing he let slip was that he had been married – although I should have noticed myself. He had a plain gold ring on his fourth finger. He didn't say anything about his wife and I wondered if he was divorced.

The bill arrived. "It's time to go back," Hunter said as he counted out the cash. "But before we go, I think I should tell you something, Cossack. Scorpia have high hopes for you. They think you have the makings of a first-rate assassin. I don't agree. I would say you have a long way to go before you're ready. It's possible you never will be."

"How can you say that?" I replied. I was completely thrown. I had enjoyed the evening and thought there was some sort of understanding between the two of us. It was as if he had turned round and slapped me in the face. "You hardly know me," I said.

"You've told me enough." He leant towards me and suddenly he was deadly serious. At that moment, I knew that he was dangerous, that I could never relax completely when I was with him. "You want to be a contract killer?" he asked. "Every answer you gave me was wrong. You tie your shoelaces with your right hand. You are right-handed. A successful assassin will be as comfortable shooting with his right hand as with his left. He has to be invisible. He has no habits. Everything he does in his life, right down to the smallest detail, he does differently every time. The moment his enemies learn something about him, the easier it is to find him, to profile him, to trap him.

"So that means you can't have preferences. Not French food, not Italian food. If you have a favourite meal, a favourite drink, a favourite anything, that gives your enemy ammunition. Cossack is fond of caviar. Do you know how many shops there are in London that sell caviar, how many restaurants that serve it? Not many. The intelligence services may not know your name. They may not know what you look like. But if they discover your tastes, they'll be watching and you'll have made it that much easier for them to find you.

"You talk to me about your grandfather. Forget him. He's dead and you have nothing more to do with him. If he's anything to you, he's your enemy because if the intelligence services can find him, they'll dig him up and take his DNA and that will lead them to you. Why are you so proud of the fact that he fought against the Nazis? Is it because they're the bad guys? Forget it! You're the bad guy now ... as bad as any of them. In fact, you're worse because you have no beliefs. You kill simply because you're paid. And while you're at it, you might as well stop talking about Nazis, Communists, Fascists, the Ku Klux Klan... As far as you're concerned, you have no politics and every political party is the same. You no longer believe in anything, Cossack. You don't even believe in God. That is the choice you've made."

He paused.

"Why did you blush when I asked you about New York?"

"Because you were right." What else could I say?

"You showed your feelings to me here, at this table. You're embarrassed so you blush. You got angry when I asked you about your laces and you showed that too. Are you going to cry when you meet your next target? Are you going to tremble when you're interviewed by the police? If you cannot learn to hide your emotions, you might as well give up now. And then there's your watch..."

I knew he would come to that. I wished now that I hadn't mentioned it.

"You are Cossack, the invisible killer. You've been successful in New York, in Paris, in Peru. But the police examine the CCTV footage and what do they see? Somebody was there at all three scenes and – guess what! – they were wearing a Russian watch, a Pobeda. You might as well leave a visiting card next to the body." He shook his head. "If you want to be in this business, sentimentality is the last thing you can afford. Trust me, it will kill you."

"I understand," I said.

"I'm glad. Did you enjoy the meal?"

I was about to answer. Then I had second

thoughts. "Perhaps it's better if I don't tell you," I said.

Hunter nodded and got to his feet. "Well, you wolfed it down fast enough. Let's get back to the island. Tomorrow I want to see you fight."

He made me fight like no one else.

The next morning, at nine o'clock, we met in the gymnasium. The room was long and narrow with walls that curved overhead and windows that were too high up to provide a view. When there were monks on the island, this might have been where they took their meals, sitting in silence and contemplation. But since then it had been adapted with arc lights, stadium seating and a fighting area fourteen metres square made up of a tatami mat that offered little comfort when you fell. We were both dressed in *karate-gi*, the white, loose-fitting tunics and trousers used in karate. Hatsumi Saburo was watching from one of the stands. I could tell that he was not happy. He was sitting with his legs apart, his hands on his knees, almost challenging the new arrival to take him on. Marat and Sam were also there, along with a new student who had just joined us, a young Chinese guy who never spoke a word to me and whose name I never learnt.

We walked onto the mat together and stood face to face. Hunter was about three inches taller than me and heavier, more muscular. I knew he would have an advantage over me both in his physical reach and in the fact that he was more experienced. He began by bowing towards me, the traditional *rei* that is the first thing every combatant learns at karate school. I bowed back. And that was my first mistake. I didn't even see the move. Something slammed into the side of my face and suddenly I was on my back, tasting blood where I had bitten my tongue.

Hunter leant over me. "What do you think this is?" he demanded. "You think we're here to play games, to be polite to each other? That's your first mistake, Cossack. You shouldn't trust me. Don't trust anyone."

He reached out a hand to help me to my feet. I took it – but instead of getting up I suddenly changed my grip, pulling him towards me and pressing down on his wrist. I'd adapted a ninjutsu move known as *Ura Gyaku*, or the Inside Twist, and it should have brought him spinning onto the mat. I thought I heard a grunt of satisfaction from HS but it might just as well have been derision because Hunter had been expecting my move and slammed his knee into my upper arm. If I hadn't let go, he'd have broken it. Instantly, I rolled aside, just missing a foot strike that whistled past my head. A second later, I was on my feet. The two of us squared up again, both of us taking the Number One Posture – arms raised, our bodies turned so as to provide the smallest target possible.

I learnt more in the next twenty minutes than I had in my entire time on Malagosto. No. That's not quite true. With HS and Mr Nye I had acquired a thorough grounding in judo, karate and ninjutsu. In an incredibly short amount of time, they had taken me all the way from novice to third or fourth *kyu* – which is to say, brown or white belt. I would spend the rest of my life building on what they had given me, and they were both far ahead of Hunter when it came to basic martial arts techniques. But he had something they hadn't. As Oliver d'Arc had told me, Hunter had seen action as a soldier in Africa and Ireland. I would later learn that he had been with the Parachute Regiment, a rapid intervention strike force and one of the toughest outfits in the British Army. He knew how to fight in a way that they didn't. They taught me the rules but he broke them. In that first fight we had together, he did things that simply shouldn't have worked but some- how did. Once or twice I glimpsed HS shaking his head in disbelief, watching his own training manual being torn up. I was knocked down countless times and not once did I see the move coming. Nothing I had been taught seemed to work against him.

After twenty minutes, he stepped back and sig- nalled that the fight was over. "All right, Cossack, that will do for now." He smiled and held out a hand – as if to say "no hard feelings". I reached out and took it, but this time I was ready. Before he could throw me, which of course was what he intended, I twisted round, using his own weight against him. Hunter disappeared over my shoulder and crashed down onto the mat. He had landed on his back but sprang up at once.

"You're learning." He smiled his approval, then walked away, snatching up a bottle of water. I watched him, grateful that in the very last moment of the fight I had at least done something right and hadn't made a complete fool of myself in front of my teachers. At the same time it crossed my mind that he might actually have allowed me to bring him down, simply to let me save face. I had liked and admired Hunter when I had eaten with him the night before. But now I felt a sort of closeness to him. I was determined not to let him down.

We spent a lot of time together over the next few weeks – running, swimming, competing on the assault course, facing each other with more hand-to-hand combat in the gym. He was also training the other recruits and I know that they felt exactly the same way about him as I did. He was a natural teacher. Whether it was target practice or night-time scuba-diving, he brought out the best in us. Julia Rothman was also an admirer. The two of them had dinner several times when she returned to Venice, although I was never invited.

I have to say that I was not very comfortable on Malagosto. It was as if I had left school after taking my exams only to find myself inexplicably back again. Everyone knew that I had failed in

New York. And time was moving on. My nineteenth birthday had come and gone without anyone noticing it ... including me. It was time to move on, to stand on my own two feet.

So I was very glad when Sefton Nye called me to his office and told me that I would be leaving in a few days. "We all agree that the last time was too early," he said. "But on this occasion you will be travelling with John Rider. He is taking care of some business for us and you will be there strictly as his assistant. You will do everything he says. Do you understand?"

"Yes."

He had been holding my latest report, all the work of the last five weeks. I watched him as he got up from his desk and slid it into the filing cabinet against the wall. "It is very unusual for anyone to be given a second chance in this organization," he added. He twisted round and suddenly he was gazing at me, his great, white eyes challenging me. "We can put New York behind us. John Rider speaks very highly of you and that's what matters. It's good to learn from your mistakes but I will give you one piece of advice, Yassen. Don't make any more."

I could not sleep that night. There was a storm over Venice – no wind or rain but huge sheets of lightning that flared across the sky, turning the domes and the towers of the city into black cut-outs. Winter was approaching and as I lay in bed, the curtains flapping, I could feel a chill in the air. I was excited about the mission. I was flying all the way to Peru – and if that went well, I would find myself in Paris. But there was something else. John Rider had told me almost nothing about himself. I was expected to follow him across the world, to obey him without question and yet the man was a complete mystery to me. Was he a criminal? He might have been in the British Army but why had he left? How had he found his way into Scorpia?

Suddenly I wanted to know more about John Rider. It didn't seem fair. After all, he'd been given my files. He knew everything about me. How could we travel together when everything was so one-sided? How could I ever face him on even terms?

I slipped out of bed and got dressed. I'd made a decision without even thinking it through. It was stupid and it might be dangerous but what was my new life about if it wasn't about taking risks? Nye kept files on everyone in his office. I had seen him lock mine away only a few hours ago. He would also have a file on John Rider. His office was on the other side of the quadrangle, just a few metres from where I was standing now. Breaking in would be easy. After all, I'd been trained.

Everyone was asleep. Nobody saw me as I left the accommodation block and crossed the cloisters of what had once been the monastery. The door to Nye's office wasn't even locked. There were some on the island who would have regarded that as an unforgivable breach of security and it puzzled me – but I suppose he felt he was safe enough. It would have been impossible to reach Malagosto from the mainland without being detected and he knew everything about everyone who was here. Who would even have considered breaking in? The lightning flashed silently and for a brief moment I saw the iron chandelier, the books, the different clocks, the pirate faces – all of them stark white, frozen. It was as if the storm was warning me, urging me to leave while I still could. I felt a pulse of warm air, pushing against me. This was madness. I shouldn't be here.

But still I was determined. The next day I was leaving with John Rider. We were going to be together for a week or more and I would feel more comfortable – less unequal – if I knew something of his background. I'll admit that I was curious but it also made sense. I had been encouraged to learn everything I could about my targets. It seemed only right that I should apply the same rule to a man who was taking me into danger and on whom my life might depend.

I went over to the cabinet – the one where Nye had deposited my personal file. I had brought the tools I would need from my bedroom, although examining the lock, I saw it was much more sophisticated than anything I had opened before. Another dazzling burst of lightning. My own shadow seemed to leap over my shoulder. I focused on the lock, testing it with the first pick.

And then, with shocking violence, I felt myself seized from behind in a headlock, two fists crossed behind my neck, and although I immediately brought my hands up in a counter-move, reaching out for the wrists, I knew I was too late and that one sudden wrench would snap my spinal cord, killing me instantly. How could it have happened? I was certain nobody had followed me in.

For perhaps three seconds I stayed where I was, kneeling there, caught in the death grip, waiting for the crack that would be the sound of my own neck breaking. It didn't come. I felt the hands relax. I twisted round. Hunter was standing over me.

"Cossack!" he said.

"Hunter..."

"What are you doing here?" The lightning flickered but perhaps the worst of the storm had passed. "Let's go outside," Hunter said. "You don't want to be found in here."

We went back out and stood beneath the bell tower. I could feel that strange mixture of hot and cold in the air. We were enclosed by the walls of the monastery. We were alone but we spoke in low voices.

"Tell me what you were doing," Hunter said. His face was in shadow but I could feel his eyes probing me.

I had already decided what I was going to say. I couldn't tell him the truth. "Nye had my file this morning," I said. "I wanted to read it."

"Why?"

"I wanted to know I was ready. After what happened in New York, I didn't want to let you down."

"And you thought your report would tell you that?"

I nodded.

"You're an idiot, Cossack." That was what he said but there was no anger in his voice. If anything, he was amused. "I saw you go in and I followed you," he explained. "I didn't know who you were. I could have killed you."

"I didn't hear you," I said.

He ignored that. "If I didn't think you were ready, I wouldn't be taking you," he said. He thought for a moment. "I have a feeling it would be better if neither of us said anything about this little incident. If Sefton Nye knew you'd been creeping about in his study, he might get the wrong idea. I suggest you go back to bed. We've got an early start. The boat's coming tomorrow at seven o'clock."

"Thanks, Hunter."

"Don't thank me. Just don't pull a stunt like this again. And..." He turned and walked away. "Get some sleep!"

* * *

I was up before sunrise. My gear was packed. I had my passport and credit cards along with the dollars I'd saved from New York. All my visas had been arranged.

There was no one around as I walked down to the edge of the lagoon, my feet crunching on the gravel. For a long time I stood there, watching the sun climb over Venice, different shades of pink, orange and finally blue rippling through the sky. I knew that my training was over and that I would not be coming back to Malagosto, at least not as a student.

I thought about Hunter, all the lessons he had taught me. He would be with me very soon and the two of us were going to travel together. He was going to give me the one thing that I had been unable to find in all my time on the island. I suppose you could call it the killer instinct. It was all I lacked.

I trusted him completely. There was something I had to do.

I took off my watch, my old Pobeda. As I weighed it in my hand, I saw my father giving it to me. I heard his voice. I was just nine years old, so young, still in short trousers, living in the house in Estrov.

My grandfather's watch.

I held it one last time, then swung my arm and threw it into the lagoon.

КОМАНДИР

THE COMMANDER

His name was Gabriel Sweetman and he was a drug lord, sometimes known as "the Sugar Man", more often as "the Commander".

He was born in the slums of Mexico City. Nothing is known about his parents but he first came to the attention of the police when he was eight years old, selling missing car parts to motorists. The reason the parts were missing was because he had stolen them, helped by his twelve-year-old sister, Maria. When he was twelve, he sold his sister. By then, it was said that he had killed for the first time. He moved into the drugs business when he was thirteen, first dealing on the street, then working his way up until he became the lieutenant to "Sunny" Gomez, one of the biggest traffickers in Mexico. At the time, it was estimated that Gomez was smuggling three million dollars' worth of heroin and cocaine into America every day.

Sweetman murdered Gomez and took over his business. He also married Gomez's wife, a former Miss Acapulco called Tracey. Thirty years later, it was rumoured that Sweetman was worth twenty-five billion dollars. He was transporting cocaine all over the world, using a fleet of Boeing 727 jet aircraft which he also owned. He had murdered over two thousand people, including fifteen judges and two hundred police officers. Sweetman would kill anyone who crossed his path and he liked to do it slowly. Some of his enemies he buried alive. It was well known that he was mad, but only his family doctor had been brave enough to say so. He had killed the family doctor.

I do not know how or why he had come to the attention of Scorpia. It is possible that they been hired to take him out by another drug lord. It might even have been the Mexican or the American government. He certainly was not being executed because he was bad. Scorpia was occasionally involved in drug trafficking itself, although it was a dirty and an unpleasant business. People who spend large amounts of money doing harm to themselves and to their customers are not usually very reliable. Sweetman had to die because someone had paid. That was all it came down to.

And it was going to be expensive because this was not an easy kill. Sweetman looked after himself. In fact, he made Vladimir Sharkovsky look clumsy and careless by comparison.

Sweetman kept a permanent retinue around him – not just six bodyguards but an entire platoon. This was how he had got the name of the Commander. He had houses in Los Angeles, Miami and Mexico City, each one as well fortified as an army command post. The houses were kept in twenty-four-hour readiness. He never let anyone know when he was leaving or when he was about to arrive, and when he did travel it was first by private jet and then in an armour-plated, bulletproof limousine with two outriders on motorbikes and more bodyguards in front and behind. He had four food tasters, one in each of his properties.

The house where he spent most of his time was in the middle of the Amazon jungle, one hundred miles south of Iquitos. This is one of the few cities in the world that cannot be reached by road, and there were no roads going anywhere near the house either. Trying to approach on foot would be to risk attacks from jaguars, vipers, anacondas, black caimans, piranhas, tarantulas or any other of the fifty deadly creatures that inhabited the rainforest ... assuming you weren't bitten to death by mosquitoes first. Sweetman himself came and went by helicopter. He had complete faith in the pilot, largely because the pilot's elderly parents were his permanent guests and he had given instructions for them to suffer very horribly if anything ever happened to him.

Scorpia had looked into the situation and had

decided that Sweetman was at his most vulnerable in the rainforest. It is interesting that they had a permanent team of advisers – strategy planners and specialists – who had prepared a consultation document for them. The house in Los Angeles was too close to its neighbours, the one in Miami too well protected. In Mexico City, Sweetman had too many friends. It was another measure of the man that he spent ten million dollars a year on bribes. He had friends in the police, the army and the government, and if anyone asked questions about him or tried to get too close, he would know about it at once.

In the jungle, he was alone and – like so many successful men – he had a weakness. He was punctual. He ate his breakfast at exactly seven-fifteen. He worked with a personal trainer from eight until nine. He went to bed at eleven. If he said he was going to leave at midday, then that would be when he would go. This is exactly what Hunter had tried to explain to me the night we met, in Venice. Sweetman had told us something about himself. He had a habit and we could use it against him.

Hunter and I had flown first from Rome to Lima and from there we had taken a smaller plane to Iquitos, an extraordinary city on the south bank of the Amazon with Spanish cathedrals, French villas, colourful markets and straw huts built on stilts, all tangled up together along the narrow streets. The whole place seemed to live and breathe for the river. It was hot and humid. You could taste the muddy water in the air.

We stayed two days in a run-down hotel in the downtown area, surrounded by backpackers and tourists and plagued by cockroaches and mosquitoes. Since so many of the travellers were from Britain and America, we communicated only in French. I spoke the language quite badly at this stage and the practice was good for me. Hunter used the time to buy a few more supplies and to book our passage down river on a cargo boat. We were pretending to be birdwatchers. We were supposed to camp on the edge of the jungle for two weeks and then return to Iquitos. That was our cover story and while I was on Malagosto I had learned the names of two hundred different species – from the white-fronted Amazon parrot to the scarlet macaw. I believe I could still identify them to this day. Not that anybody asked too many questions. The captain would have been happy to drop us anywhere – provided we were able to pay.

We did not camp. As soon as the boat had dropped us off on a small beach with a few Amazon Indian houses scattered in the distance and children playing in the sand, we set off into the undergrowth. We were both equipped with the five items which are the difference between life and death in the rainforest: a machete, a compass, mosquito nets, water purification tablets and waterproof shoes. The last item may sound unlikely but the massive rainfall and the dense humidity can rot your flesh in no time. Hunter had said it would take six days to reach the compound where Sweetman lived. In fact, we made it in five.

How do I begin to describe my journey through that vast, suffocating landscape... I do not know whether to call it a heaven or a hell. The world cannot live without its so-called green lungs and yet the environment was as hostile as it is possible to imagine with thousands of unseen dangers every step of the way. I could not gauge our progress. We were two tiny specks in an area that encompassed one billion acres, hacking our way through leaves and branches, always with fresh barriers in our path. All manner of different life forms surrounded us and the noise was endless: the screaming of birds, the croaking of frogs, the murmur of the river, the sudden snapping of branches as some large predator hurried past. We were lucky. We glimpsed a red and yellow coral snake ... much deadlier than its red and black cousin. In the night, a jaguar came close and I heard its awful, throaty whisper. But all the things that could have killed us left us alone and neither of us became sick. That is something that has been true throughout my whole life. I am never ill. I sometimes wonder if it is a side-effect of the injection my mother gave me. It protected me from the anthrax. Perhaps it still protects me from everything else.

We did not speak to each other as we walked. It would have been a waste of energy and all our attention was focused on the way ahead. But even so, I felt a sort of kinship with Hunter. My life depended on him. He seemed to find the way almost instinctively. I also admired his fitness and stamina as well as his general knowledge of survival techniques. He knew exactly which roots and berries to eat, how to follow the birds and insects to waterholes or, failing that, how to extract water from vines. He never once lost his temper. The jungle can play with your mind. It is hot and oppressive. It always seems to stand in your way. The insects attack you, no matter how much cream you put on. You are dirty and tired. But Hunter remained good-natured throughout. I sensed that he was pleased with our progress and satisfied that I was able to keep up.

We only slept for five hours at night, using the moon to guide us after the sun had set. We slept in hammocks. It was safer to be above the ground. After we'd eaten our jungle rations – what we'd found or what we'd brought with us – we'd climb in and I always looked forward to the brief conversation, the moment of companionship, we would have before we slept.

On the fourth night we set up camp in an area which we called The Log. It was a circular clearing dominated by a fallen tree. When I had sat on it I had almost fallen right through, as it was completely rotten and crawling with termites. "You've done very well so far," Hunter said. "It may not be so easy coming back."

"Why's that?"

"It's possible we'll be pursued. We may have to move more quickly."

"The red pins..."

"That's right."

Whenever we came to a particular landmark, a place with a choice of more than one route, I had seen Hunter pressing a red pin close to the base of a tree trunk. He must have positioned more than a hundred of them. Nobody else would notice them but they would provide us with a series of pointers if we needed to move in a hurry.

"What will we do if he isn't there?" I asked. "Sweetman may have left."

"According to our intelligence, he's not leaving until the end of the week. And never call him by his name, Cossack. It personalizes him. We need to think of him as an object ... as dead meat. That's all he is to us." His voice floated out of the darkness. Overhead, a parrot began to screech. "Call him the Commander. That's how he likes to see himself."

"When will we be there?"

"Tomorrow afternoon. I want to get there before sunset ... to give us time to reconnoitre the place. I need to find a position, to make the kill."

"I could shoot him for you."

"No, Cossack, thanks all the same time. This time you're strictly here for the ride."

We were up again at first light, the sky silver, the trees and undergrowth dark. We sipped some water and took energy tablets. We rolled up our hammocks, packed our rucksacks and left.

Sure enough, we reached the compound in the late afternoon. As we folded back the vegetation, we were suddenly aware of the sun glinting off a metal fence and crouched down, keeping out of sight. It was always possible that there would be guards patrolling outside the perimeter, although after half an hour we realized that the Commander had failed to take this elementary precaution. Presumably he felt he was safe enough inside.

Moving very carefully, we circled round, always staying in the cover of the jungle some distance from the fence. Hunter was afraid that there would be radar, tripwires and all sorts of other devices that we might activate if we got too close. Looking through the gaps in the trees, we could see that the fence was electrified and enclosed a collection of colonial buildings spread out over a pale green lawn. They were similar in style to the ones we had seen in Iquitos. There were a lot of guards in dark green uniforms, patrolling the area or standing with binoculars and assault rifles in rusting metal towers. Their long isolation had done them no good. They were shabby and listless. Hunter and I were both wearing jungle camouflage with our faces painted in streaks, but if we'd been in bright red they would not have noticed us.

The compound had begun life twenty years before as a research centre for an environmental group studying the damage being done to the rainforest. They had all died from a mysterious sickness and a week later the Commander had moved in. Since then, he had adapted it to his own needs, adding huts for his soldiers and bodyguards, a helicopter landing pad, a private cinema, all the devices he needed for his security. In some ways it reminded me of the *dacha* in Silver Forest, although the setting could not have been more different. It was only their purpose that was the same.

The Commander lived in the largest house, which was raised off the ground, with a veranda and electric fans. Presumably there would be a generator somewhere inside the complex. We watched through field glasses for more than an hour, when suddenly he emerged, oddly dressed in a silk dressing gown and pyjamas. It was still early evening. He went over to speak to a second man in faded blue overalls. His pilot? The helicopter was parked nearby, a four-seater Robinson R44. The two of them exchanged a few words, then the Commander went back into the house.

"It's a shame we can't hear them," I said.

"The Commander is leaving at eight o'clock tomorrow morning," Hunter replied.

I stared at him. "How do you know?"

"I can lip-read, Cossack. It comes in quite useful sometimes. Maybe you should learn to do the same."

I hardly slept that night. We retreated back into the undergrowth and hooked up our hammocks once more, but we couldn't risk the luxury of a campfire and didn't speak a word. We swallowed down some cold rations and closed our eyes. But I lay there for a long time, all sorts of thoughts running through my head.

I really had hoped that Hunter might let me make the kill. My old psychiatrist, Dr Steiner, would not have been happy if I had told him this, but I thought it would be much easier to assassinate a drug lord, an obviously evil human being, than a defenceless woman in New York. It would have been a good test for me … my first kill. But I could see now that it was out of the question. The position of the helicopter in relation to the main house meant that we would have, at most, ten seconds to make the shot. Just ten steps and the Commander would be safely inside. If I hesitated or, worse still, missed, we would not have a second opportunity. Sefton Nye had already told me. I was here to assist and to observe and I knew I had to accept it. Hunter was the one in charge.

We were in position much earlier than we needed to be – at seven o'clock. Hunter had been carrying the weapon he was going to use ever since we had left Iquitos. It was a .88 Winchester sniper rifle; a very good weapon, perfect for long-range shooting with minimal recoil. I watched as he loaded it with a single cartridge and adjusted the sniper scope.

It seemed to me that he and the weapon were one. I had noticed this already on the shooting range on Malagosto. When Hunter held a gun, it became part of him.

The minutes ticked away. I used my field glasses to scan the compound, waiting for the Commander to reappear. The soldiers were in their towers or patrolling the fence but the atmosphere was lazy. They were really only half awake. At ten to eight, the pilot came out of his quarters, yawning and stretching. We watched as he climbed into the helicopter, went through his checks and started the rotors. Very quickly, they began to turn, then disappeared in a blur. All around us, birds and monkeys scattered through the branches, frightened away by the noise. The Commander had still not stepped out at two minutes to eight and I began to wonder if he had changed his mind. I knew the time from the cheap watch that I had bought for myself at the airport. I was sweating. I wondered if it was nerves or the close, stifling heat of the morning.

Something touched my shoulder.

My first thought was that it was a leaf that had fallen from a tree – but I knew at once that it was too heavy for a leaf.

It moved.

My hand twitched and it was all I could do to stop myself reaching out and attempting to flick this ... thing, whatever it was ... away. I felt its weight shift as it went from my shoulder onto my neck and I realized that it was alive and that it was moving. It reached the top of my shirt and I shuddered as it legs prickled delicately against my skin. Even without seeing it, I knew it was some sort of spider, a large one. It had lowered itself onto me while I crouched behind Hunter.

My mouth had gone dry. I could feel the blood pounding in the jugular vein that ran up the side of my neck and I knew that the creature would have been drawn to that area, fascinated by the warmth and by the movement. And that was where it remained, clinging to me like some hideous growth. Hunter had not seen what had happened. He was still focused on the compound, his eye pressed against the sniper scope. I didn't dare call out. I had to keep my breath steady without turning my head. Straining, I looked out of the corner of my eye and saw it. I recognized it at once. A black widow. One of the most venomous spiders in the Amazon.

It still refused to move. Why wouldn't it continue on its way? I tensed myself, waiting for it to continue its journey across my face and into my hair, but still it stayed where it was. I didn't know if Hunter had brought anti-venom with him but it would make no difference if he had. If it bit me in the neck, I would die very quickly. Maybe it was waiting to strike even now, savouring the moment. The spider was huge. My skin was recoiling, my whole body sending out alarm signals that my brain could not ignore.

I wanted to call to Hunter, but even speaking one word might be enough to alarm the spider. I was filled with rage. After the failure of New York I had been determined that I would give a good account of myself in Peru, and so far I hadn't put a foot wrong. I couldn't believe that this had happened to me ... and now! I tried to think of something I could do ... anything ... but I was helpless. There was no further movement in the compound. Everyone was waiting for the Commander to make his appearance. I knew it would happen at any moment. It was strangely ironic that I might die at exactly the same time as him.

In the end, I whistled. It was such an odd thing to do that it would surely attract Hunter's attention. It did. He turned and saw me standing there, paralysed, no colour in my face. He saw the spider.

And it was right then that the door of the house opened and the Commander came out, wearing an olive green tunic and carrying a briefcase, followed by two men with a third walking ahead. I knew at that moment that I was dead. There was nothing Hunter could do for me. He had his instructions from Scorpia and less than ten seconds in which to carry them out. I had almost forgotten about the helicopter but now the whine of its rotors enveloped me. The Commander was walking steadily towards the cockpit.

Hunter made an instant decision. He sprang to his feet and moved behind me. Was he really going to abort the mission and save my life? Surely it had to be one or the other. Shoot the Commander or get rid of the spider. He couldn't do both and after everything he had told me, his choice was obvious.

I didn't know what he was doing. He had positioned himself behind me. The Commander had almost reached the helicopter, his hand stretching out towards the door. Then, with no warning at all, Hunter fired. I heard the explosion and felt a streak of pain across my neck, as if I had been sliced with a red hot sword. The Commander grabbed hold of his chest and crumpled, blood oozing over his clenched fingers. He had been shot in the heart. The men surrounding him threw themselves flat, afraid they would be targeted next. I was also bleeding. Blood was pouring down the side of my neck. But the spider had gone.

That was when I understood. Hunter had aimed through the spider and at the Commander. He had shot them both with the same bullet.

"Let's move," he whispered.

There was no time to discuss what had happened. The bodyguards were already panicking, shouting and pointing in our direction. One of them opened fire, sending bullets randomly into the rainforest. The guards in the towers were searching for us. More men were running out of the huts.

We snatched up our equipment and ran, allowing the mass of leaves and branches to swallow us up. We left behind us a dead drug lord with a single bullet and a hundred tiny fragments of black widow in his heart.

"You saved my life," I said.

Hunter smiled. "Taking a life and saving a life ... and with just one bullet. That's not bad going," he said.

We had put fifteen miles between ourselves and the compound, following the red pins until the fading light made it impossible to continue and we had to stop for fear of losing our way. We had reached The Log, the campsite where we had spent the night before, and this time I was careful not to sit on the hollow tree. Hunter spent ten minutes stretching out tripwires all around us. These were almost invisible, connected to little black boxes that he screwed into the trunks of the trees. Once again, we didn't dare light a fire. After we had hooked up our hammocks, we ate our dinner straight out of the tin. It amused me that Hunter insisted on carrying the empty tins with us. He had just killed a man, but he wouldn't litter the rainforest.

Neither of us was ready for sleep. We sat cross-legged on the ground, listening out for the sound of approaching feet. It was a bright night. The moon was shining and everything around us was a strange silvery green. To my surprise, Hunter had produced a quarter-bottle of malt whisky. It was the last thing I would have expected him to bring along. I watched him as he held it to his lips.

"It's a little tradition of mine," he explained, in a low voice. "A good malt whisky after a kill. This is a twenty-five-year-old Glenmorangie. Older than you!" He held it out to me. "Have some, Cossack. I expect your nerves need it after that little incident. That spider certainly chose its moment."

"I can't believe what you did," I said. There was a bandage around my neck, already stained with sweat and blood. It hurt a lot and I knew that I would always have a scar where Hunter's bullet had cut me, but in a strange way I was glad. I did not want to forget this night. I sipped the whisky. It burnt the back of my throat. "What now?" I asked.

"A slog back to Iquitos and then Paris. At least it'll be a little cooler over there. And no damn mosquitoes!" He slapped one on the side of his neck.

We were both at peace. The Commander was dead, killed in extraordinary circumstances. We had the whisky. The moon was shining. And we were alone in the rainforest. That's the only way that I can explain the conversation that followed. At least, that was how it seemed at the time.

"Hunter," I said. "Why are you with Scorpia?" I would never normally have asked. It was wrong. It was insolent. But out here, it didn't seem to matter.

I thought he might snap at me but he reached

out for the bottle and answered quietly, "Why does anyone join Scorpia? Why did you?"

"You know why," I said. "I didn't really have any choice."

"We all make choices, Cossack. Who we are in this world, what we do in it. Generous or selfish. Happy or sad. Good or evil. It's all down to choice."

"And you chose this?"

"I'm not sure it was the right choice but I've got nobody else to blame, if that's what you mean." He paused, holding the bottle in front of him. "I was in a pub," he said. "It was in the middle of London ... in Soho. Me and a couple of friends. We were just having a drink, minding our own business. But there was a man in there, a taxi driver as it turned out ... a big fat guy in a sheepskin coat. He overheard us talking and realized we were all army, and he began to make obnoxious remarks. Stupid things. I should have just ignored him or walked out. That was what my friends wanted to do.

"But I'd been drinking myself and the two of us got into an argument. It was so bloody stupid. The next thing I knew, I'd knocked him to the ground. Even then, there were a dozen ways I could have hit him. But I'd let my training get the better of me. He didn't get up and suddenly the police were there and I realized what I'd done." He paused. "I'd killed him."

He fell silent. All around us, the insects continued their chatter. There wasn't a breath of wind.

"I was dismissed from the army and thrown into jail," he went on. "As it happened, I wasn't locked up for very long. My old regiment pulled a few strings and I had a good lawyer. He managed to put in a claim of self-defence and I was let out on appeal. But after that I was finished. No one was going to employ me and even if they did, d'you think I wanted to spend the rest of my life as a security guard or behind a desk? I didn't know what to do. And then Scorpia came along and offered me this. And I said yes."

"Are you married?" I asked.

He nodded. "Yeah. I've been married three years and there's a kid on the way. At least I'm going to have enough money to be able to look after him." He paused. "If it is a boy. You see what I mean? My choice."

The whisky bottle passed between us one last time. It was almost empty.

"Maybe it's not too late for you to change your mind," he said.

I was startled. "What do you mean?"

"I'm thinking about New York. I'm thinking about the last few weeks ... and today. You seem like a nice kid to me, Cossack. Not one of Scorpia's usual recruits at all. I wonder if you've really got it in you to be like me. Marat and Sam ... they don't give a damn. They've got no imagination. But you...?"

"I can do this," I said.

"But do you really *want* to? I'm not trying to dissuade you. That's the last thing I want to do. I just want you to be aware that once you start, there's no going back. After the first kill – that's it."

He hesitated. We both did. I wasn't sure how to respond.

"If I backed out now, Scorpia would kill me."

"I rather doubt it. They'd be annoyed, of course. But I think you're exaggerating your own importance. They'd very quickly forget you. Anyway, you've learnt enough to keep away from them. You could change your identity, your appearance, start somewhere new. The world is a big place – and there are all sorts of different things you could be doing in it."

"Is that what you're advising me?" I asked.

"I'm not advising you anything. I'm just laying out the options."

I'm not sure what I would have said if the conversation had continued but just then we heard something; the croaking of a frog at the edge of the clearing. At least, that was what it would have sounded like to anyone approaching, but it wasn't a frog that was native to the Amazon rainforest. One of the wires that Hunter had set down had just been tripped and what we were hearing was a recording, a warning. Hunter was on his feet instantly, crouching down, signalling to me with an outstretched hand. I had a gun. It had been supplied to me when we were in Iquitos – a Browning 9mm semi-automatic, popular with the

Peruvian Army and unusual in that it held thirteen rounds of ammunition. It was fully loaded.

I heard another sound. The single crack of a branch breaking, about twenty metres away. A beam of light flickered between the trees, thrown by a powerful torch. There was no time to gather up our things and no point in wondering who they were, how they had followed us here. We had already planned what to do if this happened. We got up and began to move.

They came in from all sides. Six of the Commander's men had taken it upon themselves to follow us into the rainforest. Why? Their employer was dead and there was going to be no reward for bringing in his killers. Perhaps they were genuinely angry. We had, after all, removed the source of their livelihood. I saw all of them as they arrived. The moon was so bright that they barely had any need of their torches. They were high on drugs, dirty and dishevelled with hollow faces, bright eyes and straggly beards.

Two of them had cigarettes dangling from their mouths. They were wearing bits and pieces of military uniform with machine guns slung over their shoulders. One of them had a dog, a pit bull terrier, on a chain. The dog had brought them here. It began to bark, straining against the leash, knowing we were close.

But the men saw no one. They had arrived at an empty clearing with a tree lying on its side, nobody in front of it, nobody behind, termites crawling over the bark. Our empty hammocks were in front of them. Perhaps their torches picked up the empty whisky bottle on the ground.

"*¡Vamos a hacerlo!*" One of them gave the order in Spanish, his voice deep and guttural.

As one, the men opened fire, spraying the clearing with bullets, shooting into the surrounding jungle. After the peace of the night, the noise was deafening. For at least thirty seconds the clearing blazed white and the surrounding leaves and branches were chopped to smithereens. None of the men knew what they were doing. They didn't care that they had no target.

We waited until their clips had run out and then we stood up, dead wood cascading off our shoulders. We had been right next to the soldiers, lying face down, inside the fallen tree. We were covered with termites, which were crawling over our backs and into our clothes. But termites do not bite you. They do not sting. We had disturbed their habitat and they were all over us but we didn't care.

We opened fire. The soldiers saw us too late. I was not sure what happened next, whether I actually killed any of them. There was a blaze of gunfire, again incredibly loud, and I saw the ragged figures being blown off their feet. One of them managed to fire again but the bullets went nowhere, into the air. I was firing wildly but Hunter was utterly precise and mechanical, choosing his targets then squeezing the trigger again and again. It was all over very quickly. The six men were dead. There didn't seem to be any more on the way.

I brushed termites off my shoulders and out of my hair. "Is that all of them?" I whispered.

"I don't think so," Hunter said. "But we'd better get moving."

We collected our things.

"I shot them," I said. "What you were saying to me ... you were wrong. I was with you. I killed some of them." I wasn't even sure it was true. Hunter could have taken out all six himself. But we weren't going to argue about it now.

He shook his head. "*If* you killed..." He put the emphasis on the first word. "You did it in the dark, in self-defence. That doesn't make you a murderer. It's not the same."

"Why not?" I couldn't understand him. What was he trying to achieve?

He turned and suddenly there was a real dark-ness in his eyes. "You want to know what the difference is, Yassen?" He had used my real name for the first time. "We have another job in Paris, very different to this one. You want to know what it's really like to kill? You're about to find out."

ПАРИЖ

PARIS

Our target in Paris was a man called Christophe Vosque, a senior officer in the *Police nationale*. He was, as it happens, totally corrupt. He had received payments from Scorpia, and in return had turned a blind eye to many of their operations in France. But recently he had got greedy. He was demanding more payments and, worse still, he had been in secret talks with the DGSE, the French secret service. He was planning a double-cross and Scorpia had decided to make an example of him by taking him out. This was to be a punishment killing. It had to make headlines.

However, for once Scorpia had got their intelligence wrong. No sooner had we arrived at Charles de Gaulle Airport than we were informed that Vosque was not in the city after all. He had gone on a five-day training course, meaning that we had the entire week to ourselves. Hunter wasn't at all put out.

"We need a rest," he said. "And since Scorpia's

paying, we might as well check ourselves in somewhere decent. I can show you around Paris. I'm sure you'll like it."

He booked us into the luxurious Hotel George V, close to the Champs-Elysées. It was far more than decent. In fact, I had never stayed anywhere like this. The hotel was all velvet curtains, chandeliers, thick carpets, tinkling pianos and massive flower displays. My bathroom was marble. The bath had gold taps. Everyone who stayed here was rich and they weren't afraid to show it. I wondered if Hunter had brought me here for a reason. Normally we would have stayed somewhere more discreet and out-of-the-way but I suspected that he was testing me, throwing me into this gorgeous, alien environment to see how I would cope. He spoke excellent French; mine was rudimentary. He was in his late twenties and already well travelled; I was nineteen. I think it amused him to see me dealing with the receptionists, the managers and the waiters in their stiff collars and black ties, trying to convince them that I had as much right to be there as anyone ... trying to convince myself.

It was certainly true that we both deserved a rest. The journey into the rainforest and out again, the death of the Commander, the shoot-out that had followed, our time in Iquitos, even the long flight back to Europe had exhausted us, and we both had to be in first-rate condition when we came up against Vosque. And if that meant eating the best food, and waking up in five-star luxury, I wasn't going to argue.

We had adjoining rooms on the third floor and both spent the first twenty-four hours asleep. When I woke up, I ordered room service ... the biggest breakfast I have ever eaten, even though it was the middle of the afternoon. I had a hot bath with the foam spilling over the edges. I sprawled on the bed and watched TV. They had English and Russian channels but I forced myself to listen in French, trying to attune myself to the language.

The next day, Hunter showed me the city. I had done more travelling in the past few weeks – Venice, New York, Peru – than I had in my entire life, but I loved every minute of my time in Paris. A few of the things we did were obvious. We went up the Eiffel Tower. We visited Notre-Dame. We strolled around the Louvre and stood in front of its most famous works of art. All this could have been boring. I have never been very interested in tourism, staring at things and taking photographs of them simply because they are there. But Hunter made it fun. He had stories and insights that brought everything to life. Standing in front of the *Mona Lisa* he told me how it had once been stolen – that was back in 1911 – and explained how he would set about stealing it now. He described how Notre-Dame had been constructed, an incredible feat of engineering, more than eight hundred years before. And he took me to many unexpected places: the sewers, the flea markets, Père-Lachaise Cemetery with its bizarre mausoleums and famous residents, the sculpture garden where Rodin had once lived.

But what I enjoyed most was just walking the streets – along the Seine, through the Latin quarter, around the Marais. It was quite cold – spring had still not quite arrived – but the sun was out and there was a sparkle in the air. We drifted in and out of coffee houses. We browsed in antique shops and bought clothes on the Avenue Montaigne. We ate fantastic ice cream at Maison Berthillon on the Île-St-Louis. Curiously, this was where the founder members of Scorpia had first come together – but perhaps wisely there was no blue plaque to commemorate the event.

We ate extremely well in restaurants that were empty of tourists. Hunter didn't like to spend a fortune on food and never ordered alcohol. He preferred grenadine, the red syrup he had introduced me to in Venice. I drink it to this day.

We never once discussed the business that had brought us here but we were quietly preparing for it. At six o'clock every morning we went on a two-hour run together... It was a spectacular circuit down the Champs-Elysées, through the Jardins des Tuileries and across the Seine. There was a pool and a gym at the hotel and we swam and worked out for two hours or more. I sometimes wondered what people made of us. We could have been

friends on holiday or perhaps, given our age difference, an older and a younger brother. That was
how it felt sometimes. Hunter never refered back
to our conversation in the jungle, although some
of the things he had said remained in my mind.

We had arrived on a Monday. On the Thursday,
Hunter received a note from the concierge as we
were leaving the hotel and read it quickly without showing it to me. After that, I sensed that
something had changed. We took the Metro to
Montmartre that day and walked around the narrow streets with all the artists' studios and drank
coffee in one of the squares. It was just warm
enough to sit outside. By now we were relaxed in
each other's company but I could tell that Hunter
was still agitated. It was only when we reached the
great white church of Sacré-Cœur, with its astonishing views of Paris, that he turned to me.

"I need to have some time on my own," he said.
"Do you mind?"

"Of course not." I was surprised that he even
needed to ask.

"There's someone I have to meet," he went on.
He was more uneasy than I had ever seen him.
"But I'm breaking the rules. We're both under
cover. We're working. Do you understand what I'm
saying? If Julia Rothman found out about this, she
wouldn't be pleased."

"I won't tell her anything," I said. And I meant
it. I would never have betrayed Hunter.

"Thank you," he said. "We can meet back at the hotel."

I walked away but I was still curious. The more I knew about Hunter the more I got the feeling that there were so many things he wasn't telling me. So when I reached the street corner, I turned back. I wanted to know what he was going to do.

And that was when I saw her.

She was standing on the terrace in front of the main entrance of the church. There were quite a few tourists around but she stood out because she was alone and pregnant. She was quite small – the French would say petite – with long fair hair and pale skin, wearing a loose, baggy jacket with her hands tucked into her pockets. She was pretty.

Hunter was walking towards her. She saw him and I saw her face light up with joy. She hurried over to him. And then the two of them were in each other's arms. Her head was pressed against his chest. He was stroking her hair. Two lovers on the steps of Sacré-Cœur ... what could be more Parisian? I turned the corner and walked away.

The next day, Vosque returned.

He lived in the fifth *arrondissement*, in a quiet street of flats and houses not far from the Panthéon, the elaborate church that had been modelled on a similar building in Rome and where many of the great and good of France were buried. Hunter had received a full briefing in an envelope sealed with a scorpion. I guessed it had been delivered to his hotel room by someone like Marcus, who had done the same for me in New York. The two of us went to a café on the Champs-Elysées. It might have seemed odd to discuss this sort of business in a public place but in fact it was safer to choose somewhere completely random. We could make sure we weren't being followed. And we knew it couldn't be bugged.

Vosque provided a very different challenge to the Commander. He might be easier to reach but he probably knew we were coming so there was a good chance he had taken precautions. He would carry a gun. He could expect protection from the French police. As far as they were concerned, he was one of them, a senior officer and a man to be respected. If he was gunned down in the street, there would be an immediate outcry. Ports and airports would be closed. We would find ourselves at the centre of an international manhunt.

He lived alone. Hunter produced some photographs of his address. They had been provided by Scorpia and showed a ground-floor apartment with glass doors and double-height windows on the far side of a courtyard shared by two more flats. Although one of these was empty, the other was occupied by a young artist, a potential witness. An archway opened onto the street. There was no other way in and an armed policeman – a *gendarme* – had been stationed in the little room that had once been the porter's lodge. To reach Vosque, we had to get past him.

In all our discussions, we called Vosque "the Cop". As always, it was easier to depersonalize him. On the Saturday, we watched him leave the flat and walk to his local supermarket, two streets away. He was a short, bullish man, in his late forties. As he walked, he swung his fists and you could imagine him lashing out at anyone who got in his way. He was almost bald with a thick moustache that didn't quite stretch to the end of his lip. He was wearing an old-fashioned suit but no tie. After he had done his shopping, he stopped at a café for a cigar and a *demi-pression* of beer. Nobody had escorted him and I thought it would be a simple matter to shoot him where he sat. We could do it without being seen.

But Hunter wasn't having any of it. "That's not what Scorpia wants," he said. "He has to be killed in his home."

"Why?"

"You'll see."

I didn't like the sound of that but I knew better than to ask anything more.

Our Paris holiday was over. Even the weather had changed. On Sunday morning it rained and the whole city seemed to be sulking, the water spitting off the pavements and forming puddles in the roads. This was the day when Vosque was going to die. If we wanted to find him alone in his flat, it made sense. Monday to Friday he would be in his office, which was situated inside the Interior

Ministry. According to his file, most evenings he went out drinking or ate with friends in cheap restaurants around the Gare St-Lazare. Sunday for him was dead time – in more than one sense.

That morning, Annabelle Finnan, the artist who lived next door to Vosque, received a telephone call from the town of Orléans, telling her that her elderly mother had been run over by a van and was unlikely to survive. This was untrue but Annabelle left at once. We were waiting in the street and saw her flag down a taxi. Then we moved forward.

We were both wearing cheap suits, white shirts and black ties. We were carrying bibles. The disguise had been Hunter's idea and it was a brilliant one. We had come as Jehovah's Witnesses. There had been real ones, apparently, working in the area and nobody would have noticed two more, following in their wake. The *gendarme* in the porter's lodge saw us and dismissed us in the same instant. We were the last thing he needed on a wet Sunday morning, two Bible-bashers come to preach to him about the end of the world.

"Not here!" the *gendarme* grunted. "Thank you very much, my friends. We're not interested."

"But, *monsieur*..." Hunter began.

"Just move along..."

Hunter was holding his bible at a strange angle and I saw his hand press down on the spine. There was a soft hissing sound and the *gendarme* jerked backwards and collapsed. The bible must have been supplied by Gordon Ross, all the way from Malagosto. It had fired a knock-out dart. I could see the little tuft sticking out of the man's neck.

"And on the seventh day, he rested," Hunter muttered and I recognized the quotation from the second chapter of Genesis.

The two of us moved into the office. Hunter had brought rope and tape with him. "Tie him up," he said. "We'll be gone long before he wakes up but it's best not to take chances."

I did as I was told, securely fastening his wrists and ankles, and using the tape and a balled-up handkerchief to gag his mouth. After everything Hunter had told me, I was a little surprised that he hadn't simply shot the policeman. Wouldn't that have been easier? But perhaps, at the end of the day and despite everything he had said, he preferred not to take a life unless it was really necessary.

With the *gendarme* hidden away, we walked across the courtyard, our bibles in our hands. I thought we would go straight to Vosque's door but instead Hunter steered us over to the artist's flat and rang the bell there. It was a nice touch. She wasn't in, of course, but if Vosque happened to be watching out of his window, the fact that we were patiently waiting there would make us look completely innocent. We stood outside for a minute or two, ignoring the thin drizzle that was slanting down onto the cobblestones. Hunter pretended to slip a note through the letterbox. Then we went over to Vosque's place and rang the bell.

He must have seen us coming and he didn't suspect a thing. He was already in a bad mood as he opened the door, wearing a vest and pants with a striped dressing gown falling off his shoulders. He hadn't shaved yet.

"Get the hell out of here," he snarled. "I haven't—"

That was as far as he got. Hunter didn't use another anaesthetic dart. He hit him, very hard, under the chin. It wasn't a killer blow, although it could have been. He caught the Cop as he fell and dragged him into the apartment. I closed the door behind us. We were in.

The flat was almost bare. The floor was uncarpeted, the furniture minimal. There were no pictures on the walls. It was private. Net curtains hung over the windows and although there was a glass door leading into a tiny back garden – unusual for a Paris property – nobody could see in. A bedroom led off to one side. There was an open-plan kitchen, where, from the looks of it, Vosque hardly ever cooked anything much more than a boiled egg.

Hunter had manhandled the Cop across the floor and onto a wooden chair. "Find something to tie him up with," he said. "He should have some ties in the bedroom. If you can't find any, use a sheet off the bed. Tear it into strips."

I was mystified. What were we doing? Our orders were to kill the man, not threaten or interrogate him. Why wasn't he already dead? But once again I didn't argue. Vosque had quite a collection of ties. I took five of them from his wardrobe and used them to bind his arms and legs, keeping the last one to gag his mouth. Hunter said nothing while I worked. I had already seen that intense concentration of his when we were in the jungle but this time there was something else. I was aware that he had something in his mind and for some reason it made me afraid.

He checked that the Cop was secure, then went over to the sink, filled a glass of water and threw it in his face. The cop's eyes flickered open. I saw the jolt as he returned to consciousness and the fear as he took in his predicament. He began to struggle violently, rocking back and forth, as if there was any chance of him breaking free. Hunter signalled at him to stop. The Cop swore and shouted at him but the words were muffled, incomprehensible beneath the gag. Eventually, he stopped fighting. He could see it would do no good.

I didn't dare speak. I wasn't even sure what language I would be expected to use.

Hunter turned to me.

"You want to be an assassin," he said, speaking in Russian now. "When you were in the jungle, you told me you killed some of the men who came after us. I'm not so sure about that. It was dark and I have a feeling I was the one who knocked all of them off. But that doesn't matter. You said you were ready to kill. I didn't believe you. Well, now's your chance to prove it. I want you to kill Vosque."

I looked at him. Then I turned to the Cop. I'm not sure that the Frenchman had understood what we were saying. He was silent, gazing straight ahead as if he was outraged, as if we had no right to be here.

"You want me to kill him," I said in Russian.

"Yes. With this."

He held out a knife. He had brought it with him and I stared at it with complete horror. I couldn't believe what I was seeing. The knife was razor-sharp. There could be no doubt of that. I had never seen anything quite so evil. But it was tiny. The blade was more like an old-fashioned safety razor. It couldn't have been more than four or five centimetres long.

"That's crazy," I said. I was clinging to the thought that perhaps this was some sort of joke, although there was no chance of that. Hunter was deadly serious. "Give me a gun. I'll shoot him."

"That's not what I'm asking, Yassen. This is meant to be a punishment killing. I want you to use the knife."

He had named me in front of the victim. Even though he was speaking in Russian, there was no going back.

"Why?"

"Why are you arguing? You know how we work. Do as you're told."

He pressed the knife into my hand. It was terribly light, barely more than a sliver of sharpened metal in a plastic handle. And at that moment I understood the point of all this. If I killed Vosque with this weapon, it would be slow and it would be painful. I would feel every cut that I made. And it might take several cuts. This wasn't going to be just a quick stab to the heart. However I did it, I would end up drenched in the man's blood.

A punishment killing. For both of us.

Something deep inside me rose to the surface. I was shocked, disgusted that he could behave this way. We'd just had five amazing days in Paris. In a way, they'd wiped out everything bad that had happened to me before. He'd been almost like a brother to me. Certainly, he had been my friend. And now, suddenly, he was utterly cold. From the way he was standing there, I could see that I meant nothing to him. And he was asking me to do something unspeakable.

Butchery.

And yet he was right. At the end of the day, it was a lesson I had to learn ... if I was going to do this work. Not every assassination would take place from the top of a building or the other side of a perimeter fence. I had to get my hands dirty.

I examined the Cop. He was struggling again, his stomach heaving underneath his vest, jerking the chair from side to side, whimpering. His whole face had gone red. He had seen the knife. I balanced it in my hand, once again feeling the flimsy weight. Where was I to start? I supposed the only answer was to cut his throat. Gordon Ross had even given us a demonstration once, but he had used a plastic dummy.

"You need to get on with it, Yassen," Hunter said. "We haven't got all day."

"I can't."

I had spoken the words without realizing it. They had simply slipped out of my mouth.

"Why can't you?"

"Because..."

I didn't want to answer. I couldn't explain. Vosque might not be a good man. He was corrupt. He took bribes. But he was a man nonetheless. Not a paper target. He was right here, in front of me, terrified. I could see the sweat on his forehead and I could smell him. I just didn't have it in me to take his life ... and certainly not with this hideous, pathetic knife.

"Are you sure?"

I nodded, not trusting myself to speak.

"All right. Go outside. Wait for me there."

This time I did what I was told without questioning. If I had stayed there a minute longer, I'd have been sick. As I opened the front door I heard the soft thud of a bullet fired from a silenced pistol and knew that Hunter had taken care of matters himself. I was still holding the knife. I couldn't leave it behind. It was covered in forensic evidence that might lead the police to me. I carefully slid it into the top pocket of my jacket where it nestled, the blade over my heart.

Hunter came out. "Let's go," he said. He didn't seem angry. He showed no emotion at all.

Walking back across the city, I told him my decision.

"I'm taking your advice," I said. "I don't want to be an assassin. I'm leaving Paris. I'm not coming back to Rome. I'm going to disappear."

"I didn't give you that advice," Hunter said. "But I think it's a good idea."

"Scorpia will find me."

"Go back to Russia, Yassen. It's a huge country. Russian is your first language and now you have skills. Find somewhere to hide. Start again."

"Yes." I felt a sense of sadness and had to express it. "I let you down," I said.

"No, you didn't. I'm glad it worked out this way. The moment I first saw you, I had a feeling that you weren't suited to this sort of work and I'm pleased you've proved me right. Don't be like me, Yassen. Have a life. Start a family. Keep away from the shadows. Forget all this ever happened."

We came to a bridge. I took out the knife and dropped it into the Seine. Then we walked on together, making our way back to the hotel.

МОЩНОСТЬ ПЛЮС

POWER PLUS

We went to the airport, sitting together in the back of a taxi with our luggage in the boot. Hunter was flying to Rome and then to Venice, to report to Julia Rothman. I was heading for Berlin. It would have been madness to take a plane to Moscow or anywhere in Russia. That have provided Scorpia with a giant arrow pointing in the right direction to come after me. Berlin was at the hub of Europe and gave me a host of different options... I could head west to the Netherlands or east to Poland. I would be only a few hours from the Czech Republic. I could travel by train or by bus. I could buy a car. I could even go on foot. There were dozens of border crossing points where I could pass myself off as a student and where they probably wouldn't even bother to check my ID. It was Hunter who had suggested it. There was no better place from which to disappear.

I was aware of all sorts of different feelings

fighting inside me as we drove out through the shabby and depressing suburbs to the north of Paris. I still felt that I had let Hunter down, although he had assured me otherwise. He had been friendly but business-like when we met for breakfast that morning, keen to be on his way. He called me Yassen all the time, as if I had been stripped of my code name, but I was still using his. And that morning he had run by himself. Alone in my room, I had really missed our sprint around the city and felt excluded. It reminded me of the time when I'd broken my leg, when I was twelve, and had been forced out of a trip with the Young Pioneers.

I wondered if I would miss all this luxury: the five-star hotels, the international travel, buying clothes in high-class boutiques. It was very unlikely that I would be visiting Paris again and if I did, it certainly wouldn't have the pleasure and the excitement of the last week. I had thought that I was becoming something, turning into something special. But now it was all over.

I had already begun to consider my future and had even come to a decision. There were still parts of my training that I could put to good use. I had learned languages. My English was excellent. The Countess had shown me how to hold my own with people much wealthier than me. And even Sharkovsky, in his own way, had been helpful. I knew how to iron shirts, polish shoes, make beds. The answer was obvious. I would find work in a hotel just like the George V. New hotels were being built all over Russia and I was certain I'd be able to get a job in one, starting as a bellboy or washing dishes in the kitchen and then working my way up. Moscow was too dangerous for me. It would have to be St Petersburg or somewhere further afield. But I would be able to support myself. I had no doubt of it.

I did not tell Hunter this. I would have been too ashamed. Anyway, we had already agreed that we would not discuss my plans. It was better for both of us if he didn't know.

I was not sorry. I was relieved.

From the moment I had met Julia Rothman in Venice, I had been drawn into something deadly and, deep down, I had worried that I had no place there. What would my parents have thought of me becoming a paid killer? It was true that they had not been entirely innocent themselves. They had worked in a factory that produced weapons of death. But they had been forced into it and in a sense they had spent their whole lives protecting me from having to do the same. They had fed the dream of my becoming a university student, a helicopter pilot ... whatever. Anything to get me out of Estrov. And what of Leo, a boy who had never hurt anyone in his life? He wouldn't have recognized the man I had almost become.

For better or for worse, it was over. That was what I told myself. I had a great deal of money with me. Only that morning I had drawn one hundred and fifty thousand euros from my bank account, knowing that when Scorpia discovered I had gone they would freeze the money. I had my freedom. However I looked at it, my situation was a lot better than it had been three and a half years ago. I shouldn't complain.

We arrived at the airport and checked in. As it happened, my flight was leaving just thirty minutes after Hunter's and we had a bit of time to kill. So we went through passport control and sat together in the departure lounge. We did not speak very much. Hunter was reading a paperback book. I had a magazine.

"I fancy a coffee," Hunter said, suddenly. "Can I get you one?"

"No. I'm all right, thanks."

He got up. "It may take a while. There's a bit of a queue. Will you keep an eye on my things?"

"Sure."

Despite all we had been through, we were like two strangers ... casual acquaintances at best.

He moved away, disappearing in the direction of the cafeteria. He hadn't checked in any luggage and was carrying two bags – a small suitcase and a canvas holdall. They were both on the floor and for no good reason I picked up the holdall and placed it on the empty seat next to me. As I did so, I noticed that one of the zips was partially undone. I went back to my magazine. Then I stopped.

Something had caught my eye. What was it?

Moving the holdall had folded back the canvas, causing a side pocket to bulge open. Inside, there was a wallet, a mobile telephone, Hunter's boarding pass, a battery and a pair of sunglasses. It was the battery that had caught my attention. The brand was Power Plus. Where had I seen the name before and why did it mean something to me? I remembered. A few months ago, when I was on Malagosto, Gordon Ross had shown us all a number of gadgets supplied by the different intelligence services around the world. One of them had been a Power Plus battery that actually concealed a radio transmitter that agents could use to summon help.

But it was a British gadget, supplied by the British secret service. What was it doing in Hunter's bag?

I looked around me. There was no sign of Hunter. Quickly, I plucked the battery out and examined it, still hoping that it was perfectly ordinary and that I was making a mistake. I pressed the positive terminal, the little gold button on the top. Sure enough, there was a spring underneath. Pushing it down released a mechanism inside, allowing the battery to separate into two connected parts. If I gave the whole thing a half-twist, I would instantly summon British intelligence to Terminal Two of Charles de Gaulle Airport.

British intelligence...

Horrible thoughts were already going through my

mind. At the same time, something else occurred to me. Hunter had said he was going to get a coffee. Perhaps I was reading too much into it but he had left his wallet behind. How was he going to pay?

I got to my feet and moved away from the seats, ignoring the rows of waiting passengers, leaving the luggage behind. I felt light-headed, disconnected, as if I had been torn out of my own body. I turned a corner and saw the cafeteria. There wasn't a queue at all and Hunter certainly wasn't there. He'd lied to me. Where was he? I looked around and then I saw him. He was some distance away with his back partly turned to me but I wasn't mistaken. It was him. He was talking on the telephone ... an urgent, serious conversation. I might not be able to read his lips but I could tell that he didn't want to be overheard.

I went back to my seat, afraid that the luggage would be stolen if I didn't keep an eye on it – and how would I explain that? I was still holding the battery. I had almost forgotten it was in my hand. I unclicked the terminal and returned it to the holdall, then put the whole thing back on the floor. I didn't zip it up. Hunter would have spotted a detail like that. But I pressed the canvas with my foot so that the side pocket appeared closed. Then I opened my magazine.

But I didn't read it.

I knew. Without a shred of doubt. John Rider – Hunter – was a double agent, a spy sent in by

MI6. Now that I thought about it, it was obvious and I should have seen it long ago. On that last night in Malagosto, when we had met in Sefton Nye's office, I had been quite certain he hadn't followed me in and I had been right. He had arrived *before* me. He had been there all along. Nye hadn't left his door open. Hunter must have unlocked it moments before I arrived. He had gone in there for exactly the same reason as me ... to get access to Nye's files. But in his case, he had been searching for information about Scorpia to pass on to his bosses. No wonder he had been so keen to get me out of there. He hadn't reported me to Nye ... not because he was protecting me but because he didn't want anyone asking questions about him.

Now I understood why he hadn't killed the young policeman at Vosque's flat. A real assassin wouldn't have thought twice about it but a British agent couldn't possibly behave the same way. He had shot the Commander. There was no doubt about that. But Gabriel Sweetman had been a monster, a major drug trafficker, and the British and American governments would have been delighted to see him executed. What of Vosque himself? He was a senior French officer, no matter what his failings. And it suddenly occurred to me that I only had Hunter's word for it that he was dead. I hadn't actually been in the room when the shot was fired. Right now, Vosque could be anywhere. In jail, out of the country ... but alive!

At the same time I saw, with icy clarity, that John Rider had been sent to do more than spy on Scorpia. He had also been sent to sabotage them. He had been deceiving me from the very start. On the one hand he had been pretending to teach me. I couldn't deny that I had learned from him. But all the time he had been undermining my confidence. In the jungle, everything he had told me about himself was untrue. He hadn't killed a man in a pub. He hadn't been in jail. He had used the story to gain my sympathy and then he had twisted it against me, telling me that I wasn't cut out to be like him. It was John Rider who had planted the idea that I should run away.

He had done the same thing in Paris. The way he had suddenly turned on me when we were in Vosque's flat, asking me to do something that nobody in their right mind would ever do whether they were being paid or not. He had given me that hideous little knife. And he had called Vosque by his real name. Not "the victim". Not "the Cop". He had wanted me to think about what I was doing so that I wouldn't be able to do it. And the result? All the training Scorpia had given me would have been wasted. They would have lost their newest recruit.

Of course Scorpia would track me down. Of course they would have killed me. John Rider had tried to convince me otherwise but he was probably on the phone to them even now, warning them I was about to abscond. Why would he risk leaving me alive? Scorpia would have someone waiting for me at Berlin airport. After all, Berlin had been his idea. A taxi would pull up. I would get in. And I would never be seen again.

I was barely breathing. My hands were gripping the magazine so tightly that I was almost tearing it in half. What hurt most, what filled me with a black, unrelenting hatred, was the knowledge that it had all been fake. It had all been lies. After everything I had been through, the loss of everyone I loved, my daily humiliation at the hands of Vladimir Sharkovsky, the poverty, the hopelessness, I thought I had finally found a friend. I had trusted John Rider and I would have done anything for him. But in a way he was worse than any of them. I was nothing to him. He had secretly been laughing at me – all the time.

I looked up. He was walking towards me.

"Everything OK?" he asked.

"Yes," I said. "You didn't get your coffee?"

"The queue was too long. Anyway, they've just called my flight."

I glanced at the screen. That, at least, was true. The flight to Rome was blinking.

"Well, it looks as if it's goodbye, Yassen. I wish you luck ... wherever you decide to go."

"Thank you, Hunter. I'll never forget you."

We shook hands. My face gave nothing away.

He picked up his cases and I watched him join the queue and board the flight. He didn't turn round again. As soon as he had gone, I took my own case and left the airport. I didn't fly to Berlin. Any flight with the passengers' names listed on a computer screen would be too dangerous for me. I took the train back into Paris and joined a group of students and backpackers on a Magic Bus to Hamburg. From there, I caught a train to Hanover with a connection to Moscow. It was a journey that would take me thirty-six hours but that didn't bother me.

I knew exactly what I had to do.

УБИЙЦА

THE ASSASSIN

I had not seen the *dacha* at Silver Forest for a very long time. I had thought I would never see it again.

It had been strange to find myself back at Kazansky Station in Moscow. I remembered stepping off the train in my Young Pioneers uniform. It seemed like a lifetime ago. There was no sign of Dima, Roman or Grigory, which was probably just as well. I have no idea what I would have said to them if I had seen them. On the one hand, I would have liked them to know that I was safe and well. But perhaps it was best that we did not renew our acquaintance. My world was very different now.

It seemed to me that there were now fewer homeless children than there had been in the square outside the station. Perhaps the new government was finally getting its act together and looking after them. It is possible, I suppose, that they were all in jail. The food stalls had gone too. I thought of the raspberry ice cream I had devoured. Had it really been me that day? Or had it been Yasha Gregorovich, a boy who had disappeared and who would never be spoken about again?

I travelled on the Metro to Shchukinskaya Station and from there I took a trolleybus to the park. After that, I walked. It was strange that I had never actually seen the *dacha* from outside. I had arrived in the boot of a car. I had left, in the darkness, in a helicopter. But I knew exactly where I was going. All the papers relating to the planning and construction of Sharkovsky's home, along with the necessary licences and permits, had been lodged, as I suspected, with the Moscow Architecture and City Planning Committee. I had visited their offices in Triumfalnaya Square – curiously they were very close to Dima's place off Tverskaya Street – very early in the morning. Breaking in had presented no problem. They were not expecting thieves.

Now I understood why Sharkovsky had chosen to live here. The landscape – flat and green with its pine forests, lakes and beaches – was very beautiful. I saw a few riders on horseback. It was hard to believe that I had been so close to the city during my three years at the *dacha*. But here the noise of the traffic was replaced by soft breezes and birdsong. There were no tall buildings breaking the skyline.

A narrow private road led to the *dacha*. I followed it for a while, then slipped behind the trees that grew on either side. It was unlikely that Sharkovsky had planted sensors underneath the concrete and there was no sign of any cameras, but I could not be sure. Eventually, the outer wall came into sight. I recognized the shape of it, the razor wire and the brickwork even from the outside.

It was not going to be difficult to break in. Sharkovsky prided himself on his security network but I had been trained by experts. His men went through the same procedures, day in and day out. They acted mechanically, without thinking. And how many times had it been drummed into me on Malagosto? Habit is a weakness. It is what gets you killed. Certain cars and delivery trucks always arrived at the *dacha* at a given time. I remembered noting them down in my former life, scribbling in the back of an exercise book. Madness! It was a gift to the enemy.

The laundry van arrived shortly after five o'clock, by which time it was already dark. I knew it would come. I had lost count of the number of times I had helped to empty it, carrying dirty sheets out and fresh linen in. As the driver approached the main gate, he saw a branch that seemed to have fallen from a tree, blocking the way. He stopped the van, got out and moved it. When he got back in again, he was unaware that he had an extra passenger. The back door hadn't been locked. Why should it have been? It was only carrying sheets and towels.

The van reached the barrier and stopped. Again,

I knew exactly what would happen. I had seen it often enough and it was imprinted in my mind. There were three guards inside the security hut. One of them was meant to be monitoring the TV cameras but he was old and lazy and was more likely to have his head buried in a newspaper. The second man would stay on the left-hand side of the van to check the driver's ID, while the third searched underneath the vehicle, using a flat mirror on wheels. I timed the moment exactly, then slipped out of the back and hid on the left-hand side, right next to the security hut, lost in the shadows. Now the first guard opened the back and checked inside. He was too late. I had gone. I heard him rummaging around inside. Eventually, he emerged.

"All right," he called out. "You can move on."

It was very kind of him to let me know when it was safe. I dodged round, still shielded by the van, and climbed back inside. The driver started the van and we rolled forward, on our way to the house.

It was a simple matter to slip out again once we had stopped. I knew where we would be, next to the side door that all the servants and delivery people used. I was careful not to step on the grass. I remembered where the sensors were positioned. I was also careful to avoid the CCTV cameras as I edged forward. Even so, I was astonished to find that the door was not locked. Sharkovsky was a fool! I would have advised him to rethink all his security arrangements after a paid assassin had made it into the house – and certainly after Arkady Zelin and I had escaped with him. That made three people who knew his weaknesses. But then again, he had been in hospital for a very long time. His mind had been on other things.

I found myself inside, back in those familiar corridors. The laundry man had gone ahead and the housekeeper had gone with him. I passed the kitchen. Pavel was still there. The chef was bending over the stove, putting the finishing touches to the pie that he was planning to serve that evening. I knew I didn't have to worry about him. He was slightly deaf and absorbed in his work. However, there was something I needed. I reached out and unhooked the key to Sharkovsky's Lexus. Had I been in charge here, I would have suggested that all the keys should themselves be kept locked up somewhere more safe. But that was not my concern. It seemed only right that the car that had first brought me here would also provide my means of escape. It was bulletproof. I would be able to smash through the barrier and nobody would be able to stop me.

How easy it all was – and it had been in front of me all the time! But of course, I had been seeing things with very different eyes back then. I was a village boy. I had never heard of Scorpia. I knew nothing.

I continued forward, knowing that I would have

to be more careful from this point on. Things must have changed inside the house. For a start, the two bodyguards – Josef and Karl – would have been replaced, one of them buried and the other fired. Sharkovsky might have a new, more efficient team around him. But the hall was silent. Everything was as I remembered it, right down to the flower display on the central table. I tiptoed across and slipped through the door that led down to the basement. This was where I would wait until dinner had been served, in the same room where I had been shown the body of the dead food taster.

I did not climb upstairs again until eleven o'clock, by which time I imagined everyone would be in bed. I had been able to make out some of the sounds coming from above and it was clear to me that there had been no formal dinner party that night. The lights were out. There was nobody in sight. I went straight into Sharkovsky's study. I was concerned that the Dalmatian might be there but thought it would remember me and probably wouldn't bark. In fact, there no sign of it. Perhaps Sharkovsky had got rid of it. There was a fire burning low in the hearth and the glow guided me across the room as I approached the desk. I was looking for something and found it in the bottom drawer. Now all that remained was to climb upstairs to the bedroom at the end of the corridor where Sharkovsky slept.

But as it turned out, it was not necessary. To

my surprise, the door opened and the lights in the room were turned on. It was Sharkovsky, on his own. He did not see me. I was hidden behind the desk but I watched as he closed the door and, with difficulty, manoeuvred himself into the room.

He was no longer walking. He was in a wheel-chair, dressed in a silk dressing gown and pyjamas. Either he was now sleeping downstairs or he had built himself a lift. He was more gaunt than I remembered. His head was still shaved, his eyes dark and vengeful but now they seemed to sparkle with the memory of pain. His mouth was twisted downwards in a permanent grimace and his skin was grey, stretched over the bones of his face. Even the colours of his tattoo seemed to have faded. I could just make out the eagle's wings on his chest beneath his pyjama top. Every movement was difficult for him. I guessed that he had indeed broken his neck when he had fallen. And although the bullets had not killed him, they had done cata-strophic harm, leaving him a wreck.

The door was shut. We were alone. I had quickly taken out a pair of wire cutters and used them but now I stood up, revealing myself. I was holding the gun, the revolver that he had handed to me the first time I had come to this room. In my other hand, there was a box of bullets.

"Yassen Gregorovich!" he exclaimed. His voice was very weak as if something inside his throat had been severed. His face showed only shock.

Even though I was holding a gun, he did not think himself to be in any danger. "I didn't expect to see you again." He sneered at me. "Have you come back for your old job?"

"No," I said. "That's not why I'm here."

He wheeled himself forward, heading for his side of the desk. I moved away, making room for him. It was right that it should be this way ... as it had been all those years before.

"What happened to Arkady Zelin?" he asked.

"I don't know," I replied.

"They were in it together, weren't they? He and the mechanic." I didn't say anything so he went on. "I will find them eventually. I have people looking for them all over the world. They've been looking for you, too." He was rasping and his voice was thick with hatred. He didn't need to tell me what they would have done with me if they'd found me. "Did you help them?" he asked. "Were you part of the plot?"

"No."

"But you left with them."

"I persuaded them to take me."

"So why have you come back?"

"We have unfinished business. We have to talk about Estrov."

"Estrov?" The name took him by surprise.

"I used to live there."

"But you said..." He thought back and somehow he remembered. "You said you came from Kirsk."

"My parents, all my friends died. You were responsible."

He smiled. It was a horrible, death's-head smile with more malevolence in it than I would have thought possible. "Well, well, well," he croaked. "I have to say, I'm surprised. And you came here for revenge? That's not very civil of you, Yassen. I looked after you. I took you into my house. I fed you and gave you a job. Where's your gratitude?"

He had been fiddling around as he spoke, reaching for something underneath the desk. But I had already found what he was looking for.

"I've disconnected the alarm button," I told him. "If you're calling for help, it won't come."

For the first time, he looked uncertain. "What do you want?" he hissed.

"Not revenge," I said. "Completion. We have to finish the business that started here."

I placed the gun on the desk in front of him and spilt out the bullets.

"When you brought me here, you made me play a game," I said. "It was a horrible, vicious thing to do. I was fourteen years old! I cannot think of any other human being who would do that to a child. Well, now we are going to play it again – but this time according to my rules."

Sharkovsky could only watch, fascinated, as I picked up the gun, flicked open the cylinder and placed a bullet inside. I paused, then followed it with a second bullet, a third, a fourth and a fifth.

Only then did I shut it. I spun the cylinder.

Five bullets. One empty chamber.

The exact reverse of the odds that Sharkovsky had offered me.

He had worked it out for himself. "Russian roulette? You think I'm going to play?" he snarled. "I'm not going to commit suicide in front of you, Yassen Gregorovich. You can kill me if you want to, but otherwise you can go to hell."

"That's exactly where you kept me," I said. I was holding the gun, remembering the feel of it. I could even remember its taste. "I blame you for everything that has happened to me, Vladimir Sharkovsky. If it wasn't for you, I would still be in my village with my family and friends. But from the moment you came into my life, I was sent on a journey. I was given a destiny which I was unable to avoid.

"I do not want to be a killer. And this is my last chance ... my last chance to avoid exactly that." I felt something hot, trickling down the side of my face. A tear. I did not want to show weakness in front of him. I did not wipe it away. "Do you understand what I am saying to you? What you want, what Scorpia wants, what everyone wants ... it is not what I want."

"I don't know what you're talking about," Sharkovsky said. "I'm tired and I've had enough of this. I'm going to bed."

"I didn't come here to kill you," I said. "I came here to die."

I raised the gun. Five bullets. One empty chamber.

I pressed it against my head.

Sharkovsky stared at me.

I pulled the trigger.

The click was as loud as an explosion would have been. Against all the odds, I was still alive. And yet, I had expected it. I had been chosen. My future lay ahead of me and there was to be no escape.

"You're mad!" Sharkovsky whispered.

"I am what you made me," I said.

I swung the gun round and shot him between the eyes. The wheelchair was propelled backwards, crashing into the wall. Blood splattered onto the desk. His hands jerked uselessly, then went limp.

I heard footsteps in the hallway outside and a moment later the door crashed open. I had expected to see the new bodyguards but it was Ivan Sharkovsky who stood there, wearing a dinner jacket with a black tie hanging loose around his neck. He saw his father. Then he saw me.

"Yassen!" he exclaimed in the voice I knew so well.

I shot him three times. Once in the head, twice in the heart.

Then I left.

THE KILL

King's Cross, London. Three o'clock in the morning.

The station was closed and silent. The streets were almost empty. A few shops were still open – a kebab restaurant and a minicab office, their plastic signs garishly bright. But there were no customers.

Inside his hotel room, Yassen Gregorovich took out the memory stick and turned off the computer. He had read enough. He was still sitting at the desk. The tray with the dirty dishes from his supper was on the carpet beside him. He looked at the blank screen, then yawned. He needed to sleep. He stripped off his clothes and left them, folded, on a chair. Then he showered, dried himself and went to bed. He was asleep almost immediately. He did not dream. Since that final night in the Silver Forest, he never dreamed.

He woke again at exactly seven o'clock. It was a Saturday and the street was quieter than it had been the day before. The sun was shining but he could see from the flag on the building opposite that there was a certain amount of wind. He quickly scanned the pavements looking for anything out of place, anyone who shouldn't be there. Everything seemed normal. He showered again, then shaved and got dressed. The computer was where he had left it on the table and he powered it up so that he could check for any new messages. He knew that the order he had received the day before would still be active. Scorpia were not in the habit of changing their minds. The screen told him that he had received a single email and he opened it. As usual, it had been encrypted and sent to an account that could not be traced to him. He read it, considering its contents. He planned the day ahead.

He went downstairs and had breakfast – tea, yoghurt, fresh fruit. There was a gym at the hotel but it was too small and ill-equipped to be worth using, and anyway, he wouldn't have felt safe in the confined space, down in the basement. It was almost as bad as the lift. After breakfast, he returned to his room, checking the door handle one last time, packed the few items he had brought with him and left.

"Goodbye, Mr Reddy. I hope you enjoyed your stay."

"Thank you."

The girl at the checkout desk was Romanian, quite attractive. Yassen had no girlfriend, of course. Any such relationship was out of the question but for a brief moment he felt a twinge of regret. He thought of Colette, the girl who had died in Argentina. At once, he was annoyed with himself. He shouldn't have spent so much time reading the diary.

He paid the bill using a credit card connected to the same gymnasium where he supposedly worked. He took the receipt but later on he would burn it. A receipt was the beginning of a paper trail. It was the last thing he needed.

As he left the hotel, he noticed a man reading a newspaper. The headlines screamed out at him:

SHOOTING AT SCIENCE MUSEUM
PRIME MINISTER INVOLVED
"NO ONE HURT," SAYS MI6

It was interesting that there was no mention of either Herod Sayle or Alex Rider. Nobody would want to suggest that a billionaire and major benefactor in the UK had been involved in an assassination attempt. As for Alex Rider, the secret service would have kept him well away from the press. They had recruited a fourteen-year-old schoolboy. That was one story that would never see the light of day.

Yassen passed through the revolving doors and walked round to the car park. He had hired a car, a Renault Clio, charging it to the same company as the hotel room. He put his things in the boot, then drove west, all the way across London and over to a street in Chelsea, not far from the river. He parked close to a handsome terraced house with ivy growing up the wall, a small, square garden at the front and a wrought-iron gate.

So this was where Alex Rider lived. Yassen assumed he would be somewhere inside, perhaps still asleep. There would be no school today, of course, but even if there had been it was unlikely that Alex would have attended. Only the day before, he had hijacked a cargo plane in Cornwall and forced the pilot to fly him to London. He had parachuted into the Science Museum in South Kensington and shot Herod Sayle, wounding him seconds before he could press the button that would activate the Stormbreaker computers. There had been a furore. Just as the newspapers had reported, the Prime Minister had been present. The police, the SAS and MI6 had been involved. Yassen tried to imagine the scene. It must have been chaos.

He sat behind the wheel, still watching the house.

Yes. Alex Rider most certainly deserved a few extra hours in bed.

About an hour later, the front door opened and a young woman came out. She was wearing jeans and a loose-fitting jersey with red hair tumbling down to her shoulders. Yassen had never met her but he knew who she was: Jack Starbright, Alex's housekeeper. It must have been rather odd the two of them living together but there was no one else. John Rider had died a long time ago. There had been an uncle, Ian Rider, who had become Alex's guardian, but he was dead too. Yassen knew because he had been personally responsible for that killing. How had he become so tangled up with this family? Would they never leave him alone?

Jack Starbright was carrying a straw bag. She was going shopping. While she was away, Yassen could slip into the house and tiptoe upstairs. If Alex Rider was in bed asleep, it would all be over very quickly. It would be easier for him that way. He simply wouldn't wake up.

But Yassen had already decided against it. There were too many uncertainties. He hadn't yet checked out the layout of the house. He didn't know if there were alarms. The housekeeper could return at any moment. At the same time, he thought about the email that he had received. It presented him with a new priority. The Stormbreaker business wasn't quite over. Dealing with Alex Rider now might compromise what lay ahead. He reached down and turned the engine back on. It was useful to know where Alex lived, to acquaint himself with the territory. He could return at another time.

He drove off.

Yassen spent the rest of the day doing very little. It was one of the stranger aspects of his work. He'd had to learn how to fill long gaps of inactivity, effectively how to kill time. He had often found himself waiting in hotel rooms for days or even weeks. The secret was to put yourself in neutral gear, to keep yourself alert but without wasting physical or mental energy. There were meditation techniques that he had been taught when he was on Malagosto. He used them now.

Later that afternoon, he drove into the Battersea Heliport, situated between Battersea and Wandsworth bridges. It is the only place in London where businessmen can arrive or leave by helicopter. The machine that he had ordered was waiting for him – a red and yellow Colibri EC-120B, which he liked because it was so remarkably silent. He had received his helicopter pilot's licence five years ago, finally realizing a dream which he had had as a child, although he had never, after all, worked in air-sea rescue. It was just another skill that was useful for his line of work. He kept moving. He kept adapting. That was how he survived.

He had telephoned ahead. The helicopter was fuelled and ready. All the necessary clearances had been arranged. Taking his case with him, Yassen climbed into the cockpit and a few minutes later he was airborne, following the River Thames east towards the City. The email that he had received had specified a time and a place. He saw that place ahead of him, an office building thirty storeys high with a flat roof and a radio mast. There was a cross, painted bright red, signalling where he should land.

Herod Sayle was there, waiting for him.

It was Sayle who had sent him the email that morning and who had arranged all this, paying an extra one million euros into the special account that Yassen had in Geneva. The police were looking for the billionaire all over Britain. The airports and main railway stations were being watched. There were extra policemen all around the coast. Sayle had paid Yassen to fly him out of the country. They would land outside Paris, where a private jet was waiting for him. From there he would be flown to a hideout in South America.

Hovering in the air, still some distance away, Yassen recognized Sayle ... even though the man was dressed almost comically in an ill-fitting cardigan and corduroy trousers, very different from the suits he usually favoured, and presumably some sort of disguise. But the dark skin, the bald head and the smallness of his stature were unmistakable. Sayle liked to wear a gold signet ring and there it was, flashing in the afternoon sun. He was holding a gun. And he was not alone. Yassen's eyes narrowed. There was a boy standing opposite him, close to the edge of the roof. It was Alex Rider! The gun was being aimed at him. Sayle was talking and it was obvious to Yassen that he was about to fire. He had somehow managed to capture the boy and had brought him here – to kill him before he left. Yassen wondered how Alex had allowed himself to fall into Sayle's hands.

He came to a decision. It wasn't easy, sliding open the cockpit door, reaching into his case and keeping control of the Colibri, all at same time – but he managed it. He took out the gun he had brought with him. It was a Glock long-range shooting pistol, accurate at up to two hundred metres. In fact, Yassen was much nearer than that, which was just as well. This wasn't going to be easy.

It was time to make the kill.

He aimed carefully, the gun in one hand, the cyclic rod in the other. The helicopter was steady, hanging in the air. He gently squeezed the trigger and fired twice. Even before the bullets had reached their target, he knew he hadn't missed.

Herod Sayle twisted and fell. He hit the ground and lay quite still, unaware of the pool of blood spreading around him.

The boy didn't move. Yassen admired him for that. If Alex had tried to run, he would have received a bullet in the back before he had taken two paces. Much better to talk. The two of them had unfinished business.

Yassen landed the helicopter as quickly as he could, never once taking his eyes off Alex. The gun that had just killed Sayle was still resting in his lap. The landing skid touched the roof of the building and settled. Yassen switched off the engine and got out.

The two of them stood face to face.

It was extraordinary how similar he was to his father. Alex's hair was longer and it was lighter in colour, reminding Yassen of the woman he had glimpsed with John Rider at Sacré-Cœur. He had the same brown eyes and there was something about the way he stood with exactly the same composure and self-confidence. He had just seen a man die but he wasn't afraid. It seemed remarkable – and strangely appropriate – that he was only fourteen, the same age that Yassen had been when those other helicopters had come to his village.

Alex's parents were dead, just like his. They had been killed by a bomb, planted in an aeroplane on the orders of Scorpia. Yassen was glad that he'd had nothing to do with it. He had never told Julia Rothman what he knew about John Rider. By the time he returned to Venice, Hunter had already left, travelling with one of the other recruits. What was the point of sentencing him to death? Yassen had already decided. Whoever he might be and whatever he might have done, there could be no denying that Hunter had saved his life in the Peruvian rainforest and that had created a debt of honour. Yassen would simply blot out the knowledge in his mind. He would pretend he hadn't seen the Power Plus battery, that it had never happened. And what if Rider caused more damage to Scorpia? It didn't matter. Yassen owed no loyalty to them or to anyone else. In this new life of his, he would owe loyalty to no one.

He would still have his revenge. John Rider had betrayed him and in return, Yassen would become the most efficient, the most cold-blooded assassin in the world. Vladimir and Ivan Sharkovsky had been just the start. Since then, there had been ... how many of them? A hundred? Almost certainly more. And every time Yassen had walked away from another victim, he had proved that John Rider was wrong. He had become exactly what he was meant to be.

And here was John Rider's son. It was somehow inevitable that the two of them should finally meet. How much did Alex know about the past, Yassen wondered. Did he have any idea what his father had been?

"You're Yassen Gregorovich," Alex said.

Yassen nodded.

"Why did you kill him?" Alex glanced at the body of Herod Sayle.

"Those were my instructions," Yassen replied, but in fact he was lying. Scorpia had not ordered him to kill Sayle. He had made an instant decision, acting on his own initiative. He knew, however, that they would be pleased. Sayle had become an embarrassment. He had failed. It was better that he was dealt with once and for all.

"What about me?" Alex asked.

Yassen paused before replying. "I have no instructions concerning you."

It was another lie. The message on his computer could not have been clearer. But Yassen knew that he could not kill Alex Rider. The bond of honour that had once existed with the father extended to the son. Very briefly, he thought back to Paris. It was hard to explain but there was a sort of parallel. He saw it now and it was why, at the last minute, he had diverted his aim. How he had been to John Rider when the two of them were together, in some way Alex Rider was to him now. There would be no more killing today.

"You killed Ian Rider," Alex said. "He was my uncle."

Ian Rider. John Rider's younger brother. It was true – Yassen had shot him as he had tried to escape from Herod Sayle's compound in Cornwall. That was how this had all begun. It was the reason Alex Rider was here.

Yassen shrugged. "I kill a lot of people."

"One day I'll kill you."

"A lot of people have tried," Yassen said. "Believe me, it would be better if we didn't meet again. Go back to school. Go back to your life. And the next time they ask you, say no. Killing is for grown-ups and you're still a child."

It was the same advice that Alex's father had once given him. But Yassen was offering it for a very different reason.

The two of them had come from different worlds but they had so much in common. At the same age, they had lost everything that mattered to them. They had found themselves alone. And they had both been chosen. In Alex's case it had been the British secret service, MI6 Special Operations, who had come calling. For Yassen it had been Scorpia. Had either of them ever had any choice?

It might still not be too late. Yassen thought about his life, the diary he had read the night before. If only someone could have reached out and taken hold of him ... before he got on the train to Moscow, before he broke into the flat near Gorky Park, before he reached Malagosto. For him, there had been nobody. But for Alex Rider, it didn't need to be the same.

He had given Alex a chance.

It was enough. There was nothing more to say. Yassen turned round and walked back to the helicopter. Alex didn't move. Yassen flicked on the engine, waited until the blades had reached full velocity and took off a second time. At the last moment, he raised a hand in a gesture of farewell. Alex did the same.

The two of them looked at each other, both of them trapped in different ways, on opposite sides of the glass.

Finally Yassen pulled at the controls and the helicopter lifted off the ground. He would have to report to Scorpia, explain to them why he had done what he had done. Would they kill him because of it? Yassen didn't think so. He was too valuable to them. They would already have another name in another envelope waiting for him. Someone whose turn had come to die.

He couldn't stop himself. High above the Thames with the sun setting over the water, he spun the cockpit round and glanced back one last time. But now the roof was empty apart from the body stretched out beside the red cross.

Alex Rider had gone.

ACKNOWLEDGEMENTS

I had a great deal of help with the Russian sections of the book. Olga Smirnova reluctantly took me through some of her childhood memories and translated the chapter headings. Simon Johnson and Anne Cleminson introduced me to their friends and family, including Olga Cleminson, who cooked me a Russian lunch and helped create the village of Estrov. In Moscow, Konstantin Chernozatonsky showed me the buildings where Yassen might have lived and first drew my attention to the *fortochniks*. Sian Valvis took me round the city and told me of her experiences working for an oligarch. Ilia Tchelikidi also shared his school memories with me from his home in London. Finally, Alex Kteniadakis gave me the technical information for Yassen's computer.

A great many of the details in this book are therefore based on fact but it's fair to say that the overall picture may not be entirely accurate.

So much changed between 1995 and 2000 – the approximate setting for the story – that I've been forced to use a certain amount of dramatic licence.

My assistant Olivia Zampi organized everything right up to the photocopying and binding. I owe a very special debt of thanks to my son Cassian, who was the first to read the manuscript and who made some enormously helpful criticisms, and to both Sarah Handley at Walker Books and Harry F at HMP Ashfield who both suggested the title. I am, as ever, grateful to Jane Winterbotham, my squeamish but incisive editor at Walker Books. Finally, my wife – Jill Green – lived through the writing of this without hiring a contract killer to have me eliminated. She must have been tempted.

Collect all the Alex Rider books:

STORMBREAKER

Alex Rider – you're
never too young
to die…

POINT BLANC

High in the Alps,
death waits for
Alex Rider…

SKELETON KEY

Sharks. Assassins.
Nuclear bombs. Alex
Rider's in deep water.

EAGLE STRIKE

Alex Rider has 90
minutes to save
the world.

SCORPIA

Once stung, twice as
deadly. Alex Rider
wants revenge.

ARK ANGEL

He's back – and
this time there are
no limits.

SNAKEHEAD

Alex Rider bites
back…

CROCDILE TEARS

Alex Rider – in the
jaws of death…

SCORPIA RISING

One bullet. One life.
The end starts here.

The Alex Rider graphic novels:

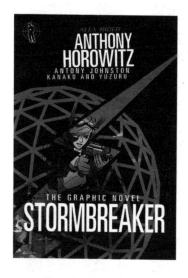

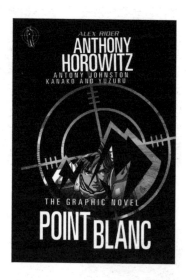

WELCOME TO THE DARK SIDE OF ANTHONY HOROWITZ

THE POWER OF FIVE

BOOK ONE
He always knew he was different.
First there were the dreams.
Then the deaths began.

BOOK TWO
It began with Raven's Gate.
But it's not over yet. Once
again the enemy is stirring.

BOOK THREE
Darkness covers the earth.
The Old Ones have returned.
The battle must begin.

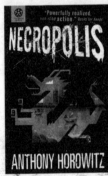

BOOK FOUR
An ancient evil is unleashed.
Five have the power to defeat it.
But one of them has been taken.

BOOK FIVE
Five Gatekeepers.
One chance to save mankind.
Chaos beckons. Oblivion awaits.

"...AND THERE WAS A GREAT WAR."

THE CHILLING POWER OF FIVE SERIES
GRAPHIC NOVELS

OTHER BOOKS BY ANTHONY HOROWITZ

London is dirty, distant and dangerous ... but that's where orphan Tom Falconer is heading. And he's got a whole assortment of vicious criminals hot on his heels.

Tom is helpless and alone until he meets Moll Cutpurse, a thirteen-year-old pickpocket. Together the two of them find themselves chased across the city by the murderous Ratsey. But it's only on the first night of a new play – *The Devil and his Boy* – that Tom realizes the fate of the Queen and indeed the entire country rests in his hands.

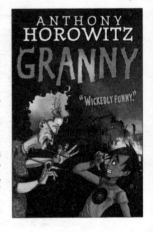

He could see it in the wicked glimmer in her eyes, in the half-turned corner of her mouth. And it was so strong, so horrible that he shivered. She was evil.

"Wickedly funny."
Daily Telegraph

"A hoot... Anthony Horowitz has created a scary and unmissable old hag."
Daily Mail

Be careful what you wish for...

Tad Spencer has everything a boy could want – incredibly rich parents, and a whole summer ahead to enjoy however he pleases. Until one evening he makes the huge mistake of wishing he was someone else.

Meet Tim Diamond, the world's worst private detective, and his quick-thinking wisecracking younger brother Nick!

"His first job was to find some rich lady's pedigree Siamese cat. He managed to run it over on the way to see her. The second job was a divorce case – which you may think is run-of-the-mill until I tell you that the clients were perfectly happily married until he came along... There hadn't been a third case."

Collect all 4 hilarious
Diamond Brothers investigations!

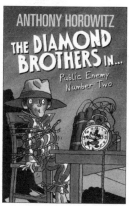

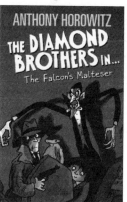

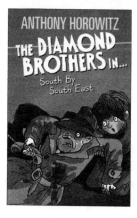